Jason Goodmaster, want
ing him. Shakily Ben released his hold on the woodwork and went back to his desk, telling himself that he was fine. He reached for the computer keyboard.

And smelled veal grease on his fingers. Things lived in grease. Invisible things. They especially liked veal grease because they could fatten on it, then swarm up fingers to wrists, elbows, armpits.

Into his eyes. Into his nose and mouth.

He had to wash.

No! He'd eaten dinner with a knife and fork; there was no grease on his skin. He reached for the keyboard again. Something tickled in his nose hairs, squirmed wetly up into the space behind his eyeball, and started laying eggs there.

Ben Ibrani screamed.

Uncle Jason didn't want him revising the article under Nicki Pialosta's byline. Ibrani cancelled everything, sent the piece on just as she had written it. If she had written it. Then he shoved back his chair and ran for the kitchen sink.

But Goodmaster wasn't through with him yet. Ibrani couldn't stop thinking about the wire brush in the trunk of his BMW, the one he used to scrape paint on his boat.

Jason Goodmaster thought he needed a lesson.

MARY KITTREDGE
AND
KEVIN O'DONNELL, JR.

A TOM DOHERTY ASSOCIATES BOOK

This is a work of fiction. All the characters and events portrayed in this book are fictional, and any resemblance to real people or incidents is purely coincidental.

THE SHELTER

First printing: August 1987

A TOR Book

Published by Tom Doherty Associates, Inc.
49 West 24 Street
New York, N.Y. 10010

Cover art by Jill Bauman

ISBN: 0-812-52066-1
CAN. ED.: 0-812-52067-X

Printed in the United States of America

0 9 8 7 6 5 4 3 2 1

THE SHELTER

FRIDAY, SEPTEMBER 21

Nicki Pialosta

All day long she had been rehearsing what she would say to him; there remained only the difficulty of saying it.

Nicki Pialosta closed her eyes. Around her the Meadbury *Bulletin*'s newsroom chattered toward another edition: keyboards clicking, telephones ringing, voices mingling in laughter, inquiry, and muttered curses.

Dear God— She forced her eyes open and sat up straight. Dear God was not going to help here. She had sought His intervention first, before that of several highly recommended psychiatrists. None of them had helped; neither had threats, pleading, or sweet reason. Only she could do what had to be done, and it was going to be painful.

Get out. Alarmingly simple, those words. Alarmingly difficult to say them aloud to Rich.

Your own baby brother. . . .

Oh, shut up. Twenty-three is no baby. Get up; get going. Get it over with—now.

Picking up her pocketbook, pulling on her coat, she strode from the *Bulletin* offices to the parking lot, where rows of cars reflected the gold of a New England autumn afternoon.

The lot attendant perched on a stool, a calculus text in his lap. He brushed back a lock of brown hair and grinned when he saw her. "Hi! Sneaking out early?"

She managed a smile in return. Just nineteen, Tommy Riley still assumed all jobs ran nine to five; his green eyes regarded the world with more innocence than she remembered ever possessing herself.

"I have an errand." He looked so earnest in his crisp blue uniform with the "Lot Manager" ID tag that she wanted to tousle his wind-tossed hair. She winked instead. "You won't tell Old Prickly, will you?"

Nearby, the managing editor's battered Dodge baked gently in the early autumn warmth, beside the wooden tub of cacti some joker had planted in eloquent comment on the managing editor's manners and reputation. Privately she suspected Tommy of putting them there, though a dozen newsroom wags claimed credit.

"You can count on me, Miss Pialosta," he said, and gestured wonderingly at the book. "You know, I'm getting this. I really am."

"I knew you would." Crossing to her Toyota, she picked a flame-red leaf off its windshield. Could you wish on the first fallen maple leaf, as on the first star of night? *If only Tommy were my brother. One foot in front of the other, it's got to be done; you can't put it off any more.* "Tommy, you keep on and someday you'll be running this newspaper."

He shrugged, clearly pleased. By the time she got the Toyota started he had bent over his book again.

If wishes were horses, she would put her real brother on one, and off he would ride. Hiccuping alcoholically, no doubt, and waving his arms, but riding away. *This time you were going to save him, this time you wouldn't be too busy to give him what he needed.*

She paused for traffic, then turned with a sigh onto Locust Street, away from downtown.

Tommy Riley

After a moment, Tommy raised his head. Miss Pialosta sure did have nice legs. And that silky black hair, jeez. Of course, he would never tell her that. Girls responded better if he talked to them like he cared mostly about their minds. What movies they liked, who was their favorite band, stuff like that. But he wouldn't know how to start asking an older woman what band she liked.

With a roaring of carburetors and a raucous oo*oo*-gah! Pete and the guys arrived in Peewee Coover's battered Ford with the slant-six engine, glass packs, and funny-car suspension. Tommy winced as they thundered into the lot and pulled up alongside the little red gate-hut.

"Hey, Riley! Come on—time to go, go, go!" Pete Cheney hung half-out the passenger window, waving a foaming beer can and laughing hysterically.

"Come on, you guys. You're early. Get that heap out of here—you want to get me fired or something?"

Peewee, all six feet and a hundred fifty pounds of him, leaned out the driver's side and gave the finger to the newsroom. Probably everybody up there was watching.

"Cut it out, Peewee. Listen, you guys, I'll meet you downtown. Okay? Go on. I'll be there in half an hour."

"Hey, should we leave you a little liquid refreshment, Riley?" Pete held out an unopened can of beer. It looked good, and Tommy was thirsty. But . . .

"No thanks, Cheney. You really are a depraved individual, you know that?"

Pete grinned and bowed, nearly falling out of the car. "And you're *so-o-o* righteous. Later, man."

"Later."

As the car swung around and back into the street, Bob Brockway stuck his head out the back window. "So *lo-o-ong,* sucker!"

Tommy sat down and forced his eyes back to the book. Jeez, those guys. He wanted to get through this calculus now so he could hang out with them later; otherwise they'd never stop riding him. But the image of fawn-brown eyes and soft red lips kept superimposing itself on the page of Σ's and *f(x)*'s.

Heck. Why had she ever had to ask him about his future, anyway? Maybe the *world* didn't have a future. Then he'd have wasted all this work. But "You're not going to park cars forever, are you?" she'd asked. So of course he had to say no, he was just passing time while he decided what to do.

"Go to college," she'd said. "Get the world by the tail—and twist it."

Then she'd smiled, showing small white teeth that were even and perfect. Her eyes crinkled up around the corners, all warm and friendly; her lashes lay thick and black on her smooth cheeks. . . . Oh, jeez. He'd wanted so bad to im-press her, he'd gone out that very night and done it —registered for college. Just night school, of course, not Ivy League, and just one class: Calculus 101, prerequisite for the next semester's economics course. And the calculus by itself was plenty hard.

He supposed he ought to stick with it, though. Maybe it would teach him what he wanted to know most of all: how to talk to a really classy lady like her. Because someday, when he got educated, with a really good job so she'd think of him like a man instead of a kid—someday he was going to ask her out on a date. A real date, with flowers, dinner, everything.

Nicki. The numbers blurred on the page as he thought about her. She sure did have the nicest legs. If the future meant legs like that, he was all for it, even with calculus.

Nicki Pialosta

This time you were going to save him.

But that was no good. Wishful thinking and useless regrets had gotten her into this mess, while he— Erasing the clear mental picture of what her brother Rich had become, Nicki eased the car up to the curb at Roundtree's Market.

The bins labeled "Keep Our City Clean" reminded her of the morning newspaper in the back seat; she snatched it up and dropped it into the container marked "Paper Only." It was like cutting her own taxes: The city sold the papers to a recycler, as it did glass, cans, and any other rubbish it could find a market for. Meadbury was nothing if not efficient.

Inside: the comforting dazzle of clean linoleum, hand-lettered signs, and a brilliant array of fruits and vegetables gleaming with freshness. Over it all, the faint scent of floor wax mingled with the perfume of baking bread.

Feeling as if she had landed on an island of safety and sanity, Nicki chose wild rice, leafy-topped celery beaded with moisture, a sack of plump mushrooms, and a sirloin steak. Enough for two. *Not three. Not any more.*

Mr. Roundtree rang it up himself. "Nice dinner there." He should know: More than two hundred pounds swaddled his five-eleven frame, and his cheeks were rounder than a squirrel's in chestnut season.

She handed him a twenty. A Strauss waltz poured from the radio on the shelf behind him. In Manhattan she'd have paid a fortune for that steak, and the music, if any, would have been taxi horns. Or gunfire . . . *Stop that.*

"New boyfriend to cook for, eh?" Mr. Roundtree smiled and tipped change into her hand.

"No." She bridled inwardly, then caught herself. He was merely asking a friendly question, although perhaps too personal a question. Still, he meant well. People in Meadbury usually meant well; she had to keep reminding herself of that. She had been in town a year, but had spent most of it in a work-numbed trance of grief and shock. Only now was she becoming aware enough of this city's attributes to get used to them: people caring, about themselves and about each other. After New York, plain friendliness felt like an intrusion; she had been right to come to Meadbury, a city in the full bloom of health.

"Just a business dinner," she said gently, regretting her rudeness. "Your store is lovely. It gives me a lift just to come in here."

To her surprise, the smile left his face. He leaned over the counter, intensity twitching the corners of his eyes and roughening his lowered voice. "It has to be this way. I've been chosen, you see. I've been given my task, and I've accepted it joyfully."

Arms full of groceries, she took an uncertain step back, startled by his flat manic gaze, his words as singsong and mechanical as if she had accidentally switched on a hidden tape.

"It has to be this way, or we're all doomed, you see. Doomed."

"Of course." Her smile, bright and taut, felt nailed on; she backed toward the door, nerves clanging. The memory of a story she had covered long ago flashed to mind as the automatic door swung open: the switchblade artist who prayed aloud as he made the ritual cuts. . . .

Mr. Roundtree relaxed all at once, leaning against the cash register, grinning amiably. "You have a nice evening now."

Startled again, she stammered that she would.

Had he joined some new religion, she wondered, or was

he just cracking in unfashionable solitude? In any case, a nice evening was most unlikely. Taking a deep breath, she got into her car, shoving her groceries onto the seat beside her.

Maybe Rich was already gone. He might have taken the hint and cleared out while she was at work. But that really was wishful thinking; Rich took a twisted pleasure in ugly scenes. Sitting in the car, knowing she was stalling, she lit a cigarette and began to smoke it.

Across the street in Goodmaster Park, lavender shadows crept over the grass, touching the long, bare limbs of girls who reluctantly gathered up blankets and pulled on sweaters. Night coming on; time to go home. Nicki fished in her pocket for the car key.

Then another, jerkier movement caught her eye as three boys melted out of the trees at the edge of the park. Breaking into a lope, they closed like jackals on a small, white-haired old woman whose fat handbag signaled easy pickings. Oblivious, she struggled over the hummocky grass as they moved up behind her.

Flinging away her cigarette, Nicki put one hand on the car door and the other on the horn.

"Hey, mama, don't you be coming alone out here, swinging your goodies for all the muggers to flash on." The tallest boy flung a jovial arm around the old woman, who beamed up at him; the other two boys strode behind like lieutenants.

Nicki fell back against the car seat, laughing ruefully at herself. *This town—* Too perfect, too good to be true. With any luck, Meadbury might banish her New York-toughened cynicism; perhaps if she stayed long enough, its caring personality would even become her own. It did seem, in its friendly ways, more like a gossipy village than a city.

"Second largest commercial center in the whole Northeast," the *Bulletin*'s managing editor had told her. He had obviously thought he was luring her from a plum of a job in Manhattan; she had not told him that to escape New York, she would take work typing the classified ads.

Small familiar warning chimes rang in her head: *Don't remember.* Obeying them, she eased the car into the homebound stream. The flagged divider guided her around the traffic circle with the smooth precision of good engineering and better execution. *Too good to be true. . . .*

She shrugged off a chill. Poor Harold Roundtree.

At the end of Saquoit Terrace stood her building—low, boxy stucco, its new lawn studded with maple saplings, which in twenty years might give passable shade. On the sidewalk outside a small girl bounced a ball, her lips moving as she chanted to herself.

Nicki slipped the car into its marked space. *I will not get angry. I will be calm, rational—* Purse in one hand, grocery bag in the other, she slammed the car door with her foot.

The little girl gave her a sullen glance. Grimy runnels of dried tears streaked her face.

"Hello, Emily." Poor thing. "Something wrong?"

"Mommy locked me out again."

"Oh." Emily Polk's mother was a lazy, neglectful slut; Nicki hoped the child had not heard what all the neighbors said about her. "Well, I'm sure she's just busy. She'll let you back in a little while."

Emily squinted up through overwise blue eyes. "Not till her boyfriend leaves. He don't like me there when he comes over. He wants me to call him Uncle Teddy. But I won't. He's not my uncle."

"Yes, well—"

"Nicki? Nicki!"

"Mrs. Margotski, yucch!" Emily said, and ran down the sidewalk.

Mrs. Margotski propelled herself over the lawn, not so much leaning on her canes as pushing off with them, crossing the courtyard in a series of hobbled leaps. Sixty-eight years old, she had the shoulders of a weight lifter. Now, pink with fury and breathlessness, she pushed her belligerent face into Nicki's.

"That boy—" She wheezed, and raised a crippled fist to her throat. "I don't want to call the police, you know, but I got to if this keeps up. The walls are too thin here. My nerves can't stand it. Nicki, I hate to say it, but that boy's trash—he's got to go."

From the windows above, her own windows, came a steady, muffled roar punctuated by thumps, as if a tool-and-die factory had been set to producing music in her apartment. "Yes, Mrs. Margotski." *I'll kill him.* "Yes, you have been very patient. Yes, I know the other tenants— Yes. I will. Yes, I remember I promised before, but—"

Upstairs, something crashed.

Thin nostrils flaring, Mrs. Margotski bristled with grim triumph. "I knew it. He's gone and kilt himself. He's gonna come flying out those windows, just watch." Her eyes shone with anticipation, as if Rich might indeed sail out headlong in a glittering shower of glass.

Marching up the front steps, Nicki thought that while Mrs. Margotski's sense of the natural progression of things might be a bit skewed, her general expectations were absolutely correct. Rich was going to come out of that apartment, if not by the window, then by the door.

Although, at this moment, I could take great pleasure in cramming him down the garbage disposal, piece by selfish, degenerate piece. Plucking envelopes from her mailbox, she stuffed them into her purse and strode tight-lipped down the hall. Snatching her key ring from her pocketbook, she stabbed the lock of her apartment door.

The door swung open. Of course he hadn't bothered with the chain or dead bolt. Aside from everything else, he thought he was invulnerable. *Well, we'll see about that.* Slamming the grocery bag onto the counter, she stalked into the living room and snapped off the stereo.

Silence descended on chaos: beer cans and ashtrays scattered and overturned, the muddy results ground into the carpet and tracked in a wavering line down the hall. The sleeves and jackets of her record collection lay about everywhere.

Behind the flowered armchair, a filthy trench coat belched, shifted, and spoke. "Hey, whereza music?"

"Get up, damn it."

Rich raised his head and peeked at her from the trench coat's creases. A foolish smile spread over his face, still so young he looked more like a mud-splashed child than a reeking drunk.

"Hey, Nicki, howza girl?"

"I said get up."

He sat up and giggled, then thrust out his hand; from his slack cuff sprouted a tattered bouquet of red silk roses. "Nothin' up m' sleeve—"

Right. Nothing. No more. The truth of it made her want to

weep. Once she had loved him for his magic, for the sleight of hand that was always quicker than the eye, for his endless capacity to delight. Once audiences had loved him too; his rise, while not meteoric, had been steady. Boston, Providence, resorts in upstate New York . . . slowly but surely, he had been making it. Even then, though, he had been drinking.

A wave of sadness swept over her, and an earlier memory: Rich at twelve, resplendent in a cut-down tuxedo, pulling a rabbit from a battered top hat to the gasps of Girl Scouts and their beaming mothers. She had been proud of him, so proud. And he had been proud of himself.

Now he could barely stand on his own two feet. A sodden degenerate creature, he could not or would not even make it from his bed to the toilet. His magic had gone away. Only the tricks remained, and the ruined trickster clambering up from her floor.

Rich's mouth curled into a sly, hopeful grin.

"It's not going to work, Rich."

The grin wavered, uncertain.

"I've asked you to get out before. Now I'm telling you."

Suddenly he coughed, a hideous racking from deep in his chest. "Never fear." He pushed up his sleeves and waved his hands in clumsy circles. A pack of miniature cards appeared on his right palm, then fell to the floor in a scattered heap. He seemed not to notice.

"Here, pick a card, any card—" Laughter wheezed into a cackle that ratcheted into another cough. Collapsing sideways onto the sofa, he held his ribs and grimaced as hacking spasms shook him. When he stopped, his face had gone as grey as the bandage on his left ear.

It was two weeks since the night he'd come in just before dawn, beaten and sniffling, dripping blood into his collar. She didn't want to think of what his torn ear might look like now, under the neglected tape and gauze; for all his demands, Rich resisted what he called "fussing." He'd refused also to tell her exactly how he'd gotten the injury—a fight, she supposed—although he'd been willing enough to let her take him to the emergency room, and to let her pay for the visit, too, because of course Rich was too free a spirit for anything so mundane as health insurance.

"My chest hurts," he whimpered now.

She stood over him. Here it was, then, the moment she had dreaded, and all she felt was dead coldness as the words, the awful words, came out of her mouth. Because this was it. This was truly, finally it. *One way or another.*

"Don't you manipulate me with your pain, damn it. No. It won't work. You have used up my sympathy. You have gobbled or guzzled me out of a year's worth of food and booze. You've alienated my neighbors and ruined my apartment. Look at this."

She gestured helplessly. "You're garbage, Rich. You're disgusting. I want you out—now."

Rich's chin quivered ominously beneath his thrust-out lower lip. "No. You can't do that t' me." His voice took on a wheedling quaver. "I'm your brother. You promised Mommy—"

"I didn't promise to let you ruin my life. You can do what you want with yours."

"Come on, Nicki, I've got to get my act together, you know that. Like, I got a lotta frustrations. I can't, like, espress myself. I need, like, a sheltered envi— environment." He passed a hand over his face, as if straightening it. "The shrink said so."

From a mask of owlish seriousness, his eyes—the same brown as her own but glazed, puffy, red-rimmed—peeped with cunning hope, measuring the effect of this performance. "Come on, Nicki, you gotta help me. All I need's a few breaks."

But Rich's need for "a few breaks" stretched back in her memory like the slime trail of a slug. Eight weeks ago he had slithered in with his talk of agents, auditions, and opening acts. A new start, he had said, a comeback—but his behavior said differently.

First he managed to "forget" appointments with the owner of several clubs. After that he stopped making them. Now her fury rose as he went on justifying and pleading and blaming—blaming everyone but himself.

"No." She flattened her voice, froze it into a spear of ice. "You have expressed yourself out of here. Granted, you are unfortunate, but if your unfortunate ass is not on that street in five minutes, I'm calling the cops. Understand?"

As if in answer, he slid off the couch. Sobbing and gasping, he snuffled into the carpet, howling and pounding his fists. Something small and white dislodged itself from the bandage over his ear, writhing about in his greasy brown hair until he rolled over it.

"Christ." A maggot. Slow hysteria crept up her spine. *No. No maggots; no creatures. He's creature enough.* "Sail your free spirit right the hell out of here, Rich. Now."

He sneaked a glance upward, caught her tone and expression, and saw that somehow, this time, his act was not producing its desired effect. And so with the slick, adaptable ease of a born stage performer, he changed it. His sad look soured, his whole face darkened. The result chilled her—it was as if he had worked magic on himself, shadowy unpleasant magic, and the trick would not end until he had what he wanted.

"Oh, sure." His lip curled. His eyes narrowed to hostile slits, through which he watched her alertly for any hesitation, any weakness he could batten on.

The moment lengthened; his face filled with mean, sneaky purpose. *Here it comes. Now he'll let me have it, both barrels.*

Only this time she was ready for him . . . she hoped. Jaw stubborn, he hauled himself upright. At six-one he stood eight inches taller than she, and he clearly meant to use every one of those inches.

"All right." His tone was sullen. "You know what it's like out there, you know I got nowhere else to go. But you don't give a damn about me. Guess I can't do much about that." He shrugged. "I mean, what the hell, I don't deserve much else, do I? I'm not the special one. Oh, no, I'm not like you."

She flinched inwardly, knowing what was coming, steeling herself for it.

"Rich. . . ."

"Oh, no." He thrust his hands out in a rough, impatient gesture of refusal. "No, forget it." His voice was rising. "You don't give a rat's ass for family feeling, I know that. And I understand."

He got to his feet and took a step toward her.

"You know why, big sister? You know why I understand?" He pushed his face, drunk and malevolent, into her own. "Because I've known lots like you, lots. You are one hard bitch, I've always known that. Under all your goody-goody shit, all that girl crap."

She retreated a step, hating herself for being intimidated.

Rich laughed, staggering. "Yeah. Can't take the truth, huh? Can you? Hot stuff reporter, except when it comes to the nitty-gritty. When the real shit comes down. Because—"

His voice dropped abruptly. Close to the bone, now; cruel, intimate. And he knew it. Damn him, he knew it.

"Daddy's little girl is just a big fat fuck-up. Really. When the makeup comes off, you're as bad as I am. And you just can't stand that, can you? Can't stand getting your nose rubbed in it. Shit." He turned away, unsteady on his feet.

"Rich, I think you should—"

"What?" He came around wildly. "Think I should what? Get out of your life? Dream on, big sister." His eyes grew cunning. "Maybe I should just go on out and die somewhere. In a gutter, huh? That make you happy? 'Swhat you want, isn't it? 'Swhat I'll do, you get your way."

"Rich—"

"Yeah. . . . Die in a gutter. Or maybe. . . ." A grin smeared itself across his blurred features. "Maybe you'd like to kill me yourself."

He advanced on her again, but this time she held her ground. "Look, we'll discuss that some other time."

"That's it, I knew it. Don't you hate me? Come on, admit it. Don't you want to carve my lungs out with a steak knife?" He bit the words off.

Astonishing. So drunk, and so accurate. A magician.

"Sure you do." His lips drew into a snarl. "Go on, you can't kid me. I know you, Nicki, known you a long time. Since you were a little kiss-ass know-it-all, mind-fuckin' the teachers an' suckin' up to the old man. Oh, I know you—hey, maybe you'll finish me off on your front doorstep, huh? Have a little instant replay, you'll feel right at home."

"Stop it." She pressed her hand to her mouth, holding it shut because he was right, he was right, dear God how she hated him now. Which was how he won, every time: knowing. Making himself so hateful, and knowing. And using it.

"Please," she said through her fingers.

"Oh, please. Please." Mincing, taunting her. "What'sa matter, sis? Can't take the facts? Huh? Big reporter?" He shoved his face into hers, his breath hot and sickening.

"You killed him," he whispered. "You killed Daddy. You let him bleed to death 'cause you just couldn't be bothered. So tell me"—his face twisted—"who the fuck are you to play Miss Righteous? Huh? You just hate me," he finished, "because I know what you did."

Sneering, he stepped away, pulling a bottle from the trench coat's pocket. Tilting his head back, he took a long, slobbery swallow.

"So watch your mouth, little Miss Righteous." He dragged the coat sleeve across his lips. "Watch your mouth, unless you want me to tell everybody else." Snorting in amusement, he fell back onto the sofa and lifted the bottle in a mock toast. He was finished with her. Winner and still champion, and he hardly even looked winded.

He's right. I do want to kill him. And I could, easily; he'll drink himself comatose, and then. . . .

And then what? Smother him with a pillow? Pour sleeping pills into him? The tormentor inside her head said, *Maybe you could slit his throat.*

Dear God. Dear God.

It did not matter what he would say, what he would tell anyone. No one, no one she cared about, would ever believe the story, or at least not the ugly twist he put on it. No, what mattered was that she could not get him out of her apartment. Even passed out drunk, he weighed too much for her to lift.

And lifting him bodily was what it would take; he had just made that clear. He would never leave on his own. He would wait until she was at work to make his liquor-store forays and be here when she returned—forever.

Determination seized her again; he would not win. Not this time. He thought he'd beaten her. But though she could not lift him, maybe she could drag him. It would take time, hauling him out the door and down the hall, but. . . .

I can do it. She could if she had to, in the case of fire or other disaster: a matter of life or death. Which it was; if he beat her this time, he would have beaten her for good. She knew it; she could feel it.

And that mustn't happen. If it did, she might as well grab his bottle and sink right down into that sodden hell alongside him. She took a step toward his crumpled form, then turned, speechless, as the door behind her opened and the lined, sallow face of a sick fifty-year-old man peered into the apartment.

The stranger blearily pushed a pair of thick horn-rims up the bridge of his long, bony nose, blinked at Nicki and then at Rich sprawled out on the sofa, and nodded confirmingly to himself as if he saw no more than what he had been expecting. Then he stepped inside and closed the door.

She found her voice. "Who the hell are you? One of his so-called friends, I suppose? Well, I'm cancelling his invitations. Get out of here right now, or when I call the cops for him they can take you, too."

The stranger's eyebrows lifted as he appeared to consider her words, then dismiss them. The stench of a public toilet thickened as he came all the way into the room, hiccuping and putting an unsteady hand on the back of a chair to support himself.

"'Scuze me. You're Nicki."

His features were blurry, as if he had begun slowly to dissolve and would go on doing so for a while. Bits of newspaper peeped through the tattered holes in his clothing, which matched only in the sense that it was all too large, all hanging together by shreds, and all filthy in the extreme.

"I," he said, "am Reginald Harper Forsten the Third."

Well, of course, that explains it. She suppressed an hysterical urge to laugh, or cry. This could not be happening. It was like a surreal off-off-Broadway play.

"At your service, and pleased t' meet you." He waved a scrawny arm at Rich, teetered, and grabbed at the chair again. "Sh-shpeaks mos' highly of you. An' of course I've read y'r articles. In the newspaper."

"You read?" Thumbprints so smeared his thick glasses that she was surprised his watery blue eyes could see through them at all. "If I make a sign that says 'Get Lost,' do you think you could read that?"

He nodded in ponderous, rueful appreciation.

"I don't shpeak highly of her." Rich giggled again. He had once more slid off the couch. "See, I'm way down here. Get it? I'm on the floor, and you're all the way up—"

In sudden fury she crossed the room, grabbed his collar,

and shook him hard; his eyes rolled dangerously. *My brother is dead, and I didn't kill him. He's done it himself, and that's why I hate him.*

"Try 'never darken my door again,'" said Forsten.

She spun on him. "Shut up. When I need your help, I'll ask."

"Wait a minute." Rich wriggled away from her, frowning as he tried to understand why things were going so bad, so suddenly; it was as if he had forgotten the scene of just moments ago.

Then he brightened. "I got it—Reg, you gotta go. You leavc, okay buddy? 'S better—Nicki an' me, we gotta talk. Nicki, he's going now, okay?" Desperately, he slung an arm over the couch and tried to haul himself onto it again.

I will not cry; I will not lower myself in front of these pieces of trash.

Forsten was silent for a moment, seeming to take in the whole situation. Then he moved, hauling Rich up with surprising strength, draping the younger man's arms over his own thin shoulders. Supporting Rich, he stood quietly, sudden pain deepening the lines in his gaunt face.

Forsten, Nicki saw with surprise, was much younger than he had looked at first. Forty, maybe. Or maybe not even that old.

"Jus' wanteda new start." Rich whimpered. "Whole 'nother chance, 'nother city. Make it big, y'know? Got a great future. . . ." His voice trailed off.

Forsten smiled sadly. "'There is no other city for you. As you have ruined your life here, in this little corner, so you have ruined it in the entire world.'"

Rich sniffled. "Huh? What kinda thing izzat to say?"

Nicki stared. "It's a poem." She wondered if at any moment the Red Queen might come bounding in, perhaps chasing a white rabbit. This was too insane to be real.

Forsten bowed as well as he could. "You see before you the Harvard man—I actually taught Cavafy once."

"Crap. Let's hear 'The God Forsakes Antony.'"

"Oh, you don't want 'Without Barbarians'?" His eyebrows lifted in acceptance of her challenge. "Very well." He cleared his throat and began to recite in clear, well-modulated tones, suddenly sober.

Cold sober. He turns it on and off. Then the poetry hit her, as it always did. Eerie, the sad, lovely words coming from that ravaged face:

"'. . . do not mourn your fortune failing you now, your works that have failed, the plans of your life that have all turned out to be illusions . . .'"

Eerie, and unpleasantly appropriate.

"'. . . and bid her farewell,'" he finished softly, "'the Alexandria that you are losing.'"

"You killed him." Rich began to struggle and snarl. "You killed him, you heartless bitch."

An absolutely cold hand seized her heart. "Get him out of here."

Not until she had spoken the words did she realize that Forsten could maneuver Rich out the door. Using his friend to remove him would be sneaky, underhanded, unfair —exactly what the big bastard deserved. And it would work. "Can you do that? Can you . . . take him?"

Forsten nodded. "I can. There is one thing, however—"

"What?"

Rich mumbled into Forsten's ragged collar. "Don't care about no one, selfish bitch. . . ." Approaching coma slurred his voice.

Forsten's face took on an oily, familiar persuasiveness. "I am, as you must know, an alkie, by nature amoral, grasping, and manipulative as hell. By this assistance"—he patted Rich's shoulder demonstratively—"I hope to earn your gratitude. Upon which, of course, I wish to cash in."

"How much?" Of course he would want something. They all wanted something, and then more somethings.

"One hot shower. Tomorrow, here." He watched her alertly.

"You don't have a shower? Where do you—" All at once she understood.

"I inhabit the city." Freeing one arm, he waved it expansively. "The city at large, that is. Unfortunately, the city does not provide sanitary facilities for its hundreds of tenants-at-large."

"You live in the street."

Smiling faintly, he nodded. "Your talent for picking the salient fact is, if I may say so—"

"No. I'm sorry. I'll pay you, but I don't want you here. Just take him and go."

He nodded again, ruefully, snatching the ten-dollar bill she thrust at him and tucking it into his pocket. "Yes. Well, it was worth a try." Bending, he slipped Rich's flaccid body into a fireman's carry, and turned toward the door. "Oh—one other thing."

"What now?" Impatience flooded through her as she considered the filthy apartment that she must restore to order, and swiftly; the dinner not yet begun; her bath still untaken.

Forsten reached back clumsily and patted Rich's pocket. It clinked. "Change your locks."

The hairs rose on her arms. "I could take his keys."

Forsten shook his head. "He has copies, you can bet on that. What you can't bet on is who else has them." He glanced at her door, at the Schlage cylinder and the dead bolt, expensive hardware she had paid a mint to have installed. Useless, now. "Change 'em soon," he said.

She nodded, wordless.

"You'll never see me again." Rich let out a wail. "I'm leavin' an' you're gonna feel bad the rest of your whole life." But he was too drunk now really to understand and he gave no further resistance, his feet making ineffectual walking motions as Forsten half dragged, half carried him out of the apartment.

She closed the door and leaned on it as Forsten's footsteps went heavily away down the hall.

You killed him, you heartless bitch.

Christ. Oh, Christ.

Meadbury

His heart thumped so loud he thought they must be able to hear it up in the street. But they couldn't hear it, and nobody knew he was down here.

It had taken him weeks to find his way through the tunnels connecting the basements of Meadbury's big downtown buildings. Meanwhile he'd had to steal all the stuff —the wire, the blasting caps, and of course the dynamite

—from different construction sites, because you couldn't just walk into a store and ask for enough explosives to blow up half the city.

Now, though, he had them, and he knew how to work them all right. Just another day on the job for the Army-trained demolitions expert, only this time he was going to off himself a real enemy.

His head hurt bad, like maybe the steel plate those Army docs put in was vibrating with the adrenaline rush. He took some deep breaths, then pulled the roll of electrician's tape out of his pocket. Four sticks on each supporting wall ought to do it. He crouched in the damp subbasement under the First National Bank, checked his map once more, and began to make packages by the light of his battery lantern. When he had twelve of four sticks each, he stopped and checked each one over, making sure he had set the detonators to the right frequency.

Okay. This was it. He had to do it, so he just wouldn't think about it any more. He was doing this for the people, right? Because something lived here, just like in Nam. He couldn't see it—it never showed itself—but he could smell it.

Because if they'd taught him anything besides how to blow things into bits, they'd taught him how to smell something bad. Something bad lived here, inside this city, just like in the villages where the Cong used to wait to kill him.

He moved through the silent, shadowy rooms of the subbasements, taping packages, saving out two. Then he went back to the map and aimed his lantern at the pipes crisscrossing the ceiling.

One was the gas main. He wired the last two packages —*careful, this is where you could screw up.* He taped the packages to the gas main and walked back to the outer room, where the transmitter box lay on the floor.

Then for one disastrous instant he let himself think of his girl, Sally, at her desk in an office twelve stories above his head. And even as it passed, he knew that one instant was his undoing.

The enemy came with a soundless rush, thickening around him, malicious and aware. His heart climbed up into his throat. The battery lantern cast great shifting shadows on the cobwebby cement block walls. Pockets of darkness lurked behind the pillars, in the corners.

It was here. He stood very still, holding his breath. Gooseflesh crept on his shoulders, his knees felt like water, and his gut was a pit of icy slush.

The transmitter was only a dozen steps away. He could reach it. He took a step, and another. Pictures invaded his head: Sally, rising in fear as the building shook, as the floor opened its concrete jaws. . . .

No. Ten steps to go. Don't think. Move. Keep moving.

He could smell it: close, real close. It stank.

. . . Sally's pink dress darkening with the blood from her crushed legs. . . .

The stink was on him now. It was inside him. Up there in his head, under the steel plate. A hoarse sob escaped his throat as he realized how badly he'd screwed up.

He knew the phrase: window of vulnerability. Thinking of Sally had opened that window just long enough to let it in. Now it sat up there in his skull, working the controls like a heavy equipment operator in his cab.

Now he couldn't hurt Sally, or anybody, because it wouldn't let him. His heart thudded. He stood stock still, an arm's length from the transmitter box.

The thing turned him, made him go back and disconnect everything. Then it rose up behind his eyeballs, forcing him to stare into the face he had never seen. All that time in the jungle, and in the coma, and in the rehab center afterward, it had been grinning at him, watching and waiting. Waiting to show him, finally, what he had been so afraid of.

And now here it was. Here for him. His heart hammered fast, faster. And faster still, until one small red explosion in the darkness under the steel plate made the hammering stop.

Made everything stop.

Nicki Pialosta

"So, you never really told me why you left Manhattan." Smiling, Ben Ibrani swirled the brandy in his glass. Six-one and one-eighty, he filled the armchair she had moved to cover the cigarette burn in the carpet.

As his sky-blue eyes studied the room, she was glad it passed muster: Those born to wealth and power disdain folks who don't scrub the ashes and beer off their floors. "I mean," he went on, "most people would give their eyeteeth to work on the *Globe.*"

Most people, she knew, would not have given just their eyeteeth for her old job. They would have cut every throat in sight and gone looking for more.

Which, oddly enough, was one reason she had left it.

"You're right, Ben. I had to kick and claw for that spot, and it was worth it. Only I didn't like Manhattan. That is, I grew to dislike it. Very much."

His eyebrows, the same reddish-brown as his hair and so neat that she wondered if he plucked them, rose in polite inquiry. They offered the opportunity to talk, but did not insist. She decided to accept the invitation.

"It's not a pretty story. My Dad was visiting—a surprise sort of thing. He was in town for the day on business and just dropped in without letting me know. And he got mugged—assaulted. And he didn't survive it."

Her hand was trembling, sloshing the brandy in the snifter. She steadied it with an effort.

"Jesus," Ibrani said. "I'm sorry. Don't go on if you don't want to."

She shrugged. "Not much more to tell. The worst thing was that he was ringing my buzzer when it happened. I thought it was kids; they'd been playing pranks, and so . . . I didn't answer." She sipped at the brandy. "After that, I understood New York. Cities have souls, Ben, and New York's soul is rotten. It wants to hurt. It wants to kill."

"Yeah. I know what you mean."

"No, I don't think you do. Not really. I've lived in twenty different cities; Dad was in the Air Force, and Air Force brats see the world. Every city was different. Every place had a different personality. You could sense what it was, and how it reacted to you."

She stopped, afraid he might think her a bit unbalanced.

But he smiled tolerantly. "Interesting theory. What personality do you think Meadbury has, or is it too small to have one?"

"Oh, no, it's got one, all right. Benign, well-meaning—interested. Funny, it reminds me of Dayton, except that Dayton's probably the litter capital of the world. Around here if I drop a gum wrapper in the street I feel like a barbarian. I mean, any city that recycles its sewage sludge to fertilize its parks. . . ."

She shook herself inwardly, straightened. "Anyway, after what happened I didn't want to live there any more." *To put it mildly.* "So, to get back to where we do live, what do you think of my story idea?"

"I don't like it." But he sounded unsure.

She leaned back in her chair and sipped her drink. "You're the editor; I'm just the lowly reporter. May I point out, however, that this is your chance to give Old Prickly his hard-hitting, in-depth feature? What was it he said about the last one?"

Ibrani made a glum face. "Too upbeat. And in a way he's right. This is a one-paper town, and that gives us a responsibility. If we don't rake the muck, nobody will. Those jokers over at Channel Six think a story is something you tear off the AP wire."

"So what's the problem?" *Careful, careful; one must be ambitious, assertive—but always ladylike.* She had learned, by God how she had learned, to take care of herself. The knights in shining armor were dead.

"Well, for one thing, it's really a Metro story. It doesn't belong to us. I'm not sure how the Metro guys will like you horning in on their territory, even if I get Will Rifkind to agree to it. And if I do get it past him, who's going to do all the features you would have been doing?"

"Ben, you hired me as a reporter, not a gallery-and-restaurant reviewer. I can cover the circus and the county fairs with one hand tied behind me, and you know it. And as for Rifkind, well, we'll make sure it looks like a feature, that's all. It will be a feature. I'll write it that way. We can have the story for our section without stepping on anybody's toes, if we're careful."

He still seemed uneasy.

"What else?" she said.

Finally he did smile, capitulating. "I just don't like the thought of you out on the street with a bunch of degenerates. I know it's not the modern way to think of things, but I was raised the old-fashioned way."

Familiar refrain: Don't try, you might hurt yourself. Kind, but wrongheaded.

"I can't do this in the library, Ben." She took another swallow of brandy; it felt good, burning down, easing the lump that had been in her throat since this afternoon's ordeal. "And I can take care of myself out there. You know from my clips that I've done it before. But if you don't want the story, there's not much point to my writing it. Maybe I should just wing it at Rifkind, let him assign it to one of his guys?"

"No," Ben said at once, as she had known he would. "No, you're right. 'Tenants-at-large—' It'll make a great feature. This city needs features like that. I guess I'm too conservative—and Old Prickly will love it. Go ahead." He grinned. "But don't tell him I called him that. And don't tell Rifkind. I'll ease him into it myself when the time comes."

She smiled back. It was only fair. She had gotten the idea while scrubbing the corner where Rich had thrown up. I want something for this, she had thought, and had known at once what it must be: the article that would make her reputation on the *Bulletin.*

She needed it. The stories she had written in Manhattan counted for nothing up here. Managing editors did not care what reporters had done for other papers, other towns. To stand out, to get ahead, she had to do something in Meadbury.

The vagrants were perfect. Meadbury: The City That Cares—how could it be, when people lived in its gutters? Only fair to tell the city that, under her byline of course.

There was one small problem: Rich. Reporters were supposed to be objective. They were not supposed to have brothers drowning in the very muck they proposed to rake. And yet, if she didn't rake it, who would? The fact was, no one else cared. No one else thought abandoned people and ruined lives were newsworthy.

But they were, and that was the bottom line. If the story worked, she would be golden. If not. . . .

Well, she wouldn't tell Ben about Rich; not yet. Time enough when the story was rolling, when the photographers were assigned and the researchers burrowing. Time enough when the ads for the extra pages had been sold.

"I'll start tomorrow," she said.

Ibrani sighed, running a manicured hand through his perfectly-razored auburn hair. The dull, authentic glint of gold flashed at his tailored cuff. "Why do all my reporters have to be so damned aggressive?" But his tone held a grudging hint of admiration.

A distinctly respectable catch. Awful thought. Cold bitch. Yet once he would have seemed exactly the answer to her prayers: intelligent, good-looking, even rich. And not nouveau riche, either.

Benedetto Ibrani's family, he'd told her, had come to America in the heyday of Giuseppe Garibaldi, abandoning in the mountains of northern Italy the title they didn't want any more, and the estate a rebel wanted more than the Ibranis wanted to die for it. They got the gold out, though, along with the paintings and the five hundred years of aristocratic experience.

Once he would indeed have been the answer to Nicki's prayers.

But she hadn't said those prayers since her father's funeral. At this remove, she felt only curiosity about the woman she had once been—and regret.

Later, when she and Ben had bantered their way through more small talk and consumed more brandy than was entirely prudent, he asked what she wanted out of life.

Your job, and after that, Old Prickly's. And I'm already reaching for both of them.

Then she proceeded to lie; quite charmingly, she thought.

Tommy Riley

He chugged down the last of the warm beer and tossed the can to the floor of the car. All this cruising around was getting boring, especially since Pete was stoned and he wasn't.

"Oh, man." Pete slowed as two girls—one blond, one brunette—teetered across the street on high-heeled wooden sandals, rumps twitching in their tight white jeans. "Howdja like to pick up some of that?"

"Jeez, will you say something else for a change?" Tommy gazed irritably after the girls, who most likely had very large boyfriends.

"Oh, I get it. I ain't intellectual enough for the college boy now." Pete glanced at him. "Hey, you wanna do a number on Old Man Roundtree?"

"How come?"

"'Cause he threw me out of his dump. Said I was shopliftin'."

"You probably were."

"So what's that got to do with it? I'm gonna do a job on those windows of his some fine night."

"Yeah, well. Count me out. Those windows are money. They'll have your ass." Tommy picked another beer from the six-pack, decided he didn't want it, and pulled the tab on it anyway. Warm beer, jeez.

Pete swerved out around a bus and cut back hard in front of it. The bus horn bleated.

"Hey, watch it." Beer foamed down the front of Tommy's shirt.

"Relax, my man. Everything is under control. Captain Pete's at the wheel. Hey, you wanna go down to the video arcade?" Pete snapped on the radio; the Doors blasted out at top volume.

According to Jim Morrison, the blood in the streets was up to their ankles.

Jim Morrison was a big, dumb, loudmouth loser, and now he's dead because he was dumb. The thought shocked Tommy. He liked Jim Morrison. He liked the Doors.

Only he didn't. Not any more. He turned the radio down,

ignoring Pete's peevish look. "I gotta go home. Got a calculus quiz tomorrow."

Pete frowned straight ahead, aiming his father's big white El Dorado down Locust Street, which luckily was not very busy. "Sure. Okay. Whatever you say." He swung onto a side street and headed back toward Tommy's house. "You're gettin' to be a real big drag, you know it?"

"Yeah. I know it. See you tomorrow."

The El Dorado roared away down the street, leaving Tommy staring after it.

Jeez, education, man. He hoped it wasn't seeping in too deep, rotting all the fun centers out of his brain. That was no joke—he was feeling it already. If he wasn't careful, he thought, it might change him forever.

Then he went inside to study for the quiz.

Nicki Pialosta

She remembered the lock when Ibrani was leaving, his steps crunching distantly on the gravel drive. The brass knob of the dead bolt glittered at her. The chain clattered as she hooked it into its slot.

Who might have her keys? Who might have copied them? Anyone could have weaseled them out of Rich, extracted her name from his drunken maunderings. And her address was in the book.

The telephone rang: a shrill, nerve-jangling peal.

She grabbed it: silence. "Hello?" The line was open: someone listening, waiting, not speaking. She hung up. It rang again.

This time she picked it up without speaking, but a matter-of-fact voice said, "This is Mr. Ibrani's service." It was a woman, talking through her nose. "He left this number to reach him. Is he there?"

"No." She collapsed into a chair. *Silly goose, you're getting paranoid.* "No, he just left. You can probably reach him at home in a few minutes."

"Thenkyew." The line disconnected.

She checked her recorder a final time, then began to gather the cups and glasses, to empty the ashtrays. The coffee and brandy had put her at loose ends: too nerved-up to sleep, too tired to work. She leafed through her mail, which she had not had time to look at earlier; among the notices, catalogs, direct-mail ads and her credit-card bill, she found an envelope addressed in a familiar, looping hand and tore it open.

Inside, Mr. and Mrs. Henry Callendar announced the engagement of their daughter, Mary Anne, to Brockton Barnes Waite, Esquire. On the other side of the card Mary Anne had written "Hope you can make the wedding. We'd love to see you."

Nicki checked the date, thought about going, then dismissed the idea. Mary Anne Callendar. A nice young woman who had needed befriending when she'd started at the *Globe* as a food writer. Rapidly, though, she'd found her niche, as willowy blonds with big blue eyes were apt to do. Soon, when they went out, Nicki was Mary Anne's sidekick instead of the reverse. Once Brock arrived on the scene Nicki felt like an appendix that needed removal, although Mary Anne continued urging her to tag along.

After the wedding Mary Anne would no doubt quit work to have a baby. She could practically hear Mary Anne: "Oh, but you don't need a man, Nicki, you're so lucky. You've got your career."

Much good it's doing me this minute. Nicki caught herself, told herself to stop. She was just tired and grouchy.

Tired, but not sleepy. Setting the invitation aside, she paged through a magazine, flicked the TV on and off, wanted a shower but felt oddly reluctant to take one. Standing naked in it, she might not hear—

What?

She could go to the Park Plaza for the night, but probably more low-life types had keys to hotel rooms than were carrying the ones to her apartment. Besides, if anyone wanted to get in, the motive would surely be burglary. And burglars wanted people to be away from home. She could come back to find the place cleaned out.

No, better to stay. Tomorrow she would call the locksmith. She turned the television on low and left a light burning in the living room, then at last gave in and took half a Valium. On top of the brandy she'd drunk, it knocked her solidly out.

So that not until morning, struggling through a muzzy

hangover, did she wonder: Had she heard something, or only dreamed it?

She got up, plodded from the bedroom. Coffee, news magazine—she turned toward the front door and stopped, her cup jittering hard in its saucer as she stared at the door.

Which stood ajar two inches, restrained only by its flimsy chain.

SATURDAY, SEPTEMBER 22

Meadbury

The two men walked stealthily down the long, shabby corridor, sloshing gasoline into the doorways and leaving a dark trail of it in their wake.

Wally, the middle-aged one with the three-day stubble, spoke in a whisper. "Charlie, why the hell are we doing this in broad daylight? Shoulda done it last night."

"What are you, crazy?" Charlie snorted. "People sleep here at night; don't wanna torch a place when people are sleeping, too many of 'em go up, you know? That's called murder one, old pal, and murder one is somethin' I don't ever wanna have to deal with."

He opened an apartment door with a passkey and soaked the rug leading from the hall to the living room. "This is killing me, you know?" Straightening, he kneaded the small of his back, and grinned. "Those drapes are perfect. They'll catch if you breathe heavy on 'em."

"Jackie says you've got two hundred g's in insurance on this place."

"Jackie's full of it, you know?" Charlie walked out of the room, propping the door open as he left. "Just like a chimney."

"Well, Jackie says—"

"Hey." Charlie spun on his helper. "Jackie don't own this place, Jackie don't pay the bills on it, and Jackie ain't going broke from tenants who don't come up with the rent. So don't tell me what Jackie says, okay?"

Wally backed away. He had five inches on Charlie, but Charlie had the temper. "Okay, man, okay." He held up his hands. "Whatever you say. You sure it's empty upstairs?"

"I doubt it. Gotta be somebody home."

"I thought you said—"

"It's daylight, turkey. Nobody's asleep up there."

"But—"

"And there's a twenty-thousand-dollar fire escape, so don't worry about that. And I got the inspector in my pocket, so don't worry about that, either. Come on. Let's just get the basement, then we're done."

"Yeah, the sooner the better."

Charlie hit the switch at the top of the basement stairs; the light bulb popped into brilliance, then died. "Shit. Place is falling apart." He started down. "There's a flashlight at the bottom. Walk careful. I don't think my insurance'd cover you if you broke a leg trying to burn the joint down."

Wally followed, wading into an ocean of ink, feeling for the treads with the tip of his shoe. The stairs creaked. The railing wobbled in his hand. From below rose Charlie's sigh of relief, accompanied by a click and a sudden pool of yellow light on the cement floor. Shadows wavered on the walls.

"Come on, bring the gas." Charlie's voice came from over by the furnace. Wally lugged the can to him, but as he set it down, something wet splashed on his shoe. "Hey, the can's leaking."

"So? Ain't like we're gonna use it again."

Through the thick masonry foundations came the rumble of heavy vehicles and the high keening wail of sirens. Wally frowned. "What's going on out there?"

"Damn if I know. Let's get this done with and then get the hell out. G'wan, I'll hold the light, you pour—" The flashlight's batteries failed abruptly; the shadows closed in. "Shit. I can't see a damn thing."

Neither could Wally. But it felt like some third person had suddenly joined them. "Charlie," he whispered to the darkness on his right. "Is that you?" Silence. Then booted feet thudded on the floor overhead. "God, they're here!"

"Just stay quiet." The voice came from Wally's left. Then who was that on his right? Wally frowned at the darkness, not wanting to turn his back on it. "Hey," he said unhappily.

"Hold on," Charlie said, "there's more batteries in the cupboard." His footsteps shuffled away.

Now the darkness pressed against Wally's face and mouth like a thick, damp rag. To distract himself from his nervousness he found himself wondering about Charlie's tenants, where they'd go, what they'd do, how they'd make it without the few possessions they'd managed to collect.

The darkness reeked of gasoline. Something rustled next to him, very near. Not Charlie, though. Charlie was rummaging the cupboard, way over there.

"Got 'em!"

Wally's mouth opened wordlessly. Charlie, he wanted to say, but couldn't. All of a sudden this idea of Charlie's didn't seem so hot. It was wrong to burn people out of their homes.

Charlie, he tried to say again, but something snapped his mouth shut, something that was in him now, moving him aside and taking control. As if from a distance he felt his hand worming into his pocket, felt it searching about in there. What the hell, he wondered, was it after?

As if in answer, his fingers closed around his cigarette lighter. Huh? Wally thought, and then all became clear to him.

No. He moaned inwardly. Oh, no. Please don't do that. But his hand continued on its errand, drawing the cigarette lighter out of his pocket.

Meanwhile Charlie had gotten the new batteries into the flashlight, and snapped it back on. Now the bright white beam crossed the cellar floor and lit on the red gas can. "There," Charlie said.

"Yeah, thanks," said Wally's mouth, as his body began moving stiffly, puppetlike, his shoes scraping on the rough concrete floor.

"Hey," Charlie began in alarm, spying the cigarette lighter. "Hey, what the hell are you—"

Flick, Wally thought simply, glimpsing his thumb as the lighter flared.

Just one tiny flame.

Which grew at once into a fireball, swallowing both of them.

Nicki Pialosta

By midmorning, downtown Meadbury bustled with shoppers and office workers enjoying the warmth of a razor-bright fall day. Jovial Pilgrims and accommodating turkeys eyed each other in department store windows. The crisp tang of fallen leaves carbonated the air and the clear, slanting sunshine, through which everything looked unnaturally vivid, sharp-edged.

Nicki leaned against the brickwork between two of the store windows and lit a cigarette. One display held a calendar that announced "Only 72 Shopping Days Till Xmas!"—an anxiety that the foresighted parent might relieve by purchasing the model railroad laid out alongside the calendar.

The little engine tootled importantly around yards of track. At a crossroads lay a perfect toy city, its gate jerking up and down at just the right moment, its perfect little people going in and out of their tiny, perfect houses. Each cunning figure was controlled by a wire attached to a tiny, hidden switch. In ten-pitch caps the station sign read "MEADBURY."

Nicki turned away, shivering despite the sun. The miniature city made her inexplicably uneasy. It was almost too lifelike, too real, except for the expressions of the miniature people, grimacing with taut, frozen hilarity as they jerked through their unchanging routines.

Stop it. Stop letting your imagination run away with you. You have things to do. Work, for example. Guiltily, she remembered the assignments waiting on her desk: a restaurant review, an interview with a local author whose first mystery novel had just been published, a crafts fair, and a rags-to-riches story on a local artist who designed sets for Broadway plays.

The crafts fair piece and the restaurant review would be dreck. The other two might turn out worthwhile; writers and artists could be dears, or asses. None of the stories interested her, but when she got back she would write them just the same; she lacked the clout to pick and choose her assignments.

For now. She turned her attention to the project at hand.

A large woman laden with shopping bags caught her eye and smiled as she passed. A man jostled her arm and tipped his hat in apology. On the street a truck slowed to let an old man falter to the opposite curb; the driver grinned down as the man waved his thanks. A DPW employee wearing faded blue coveralls pushed a broom along the walk, pausing now and then to sweep accumulated debris into a dustpan and then to empty that into the wheeled garbage can he towed behind.

Soothed by the rhythms, by the warmth, Nicki lit another cigarette and settled in to watch her target pick his own.

Thirty feet down the sidewalk, striding briskly and squinting into the sun, the man with the topcoat over his arm did not see Forsten.

Forsten's head came up an inch, as if to sniff the air. Rocking on the balls of his feet, he waited until the man was almost alongside, then stepped directly into his path.

"May I have a dollar, please?" He stuck out his hand.

His target recoiled. "A dollar? What for?"

"Wine. I need it, sir. I need it badly." Although Forsten's voice was firm, his extended hand trembled. "Please."

"Good heavens." The man searched his pocket. Pedestrians streamed by on both sides, their eyes averted. "Have you no pride?"

"None at all, I'm afraid." Forsten hung his head. "I do have a nice stock of grovels, though. How will you have it—down on one knee or flat on my belly? I'll clean your shoes while I'm there, if you like."

"God." The man thrust out a dollar. "Get away, man. Let me by."

Forsten's fingers closed on the bill with a nearly audible snap. "Thank you."

The man scurried on. "In broad daylight!" He cast back an outraged glance. "Right out in the street."

Forsten scanned the crowd for his next mark.

Nicki moved up, chuckling in spite of herself. "Some technique."

Thick lenses enlarged his puzzled, watery blue eyes, magnifying their yellow tinge. He stank. He stared, but did not acknowledge her.

"I'm Nicki. Last night? My apartment?"

He laid a palm to his forehead. "Of course. Do forgive me. Short term's the first to go, they say. Soon I'll recall only poetry. Nicely furnished, but no one at home, so to speak."

She edged him out of traffic, over to the windows. "Look, Reg—"

"Not having second thoughts, I hope?" He shook an admonishing finger in an oddly schoolmasterish gesture. "Writhing about in the toils of guilt? You cannot keep him, you know. He may be magic, but he's not housebroken."

"Reg, it's not about Rich. It's about you."

He cocked an eyebrow. "Really?"

"Really." She took a deep breath, caught too strong a whiff of him, and almost gagged. "I'm sorry I was so rude. I was upset. You were a great help, and I've decided you can use my shower."

He nodded, considering this. "Do you have a dollar?"

"Um, yes, I do." She fumbled, dug it out of her purse. "Why?"

He plucked it from her fingers and tucked it away. "Time is my stock in trade." His voice was flat. "Let us stroll to my office."

"Reg, I don't—"

"Unless you're afraid? You needn't be. I'm quite harmless. Chemically caponized, in fact; the alcohol does it."

"I'm not afraid of you, Reg." Eyeing him—fifteen pounds and maybe three inches he had on her—and the alley he was heading for, she hoped the statement sounded true.

His smile spread, dark and unfooled. He pointed ahead. "Shall we reason together?"

Mistake. Big mistake. Still, she followed him into the passageway. It was almost a tunnel. Windowless brick walls rose eight sheer stories, seeming to meet overhead, closing out the light. Her shoulders brushed them on both sides. Unidentifiable things crunched and squished underfoot; she did not want to think about what they might be. *Meadbury's clean-up crews ought to tackle these alleys.* Nervous, she peered ahead. If she screamed, no one would hear her; no one would ever know.

Then she relaxed. The alley, after widening into a paved yard beside a loading dock, continued out to Elmwood

Avenue. Ahead, men pushed hand trucks piled high with cartons through the open stockroom doors. But Forsten had vanished.

"Here." His voice came out of an archway on her right.

One of the workers, glimpsing her, shifted the chewed cigar in his mouth and shrugged as if to say, "Your funeral, lady."

She hoped distinctly that he was wrong.

"You're wasting my time, not to mention my patience."

She followed the voice into deeper shadows.

Hands seized her shoulders; a small shriek escaped her. "Reg! Don't scare me like that."

His laugh rang harsh, almost bitter. "Step over this—" He waved at a large, vague shape.

She did so with care. "What is it?"

"Friend of mine. Jamallah. Nice fellow, unless you hurt him. The raveled sleeve of care takes a good deal of knitting in his sad case."

Farther in, the light strengthened; stray beams slanted down from one square of open sky. She blinked, and picked her way behind Forsten to the foot of an air shaft. Untidy stacks of cartons, toppled and leaning, mounted on either side; through cracks in the pavement, a few famished weeds strained toward the sun.

"Home at last." He kicked aside a large carton of newspapers. "Sorry the bed's not made. I generally entertain at my club." Indicating an orange crate, he pulled up another, and sat. "Now. What is it you want?" His gaze lacked the humor she thought she recalled.

The crate wobbled beneath her. "I told you, I've decided—"

"Bullshit. I'm a drunk, not a fool; there is a difference, you know. You want something, or you wouldn't be here. I don't know what it is, and I don't know what you're willing to trade. That makes, so far, perhaps one-third of a deal. You may care to elucidate further, or perhaps you've changed your mind." He stopped and waited.

"No. I haven't changed my mind." Heat crept up her neck. "Am I that transparent?"

"Let's say I've had practice looking. Young ladies do not generally follow me down the street to offer the use of their showers. Ergo: ulterior motive."

She glimpsed, then, how mean it was, this life lived so desperately close to the bone. It had not occurred to him that kindness might be a motive.

And of course he was right. "I need your help."

"In that case, you are in deep and serious trouble. How do you think I could help you?"

"I need to see your kind of life. I need to *feel* it, so I can write it. Maybe then things might change, for you and for other people."

"One of the changes being, no doubt, your professional standing."

"That too." No point lying; he understood self-interest.

"And perhaps a sop might be thrown to guilt over a certain unfortunate younger brother?"

She said nothing.

Quiet, motionless, he considered her.

"By God," he said at last, softly. "Have I found my Boswell? Shall you trail in my wake, scribbling notes, while I piss in doorways, match wits with rats, and guzzle cheap wine till it drizzles into my clothes?"

"Reg—"

He jumped up, voice rising. "Shall I suffer your pity, ineptly disguised as compassion, while I twitch and shriek and befoul myself? You? How low, indeed, have I sunk." His voice, sulphurous, bubbled up from his own private hell.

"No, Reg, listen—"

His face changed, brightened. "But what an appropriate chronicler: a junior scribe from a smug little sheet in the garbage-recycling center of the nation. And truly, we deserve the attention. After all, we're a vanishing species, dying off in September now instead of in cruel winter. No doubt the city will soon discover a rich source of organic phosphates in our corpses."

"Reg, I didn't mean you!"

He sat back down, the wild glitter fading from his eyes.

"I thought . . . a woman. You could introduce me, arrange things. I really think a woman would be better for my purposes. What's so funny?"

"For your purposes. . . ." Shoulders trembling, he lowered his face to his hands. "Oh, my dear girl." He made noises of bitter mirth and peeped between fingers so skinny their knuckles looked like beads on string. "For your purposes." For several moments he gasped with helpless laughter.

At last he brushed the tears from his eyes. "Oh, Nicki, your simple faith is truly appalling. Whatever your purposes, the women among us can hardly be better for them. If anything, they're worse, as you shall see. Pride flees, my dear, before your innocent wish to do good."

"Then you'll find me someone?" As she stood, her left stocking snagged on the rough crate; she tore free heedless of the damage. This was worth a new pair. Several new pairs, in fact.

"No need to find her. She'll find you, if there's dinner in it. Dear old Sarah, the scourge of South State Street. Be at the Greyhound station, five o'clock tonight. Dress warmly. You can't imagine how cold it can be. And do be careful. There are other things you can't imagine."

Not after thirty months on a Manhattan beat. "Thank you, Reg."

"Thank me with a twenty." Stepping suddenly much too near, he thrust out a demanding hand.

Under his hungry stare she withdrew her wallet, and from it two tens. As she sensed the effort it cost him to wait, not to snatch away the money, her forgotten fear returned with a sickening rush.

"A pleasure doing business with you." His voice was expressionless as he stuffed the bills into the rags of his jacket. Then with a curt nod he slipped by and disappeared into the dark alley.

Nicki stared after him. *The least you could do is get* me *out, too.*

Something squeaked, ratlike. She jerked around. The walls looked down, blank and silent. Biting her lip, she took a step into the narrow passageway and stumbled on something soft, something yielding.

Jamallah lurched and reared up, tumbling her hard against the brick wall. He staggered, blocking the exit, and roared.

"Oh, mon, the city sing so loud today—" A huge black fist slammed into the wall just over her head, raining down crumbs of brick. His enormous shaven head was at least seven feet in the air. "Too loud she sings, too loud!"

If I can reach the alley, the street—

His fingers scraped the masonry again, searching it, inches from her face. Then his eyes, gleaming golden in the shadows, focused on her. He smiled.

Nicki bit back a scream.

"Oh, but she sing me a pretty tune today, a pretty." Golden eyes smiling, seeing God alone knew what, Jamallah reached tenderly for her throat. His cold, strong fingers found it, encircled it, and began to close.

She wrenched away, pushing off from the bricks like a sprinter from the starting blocks. Ducking under a forearm the size of a tree branch, she ran. A howl of outrage propelled her faster. Risking a glance back, she tripped and fell. The broken pavement slammed the air from her lungs. For a moment she lay sprawled, panic-stricken. Very close behind, a garbage can crashed to its side.

As she scrambled up, her hand closed on something small and strangely familiar. Jamallah's mad, tuneless hum droned in her ear; his workboots crunched on gravel and glass. Nicki charged down the alley, turning her ankle, bashing her wrist against the wall, at last half falling into the blessedly busy street.

Sunlight dazzled her eyes. Blinking, she sucked great, sobbing gulps of air; clean, fresh air. Pedestrians passed by without comment or sidelong glances. Meadbury was caring, yes, but not intrusive; no one sought thrills from others' discomposure.

Only after she had caught her breath, after the worst of the terror had gone, did she open her clenched fist.

A set of keys lay on her palm: the keys to her apartment. The keys she had given Rich, on the chain with the tin four-leaf clover. "For luck," she had told him back on that first day, and they had laughed because everyone knew magicians already had luck.

Confused, she peered back into the alley. Then she realized: Of course. Rich had been here with Reg. Lost the keys.

The alley held nothing at all. No murderous monster grinned there.

Silly. He wouldn't really have hurt you. Another wino who

might take your purse, which by the way, you should have left at home. Another wino, another big baby like Rich. That's all.

Still, the alley seemed to leer, smug in its shadows, its scabby frights.

In the store window the little train hurried through the toy town. The flagman leapt onto the track, whipped his flag out, and jumped back from the engine's path as it rushed by.

Nicki thought she knew just how he felt.

In the alley behind her, someone chuckled.

Clutching the keys, she walked on trembling legs to her car, and drove off without looking back.

Meadbury

Arthur "Jayman" Shipman ambled along a downtown street, talking loudly. Those within earshot probably thought he was talking to himself. He was not. He was conversing with his Uncle Bubba, who had shared his head since that day ten years ago when Uncle Bubba had followed his arm into the threshing machine.

Actually, Bubba did most of the talking.

Do it here, Artie boy.

It felt wrong. "Uncle Bubba!"

Here. Now!

He didn't want to. It was his favorite place, sure, but there were only twenty or thirty people in the fast-food restaurant. He liked it best when the place was crampack-solid, because then all the tables by the big windows had as many people sitting at them as could fit, and half of them'd be staring at the sidewalk.

Artie!

That was the don't-mess-around-any more tone of voice, the one he always obeyed because if he didn't the pain would happen inside his head where Uncle Bubba lived, and so—

Edging out of the pedestrian flow, Arthur "Jayman" Shipman took off his clothes. All of them. Saving his socks for last. Then he pressed up against the window and waggled his dong until the lady drinking her milkshake through a straw looked up. Her jaw dropped and she turned purple, starting to choke as she raised her right hand, pointing. All the people inside turned their heads.

"Jayman!"

"Darn you, Uncle Bubba, now look what you done!" The black cop who'd busted him last time was coming, already pulling out his nightstick even though Arthur Shipman hadn't done anything to deserve getting hit for. He scooped his clothes up into his arms and sped around the corner, heading for the alleys, alcoves, and dark secret crannies at the heart of the city.

The cop pounded along right behind him.

Late afternoon air washed Arthur's skin. He laughed as he hurdled the garbage cans. *Like a deer!* He wished he had left his shoes on, though. The broken glass was cutting into his feet something fierce, and the blood would mess up his only pair of socks.

"Jayman!" The cop was gaining, even though he was weighted down with gun and cuffs and stick and radio and all the other technical stuff cops slung on their belts. Of course, he was black, and everybody knew no white guy could outrun a black guy, especially when the white guy's thirty-eight years old and sharing a skull with Uncle Bubba. Arthur knew he had to do something, fast.

He dove under an archway and slipped, scraping his ass on the cracked cement. Something rolled away from his foot. He reached for it. His hand closed on a metal cylinder. A piece of pipe. Heavy. About two feet long, just the right size for a—

Uncle Bubba spoke. *Don't you do that, boy.*

"But he's gonna get me!"

You hurt that man, you're on your own.

"I don't care." Slipping to his feet, hugging the wall, he waited till the cop came tearing past. He raised the pipe. "Hah!"

The black face turned, eyewhites rolling. Arthur Shipman brought the pipe down right in the middle of the blue hat with the shield on the front. The eyes closed and the hat bounced away and the cop folded up with a grunt.

Arthur Shipman stood in the shadows and pulled on his clothes. He hadn't hit the cop very hard, only hard enough to be sure that was one cop who wouldn't be chasing Arthur

Shipman the rest of the night.

"So what do you think of that, huh, Uncle Bubba?"

No answer.

"Okay, you be that way, old man, see if I care." It'd be funny, though, living without that familiar voice. Arthur already felt a little bit lonesome for it.

Then he froze. Had something over there moved? Was somebody watching?

He squinted, then relaxed. No. Just a funny-looking shadow, that was all. He walked around the corner and down a flight of stairs to a cardboard-lined landing, sat down, and promptly fell fast asleep.

Tommy Riley

"So why'ncha pick up somethin', Riley? There's girls like crawlin' all over. Even you could get one." Peewee Coover leaned against the Space Invaders game and hammered the buttons. "Wham! I got me another alien bastard! Man, I'm beatin' the livin' shit out of those crafty little buggers."

Tommy sipped the Coke he'd bought to wash the taste of beer from his mouth. Funny, he didn't like beer so much any more.

"Hey," Peewee said, not looking up from the game, "you got any q's?"

Tommy dug a handful of quarters out of his pocket and stacked them by Peewee's right hand. He was well supplied with quarters nowadays, partly because he was earning them regularly and partly because he had so little time to spend them. "Listen, I'm gonna split."

Peewee shrugged and blasted another alien out of the sky. All around the bright fluorescent-lit room, video game machines flashed and jangled as teenaged spacemen turned back the murderous alien tide. From monster speakers set up in the corners, Southside Bruce and the Asbury Johnnies blared; the noise was giving Tommy a headache. "See ya."

Peewee grunted. "Wham!"

As Tommy passed the door, Pete Cheney lifted his blond head. "Hey, Riley, when you gonna help me take out you-know-who?" His blue eyes glittered dangerously; probably he was on something again. Cheney would eat anything in pill form; mostly the stuff turned his brains to twisted wires.

"Come on, Pete, you still all hot about Roundtree? Leave it alone, man, you don't want to bust his windows. You really don't."

Pete made a sour face. "Fuckin' candy-ass. You burn my tail, you know that? You're such a big, fat, holier-than-thou." Then a sly smirk came across his features as a new thought occurred to him. "Hey, you get lucky yet with that newspaper broad you're so stuck on? I know her. She interviewed my old man. Her name was underneath the article—Nicki Pialosta. Yeah, old Tricky Nicki."

Tommy lunged across the machine and had Pete by the collar before he could think. "Shut up. Just shut up, okay?"

Pete held up his hands. "Okay, okay. I mean, you don't have to get so violent. She's just a chick, you know?"

"Don't let me hear her name come out of your mouth, you got it?"

"Sure. Whatever you say, man. Jesus." Pete returned to his game, shaking his head.

Tommy stepped out into the twilight and took deep breaths of fresh air. He shouldn't have gone after Pete that way. Maybe he ought to go back in now and apologize.

He looked over his shoulder at the arcade, practically rocking off its foundations with the noise of the games and the music and all the kids yelling their heads off.

Forget it. He could apologize tomorrow. After work, maybe.

Yeah, tomorrow.

Nicki Pialosta

Oh, sure, it's a great idea, Ben, but on second thought I'm just too scared. Why don't you put me on cooking, or contests, something cozy and safe and anonymous?

Standing in chilly dusk, breathing bus fumes in front of the Fourth and Edge Street bus station, Nicki forced herself not to flee. It had taken an enormous effort to come at all. Fog haloed the murky neon signs of the taverns on desolate Edge Street, and she was assailed by a strong temptation to pack it in and get herself home.

Home was safe, now. The super had gotten her note, and Nicki had returned just as the locksmith finished installing a stout, gleaming new Block lock. Unpickable, he said, and the Block Corporation guaranteed no key but this lock's own would ever open it.

"So you don't give this key to nobody." He had dangled it before her eyes. "Pretty girl like you. There's maniacs out there."

She considered going back to her apartment and putting that great big lock between her and the world. Still no sign of Sarah, if such a person even existed. Reg might simply have drunk the whole twenty, might even now be chortling about how he'd snookered a gullible reporter. At least the sun had not gone all the way down. Yet.

And she was on her own here. No one knew she had already started on the piece; Ibrani had not finished "thinking it over." To win his final approval, she would have to show him something so good that he would ache to print the story.

A figure shuffled from behind the rusted dumpster across the street. Something that looked like a heap of burlap sacks dragged a shopping cart over the curb. The cart squealed the plaint of pitted metal, apt accompaniment for the hoarse chant pouring tunelessly from the rag heap.

It stopped before her. The face resembled the kind of freak vegetable seen at roadside stands: misshapen blob of a nose, jutting chin, bristly whiskers sprouting from various warty protuberances. Steel-grey hair strained back from the wide, shiny forehead.

"H'lo." A red hand shot out from among coats layered one on top of another. The hand clutched a stick of gum. "Here."

Nicki took it. "Thank you."

"Cuts the stink. Stink'll keep you warm, though, remember that."

"I will." Nicki put the gum in her mouth.

"Well. I'm Sarah. How 'bout a hamburger? Good hash house over there." She gave a gravelly laugh. "We c'n hash things over."

Sarah's laugh was infectious. To Nicki's surprise, she liked the old woman at once, though a Martian dropped out of the sky could not have seemed more alien.

Inside the diner, Sarah peeled off three coats and shoved them ahead of her into the booth. "So you wanta see th' life. You wanta see normal, or you wanta see funny?" She gave the word "funny" a scornful, scathing twist. Her blue eyes, startlingly alert, fixed Nicki with a quick sharp look.

"Normal." Nicki paused to give the waitress their order, then went on carefully. "I write articles for the newspaper. The paper wants me to tell people about all of you, and get the city to help you. But I don't know what you do"—she gestured at the window, beyond which dusk thickened into night—"out there."

"Hmph." A hint of grudging respect crept into her voice. "Nobody docs, and don't many wanta learn."

The waitress crashed cups and plates onto their table, scowled at Sarah, and left.

Sarah ate steadily for a while, engulfing two burgers, a heaping plate of home fries, a wedge of pie with ice cream, and three cups of coffee. "Good grub." Her cup clattered into its saucer. "You oughta stoke up, too, honey."

The coffee smelled of soap. "I . . . ate before I came."

"Oh." Sarah blinked. "Yeah."

Nicki paid, and they stepped into the clammy twilight, heading down Fourth to Elmwood Avenue. Cars sped by more frequently there than in the decayed district they were leaving. What did their drivers think: a cop sweeping up yet another bit of human rubbish? A bag lady and her apprentice? Nicki raised her collar against the wind.

It seemed to her, then, that this was the true but secret heart of Meadbury: these ruined, abandoned blocks where the buildings slouched downhearted and desolate, where the people survived by gathering empty bottles for the nickel the recycling center paid for each.

Sarah, still pulling the squealing cart, kept sneaking mystified glances at Nicki. "You sure a pretty little thing like you wants ta hang out all night with a ol' bag like me?"

"Sarah, I can't do this without you." Somehow, meeting Sarah had stiffened her resolution again. If she should not be out here, then neither should Sarah, who really belonged in a neat snug room complete with teapot and carpet slippers. "I need you, I really do."

Sarah stopped, her cart halting behind her with a crash of rusted metal. "Well. Been a long time since anybody said that t' me. Sounds real nice." Her smile exposed four spade-shaped teeth, widely separated.

Several blocks away, a figure shambled onto the sidewalk, a shadow-shape cut from enormous sheets of black paper. Nicki blinked; the figure vanished. Had it been there at all? She shook off a chill.

"Come on, honey." Sarah gave the cart a yank. "Let's go shake ourselves down some college kids."

On the narrow, tree-lined campus streets, fresh-faced youngsters loped along, wearing designer jeans and Frye boots with an air of casual entitlement.

Sarah plopped heavily onto a bench outside Whillikers, the college hangout where ferns outnumbered people and everything but the drinks came smothered in bean sprouts. "Git about ten feet away, honey, so you don't confuse 'em."

Her technique, while different from Forsten's, was no less practiced, no less flexible. To a football jock it was, "Come on, Herkales, cough up a buck for a poor old lady. You c'n spare it!" A demure young woman hailing a cab got, "Honey, can you find a dime for me?"

A blond-haired boy strolled up the walk. Hands stuffed in his pockets, he studied the menu tacked to the restaurant door, then responded to Sarah's pleas with a handful of change. "You take care, now."

"Take care of you, boy, if I was a little younger an' not so stiff."

Nicki smothered laughter because a large walrusy fellow was approaching. He looked familiar but she couldn't quite place him. With a pipe clamped between his teeth, and his tweed jacket clutched at the neck, he shaded his eyes from the neon sign overhead and looked through Whillikers' window. Then he turned and squinted closely at Sarah.

"Here you are." He held out a bill folded lengthwise. Something glittered inside it.

Sarah screeched as he went through the restaurant door. "A fiver! An' what's this he gimme alongside?"

Nicki leaned over her shoulder.

"Keys." Two keys, and a four-leaf-clover charm. The wind blew cold all at once.

"Hmph. What do I want with keys? Ain't got nothin' to open."

"Wait here." Nicki strode into the smoky interior. "A

man," she said to the boy at the register. "Tall, pipe, tweed jacket." She scanned the room in vain. "Just a minute ago, I saw him come in."

The boy shook his head. His look suggested that she was too young to have gone that senile. "I'd have noticed, I think. We don't get many, ah, older people in here."

She understood: Whillikers played music loud enough to stun. No one in sight sported a walrusy mustache.

Mystified, she went back outside.

Sarah was tapping the handle of her cart. "Come on, honey, time to blow this action."

Nicki hurried along beside her. For a stiff old lady, she moved surprisingly fast. "Sarah, will you let me see those keys again?"

"Huh? Nope. Tossed 'em. Let's go to th' train station. Warm there, and they got candy machines. Why? You think them keys were valyable?"

"They were mine. I mean, I think they used to be mine."

But surely that was ridiculous. It was one thing to copy keys, but quite another to copy the chain and clover charm. Silly. Probably there were thousands of clover charms.

But her door had been opened, and Rich's keys had appeared in her hand, in the alley; and then, an hour later, when she had searched her purse for them, she could not find them. Confused and uncertain, she found herself pouring the whole tale out to Sarah, who listened with absolute attention.

"And I don't know what to think," she finished. "It all just seems so odd."

"Funny, ain't it?" Sarah said. "I mean, the way things fall. First one little thing, an' then another little thing. Like the pretty gadgets you look through, with the colored bits. Just touch 'em, y'know, and they fall all different ways. Now you, you ain't got no colored bits, but you feel like they're comin'. Little things fallin' into some nasty shape. Is that it?"

Nicki sighed. "Exactly. And it's so silly."

Sarah shook her head. "Ain't silly, girl. Don't go off half-cocked, but pay attention. That's my advice. You don't pay attention to th' nerves on yer own insides, why, you ain't got much to go on in this life."

Inexplicable tears stung Nicki's eyes. "Thank you."

She shrugged. "Ain't nothin'. You hungry? I am."

"Wait." While they stood on the corner of Elmwood and Goodmaster Drive, Nicki rummaged in her bag. "Apple?"

Sarah spat. "Ain't got the choppers I used to."

Embarrassed not to have noticed that, Nicki dug again. "Milky Way?"

Sarah's breath came out in a soft hiss. She snatched and unwrapped the candy in one greedy motion, her first bite taking a full half of it. "Thanks," she said through the mouthful.

They paused on the edge of Meadbury Commons, then jaywalked over to the bright, shopping-mall side.

"Sarah, how old are you? I mean, if you don't mind my asking. It's for the article."

"Don't mind a bit, not f'r th' article." She polished off the rest of the candy. "Last week was m' birthday. Bought m'self this hat. Like it?" She pulled back several layers of hoods to reveal a child's coonskin cap, jammed far back on her skull. The tail dangled over her left ear, which stuck out from her skinned-back grey hair like the handle on a jug.

"It's very nice," Nicki said gravely. "Looks warm."

"Is warm. Sometimes I stick my hands in it at night." She dragged the hoods back up over it. "A real nice present."

"But which birthday was it?"

"Oh, I dunno." She peered at a window display of silk shawls from India. "Lookit them damn fool things. Wouldn't keep the rain off for a minute. Sure do like the colors, though. Oh, m' birthday. Thirty-six, thirty-eight. Thereabouts."

Nicki felt stomach-punched. Without thinking she had put Sarah on the far side of fifty. "How long have you been on the street?"

"Since I was seventeen." Sarah gazed up at a window whose posters read "Rio*Bermuda*St. Thomas." A laughing brown girl in a red swimsuit ran through white surf, beneath a blue sky. "Kinda pretty, ain't she? Too skinny down the leg, though."

She turned from the window and shrugged. "Ma kicked me out, see. I was pregnant, an' she was the real old-fashioned kind. Called me garbage. Guess she's gone, now. I ain't sure."

"So you've got family? A son or daughter somewhere?"

Sarah's eyes went suddenly agate in the bright store-window lights. "Nope. Died. We gonna stand here flappin' the breeze all night?" She gave her cart a pull and shuffled away down the sidewalk.

Nicki followed, mentally kicking herself once again. *Tactless fool.*

They rambled for several more hours before Sarah decided it was time to turn in for the night.

Flashlight, I should have brought a— In the darkness of the alley, something small ran past Nicki, chittering.

"Damn." Sarah wheezed. "Brassy little suckers, ain't they?"

Shuddering, Nicki shrank back, then stiffened herself for a plunge after her guide, who led the way through the garbage-strewn gloom. "What was it?"

"Rat." She gave the word a vicious inflection. "Nasty, filthy, mean little bastards. A rat'll fasten right into your throat while you sleep. See, they got these little curved teeth, like razors. They'll just chew an' chew until—"

Oh, stop.

"Why, one morning I wake up an' there's a rat sitting right on my chest. Fat one, too. Me looking at him, an' him lookin' at me."

"What did you do?" *God, it's cold out here, cold and dark.*

"I just took ol' Mr. Rat by his long tail and bashed him smack against a wall." Sarah's head popped up again. "That was one croaked rat."

"I'm sure it was." Spending the night with Sarah seemed even less attractive than it had a moment ago. "What's back there?"

"Hid m' friend somewhere right along— Here. Gotcha, you little devil."

Straightening, Sarah brandished a baseball bat studded with roofing nails. "Don't fret, honey, ain't for you. I keep it here during the day 'cause the cops don't like t' see me totin' it. Bastards took my last one, can you believe it? But I sleep better when I got Louie here in m' arms."

Nicki shivered. "Oh." As she began again to pick her way through the dark behind Sarah, she nonetheless felt more secure.

"So you've been out here, what, about twenty years?"

"Yep. Rain er shine. More rain than shine, seems like."

They edged between rows of trash cans. "You're sure this goes somewhere?"

From the shadows ahead, Sarah snorted. "Think I can't find m' own hidey-hole? Think I'm stupid?"

The snort reassured Nicki as much as anything could. Sarah did seem to know where she was going, which Nicki most emphatically did not.

She had had to promise solemnly never to reveal the location of Sarah's spot, her hidey-hole. "It's tucked back a ways," Sarah said. "Took me a deal o' time t' find it. Got electric light and all. Wouldn't wanna get evicted. Can't get evicted much further, 'cept maybe into the boneyard. An' I ain't ready for that."

Nicki bumped a wooden fence wet with rot and dew, gasped automatically, then continued to grope toward Sarah, who abruptly stopped muttering.

The silence held for a long moment. Then Sarah screamed, a howl of fury and outraged grief. "God damn you, you scum! Garbage! Thief! Jayman, you get y'r filthy ass outta my spot right now!"

Nicki struggled through a tangle of weeds, newspapers, and overturned trash cans to a cement stairway leading down. Two battered delivery trucks stood on the strip of cracked asphalt alongside the warehouse. Although screwed-down sheet metal blocked the door into the cellar, a dim yellow bulb still burned over the staircase. The place was the perfect small hideout, just the right size for someone to crawl into.

Someone had.

At the foot of the steps a man sprawled. Wearing stained blue work pants, shoes visibly reinforced with cardboard, and a tattered red-plaid lumber jacket, he lay with his knees drawn up and his face burrowed into the cradle of his curved arms.

Something about his head looked wrong. His heaving chest, also, was much too broad to match the skinny wrists jutting out of his sleeves.

"I'll douse you with kerosene and touch a match to y'r filthy, thieving hide!" Sarah sobbed. "I'll burn ya, see if I don't."

"Sarah, I don't think—"

"I'll haul y'r ass outta there." Tears streamed down her red, chapped cheeks. Clutching the baseball bat, wheezing, she struggled heavily down the broken steps. "It's my place, mine." Leaning on the rusted rail she reached down, grasping the figure by the collar of its jacket. "An' then, by God, I'll—"

The figure flopped over. From its jacket front poked the narrow grey face of a rat, its eyes glittering as it sprang straight at Sarah. With a feral hiss it scuttled up the steps, leaped over Nicki's bag, and vanished.

Sarah screamed steadily. The hoarse wails reached Nicki as if from afar, rising and falling like a siren. Gripping the rail, she struggled to control her sudden, violent shaking.

From the foot of the steps, a featureless corpse stared at the sky, its throat chewed by the rat into a pulpy red hash. One torn strip of cheek hung over its ear. Cartilage poked from the gnawed, ruined nose. Its eyes were clawed sockets, cratering the face.

Flesh above, skull below, Jayman grinned up to the stars.

From the nibbled fingers of his right hand, two hideously familiar keys dangled, on a chain whose bloodied four-leaf-clover charm had not brought Jayman any luck.

Nicki turned away and was thoroughly, frightfully sick.

SUNDAY, SEPTEMBER 23

Tommy Riley

She looked awful, just awful: eyes red and puffy, skin dull as paste.

"Uh, hi, Miss Pialosta." Jeez, had somebody hit her or what?

"Hi." She leaned against the gate-hut and tried to smile, then tilted her head back and closed her eyes. "Tommy, don't ever let anyone tell you reporting is a glamorous job."

"Gee, Miss Pialosta, you shouldn't work so hard."

She laughed. It sounded like she might cry. "Right. What are you doing here on Sunday, anyway?"

"Filling in for Bradley. He had a choir concert. I'm getting off now, though." And just in time, too. He had a headache, and lots of homework. At least his mother had given him the car; he didn't feel like walking home.

She nodded, not opening her eyes, holding her face to the sun and rubbing the bridge of her nose with her fingers. It practically tore his heart out to see her looking that way.

"Uh, listen. I hope you won't take this wrong. I've got my mom's car over there. Would you like to go for a ride? Just get a little air? We could go down past the harbor." He held his breath.

Her eyelids parted; she blinked at him. "You know something, Tommy? I think I'd like that very much. I think a ride is just what I need."

Suddenly his head felt a whole lot better. He held the car door for her, being careful not to slam it on her dress. Then he settled himself behind the wheel.

Okay. You're in neutral. Turn on the key. Press the clutch. He got the car out of the lot and into the street without doing or saying anything stupid. But soon he was going to have to say something. *Jeez. She's here. Right here in the car.*

"Uh, nice day, isn't it?"

"Very nice." She sagged back against the seat, eyes half-shut, letting the breeze riffle through her black, wavy hair.

"So, uh, you got a hard story to work on?"

Small, white front teeth bit into her soft lower lip. "Uh-huh."

Tommy sensed he shouldn't ask any more about that. Slowing the car, he turned onto Harbor Drive and got into the right lane where he could idle along.

Out on the water, a single rainbow spinnaker bellied out in the chilly northeast breeze. "You won't get fired for taking off like this, will you?"

She sighed. "At the moment, I wish I would. But no, I won't. As long as I meet my deadline, I can keep on killing myself for the Meadbury *Bulletin.*"

"That's good. I mean," he said through her laughter, "I'm glad you won't get fired. I got fired from my last job. It was awful."

"My goodness, what happened?"

He eased onto a wide, grassy shoulder where other cars were parked, overlooking the water and part of the yacht club dock. The smell of salt and diesel fuel and creosote rode bracingly on the air. Choppy green waves slap-slapped the pilings. "It was just a mix-up. I was running cars from the country club to the parking lot just down the block. Valet parking, you know. So this guy comes out and says he wants the silver Porsche, and I went and got it for him, and he gave me five bucks and drove away."

"So what was wrong with that?"

He turned and looked at her. Her cheeks were pinking up, and her eyes had some sparkle back. "It wasn't his car. The owner never saw it again."

She laughed. She sank down in the car seat and laughed until the tears ran, holding herself and shaking until he thought he might float away with how wonderful it was, making her laugh like that.

"But the worst part was when the owner came out and asked for his silver Porsche, and I told him not to con me because I'd already given it to the real owner."

"Oh, no. Oh, Tommy, that's just awful."

He was laughing too. "Yeah, I guess. The country club manager thought it was. He said he was going to get the roller and make a new putting green out of me. But it was okay, because then I got the *Bulletin* job. Old Prickly said if I could get Fucked-up Finnegan to dump me, I must be all right."

He stopped abruptly; his face burned. "Uh, sorry. I mean, I'm sorry I said that word to you."

She pulled a cigarette out of her purse. "Tommy, I'm not your maiden aunt, okay? I've heard that word before." She punched the cigarette lighter, but when it popped out he beat her to it.

Willing his hands not to shake and his armpits not to sweat and his breath not to be too awfully bad, he leaned over and lit her cigarette.

Oh, jeez.

"Thank you," she said, like it was no big deal at all.

MONDAY, SEPTEMBER 24

Nicki Pialosta

Monday noon. Nicki sat at her newsroom desk, going through a heap of press releases: a poetry co-op with a new book out, all twelve contributors angling for publicity interviews; a "radio personality" forming an investment company to buy a local department store; an animal hospital that specialized in reptiles and amphibians, and made house calls. This last, with a sense of profound disinterest, she set on the "follow up" stack. Like it or not, strange animals always made good copy.

Almost as good as dead people. Nothing like a corpse to jazz up a story, and hadn't she been lucky to be right on the spot?

Other bits of paper littered her desk top: notes to be filed, scribbled memos already recopied, fragments needing to be deciphered before they could be tossed out. In places her hasty scrawl was illegible even to her. The clatter and chatter of the newsroom reached her faintly; she was grateful for it, and for this stupid, rote chore of desk-cleaning. It gave her mind's eye something to do.

When it had nothing to do, it saw Jayman.

She paused over one sheet torn from a looseleaf note-book. Her writing? Her fountain pen, surely; no one else used fountain pens any more. "You are cordially invited," it read. What the hell had she meant by that?

She put the piece of paper in the "to be dealt with" pile, then lowered her face into her hands as without warning another wave of dizziness hit her. A too-hasty gesture, a too-sudden turn of the head unleashed swimming nausea.

God, I've got to go out and see that damned crafts fair today.

Jimmy Conklin's tenor voice rose above the newsroom murmur, demanding attention. "Cripes, what sicko put this in here?"

"Put what in where?" She lifted her head cautiously. After the marathon of questions and statements at the police station had come the marathon writing session, stretching late into Sunday night. Deadlines did not wait for dead people, nor for unfortunate live ones in shock from discovering the remains. Her only respite throughout the disastrous weekend had been the hour with Tommy. Such a sweet kid.

And on top of everything, she still had Ibrani to talk to; or rather, to listen to. Ibrani was now in conference with Old Prickly, the Metro editor, and the paper's legal counsel; she didn't know what he was telling them, but she hoped to hell he was making it good.

She hoped, in fact, that he was saving her ass. If it weren't in jeopardy, she thought, she would be at that meeting herself. Apparently Old Prickly took a dimmer view than she'd realized of reporters nosing around in other reporters' territories, unsanctioned by editors.

Just another difference between Manhattan and Meadbury, she thought; in Meadbury, unbridled personal ambition was unfashionable.

All for one, and one for all. So let's hope Ibrani lies, and sanctions me retroactively, because if they dump me off this job I will *be typing classifieds somewhere.*

"I mean, what is this in here?" Conklin's voice held outrage now.

"Jimmy, what are you talking about?" *Please don't make me get up.*

His radio, tuned as always to the police band, rasped static, through which a woman's voice began dispatching patrol cars. "Just a sec."

Even the sight of her piece splashed on the front page of the Metro section failed to lift her spirits. A couple of Metro writers, jealous of their turf, had already given her dirty looks. If Conklin weren't such a nice guy he probably wouldn't be talking to her either.

Nicki let her eyes drift closed; behind their lids the wedge of newsprint dissolved again into Jayman's face: sightless, accusing. Although that was silly. That was nerves and fatigue and what Rich's shrink would label misplaced guilt. *Maybe I ought to dig out that shrink's name and give her a call.*

There had been no chain, no keys. No dangling, blood-smeared four-leaf clover. The police detective had looked at her oddly when she asked.

". . . but I really thought I saw—"

No. Nothing in the hand, nothing fallen. Of course the area had been thoroughly searched, which meant either that she had imagined the keys or that someone had picked them up. Which? Neither choice was attractive in its implications.

"The things these wackos—" Conklin's telephone buzzed before he could go on.

When her own phone rang, she ignored it. *Whoever you are, I don't want to hear your problem.*

It buzzed again. *Dear God.* She answered.

"Jason Goodmaster here." Good breeding and better bank balances had endowed the voice with total assurance.

Startled into alertness, she sat up straight, scribbled the name on a pad, and waved it at Conklin. "Mr. Goodmaster, what can I do for you?"

"It is what you have already done that I wish to discuss, Miss Pialosta."

Wonder if I could arrange a trade. Although Goodmaster's name adorned half the parks, school buildings, and cultural centers in Meadbury, the tycoon himself had not been interviewed or photographed in the last twenty years, nor even glimpsed by anyone who would talk about it. He existed as a voice on the phone, and as signator on large checks to local charities.

"Yes?" she said cautiously.

"Your article in today's *Bulletin.* I find it disturbing, very disturbing."

He did not sound like a man accustomed to being disturbed. *He probably hires people to be disturbed for him.*

"What I wrote was the truth, sir. It was intended to, ah, affect people." *And I don't plan to be bullied about it by a stuffy old hermit.*

"Miss Pialosta—" Gentle reproof infused his words. "Miss Pialosta, Meadbury is special. It is a jewel of a city, and I have spent a good deal of energy polishing it, bringing it to near perfection."

"Mr. Goodmaster—"

Smoothly he overrode her. "You, Miss Pialosta, have told Meadbury's citizens that their diamond is paste. You have said that Meadbury does not take care of its residents."

She was too tired for polite sparring, no matter how rich he was. "I did my job, Mr. Goodmaster. If you don't care for the results, you c—"

"Miss Pialosta—"

For such a ritzy guy, you've got rotten telephone manners.

"—I do care for it. I am, in fact, most appreciative. You have performed your function, performed it well. I'm calling to thank you."

"Oh. Well, ah, you're welcome." All at once she felt foolish in the extreme. *Paper tigers. . . .*

"It now becomes my function," he said, "to see that you have not performed yours in vain. In fact, I have already taken steps to assure it. Your work has intensified my concern, and my efforts."

"I see." She flicked on her VDT, ready to interview him right then and there. "Well, sir, how do you plan to—"

A passing copy editor tossed the evening final onto Nicki's desk. The headline froze her: 3 VAGRANTS STRANGLED, AUTOPSIES SHOW.

"Miss Pialosta?"

She looked at the phone and remembered she had been speaking. "Yes, I'm sorry, Mr. Goodmaster. I just got tonight's final. There've been some further developments."

She scanned the lead column and read aloud. " 'Three area vagrants, found dead in different parts of the city over the past ten days and originally thought to have died of natural causes, were strangled, State Coroner Michael D. Tapli said this morning.

"'At a 10 A.M. press conference at police headquarters, Tapli listed manual asphyxiation as the probable cause of death in all three cases. Chief of Police Keith Winkle said an investigation is in progress, but declined further comment.'"

The phone lines whispered busily until Goodmaster spoke. His gentility had vanished, leaving behind a cold, disembodied-sounding anger. "The situation shall be rectified, Miss Pialosta; the cancer shall be excised. I shall see to it. Personally, if necessary. And one more thing. I understand that your zealousness may have put you in an awkward situation. You needn't worry. I'll see to that, too." The receiver clicked.

She stared at it. "I'll be damned."

Conklin touched her elbow. "Goodmaster? The lord of all he surveys?" The awe on the redhead's broad, freckled face was only half-mocking. "What'd he want?"

Except for the part about saving her ass, she told him.

"Can't say I disagree." He sat on the edge of her desk, his high-heeled cowboy boots not quite touching the floor. "It is really tacky, all those dead winos littering the sidewalks. You think he'll get an ordinance passed or something?" He gave a wry smile. In his three years on the police desk, he had seen worse than Jayman.

Nicki tapped the article with a pencil. "How come you didn't tell me about this? That is your byline, isn't it?"

He grinned wickedly. "'Fraid you'd scoop me."

"Jimmy, I did not go out there to—"

Putting his hands up, he stopped her. "Just kidding, just kidding. First you were busy, and then I was busy, and anyway, you know now. What I wanted to ask you about was—"

His phone rang. "Cripes. This." He tossed down his copy of the final, folded open to the classifieds, and ran for the phone. "Yeah?"

She glanced down. Conklin's voice faded to a background staccato.

Between the personals and the novenas to St. Jude ran the memorials: short poems or prayers people put in to mark the anniversary of a loved one's death. The last in the column, boxed in black, read:

IN MEMORIAM
Arthur "Jayman" Shipman
1946–1984
free at last

The four lines of type melted into a skull, into Jayman's face. The quiet dignity of the ad in no way conveyed the horror of his death. *Which is just as well. I'm tired; God, I'm so tired I'm hallucinating.* Brushing aside her sudden unease she turned back to Conklin. "Do you know who put this here?"

But he was running, yanking on his jacket as he dashed for the door.

"Hey! What's up?"

"'Nother stiff," he called over his shoulder. "Down behind Gimbel's. Cops think it's croaked wino number four."

It was not the first time she wished he could use euphemisms like everyone else.

There was something else, too: a snapshot of memory she wished she could either make sense of or forget. Amidst the squad cars' strobing blue lights and the ghoulish spectacle of the ambulance attendants trucking Jayman's bagged corpse away like so much rubbish, her mind's eye held clearly another image: a uniformed cop speaking quietly to Sarah, whose creased face grew still with an odd mixture of fear and guilt as she slipped something glittery into his hand.

TUESDAY, OCTOBER 2

Meadbury

The sunlight was warm and the breeze was cool. Red-orange leaves tumbled by the bench in Goodmaster Park like auditioning gymnasts. Michael Quincy Lynch lifted his chin high. A guy could never have a good enough tan.

"Hey, Mike!"

Lynch looked up and waved to a large man with a walrus mustache and a briefcase. "Ferdie! How's the assessor's office treating you these days?"

Ferdinand MacGregor, Assistant City Assessor, groaned as he sank onto the bench next to Lynch. "We got auditors in, and they find out our computer programmer's spending half an hour a day on our stuff and seven and a half on other people's, so the boss canned him. Only then do we find out this guy figured to suck off the Meadbury tit forever. He programmed that computer so if he doesn't feed it a code every seventy-two hours, it crashes. Which, since he left Friday and ain't been in since, it has done. It is down, down, down. But the bills still go out, see. By hand. That answer your question?"

"Uh-huh. So how's the assessor's office treating me?"

"You got the envelope?"

Lynch reached into his jacket pocket and brought out a fat, sealed business envelope. "You got me at twenty-five like you said?"

MacGregor shrugged. "Round numbers make people suspicious. Twenty-five thousand, four hundred sixty-nine dollars. Not bad, huh?"

Lynch frowned. "You said twenty-five, though."

"So I'm half a bill high, big deal. I mean, your place has gotta have a fair market value of sixty-two, sixty-three thousand. You'll save about seventeen hundred dollars every year from now to the 1994 revaluation."

"How many, ah, clients do you have, Ferdie?"

MacGregor shot him a reproachful glance. "I do this for you, Mike, you, out of friendship and goodwill."

"And for a thousand bucks." Lynch slapped the envelope into MacGregor's open palm. "All small bills, just like you said."

"Excellent, excellent." MacGregor tucked the envelope away. "And now, lunch hour being over, duty calls. More bills to post."

Lynch walked with MacGregor to the parking lot. He felt good. Deals always made him feel good. "Catch the Pats on Sunday? I got tickets."

"Sure, gimme a call Friday late, we'll set things up."

"Will do." Lynch slipped into his Buick. The sun had warmed it. The air was stuffy and the plastic seat covers sticky. He opened the window. Once he got moving, a chilly breeze swept through the car. He shivered and rolled the window back up.

Dappled sunshine fell on his face and gravel crunched under the Buick's tires as he slowed for the bridge over Locust Creek. *Wish they'd fix this sucker, widen it, repave it, like going over a washboard. Hell, what could it cost? Fifty, a hundred thousand? Maybe I shouldn't've bribed Fergie. I mean, if everybody did it, how'd the city ever pay for anything? But—nah, fuck the city.*

But his unease did not fade. If anything, it deepened, chilling his Irish-lapsed-Catholic conscience with visions of saints and angels scowling down from heaven, glaring at him through a window in his soul. It was guilt that had opened that window, he knew, and Michael Quincy Lynch was used to guilt.

What he wasn't used to was the thing, the thing slipperily invading him through the opened guilt-window. He stiffened with the mental glimpse, just a flicker, of something so horrid he was sure he must be having a stroke, or maybe the Russians had pushed the button and the bomb had already fallen and he was dead, flash-fried into atoms and looking into hell.

Then he was alive again, driving across the bridge, and he couldn't see the thing anymore because it was inside him, all the way inside. And in control.

Lynch's own hands spun the wheel. The car swerved hard to the left. "Hey, what the hell? Are you nuts, Mikey?" Lynch heard his own voice pleading. "Get back on the road!" An icy something stiffened his spine, pulled his arms back. Disbelieving, he watched his fingers open, felt his right foot floor the gas pedal.

The Buick's engine roared. The guardrail broke away in a cloud of splinters. Eighteen feet of water swirled up over the Buick's hood, foaming greenly on the windshield as it rose, closing over the car top.

He lunged for the door handle.

The water outside held the door shut.

Bracing himself, Lynch took a deep breath and grabbed the window crank.

But the something inside him would not let him turn it.

MONDAY, OCTOBER 15

Nicki Pialosta

Red-white-and-blue banners draped over the back of the speaker's platform said: We Take Care Of Our Own. To one side, in front of the platform, the Junior League had set up a table: red-and-white-checked cloth, shiny four-color brochures, printed contribution envelopes. Bottles of white wine and clear plastic cups stood on the table, too; the bottles emptied rapidly as the Junior Leaguers profferred smiles and refreshments to business-suited men and women. Glimpsing familiar faces, Nicki thought every banker, builder, real-estate broker, and politician in town had showed up for the ground-breaking of the Meadbury Shelter for the Homeless.

A few were already looking plenty refreshed. Those Junior Leaguers knew how to make folks feel right at home. And there was nothing like a little lubrication to help separate the rally-goers from a couple or three of the twenties moldering in their wallets.

Well, booze in the afternoon was nothing new for most of those folks, she thought, and frowned, glimpsing an altogether too familiar face. *Oh, no—Rich.* A little thinner than when she'd last seen him, but still wearing his irrepressible grin and holding his hand out for a drink.

Her heart sank. Somehow he'd managed to clean himself up: decent suit, new tie, fresh haircut. His ear had healed; no bandage any more. Only his shoes betrayed him: sneakers, above which his bare ankles flashed white. But no one was looking at his ankles. They were smiling, nodding appreciatively at the handsome, affable stranger who told such great stories, delivered uproarious jokes with such polished skill. He still had the touch, the line of fast patter, the buck-and-wing flash that used to roll them in the aisles.

Who was he? she could see them wondering. And how can we get him to sell our—real estate, mortgages, tax shelters. Fill in the blank. Everyone wanted Rich, at first. For a while. Ten days, two weeks.

Or twenty minutes, if there was anything around to get loaded on.

Someone offered Rich another plastic cup of wine. "And then—" He knocked back a swig of the stuff, enjoying the rich, vibrant sound of his own important voice. "—and then, I swear this is true, the guy gets up on the stage, and he looks down at the front of his pants, see, and. . . ."

His voice dropped to a confidential murmur; a roar of laughter erupted around him, although not from everyone. The two women who'd made up part of Rich's audience turned away abruptly. One of them, the older one, was pink with embarrassment, the other flushed with what looked a great deal like fury.

Up to his tricks already; oh, hell. Let him stay over there, away from me; let him shut up, or pass out. Or drop dead.

"Hey, wait a minute, y'gotta hear this one. . . ."

Nicki frowned, trying to ignore him. The smell of fresh pine boards drifted off the stage; applause spattered around her as a balding, bespectacled fellow in a cashmere jacket and dark slacks stepped up to the podium.

Good. Now Rich will have to zip his lip. On the other hand, speeches would give him more time to guzzle. She forced her mind away from the thought of him, uncapped her fountain pen, and steadied her notebook on her lap.

The speaker adjusted his vest and his glasses, and tuned his smile down to somber. The sunlight played on his sandy hair; he patted his slight paunch, drew himself up to his full five-nine, and began to intone.

"Ladies and gentlemen, a killer walks among us."

That was not what progressive, profit-seeking civic leaders wanted to hear; they shifted from one foot to the other. Those who were sitting moved uneasily in their hard folding-chairs.

Ben Ibrani slipped into the seat beside Nicki. "This guy is a toad."

She gave her ex-editor a look. She was Rifkind's reporter, now, on loan to Metro for special assignment until further notice. How Ibrani had worked that out, she hadn't asked; she only knew she owed him one.

Him . . . and Jason Goodmaster? She didn't know, and thought it best not to push her luck by asking; at least, not yet. *Let the dust settle, first; things could still go wrong.*

"He's very competent." She indicated the man on the platform. "Number one salesman for the dealership on Eighth Avenue, and he's raised thousands for the PTA."

"Yeah? And where was he before that?"

She did not answer. Privately, she had reservations about the speaker. Raising money was one thing; directing its spending was quite another. And Jason Goodmaster had apparently handed the whole project over to Ned Gorman. Not having memorized the car-salesman Hall of Fame, or the PTA Volunteer Directory, she had never heard of him until his appointment two weeks earlier.

At any rate, Gorman had yet to give any cause for complaint, even if he was a little overbearing.

". . . a killer who preys on the weak and defenseless . . ."

"Ah, shit," Ibrani muttered.

". . . who stalks by night . . ."

"He'd do it himself if he thought he could make a fast buck."

Nicki glared at him and lit a cigarette. So far, Gorman was sticking to the text of the speech his PR people had already given her; no need to scribble it down again.

"Well, he would," Ibrani went on. "He'd hold wino shoots to make his fund-raiser succeed. He's making his name on this thing, you know, not to mention his living. By the way, have I told you you're smoking too much?"

"Not in the last ten minutes."

". . . but we shall overcome this villain's senseless treachery . . ."

"Also, he steals lines from dead black heroes."

". . . housing our homeless securely, safely, before the snow flies." Gorman paused. "I have in my hand a check for ten thousand dollars." He bowed his head.

"The guy's gonna cry."

She jerked around. "Ben! I'm here to cover this, not listen to you."

"He could stand some covering. I vote cement."

". . . Mr. Jason Goodmaster, who sends his greetings and his regrets, along with his generous check . . ."

She *tsk*ed in exasperation. "He didn't show up. I wanted an interview." Although not necessarily for publication; what she really wanted to know was whether he'd gone to bat for her. She didn't think so; no one was showing her any of the resentment such intervention would have caused —assuming Goodmaster held any real sway at the *Bulletin*, which was unlikely. Old Prickly hadn't gotten his nickname for nothing.

Still, how the hell had Goodmaster known she was in trouble in the first place? But he wasn't here, so she wasn't going to get to ask him.

"Promise 'em anything, give 'em ten grand," Ibrani said. "Works every time. You'll never see him. I haven't seen him in eighteen years, myself."

". . . and as chairman of Meadbury's ad hoc Committee to Shelter the Homeless, I am proud to have turned the first spadeful of earth." He pointed to the right of the platform, where the shovel he had dropped lay beside a tiny mound of dirt. "And to announce that we have now exceeded our goal. In just four weeks our generous citizens have donated two hundred thousand dollars, not counting today's wonderful effort. . . ."

Ibrani's eyes were glazing. That was Gorman's secret: provoking unbearable boredom. Getting money had to be easy once the mark was hypnotized by the rise and fall of his voice, by the empty phrases through which one could sail headlong into a trance. Her own eyes unfocusing, Nicki gazed up numbly.

Sudden silence sucked her attention back, as it was meant to.

Gorman leaned forward, a stricken look on his face, his glasses clutched in his fist. A masterful pose. He must have copied it from someone. "Six people."

"I'll be damned." Ibrani, alert all at once, watched admiringly.

"Six people, killed in our streets."

Nicki's pen raced across the notebook page; the PR handout hadn't included these lines.

Again Gorman let his words echo into the surrounding park while the territorial aspects of his statement sank home.

"Not New York, not Los Angeles, not any one of those towns where human trash has taken control. No. Right here in our home."

Ibrani's eyebrows went up. "This guy's getting good."

"And we are not going to let it go on." Gorman glared over the audience like an eagle. "Meadbury's senior citizens do not sleep in the streets. In New York, maybe, but not here. Not in my town. No, sir."

His voice dropped to intent urgency. "In my town, human beings sleep in clean beds. They wear clean clothes; they have food to eat, shoes to wear. They live like civilized people, in safety and in harmony. That's what a human being is in my town, and we will do whatever it takes to make sure that's how it stays. Am I right? Are you with me? Are we going to show the world that our system works?"

"The little sucker's making his move." Ibrani snapped his fingers. "He's running for mayor."

Applause began faintly, a hesitant riffle that built and built, buoying Gorman until he flushed, nodding and smiling. "Thus we raise this shelter at the exact geographical center of town. As the heart is the center—"

"I'm leaving," Ibrani said.

"Why?" She tore part of her attention from Gorman even as she continued writing.

"Because he disgusts me. He's making career moves on dead losers."

Nicki looked speculatively at Gorman. "Do you suppose he's putting those ads in? Just to keep up the pressure, or something?"

The clerks had been told to continue taking the eerie "death boxes," but to report the name and address of anyone placing one. Each swore no such ad had been placed, yet they continued to appear, one after each murder. It was driving the cops nuts, and giving the classifieds director an ulcer.

It was also making Nicki more nervous than she cared to admit. What had Sarah said? ". . . little bits, falling into some nasty shape. . . ."

Ibrani pulled his coat on with a sharp angry shrug. "I wouldn't put it past him. Your story; you listen. I'm going downtown; that guy gives me the creeps." He strode off through the dry leaves.

A moment later, she was glad he had gone. Gorman was back to his prepared notes, but now Rich was shambling up onto the platform. From his unsteady gait, Nicki could tell that the wine had not been his first alcohol of the day. He'd obviously started earlier—much earlier—with the hard stuff, and now he was thoroughly drunk. Still, he seemed delighted to be on stage, and looked as if he fully expected the audience to be delighted, too.

From either side of the platform stepped an alert, dark-suited man; neither looked delighted at all. Their appearance jolted her, even through her embarrassment. *Guards? Gorman has guards?*

Gorman stepped aside but made no protest as Rich grabbed the microphone.

"Ladies 'n' genulmun!" Rich clapped his left arm around Gorman's plump shoulders; his right arm shot out. The familiar spray of tattered red roses shot from the sleeve of the new suit, obscuring the microphone.

The audience laughed uncertainly. Rich made an ace rise out of a pack of cards. The laughter strengthened; perhaps the audience assumed this was some sort of arranged entertainment.

But once sure of their attention, Rich lost his smile. Gorman, no doubt sensing better publicity than he could have arranged, let him go on.

Rich's voice boomed through the microphone. "I came t' tell you. My friends're dying, an' you're gonna be next."

Gorman all at once did not look so happy.

"See, you don't understand. I know, though. I live out there, onna street. Th' suit's a disguise, see; I really came here so I could tell you—they're all around, watching!"

As the guards nodded to each other and moved, Rich began to hurry. The words tumbled out of his mouth: "You think it's just us, see, all us bums. My friend died, his guts were out on the sidewalk, and the bugs . . . and there was this dog. . . ." He shook his head and looked around helplessly.

"An'—an'—my sister! They're watching her. They wanna—you gotta—"

The guards advanced to within two feet of him. Glancing from one to the other, Rich burst into tears and fell on Gorman with loud, slobbering sobs, pressing his face into Gorman's immaculate jacket.

Gorman's smile looked forced as he struggled to hold Rich's weight.

"All right, my friend." He gestured for the dark-suited men to back off, then retrieved the microphone and spoke into it while Rich's weight bore him steadily down. "Everything is all right. Our friend is a little overwrought, but given the circumstances, who can blame him?"

Rich's knees buckled. Gorman kept smiling as he hit the boards. He smiled ferociously, wriggling out from under Rich. He smiled and smiled, clambering unsteadily to his feet.

Ibrani was right. Gorman's a fake. Nobody smiles, dealing with Rich.

Reg Forsten bobbed up in front of the platform, waving frantically and calling Rich's name.

Rich squinted blearily down at him. "Sorry." He caught Gorman's wrist and hauled himself to his feet. For a moment he swayed back and forth.

"And for my last trick—" Wavering, he stepped straight off the stage and fell in a boneless heap. The audience gasped.

It's a trick, all right; if he weren't so drunk he'd have broken his fool neck.

"Do not be alarmed!" Forsten's stentorian tones drowned out the buzz of consternation, the Junior Leaguers and business tipplers nudging each other and muttering about ". . . that fellow, knew right away there was something odd about him. . . ."

"I shall take charge of this unfortunate young man." Looping Rich's limp arm over his shoulder, Forsten heaved; for a second, the two almost collapsed. Then Forsten staggered toward Nicki, half carrying and half dragging his burden in a way Nicki found both sad and familiar.

"Let them pass," called Gorman, brushing squeamishly at his wet lapels.

Right, let them pass, preferably without noticing me. But Rich, somehow still conscious, did notice her. He muttered to Forsten, who slowed, although reluctantly, as he approached Nicki's aisle chair.

"M' sister." As Forsten released him, she cringed, hoping no one heard. "She'll gimme li'l drink."

"Rich." She struggled to keep her voice low, and firm. "Rich, you've had enough. Go on, Reg will take you."

His eyes snapped open, wide and terrified. And furious. He fumbled with his clothing.

"Oh, yeah?"

Almost at once she understood what he was doing and tried to slide out of range; unbalanced, the wooden folding-chair collapsed, dropping her to the damp grass.

"Oh, yeah?" he snarled as Reg tried ineffectually to drag him backward. "Well, piss on you!"

And to her shock and humiliation, he did just that.

His stream, clumsily directed, still managed to reach his target. She recoiled, but not quickly enough, warm wetness striking her right knee and trickling down the side of her leg. Its pungent odor filled her nostrils, sickening her as she squirmed backward over the grass, until at last she was out of his range.

"You—you bastard," she whispered from between clenched teeth. Only the crowds around them prevented her from leaping up to throttle him on the spot, bashing her fists into that slack, stupid face.

"It falleth as the gentle rain from heaven." Forsten's eyes twinkled wickedly. Then, demonstrating once again the surprising strength still hiding in his ruined frame, he tackled Rich, hissed something about cops, and dragged the bigger, younger man away.

Gulping back tears, still rigid with the wish to smash Rich, Nicki mopped at her stocking and the side of her skirt with a bunch of napkins one of the Junior Leaguers thrust at her. The rest of the audience had turned their attention tactfully away, leaving her to her humiliation, but she felt their embarrassment for her and shivered with fury at having to bear it. By the time she could raise her head again, her brother and Forsten had vanished and Gorman was at the microphone once more.

"That, my dear friends, is why our city needs the noble project upon which we have embarked today."

She strained to see which way the two might have gone, but could not. She had no idea where they were going, what they would eat, where they would sleep. Through her anger she realized that she did not care, or at least not much. And what had Rich meant by that crack about "them" watching her?

Nothing, probably. God only knew what was percolating through that sodden brain. At least now, he would be safe for a while. He wouldn't be victimized by some street bum like that crazed Jamallah, or allowed to get into too much trouble.

No sir, not after today, not after having his arms around Ned Gorman, the new mayoral candidate.

After that stunt, the cops would be keeping a real close eye on him; he could hardly be any safer in a jail cell.

Which is where he might yet end up. Maybe where he belongs.

Oh, Rich. Oh, damn you.

Tommy Riley

He stood a moment on the upstairs back porch; then, dropping into the straight wooden chair his mother used to air blankets, propped his chin in his hands. Inside, the telephone rang.

"Tommy, it's for you!" His mother's soft soprano came from downstairs.

"Tell 'em I'm busy. I'll call 'em back." He heard her bustling to the phone, then the low murmur of her voice, apologetic.

He probably wouldn't call back, though. He didn't feel much like talking to anyone. Overhead, dead leaves on the trees made a dry, chill rattle in the wind. From beyond the branches, the pale sun shone onto the grey-painted floor of the porch, building a shifting pattern of bars around his shadow.

Winter coming. Good. Soon he could stay inside without having to make up excuses. He was glad he didn't have to work until this afternoon. He had an awful lot of studying to do; he would have to take the book down to the lot with him.

He didn't like having to do that; work played heck with his concentration. It seemed like all he really wanted to do lately was . . . concentrate.

Musing, he let his mind stray off into the complexities of the differential equations he'd been working on. Calculus was difficult for him, and the teacher was covering the material awfully fast. Still, when his eyes weren't tired and his head didn't ache and his neck wasn't sore from bending over that damn book hour after hour. . . .

Funny. Even with all that, there was somcthing pleasant about it. You didn't have to decide the right answer; all you had to do was figure it out. Move the formulas around, like in a puzzle with rules for solving.

Those were the kinds of rules he liked: rules he was in no danger of breaking. They couldn't be broken, so they could protect you . . . and why in heck was he thinking that?

"Tommy? Are you all right out here?" His mother stood in the doorway, asking gently, not wanting to anger him by acting worried and treating him like a baby. Her mild brown eyes, though, said all the things she wouldn't: You're working too hard. You're not eating right. You're not getting enough sleep.

She didn't understand.

"I'm fine, Mom. Honest. I just took a break from studying. I'll be back in soon."

He wondered if she knew how much he loved her. Lately he kept wanting to tell her, not for any real reason. Just because.

Jeez, what was it with these feelings all of a sudden?

He leaned on the porch-rail banister, and looked out across the lawn. Somewhere a door slammed; a dog barked. Down in the street, a car moved slowly along. From the Walkers' house next door, a television yammered.

It all felt good, normal and safe. Up and down the block, inside the houses, families he had known his whole life were doing what they always did: playing, cleaning, watching TV.

Sudden hot tears lumped in his throat. Gritting his teeth, he swallowed impatiently. *Take care of them, please. And . . . don't make me go away.*

Jeez, he was getting soft in the head. He should go in, make a sandwich, study some more, and then get high and listen to real loud music through his headphones. That would straighten him out. He got up.

Nicki. He would see her at work today.

Yeah. Not that he could or would do more. But jeez, she put a flash of sweetness in his day when she waved at him from across the parking lot. It almost made everything worthwhile. She was special.

He turned toward the door, and stopped.

At the rear of the yard the trees opened up to let a shaft of sunlight through to the ground. In that bright patch stood a. . . .

Something. It was still, and formless, and as black as a midnight shadow.

And it was staring at him.

It held him in its dark, unmoving gaze several moments more. Reluctant to move, he tried to fit some explanation to its hunched vagueness. Then it scuttled sideways out of the patch of sunlight and vanished.

He rubbed his eyes. What the hell had it been?

And where had it gone?

He went inside, locking the screen door behind himself and then the inside door, too. From the living room everything looked all right, perfectly normal. The shadows shifting across the lawn, under the bushes at the back of the yard—that's all they were, bushes. Shadows of bushes. Weren't they?

Weren't they?

Nicki Pialosta

Swinging into the *Bulletin*'s lot, Nicki passed Tommy perched on his stool just inside the gate-hut, frowning into a book. In the last month he seemed to have lost weight, and lost his smile as well. He answered her wave with a halfhearted flick of his hand.

She parked the Toyota, then went back to him. "Still working hard, I see."

Not looking up, he sighed heavily. "Yeah. Exam in a

couple of weeks. I'm going to have to take off work and everything."

"Hard stuff?"

He gnawed a thumbnail. "Yeah. I gotta pass."

"I'm sure you'll pass, Tommy. Look how hard you're studying. That's really all it takes. And even if you don't pass, it's not the end of the world. Everybody fails sometimes. It's how you try that counts."

He looked up. "You don't understand. This is the test. If I don't pass it, I flunk the course. And I'm not gonna flunk my first college course. I'm just not, that's all." He bent back to the book.

"Well." She hesitated, wanting to offer more reassurance. "Listen. I think you're right. No one wants to fail on their first try. But if you do. . . ." His face darkened. "If you do, you can take the course again. Next time you'd be way ahead, you'd ace it for sure. I mean, I know that's not the glorious victory you had in mind. . . ."

His green eyes flickered with a hint of the old humor.

"But hey," she finished, "who's counting?"

He shrugged. "I guess so." But he didn't look convinced.

Inside, she hung up her coat and dropped her purse beside the morning's stack of mail. Through the open door of his office, Ben Ibrani nodded curtly and went back to a letter he was reading. Whatever it was seemed to have unnerved him; he had scratched his reddish-brown hair into disarray, and was lighting a fresh cigarette from the butt of the last.

And you dare to lecture me, huh? She hefted the mail, planning to sort through it while trying to solve the day's next problem: how to write the Gorman debacle under her own byline without announcing her relationship to Rich Pialosta. One of them was going to have to get a pseudonym.

Not that it would help. So far, all that had been destroyed were a skirt and a pair of stockings; she'd had to stop at home to change. But sooner or later the whole thing was going to come out: her vagrant brother, her objectivity-destroying ulterior motive for wanting to write about Meadbury vagrants. And if she'd thought she was in trouble before . . .

Her only choice now was to make the story big enough, good enough, so that when Old Prickly learned the truth, the paper would be in too deep to abandon the stories, or their writer.

A stiff, square envelope addressed to her in a fine copperplate stopped her musing. She tore it open, wondering who else could be getting married, then halted. The creamy, expensive card-stock was entirely blank, except for four letters in the lower left hand corner: RSVP.

What the hell? All right. Some nut's idea of fun. It goes with the job, and it sure beats heavy breathing on the phone at two in the morning. About to pitch the card into the wastebasket, she caught herself. Ibrani's office door was closed. She went over, knocked, and entered.

He was sitting behind his desk, gazing blankly at the wall. "Huh? Oh, Nicki. I was, ah, thinking." He laughed. "What's up?"

"I just wondered if you'd been getting any odd mail lately."

"Not unless you count the stuff my broker sends me." He looked mystified, but slightly amused. "Why? You getting mash notes?"

"I don't know." She flipped the blank invitation onto his blotter. "I was wondering if everybody got one of these, or just me."

Something moved in his eyes, and was gone. "That's strange." He snapped one stiff corner of the card between two fingers. "Good stock, too. If it's a practical joke, somebody spent some money on it. No return address on the envelope, I take it?"

She shook her head.

"Well, let me ask around." He tossed it into his center drawer. "Gorman give 'em their money's worth?"

"Oh, sure. They were rolling in the aisles."

"Rifkind treating you okay?"

"Sure. He's not around much, is he? I mean, I get assignments from him and hand stories to him, and that's all."

Ibrani shrugged. "That's just the way he is. Don't worry about it."

Returning to her desk, she sat motionless for a few minutes, until the clacking of Jimmy Conklin's ancient

Underwood reminded her of her own approaching deadline. Flicking on her video display terminal, she shrugged at his audible sniff; he refused to compose at a VDT, claiming it gavc off bad vibrations. Quirky behavior for a hard-headed guy, but she liked him for it; his pounding away reassured her, somehow. She settled down to work.

Tommy Riley

Still perched on his stool by the gate-hut, he stared into his book and thought about what Nicki had said to him. She'd meant it to make him feel better, hc knew, and in a way it did, because it was true. He could take the course again, and it would be easier the second time. And yet—

And yet what she'd said—who's counting?—made him uneasy, too. Because somewhere, in some illogical part of his mind, he felt the question hooking itself to the shadow-shape he'd seen in the yard this morning.

And that was nutso. Really. Much more of that, and he would be writing those test answers in blunt crayon, inside a rubber room.

Still, the uneasy feeling was stubborn, hanging around inside his head like the feeling of a bad cold coming on. Or like when someone kept staring at you. . . .

Cut it out, Riley. He shook himself, throwing off the question, pushing it to the back of his head where it lingered dimly, even though he forced himself to ignore it—

Who? Who's counting?

—until at last with a final shrug he threw it off entirely.

THURSDAY, NOVEMBER 8

Meadbury

Ferdie MacGregor stared into the bathroom mirror, hoping the sight of his own face might tell him where he had been and what he had done. The sad hound-dog eyes, the droopy mustache and sagging jowls told him nothing, nothing at all. He lifted the glass of scotch and ice from the sink and took a big gulp.

The blackouts were hitting more often, and lasting longer. The time before this he had been AWOL from his head for hours, losing it as he went up the sidewalk toward that college café—Whizzikens?—and not coming to until he had let himself back into his apartment. He did remember how unpleasant his keys felt in his hand. But why should keys, his own keys, make him so uncomfortable?

He searched his mind, wondering if this latest blackout had somehow uncovered any events from the one before, there in front of the cafe, but no, just that same blurry image of a shocked white face . . . which he recognized now. The newspaper dame, the one from the *Bulletin.* He must have asked her to put out, or something. God, he'd been juiced.

His mirror image frowned at him. Christ, that was all he needed, a newspaper on his case. First they'd nose into why he was talking smut to broads on the street; next thing you knew, they'd be rooting around in his business deals. And that would be the end of him.

"I'm getting out of here," he told the mirror. Too many

things going bad, deals going sour, too much flak coming down on Ferdie MacGregor.

At least I remember my own name, he thought. He bent to splash handfuls of cold water on his face, then picked a towel from the damp heap on the floor.

No blood on him, thank God. He had read about psychopathic killers who never even suspected themselves because they were afraid to remember. He was pretty sure he had done nothing too dreadful, and he wanted to remember. This amnesia was the strangest sensation, like someone had put a hand in his brain and yanked out a whole fistful of memories.

Well, soon enough it wouldn't matter. He was just about to commit something truly dreadful, and the only blood involved would be the bullets he would be sweating while he cleaned out the city of Meadbury's pension fund. After that it was hello, Tahiti, and good-bye, rotten old life. What would it matter if he lost a few memories there? Every day would be the same anyway: sun and rum and blue sky and little brown girls.

In for a penny, in for a pound. MacGregor poured another scotch and sat at the littered kitchen table. Somebody else could clean up the grimy cups, the egg-caked forks and plates. A cop, probably.

He had to get away quickly, because they were going to catch him sooner or later. So far it had been a hundred here, a favor there, and how about that asshole Lynch taking his car off the Locust Creek bridge? He had had to scramble to get that assessment back up to its fair market value before the bank and the tax people got suspicious.

And then there was that old bastard, Goodmaster, calling him to check on the tax bills. Calling him on the phone, for Christ's sake, to make sure things were proceeding in orderly fashion while the computers were down.

That's what the old bastard said. "In orderly fashion." Like it was any of his goddamn business. Only, Ferdie had a hunch that wasn't really the purpose of the call; there'd been some sort of warning in the old guy's voice, as if Goodmaster knew it was only a matter of time before good old Ferdie MacGregor got himself into a spot he couldn't scramble out of.

Knew it, and was amused by it. In fact, Ferdie had the uncomfortable feeling Goodmaster might be onto him already; Goodmaster, or somebody. Those handwritten tax bills could have tipped someone; unlike bills sent out by computer, handwritten ones had to be looked at by human eyes. Looked at, and thought about, maybe by someone who'd noticed discrepancies.

Maybe the whole computer crash was a set-up. Even now Ferdie had no real evidence of this, but he did have a prickle down his spine: the sensation of someone very near, waiting to pounce.

Well, they weren't going to. Ferdie MacGregor was still fast and sly, ready to make hay or make tracks, whichever. Three hundred twelve thousand dollars should last a while, and when it ran out, why, he could write a book about how he had stolen it, and make more. He downed the drink and left the glass on the table. Too bad about Meadbury. Dull, juiceless little burg—what had it ever done for him?

Sun, sand, and sea; just like that painter, what's-his-name, who said to hell with it all and ran. Ran for his life, really, before dullness could rot him to the bone.

On the other hand, dull is safe, isn't it? Excitement, that's what you get when you risk something important—like your life. In Boston, just crossing the street's exciting. But Meadbury . . . Meadbury protects you.

Unaware of the window he had just opened, he spat into his empty glass. "Fuck protection," he said aloud, unaware that by entertaining even the tiniest second thought, he had forfeited all the protection he'd ever had. "Fuck it," he repeated. "I want a blazing sun and burning brown girls."

He wandered yawning into the bedroom, comforted by the idea that he was not really going to be stealing. He was running for his life, and who could fault him for that?

Standing in darkness, he groped for the light switch, missed it, and banged his knuckles on the door, which slammed shut.

"Damn." He pressed his hand to his mouth, then felt for the switch again.

And froze, struck by the sudden absolute certainty that someone was in his living room. Someone who had no business being there. Someone whose purpose could only be grievous trouble for Ferdinand MacGregor.

He had to hide. Quickly.

But where?

Not the closet. Not under the bed. Not any of the obvious places, the spots they'd check first, but—

At that moment something popped into his mind. Something friendly, something helpful, something that suggested. . . .

The suitcase. The three-suiter. Yes, they'd never look there.

A great calm descended on him. He slipped out of his shoes, the better to tiptoe across the room. He opened the suitcase and knelt down in it.

His feet stuck out.

Calm fled; panic flared. Ferdinand MacGregor wondered what the hell he thought he was doing.

A giant shudder wiped him clean of all emotion.

Your feet stick out? It was the other resident of his head, the one who had slipped in quietly with his second thoughts and stayed when they were banished. *No problem,* it said. *Feet are an easy fix.*

Then it offered a suggestion. Following this suggestion, Ferdie broke each of his ankles and twisted each one ninety degrees.

There. Perfect fit. And it didn't even hurt. Still—

He scrunched down. The suitcase would not close: His butt stuck up too high.

Actually, it wasn't his butt, it was his torso, which lay on top of his thighs, which themselves pressed against his calves, making sort of a three-decker sandwich, as it were. But that was an easy fix, too, because his headmate had another idea, one that Ferdie alone would never have thought of.

By grabbing each lower leg firmly just below the knee joint, and twisting *real* hard, he could dislocate each knee, and then tuck his thighs inside his calves.

Clever, so very clever.

There was, in fact, just one detail remaining: His head still stuck out.

But if he bent his head— Nope, not enough, not quite.

Ferdie, you can wedge it in a little farther if you just—

Ferdie listened. Then he worked his hands around to the base of his skull, laced his fingers together, and gave a mighty yank.

His neck snapped neatly. The lid of the suitcase clicked shut.

Ferdie lay in darkness, waiting for the dangerous someone in the living room to go away.

Instead, though, his helpful brainmate went, taking its tranquilizing, anesthetizing qualities, leaving Ferdie alone inside his head, and inside the suitcase.

Pain exploded in Ferdinand MacGregor. He could not even scream.

It took him forty-eight hours to die.

And for most of those forty-eight hours, he could not stop thinking that he had finally gotten himself into a spot he couldn't scramble out of.

MONDAY, DECEMBER 3

Nicki Pialosta

The windshield wipers slapped away dawn's early sleet as Nicki turned onto Edgewood Avenue, heading for the shelter.

Rich must be cold. Classic no-win situation: I feel like shit no matter what I do. He ain't heavy, he's my brother—

But Rich was heavy, and it was already December, and a maniac still prowled the streets. She could not take him back, but—

Face it. You can't write him off completely. Once a day, every day, she had to check that nothing awful had happened. As soon as she saw he was still alive, she could go off to work, relieved until the next morning.

Of course, he had been carrying a grudge since the day of the rally, when he'd expressed his anger over being thrown out of her place as pointedly as a tomcat spraying in resentment.

No, don't think of that; it will only make you want to throttle him all over again.

But at this remove she could almost laugh about it: dear old Rich, the master of "espressing" himself. And how like Rich, too, to maintain even now that she had wronged him. Some things never changed, including the fact that, despite everything, he was still her brother.

At the far end of the park, the half-built shelter's dark, angular skeleton loomed over bare trees. Rich and his cohorts had begun sleeping on the construction site three weeks ago. Workers and contractors groused, but as Ned

Gorman pointed out, they had safe, warm homes. Permitting the vagrants to sleep inside the eight-foot cyclone fence, under the wary eyes of patrolling guards, at least gave them security. As for warmth, well, volunteers bearing blankets and steaming buckets of soup helped some, but were no substitute for a roof and four walls.

She peered through the windshield. Ahead, a yellow-ponchoed cop with a plastic bag over his hat was waving traffic onto Pine. Beyond him, half a dozen squad cars studded the construction site with blue and white, their dashboard and light-bar beacons whirling yellow and red.

Nicki's heart lurched, and lurched again as an ambulance loomed in her rearview mirror. Two more followed close behind. All three screamed by, and into the shelter drive. Curious passersby pressed against the wire fence; inside, just past the site-office trailer, photographers flashed away at something. Several somethings.

She wrenched the car over, leaped out, and ran, digging into her purse for her press card. "Who's in charge here?"

The young cop holding the green umbrella looked sour. "He's busy." He jerked a thumb at an older man in a shiny black slicker, who stood by a stack of two-by-eights. Before him huddled a dozen vagrants, including Reg Forsten and Rich.

Her feet slurping in the mud, Nicki approached. "Lieutenant—"

He acknowledged her just enough to avoid bumping her as he brushed by.

"Lieu—"

"Hey. I got enough troubles. Get lost."

"I'm a reporter. *Bulletin.*" She showed her card.

"Yeah, well, we'll throw you a party later, answer all your questions then." His galoshes squished in the yellow muck. "Hey ghouls, you got your pictures? Lab guys finished? Haul 'em out, then, it's fuckin' rainin'! Ain'cha got no respect for the dead?"

"Who's dead?" She grabbed her notebook. "How many? What happened?"

He stopped short, leveling a finger like a gun. "Look. I got three stiffs here. I gotta find out why they're stiff, when they got stiff, how they got stiff, and who made 'em that way.

Especially who made 'em that way. I don't know any of that, yet, so you wanna lay off till I do?"

And a nice day to you, too. As the lieutenant stomped off, she spied Jimmy Conklin inside the trailer's open door, leaning toward a hard-hatted man in sweatshirt and work pants. Conklin scribbled intently.

Relieved of professional duties, she moved to where the flashguns had strobed.

"Hey, move 'em out," yelled the man in the black slicker.

Two youngish fellows in identical yellow sou'westers plodded glumly from the first ambulance. "I ain't up for this," said the taller youth. "I hate rain. Makes 'em slippery."

"Hey, at least you had breakfast." The other pulled what looked like a plastic trash bag from inside his coat. "I'm still running on last night's pizza."

The taller one took the bag and shook it open. "You frag 'em, we bag 'em," he said unhappily.

"Shut up, will ya?"

Grim-faced, they approached the first body, which lay with arms and legs flung out at odd angles.

Nicki moved closer, wanting and yet not wanting to see. Intent on their grisly chore, they ignored her.

"Okay, you take the shoulders."

"Hey, I took the shoulders last time."

"C'mon, I got the bag."

"Oh, all right, what the hell. Hold it open, now. One, two, three—"

The corpse rose up smoothly; its feet slipped into the bag. Its head fell off, and bounced once.

"Oh," Nicki heard herself say, and went very cold.

The young man at the foot end of the bag dropped it, swiveled rapidly to his right, and lost his breakfast in a single convulsive rush.

The other lowered the shoulders and frowned. "Hey, come on, you've seen—" Then he glanced down. The severed head lay between his feet, face up. "Oh, God. Oh, Jesus, I'm gonna be— Hey, somebody get over here." He was fighting tears. "Oh, come on, he's getting all over my shoes—"

"Hey." Conklin tapped her on the shoulder. "What're

you doing here?" The pages of his notebook curled in the dampness. "Damn, you got a waterproof pen? My backup just died on me."

"No, only a fountain pen. Wait, I've got a pencil. Here." Her hands trembled badly; she plunged them into her coat pockets. "I've got to see somebody over there. Then I'm going downtown. You need reinforcements, call."

"Yeah." Distracted, he moved forward. "Thanks." Pad open, number two lead at the ready, he closed in on another aspect of his story.

Rich slumped in a half crouch against the wire fence, oblivious to the mist and everything else. Behind him milled Gorman's volunteers, goggle-eyed, buzzing, and nervous. Clouds of white steam rose from a galvanized coffee urn perched on the trunk of an '83 Cordoba. Someone had given Rich some coffee; the paper cup lay on its side in a puddle by his foot.

She squatted beside him, peered into his face. It was blank and vacant; deliberately, she thought. As if he'd gone deep inside to hide.

"Rich?" She touched his sleeve. He jerked away from her.

"Leave me alone." His fingers toyed absently with two linked metal rings.

"Rich, come on. Get up now, Rich. You can't just—"

Forsten's voice was chill acid. "May I suggest that you remove yourself from our grief? Those three butchered losers were our friends, difficult as you may find that to comprehend."

She swung around. "I comprehend it just fine, Reg. You don't have a monopoly on feelings."

He looked at her. "No? The evidence suggests otherwise. If you'll excuse a homeless bum for offering an opinion."

She turned away from him. Rich raised his eyes. She bit her lip at the pleading in them, willing herself to remember how bad things had been: bad enough so that she'd paid Forsten to drag him away.

Drag him to this. But I can't take him back. It's terrible now but taking him back won't solve anything.

"They're killin' us." His voice seemed much deeper than Nicki had remembered, as if it came from the bottom of his soul. "Can't you feel it? Closin' in real slow."

She got to her feet. "Please," she said to Forsten. "Please

take care of him. I'm so sorry." She stopped as tears threatened her.

Forsten smiled without friendliness. "I should have thought a chain link fence, sodium-vapor lamps, and two armed guards would have taken care of all of us nicely. But then, sheep must feel safe, too, inside the slaughtering pen." His cold eyes met hers. "Whose plan was that, do you suppose?"

With disbelief, she understood him. "That's crazy. You're crazy!"

His grin opened wide as a trap. "Go away," he said in a whisper. "You've done enough, now. You've taken care of us all."

Furious, she turned on her heel and left. She had gotten everyone interested in them; she had gotten this shelter idea rolling, and now they were blaming her.

Slick with mist, the shelter's orange beams reflected the squad cars' whirling lights. Over the chatter and static of their radios, the lieutenant yelled, "Bring 'er down!"

She followed his slit-eyed gaze up into the jungle-gym structure. Three stories above, half-obscured by slanting rain, a man's face peered down. Then the caged platform on which he stood shuddered, and began to descend. Gears meshed and clashed metallically.

Conklin came over to her. "Somebody up there jammed the safety. They sent that poor slob up to get it."

The platform lurched to a stop. Six uniformed men ringed it alertly, automatics in hand. Meanwhile a burly patrolman, trying without success to pretend that he controlled his captive, guided the handcuffed prisoner off the platform by the shoulder. The cop's other hand held a floral-print shopping bag, from which protruded a wooden handle.

Blinking with confusion, a huge black man stumbled into the hostile blue circle.

"Jamallah—"

Nicki had not seen him clearly that morning in the alley, but there could be no other like this dark giant whose sheer bulk made his captors resemble children in uniform. Rain ran off that gleaming shaved head, trickling down the broad, devastated black face which must once have been handsome. Dark crimson clots stained his tattered clothing.

As flashguns popped, his wide lips curled back in a dazed grin. "She sing, mon," he said slowly, sadly. "The city sing, and Jamallah play the drum for her. Play an' play an' play. . . ."

"Jesus sweet Christ." Conklin scribbled frantically, transcribing the giant's mad plaint.

"Awright, awright, get 'im outta here." The lieutenant shook his head in disgust. "Fuckin' degenerates."

". . . sing and sing. . . ." They led Jamallah to the open squad car. "All the night long she be singing and sing—" The door slammed.

Gingerly the lieutenant peeked inside the shopping bag. "Shit. The guy's got a fuckin' meat-ax in here."

"Anything on it?" one of the suited men asked.

"Yeah." The lieutenant grimaced. "Meat."

Tommy Riley

The day of the test, and today of all days they had to have a different instructor, a sandy-haired guy with thick glasses and a three-piece pinstripe suit. Tommy supposed Mr. Corcoran didn't feel like taking time off from his day job just to watch thirty people sweat his exam.

But jeez, if I have to sit through it, he ought to sit through it.

Tommy leaned back, resting his arm on the little table attached to his chair, and waited while the substitute passed out the blue test booklets and the sheet of questions. He felt pretty confident, despite the fluttering feeling in his stomach. He always got that. But he knew how to get the answers, for sure. He made himself concentrate: *f(x)*'s and Σ's. Move them around. He could see where they were supposed to go, almost like one of the games down at the arcade. A game with rules.

But that guy, the substitute teacher—Tommy could almost swear he'd seen him before. Or his picture, maybe. He hadn't told them his name, just that he was subbing for Mr. Corcoran.

"Ladies and gentlemen." He had a fruity kind of voice. "You are to answer the questions you find on the sheet as correctly and completely as you can. Please do not skip any questions. If you do not know an answer, construct one from what you have learned. If you cannot construct one"—he looked straight at Tommy—"make one up."

What? Had he heard that right? Make up an answer? He raised his hand.

The sub shook his head firmly. "Begin, please."

Tommy looked down at his sheet. The others had begun already; their pencils scraped faintly as they worked their problems in the blue booklets.

#1. What is the thing you want most in the world?

Tommy looked around. Behind him, Bill Henderson frowned and scribbled down a number.

"Sir, I think I've got the wrong test."

The teacher came to stand beside him. "No, Mr. Riley. You have the correct test. Answer the questions."

"But—"

"Answer the questions, please, Mr. Riley. A great deal depends on your passing this examination. Trust me. I don't want you to fail. I want you to succeed. I know what I'm doing, Mr. Riley."

His mouth felt full of cotton. "I didn't tell you my name," he whispered.

The teacher smiled. "No, you didn't. I know your name. I know a lot about you." He gestured at Tommy's desk with a plump hand. "Answer the questions, boy." His voice was almost gentle.

Almost.

Tommy didn't know what was going on, and he didn't like it one damn bit. It made him feel funny to have a different test than the others. What about the real exam? He'd probably have to take it over. Irritably, he read the questions:

#1. What is the thing you want most in the world?

#2. What are you willing to do to get it?

#3. What is the thing that most frightens you?

#4. What will you do to vanquish your fear forever?

What the heck kind of questions were those?

"You must answer truthfully, Mr. Riley. You cannot pass the test by telling lies." The sub moved to the front of the room and sat down at the desk.

Tommy sat there, feeling robbed. Calculus, he wanted to say. I came here for calculus. And I studied so hard.

But something in the teacher's look stopped him from saying anything.

Tommy picked up his pencil. All right, he would answer the fucking questions.

Nicki Pialosta

By the time Nicki got downtown, the mist had thinned to drizzle; the sky was lightening to pearl grey. Tommy was nowhere around, but she could not stop to worry about him. Bracing herself against the chill air, she hurried into the newsroom.

The morning edition lay on her desk; she pulled out the Metro section. SHELTER NEARS COMPLETION, ran the 24-point head to her story, there on the right below the fold of the section's first page. All right. Rifkind might be a cold fish, but he gave her the one thing she wanted: column-inches, and in all the right spots. She skimmed the piece, checking the editing. It ended with "continued on page 14."

She flipped through the rustling sheets. Page 15 held the slop-over section of the want ads; a somber black box caught her eye, and a chill went through her.

IN MEMORIAM
William "Corky" McDougal
1930–1984
Jefferson Lincoln White
1956–1984
Alfredo "Chico" Hernandez
1946–1984
Jamallah Abdul Stevenson
1946–1984
free at last

Again. My God. Again. She looked up a number in the centrex directory and dialed it.

"Classified," said a woman through a snap of chewing gum.

"This is Nicki Pialosta, from Fea—"

"If you wanna know about that ad—"

"Well, yes, I—"

"I told the managing editor, I told the police, I'm tired of telling—"

"But—"

"No. I didn't get a name because nobody placed that ad. Period. We've got no records on it. Now it's Monday morning, my phones are going crazy and my helper's out sick again for the fourth time in two weeks, so you want to talk to anybody about it, you talk to those people over in the computer room. I swear they're doing it all, just to throw this thing on me. Good-bye!" She slammed down the receiver.

Nicki replaced her own receiver only a fraction more gently. Almost before she had lifted her hand from the phone, it rang again.

"Nicki?" Conklin's voice was urgent. "You won't believe what just—"

"Jamallah's dead."

"How did you know?" People babbled in the background. "Hang on."

She stared at the boxed memorial. *So simple. You pick them out—you have to know them, of course—and then you get the ad into the paper.* There were computer hacks —wizards of electronics, some with a bent for illegal tinkering—who could break into any system, including the *Bulletin*'s. That had to be how it was done. Even the police thought so.

Then you go to the shelter while they sleep on their sheets of cardboard and newsprint. You walk among them, looking into their sunken faces, and then you—

Conklin came back on the phone. "Hey, Nicki? Jeez. You wouldn't have believed it. Listen, is Ibrani around?"

"How did it happen, Jimmy? How did Jamallah die?"

"He was the strongest mother I've ever seen. They put him in a fourth floor cell; it looks like he ripped the bars off the window with his bare hands. I mean, those are cemented in, you know?"

"But how—"

"He took a dive right out that same window. Landed smack on that iron spike fence outside. Hey, how did you know about it?"

"Jimmy, has anyone got the paper down there?"

He paused, puzzled. "Yeah. Why?"

"Look at page 15."

"Huh? What is this, a joke?"

"I don't think so." As she set the receiver back in its cradle, weariness washed over her. She hoped Jamallah's voices had kept on singing. She had a sudden clear picture of him dying; she banished it, but not quickly enough. Nowhere near quickly enough.

There he hung, impaled and bleeding—*but please God, dead already, please.* She hoped the big black man had thought the voices were welcoming choirs of angels. If there was any justice, he had; if there was any mercy, which she was beginning strongly to doubt, he was hearing them now.

The stack of envelopes on her desk reminded her that life went on. One looked familiar: heavy cream stock, invitation-sized. It was the seventh she had received; no, the eighth. Inside, she knew, would be a card, blank, except for the lower left-hand corner: RSVP.

Sorry. Joke's gone tired, doesn't work any more. After what I've seen today, it'll take a lot more than a blank card. . . . She tossed the envelope unopened into the wastebasket. Picking another, this one cardboard-reinforced and addressed in an unfamiliar hand, she slit it open carefully.

Two keys and a clover charm clinked out onto her desk.

Slowly she picked them up, hefting them. They were not imaginary. And therefore she was not imagining them. They were absolutely, solidly real, clinking musically as she dropped them into the metal top drawer of her desk, which she locked.

Real or not, when she opened the drawer an hour later to peek at them, they were gone.

MONDAY, DECEMBER 10

Tommy Riley

"Yes, Mr. Riley," the woman on the other end of the telephone said patiently. "That's correct. Your grade for the autumn semester of Calculus 101 is A-plus." Her voice grew amused. "I must say you're the first student who's ever called to question such an excellent mark. You don't really want me to try to change it, do you?"

"No," Tommy said. "I mean, yes! That is . . . I mean I don't really know what I mean, but there's a mistake, I'm pretty sure of it, and—"

"Let me just check your file," the woman at the other end said. "Hold on, please."

Tommy held on, shifting impatiently in his chair at the kitchen table. From the front of the house came the sound of the mailman dropping envelopes through the mail slot, then clomping away down the front porch. On the table before him lay his grade report, a computer-generated form from the Meadbury Community College Division of Undergraduate Records. Almost twenty-four hours, now, since he'd ripped the envelope open; twenty-four hours during which he'd tried to figure out what, if anything, he should do about the grade. Because it was wrong, absolutely wrong. How could he get an A+ without taking the final?

Finally he'd called Peewee Coover. True, he hadn't been hanging out much with Peewee lately, but they'd been pretty tight once upon a time. And Peewee always had good ideas about keeping out of what he called bummer-type situations, or getting out of them once they'd been stumbled into.

"A-plus my ass," had been Peewee's comment once he was finished being sarcastic about the college dude who found out that his old buddies were good for something after all. "This, my man, is some sort of trap."

Popping open a can of Pepsi, Peewee had settled himself in the same kitchen chair where Tommy was sitting now, guzzled half the can of soda, belched, and gone on to say what Tommy had been half dreading and half hoping he would say:

"You gotta get this straightened out, my man. Or somewhere down the line, when push comes to shove, your ass is gonna be in one mighty mother of a sling. Those college people just wanta find out if you're some sort of asshole sleazebag, find out if you'll take a good mark you didn't really get." He had gulped the rest of the soda. "That's the Peewee pronouncement on this bag of shit, man, an' you can believe it."

Tommy did. It made sense—sort of. Which was why he was sitting here now, waiting for the secretary to come back on the line. Although—

The telephone clicked. "Mr. Riley?"

"Uh, yeah? I mean, yes. I'm here."

"I'm transferring your call to Mr. Corcoran's office. Hold on."

He didn't see why he was important enough for the college to check out. Lots of sleazeballs graduated from college, didn't they?

The phone clicked again, and Corcoran picked up.

"Riley? What's this story about your not taking the final?" Corcoran sounded hurried, a little impatient.

"Well, sir, I didn't, and I still have to make it up, so the grade—"

"You earned that grade, Riley. You deserve it, and you're keeping it." The teacher's voice sounded friendlier, heartier now.

"But the final, sir—"

"Riley." Corcoran's tone grew stern, almost fatherly. "I don't know what the problem is, son, but it's not with the final. I gave it, you took it, I've got your test booklet right here in my hand."

Tommy felt his jaw drop. "What?"

"You scored a hundred percent," Corcoran went on. "I remember that, even if you don't. So listen, guy, why don't you relax a little? Take it easy over semester break, and I'll see you in class, all right?"

"S-sure," Tommy managed.

"And son, if you have any more of these little memory lapses—"

"Yeah," Tommy said. "Yeah, all right, Mr. Corcoran. Thanks. See you in January."

Slowly, he hung up the phone, feeling as if he'd suddenly fallen into a *Twilight Zone* episode. Distantly, Peewee Coover's voice echoed in his memory: ". . . push comes to shove. . . ."

"I don't get this," he muttered, picking up the grade report and wandering out into the living room with it. "I just don't get it at all."

Today's mail lay on the floor just inside the front door; I may have already won ten million dollars, he thought as he gathered it up. That was what he thought every day when he looked through the mail, and of course he never had won yet. But the way things were going, you never knew—

The second letter in the pile was addressed to him, the envelope heavy cream paper with a return address embossed in blue. He tore it open at once.

Ned Gorman
Meadbury Guaranty Corporation
Main Street
Meadbury
555-1000

Dear Mr. Riley,

Congratulations on your fine scholastic performance over the recent months. Young men like you are among our town's most valuable assets, and I want you to know that I recognize and appreciate your excellence.

It has come to my attention that your merits are not being utilized, nor your potential developed to the extent that you deserve—and require. Your present employment, in particular, fails to exploit your obvious ability.

Therefore, I extend an invitation to meet with you this evening at 7 P.M., in the conference room of the new Meadbury Shelter for the Homeless, where I will outline a program that I believe will put your fine qualities to better use.

As you may know, I have become active in helping our town become the best that it can be—and that means helping young men like yourself attain positions of civic leadership. My methods may seem unorthodox, but they are time-tested and work well; please do me the honor of learning more about them from me personally.

Of course, our meeting will put you under no obligation whatsoever. But I hope that once you have heard my plans you will realize the unusually fortunate nature of the opportunity I intend to offer.

Your future is in Meadbury, Mr. Riley—and Meadbury's future is in you. I look forward to assisting you into that future, and to meeting with you this evening.

Most sincerely yours,
Ned Gorman

Tommy smacked his forehead gently with the heel of his hand, still staring at the letter. Jeez, things were all screwed up; this Gorman guy—

He snapped his fingers. Of course! He thought he had recognized the substitute teacher at the exam. It was Ned Gorman himself; Tommy had seen his picture in the paper. But why? And why would Mr. Corcoran say—

Maybe Gorman was looking for hotshot assistants, recruiting for his political campaigns or office staff or something. Not that he'd find many hotshots out at Meadbury Community College, and one A+ grade didn't add up to genius, either.

And the grade was wrong. He knew it, and he was pretty sure Mr. Corcoran knew it, too, no matter what he said. And Mr. Gorman must know, since he was the one who'd given him that weird questionnaire in the first place.

So what was going on? Test, Peewee had said. They

wanna find out if you're a straight-ahead guy, or one who'll take shortcuts.

Sighing, Tommy shook his head. Peewee's explanation would make more sense if Tommy were in State Trooper school, maybe, or applying for a bank job, but—

He looked at the letter again: ". . . fortunate opportunity. . . ." That sounded decent. For a moment Tommy thought of letting things just stay the way they were, taking the grade, showing up at the meeting. Keeping his mouth shut, and getting in on whatever Mr. Gorman offered.

But no. Sooner or later he'd be found out—whatever there was to find out; he was beginning to think that things were just too screwed up for him to understand—and Mr. Gorman didn't sound like the kind of guy you'd want to be in trouble with. Tommy figured he'd better call up and set the man on the right track.

Returning to the kitchen, he dialed. The phone rang once, then clicked as a receiver was lifted. Tommy sat up straight.

"Meadbury Guaranty."

"Hello? Is Mr. Ned Gorman there, please?"

"One moment."

There came a whirr and a hiss and a run of musical tones. "Gorman."

"Hello, Mr. Gorman? Uh, this is Tommy, um, I mean Thomas Riley. I got a letter from you today, and I think there's a mistake. I mean, I think maybe you've got me mixed up with someone else?"

"Indeed. Go on, Thomas."

"Uh, the thing is, I'm not who you think I am. I mean, I am who you think I am, but I didn't get the grade I got, even though the college thinks I did. See, what happened was—"

"Yes, Thomas, I know." The voice was gentle now. "There's no mistake. I know all about it."

"Uh, you do?" Of course he did; he'd been there the day of the test.

"Yes. Don't worry, I know who you are. And don't worry about disappointing me; I didn't choose you on the basis of your calculus grade. But I do look forward very much to meeting you properly."

"Uh, sure," Tommy said. "I mean, yes, sir. I'll be there.

It's just that I didn't want you to think—"

"I know," Gorman said gently. "Don't worry. It was right of you to call. Until this evening, then?"

"Until this evening," Tommy repeated, not realizing how stupid he sounded until the receiver clicked in his ear.

He was still staring at the phone when his mother came into the kitchen, laden with grocery bags.

"Oh, there you are." She hefted the bags onto the counter. "Do you want leftover lasagna, or shall I defrost—"

Take it. Just take it. He wants you to go see him; go and see him. What've you got to lose? Not a whole hell of a lot.

He got up. "Mom, listen, I gotta go out tonight. I'll help you put that stuff away, but first come and help me get out my suit, okay?" He headed for the stairs, his mother following bemusedly after him.

"Jeez, that spot on the cuff," he said, "I hope the cleaners fixed it. Do I have a good shirt, a dress shirt? And can I borrow Dad's cuff links, the gold ones? I will not lose them, I promise."

He turned on the landing, looking down into her round, pink face, her greying hair mussed into fluffy little curls, and a moment of tenderness surprised him. She was so good to him, and she wanted so much for him.

And although he still wasn't sure what was going on, if this was opportunity knocking he was going to answer it. Heck, maybe Peewee was right; maybe this was all some sort of honesty test, and he'd just passed it.

He was going to make his mother proud of him. Her, and maybe even Nicki.

Wonderful Nicki. Wonderful life. His mother came up onto the landing beside him, smiling her what's-my-boy-up-to-now smile of amusement.

"Your suit?" she said. "And cuff links? Tommy, do you have a fever?"

He put his arm around her. Not much time; it was already after four, and if he didn't have a clean white handkerchief—two handkerchiefs, one for show and one for blow—he would have to go out and buy some.

"Mom," he said, "you're not going to believe who I just talked to."

TUESDAY, DECEMBER 25

Nicki Pialosta

Christmas morning. She snapped the clock radio's spine-stiffening buzz to "Morning Music," a luxury generally not permitted by her schedule. Handel's *Messiah* and no deadline, now there was a Christmas present. Today's agenda consisted of no agenda at all. Tossing back the covers, she thought how right she had been to turn down Jimmy's invitation. Other peoples' relatives were remarkable chiefly for being even more boring than one's own.

Not that yours are going to bore you, said an unpleasant voice at the back of her mind. Not unless they come back from the grave, or from the institution where you've warehoused your only brother.

No. Swinging her feet out of bed, she rejected the guilty thoughts. No more guilt. She had tried; she had failed. Rich was someone else's problem now.

Meadbury Shelter's opening ceremonies, conveniently held on Christmas Eve, marked the loosening of Rich's grip on her time, her conscience, and her life. She had considered attending the opening, then thought better of it since the shelter's first residents—Rich among them—were the guests of honor.

Which made it his night, not hers; he didn't need to see her there. He would do better, something told her, if he didn't. Besides, she didn't want the chance of another scene like the one at the ground-breaking.

Humming, she ducked into the shower. Hallelujah, indeed, she thought, toweling off.

Coffee, and no morning newspaper, thank you. Under the little aluminum tree, a compromise between sentimentality and convenience, lay her Christmas gifts to herself: a pair of comfortable, ugly slippers, the fuzzy, dowdy kind never worn by glamorous young career women—hah, she thought, slipping her feet into them; a complete set of Jane Austen; and one inexcusable extravagance, a chess computer. Its blank screen seemed to leer mischievous challenge.

For an unexpected instant the memory of a long-ago Christmas pierced her: Rich and herself by the huge tinseled Scotch pine, warm, homey air full of turkey-and-pie smells, the rattle of ribbons and wrappings, the voices of Mother and Dad. By contrast her own apartment seemed all at once too empty and silent.

She shut the memory away; later she would think of them and allow herself to miss them. But not now, not when the day stretched before her, ready to be whatever she made it. Straightening, she went to take her Christmas dinner, a Cornish game hen, out of the freezer.

Jimmy Conklin's gift, embarrassingly unexpected, looked no more out of place on the kitchen counter than it did anywhere else. The deep-blue velvet box held a complete set of gold Cross pens, ball-point, felt-tip, pencil, and wonder of wonders, even a fountain pen. Gorgeous, and extravagant even at the discount she hoped he had gotten —dear Jimmy. Anyone else would be thanking God for him; last night when he had shown up, wrapped gift in hand, she had had to talk fast to convince him she had plans for Christmas Day.

She had plans, all right: one entire day of total silence, unbroken by telephone (already unplugged), doorbell (to go unanswered), or natural disaster (which, should it occur, she resolved to ignore).

Still, it would not do to leave the pens lying around. Scooping up the silk-lined case in which the gleaming things reposed like cosseted princesses—and about as useful to one who lost a couple of Parkers every week—she opened a kitchen drawer.

In the drawer, among the scraps of mismatched silver and kitchen gadgets, lay a pair of keys. The clover charm winked up nastily at her.

For a moment she felt nothing except disorienting fear.

Again. Someone—here. In my apartment, someone opened this drawer, and—

Then realization hit. Rummaging, she snatched up the first weapon that came to hand: scissors. Clutching them, she searched the apartment, door to door, window to window, under the bed, in the backs of the closets. Finally she yanked hard on the door and chain. No one.

Not now. But someone was here, opening drawers, looking, touching. Waiting.

She backed into the kitchen, holding her robe closed at the throat, feeling as if the someone might appear any moment.

When? In the night, while I was asleep? Or watching from the street, waiting for me to leave? While I stood in the shower? While I ran out to check the mail, or get cigarettes?

One last check. One horrid, almost unthinkable possibility. Fearfully, clover charm dangling from her hand, she approached her front door.

Because otherwise how had those keys gotten into that drawer? She opened the door, slipping the chain, and inserted the old key into the new Block lock. Unpickable, guaranteed. . . .

Slowly the key began turning. Nicki's heart hammered her breastbone. Please, she prayed, please.

The key stopped. She rattled it firmly, tried the second one. No; they would not open the new lock. She sighed with relief.

So how had they gotten into the drawer? Because they were real; they existed, and by extension all the others had been real, too. The set in the alley. The pair from the walrusy-mustached fellow.

Again, in Jayman's hand. And yet again in an envelope, mailed to her.

Real. On the car seat, gone before she could blink. Inside Tommy's gate-hut in the *Bulletin* parking lot. Tommy off somewhere, the hut sealed, the keys no longer on the ledge just inside the little window when she returned with the maintenance man to open the padlock.

Each set appearing on the day of a murder and a death-box ad; each gone before they could be seized, or after they had been seized. Leaving nothing to show to the police, nothing to tell them. *Nothing you could tell anyone at all—unless you wanted to be locked away yourself.*

But they existed. Not hallucinations, appearing and vanishing at the whim of a mind shaken with worry and strain. Real—she clutched them, grateful for their sharp edges biting into her palm, because the pain made her sure they were not imagined. Not this time.

Real, unless they disappear out of my hand.

And if I'm not crazy—Q.E.D.—then someone else is.

Finally she snapped the dead bolt open and shut again, slammed the chain off and on, and stood there wishing for a stout iron crossbar. *And a moat. With alligators.*

Then she steadied herself. With another cup of coffee, the Cross pens—that's what they were for, detective notes—and a fresh spiral pad, she went to the sofa. Still she could not arrange herself comfortably until she had gotten up and rummaged in the hall closet. The length of metal tubing from the vacuum cleaner hardly matched Sarah's nail-studded baseball bat; still, with it near to hand, she could turn her attention to the questions.

Who? Why? How?

All right. The keys. And the ads. And the killings. All of which are connected, if only by time. Since the police feel free to assume the killer placed the ads somehow, let's say they're right. How do the keys fit in, if they do?

She sipped cooling coffee and lit a cigarette. *Face it—they do. Once is accident, twice is coincidence, three is on purpose, and the fourth is wake up, dummy. Especially since this makes more than four, and it's in your own house, behind your locked doors.*

So—a psycho killer sends me keys—my own keys, except that my locks are changed. Delightful thought— Merry Christmas to you, too. Got the keys from Rich, of course. Dear, thoughtful brother—I wish he were sheltered on the moon.

Except, my dear miss newspaper writer, the killer is not sending you keys, he's practically handing them to you. And taking them away again. He's close enough to touch you, anytime he wants.

She looked at the makeshift club. Much too small.

What else is he doing, aside from slaughtering bums? And why is he doing it to me?

Keys. Ads. The killings, and. . . .

The missing link popped into place all at once.

The notes. The mysterious invitations. RSVP. Ten of them now, as if someone did not want her to forget; as if. . . .

Respond, if you please. I kill. I want your attention. Respond.

Dear God—my attention. A newspaper-writer's attention, because. . . .

The gold fountain pen moved fluently over the page, its smooth sweep seeming on its own to make sense of what she knew. Too much sense.

He wanted to get caught. Not by cops (who did not know about the keys; there were no keys to show them). Cops might shoot; he wanted to live.

To live, with a writer knowing about him.

He was smart. He had to be, to break into the computers. He knew that if he lived, he wouldn't go to jail: He was insane.

Crazy like a fox.

And crazies only wanted writers for one reason: to write their stories.

So when the shrinks finally called him cured, he could walk straight out of the booby hatch to the bank: do not pass go, do not collect two hundred dollars.

Collect two million and movie rights instead.

But he was too smart, even for me. Too subtle. I didn't respond to the notes or the keys. Not the way he wanted me to; his message was too distant, too indirect.

So he moved in closer.

In here, where I live.

Jesus God. He's been everywhere—he was there on that first day, back in the alley. At work. In my car. Here. He's right in my footsteps, has been all this time.

What happens if I tell his story wrong?

And where is he today? Because between you and me, dear notebook, I think the cops had better find him before he gets in touch with me again.

Closing the notebook, she reached for the keys, which she'd laid on the arm of the sofa.

Gone.

Furious, she plunged her hand down between the sofa cushions. But the keys wouldn't be there, she felt sure;

nothing would be there except maybe a lost pen and a few stray fluffs of lint.

Nothing. Gritting her teeth, she forced her hand deeper. Her fingers brushed, then closed around the familiar metal shapes.

Sighing, she drew them out. *No you don't, dammit. Not this time.*

Clutching the keys, she picked up the phone. No dial tone. A lump of fright rose back into her throat before she remembered and leaned down to plug the damned thing back in.

A merry, merry Christmas to you, too, she thought as she dialed the police. And how was she going to explain all this to a cop?

WEDNESDAY, DECEMBER 26

Nicki Pialosta

Lieutenant Forbes nudged the keys and charm on his scarred desk with a thick forefinger. He sighed heavily. "All right, Miss, uh, Pialosta. You say you got, or saw, seven sets of keys like this."

Nice of him not to say "alleged" keys when he clearly did not believe her. "Yes. But I only have this one set, because the others disappeared." It sounded crazy even to her.

Bushy grey eyebrows rose and fell. "And these invitation things. Where are they?"

"I told you, I threw them out. I didn't pay attention. I didn't even think they were important until—"

Until you came up with this crackpot theory, his face said.

"Wait, I did give one to Ben Ibrani, my editor. The first one. He thought it was odd, too, so I'm pretty sure he'll remember."

Forbes rubbed the tip of his flattened nose. "Okay. We'll ask him. Meanwhile I think I've got everything here. We'll keep the keys, if that's okay with you; see if we come up with anything on them. Thanks for coming down. We appreciate your help. If anything else happens, get in touch."

He was humoring her; it was in his voice. She got up, reluctant to leave. "Lieutenant Forbes?"

"Yes, Miss Pialosta." His patience sounded forced.

"Lieutenant, I realize what I've told you sounds like

absolute nonsense. I wouldn't believe it myself, except that it's happening to me."

"Of course."

"And I know I haven't given you much to go on, but I'm frightened. I guess that's really why I came. Please believe me. I'm not imagining things, and I'm not making anything up. I'm really worried. If some nut has picked me to be his link to the world. . . ."

Forbes sighed again. "Miss Pialosta, at this point what you've told me doesn't sound any more nuts than the rest of what we've got on this case. I assure you, we're not going to ignorc what you've said. Now, I'm going to put light surveillance on you, just to be safe. Just to check things out. So don't be alarmed if you see more uniforms than usual for a while. You'll be watched at home, in your car, at work."

He smiled for the first time, tolerantly. "Does that make you feel better?"

"Yes. Yes, it does. Thank you very much, Lieutenant."

"You're welcome. Good-bye, Miss Pialosta." Swiveling, he pulled a file folder out of a drawer and immersed himself in it before she escaped his dingy, windowless office.

On the sidewalk, with the clean winter wind in her face, she took a deep breath of relief. Surveillance—it did make her feel better just to know she wasn't all alone with some maniac lurking nearby. She strode to her car, past a blue-and-white parked at the curb. The cop at the wheel looked familiar, but she could not place him. As she edged out into traffic, the cruiser followed. Had the surveillance begun already?

She drove slowly, glancing into her rearview mirror every block or so. Apparently the lieutenant meant what he said; the squad car stayed half a car length behind her until she hit a red light and had to stop. Then it came alongside.

The cop at the wheel turned and smiled at her. She swallowed hard and nodded back.

Black curly hair; gold wire-rimmed glasses; a curved white scar elongating the corner of his lip: the cop from the alley, the night Jayman died. The cop who talked to Sarah.

Watching—at home, at work, in your car. Does that make you feel better? Oh, yes, Lieutenant.

The squad car dropped back into place behind her as she pulled away from the light.

At least, I think it makes me feel better.

SUNDAY, JANUARY 6

Meadbury

Jesus, the kid was going to drive her freaking nuts, bouncing that ball.

"Emily, cut that out! Dammit, I told you—"

Ginny Polk stomped down the hall of the tacky two-bedroom apartment she'd had to move into last year when Howard split. It hadn't gotten any better since, not with crayon marks on the walls, and books and toys strewn everywhere.

The place was a goddamn dump. This was what she got for ten years of scrimping and making do while goddamn Howard promised and promised. Always someday; never today. And when someday finally came and he hit it big on those goddamn condos he built, what did he do?

Split to goddamn California with his goddamn secretary.

Leaving behind a twenty-two-year-old wife, damn near unemployable because she'd dropped out of high school for him, and a five-year-old daughter who'd promptly started wetting her bed again.

Till death do us part, you said. If I'd guessed what you were up to with Wilma the Willing, it would have been death that parted us. Yours. You prick.

Ginny flung open the door to her daughter's room. "I told you to pick up your toys, didn't I? Didn't I?"

Emily gave her a sullen look that Ginny wanted to smack off her grimy face. Where the hell did she get off, six years old and thinking she knew so damn much? Say two words and she fell down on the floor screaming. Rude as hell when anybody came over, and just try to leave her a couple of hours with a sitter. And she looked like her goddamn father.

"Pick up those toys right now." Teddy was already on his way over; she didn't want him to see the mess one little girl could make. It would turn him off, and Ginny didn't want to turn him off.

She needed a couple of hours just relaxing, having a few drinks, a few laughs. She needed Teddy—God forbid he should ever find out how much.

She strode over and grabbed Emily's skinny arm. God, the kid's T-shirt was filthy. Couldn't she stay clean for five minutes? "I'm going out. Pamela's coming to babysit."

Emily stared at the floor. "Don't like her."

"I don't care if you like her or not, she's coming." Black smudges marked the wall where the kid had been bouncing that damn rubber ball against it. Over and over, bouncing the damn thing until Ginny was ready to wring her neck, all the time talking to that obnoxious invisible friend of hers, Mr. Good.

Mr. Good. That was a hot one.

"I'm hungry."

Ginny checked the mirror on the back of the closet door. God, she would have to fix her mascara. If she hadn't been chasing after Emily all the time, she'd have gotten a chance to hot roller her hair.

"Pamela'll fix dinner. There's half a can of Spaghetti-O's in the fridge."

"Don't like Spaghetti-O's."

Ginny spun around, grabbed Emily, and shook her. "You'll eat them and like them, dammit, or you won't eat. Understand?"

"Mr. Good says you're a bad, bad mommy. He says he's going to eat you up. And I'm glad." Emily's face, six inches from her own, twisted into its usual bratty expression. "Bad, bad Mommy," Emily sang in that infuriating kid's chant.

"Shut up."

"Bad, bad, Mom-my. You're gon-na get it." Emily stuck her tongue out and blew a wet, noisy raspberry in Ginny's face.

"All right, dammit, that's it." She grabbed a handful of Emily's hair and yanked the child across her knee. "That's it, once and for all, that's it!"

She struck her daughter, then, and in the blow realized her power, and in the realization saw the promise of freedom: *just me and Teddy.*

A portion of her recoiled, scrambling back and away in horror, praying: *Don't let me kill her!*

A very small portion. Not enough to stop her hand. Just enough to open a window. Not thinking of what she was doing, now, or of the tremendous force with which the blows struck—

"You're driving me crazy you goddamn brat I can't do a goddamn thing—" Hit and hit, because the pain was so bad and Ginny was helpless against it; hit and hit—

Something came into her head, then, piercing like a frozen arrow.

Ginny's hand stopped in midswing; her mouth in mid-curse.

Emily slid to the floor and backed away. She smiled at something only she could see. "Bad Mommy," she whispered. "You're gonna get it."

Ginny's hand, pink and swollen from spanking, wobbled ever-so-slightly in midair, like the hand of a puppet suspended from invisible strings. My hand? she thought confusedly, not quite recognizing the chapped knuckles, the freshly polished red nails.

"Bad Mommy," Emily said with satisfaction.

The hand moved toward Ginny's mouth, and into it. The red nails clicked against her teeth as she tried to close her jaws; the fingers—whose fingers? she thought—pried her teeth apart and forced on past them.

Emily giggled, and began to bounce her ball.

Fingernails scraped the back of Ginny's throat, gagging her.

"Bad Mommy," Emily said again, and turned away.

Please, no, this is not happening to me it's not it's not hap—

But it was. Ginny knew it for sure as the fingers clenched into a rough fist.

MONDAY, JANUARY 7

Nicki Pialosta

Another morning in January, the sun a pale cold star in the frigid sky. Nicki slammed out of her apartment, through the traffic lights, and into the office in an evil mood that curdled further at the sight of Jimmy Conklin in her chair, his scuffed cowboy boots propped proprietarily on her desk.

She stripped off her coat and hung it on a hook. "The concept of private property," she said crisply, "is an old and honorable one."

Conklin shrugged. He was impossible to embarrass, and almost impossible to suspect— Almost.

"Just comparing notes." He raised the folder she had filled with clippings about the so-called Meadbury Slasher. "Got to you, huh?"

"Yes, it got to me." Forcing him out of the way, Nicki dropped her purse into her center drawer and picked up her mail. Circulars predominated. Conklin kept paging through the bulky folder.

She tapped his shoulder. "If you must inspect my papers, would you mind taking them to your desk? Some of us have work to do."

The chair squeaked as he got to his feet. "You know, like my ma used to say, you can't be a doormat until you lie down."

"What's that supposed to mean?" She slipped into the warm seat and brushed sand off her blotter.

"It means you're letting your little brother spoil your disposition."

Her heart lurched, even as she slapped down the wad of envelopes. Here it was, then: the moment of truth.

"And just how the hell do you know I have a little brother?"

Not from the article on the shelter's ground-breaking, that was for sure. After a tussle with her conscience, she had decided to name in full the derelict who had barged into Gorman's speech, although she had omitted describing his excretory encounter with "this reporter." Then, in a moment of unusual grace, the computers had chosen that paragraph to screw up. It had appeared garbled and totally unreadable. "Well?"

Conklin perched on the edge of her desk and ran a hand through his bright red hair. "Look, Nicki, the cops checked out every one of the bu— I mean, guys—on the site that morning. I mean, they checked them. There aren't a whole lot of Pialostas in town, you know."

Staring at him, she thought of a desert island somewhere. A tiny island, marooned in an azure sea. No people, no phones; just sand and sea and silence. *And did the cops check you, my little crime-reporting friend?*

"I suppose now everyone knows I've got a wino brother."

His freckled face twitched in surprised hurt, or a good imitation of it. "Gee, no. I wouldn't do that."

She closed her eyes.

Of course not. He's a friend, isn't he? Isn't he?

"That was kind of you. Not saying anything, I mean."

"Yeah, well. Don't thank me. I'm not the only one who reads police reports, you know. If I were you, I'd get ready for a shit storm—Rifkind isn't going to like your not telling him sooner. Some folks might say the paper got the town to build the whole shelter just for your brother."

"Right. Nice of you to remind me."

"As if you needed it, huh? But I could be a whole lot nicer, you know. If you'd just drain the moat, let down the drawbridge, and take those pots of boiling oil off the parapets, a guy could get closer."

"My, aren't we poetic this morning." She slipped a renewal notice from the *Columbia Journalism Review* into her desk drawer, carefully set aside a single cream-colored envelope marked "Personal," and roundfiled all the rest.

"Yeah, well," he said, "since we are clearly not going out

on the town tonight, how about a little advice?”

She tried to smile, her glance straying unhappily to the envelope. “Sure. What kind of advice do you need?”

“Very funny. I don’t know what the hell to tell you about Rifkind. You gotta wing that one. But as for your brother, hey, the guy’s got three squares, a roof over his head, and people to watch out for him. You can’t do any better, unless you want to take him home and keep him on a leash. Jeez, will you quit staring at that thing and open it?”

She picked it up.

“Let me guess,” he said. “Heavy cream card-stock. Embossed. RSVP. No signature, no anything else.”

Shc stared at him. “IIow did you know that?”

“I told you, I hang around with cops. And I got one Saturday.”

She pulled the card from its envelope. It was identical to the ones she had received before. Then, torn, she looked up at Jimmy’s round, honest face. Or was it? Whoever was sending the cards, planting the keys, was someone very close.

Is it like the card you got Saturday, Jimmy, or like the one you’re planning to send me tomorrow? And if not you, then who?

“Did you tell the police?” she asked.

“Yeah, I took it down to the shop, not that they’ll find anything on it. In fact, I’m going down there now. Want me to take this one, too?” He extended a slim strong hand, stained at the fingertips from changing typewriter ribbons.

“No! I mean, no, thank you. I’ll take it.”

He tipped his head curiously at her, then shrugged. “Suit yourself.” He hopped down, started to walk away, then turned back. “Um. I know it’s none of my business, but be careful, okay? I don’t like this. Cops don’t, either. Somebody in this town is not playing with a full deck.”

Full deck of cards, she thought, and let her breath out hard. “I know.”

“Don’t do anything brave and stupid, okay?”

She bit her lip. “I won’t.”

He nodded. “I didn’t mean to zing you about your brother.”

“Forget it. It’s good to find out someone cares enough to speak up.”

His green eyes brightened. "In that case, there's a great little Italian restaurant—"

"Thanks. But I've got a lot of work to do."

"Yeah, okay. I get it. Back to the cop watch." He made a wry, undaunted face and strolled out of the office.

She watched him go. It was like that old TV game show—*Who Do You Trust?*

She looked back at the card.

Yeah. Who the hell do you trust?

Finally she set the card aside, called the switchboard, and asked the operator to find Will Rifkind.

Because the other game show for today was *Face the Music.*

Tommy Riley

Pete parked in front of Tommy's house, left the motor running, and slumped in disgust behind the steering wheel. "Come on, Riley. Can't you call in sick or something? It's only eight; they'll have time to find a sub."

Tommy settled back in the passenger seat and sighed. Pete just didn't understand, not at all. How could he when he treated life as one long beer blast that would never end? The snow-lined front walk drew his eye to the front door. His mother was out. If he went in now he would have time to be alone, time to sit and . . . well, sit and think. More and more, that was all he wanted to do, sit in his room with the shades drawn and examine the new kinds of knowledge developing inside him.

Knowledge that Pete would have to find in his own way.

"I've gotta go change."

"Oh, man, you are getting so dull, you know? Next thing, you'll be settled down with some chick in a trailer park. Like Brockway and Sooz." Pete thrummed his fingers on the wheel. "We could still hang out for a while, get some coffee. You've got time. Hey, what's the news with Nicki?"

A black, dangerous anger stirred in Tommy. "I told you not to talk about her." He did not want to loose the anger on Pete. Pete was his friend.

"Okay, okay." Pete held up both hands. "I didn't say it."

Tommy reached for the door handle. An hour, he would have a whole hour to be alone, to . . . listen.

That was it. It was like listening. He needed to listen to his own thoughts, which in recent days had taken on a deep, unfamiliar resonance. First they had frightened him, then fascinated him; finally they had taken him in thrall. They spoke to him, and he no longer found that strange.

An gnat buzz in his ear made him turn to Pete.

". . . later," Pete was saying. "I'll pick you up. It's Coover's goddamn birthday— Christ, he's such a little kid. We got a chick comin' over for him, give him a little happy birthday surprise. I got a keg in the basement, we'll grab some pizza, and Brockway's gonna score some smoke if Sooz'll take the chains off him for the night. Anyway, the guys are gonna be down at the arcade; we'll pick 'em up." He grinned. "Right after I deliver a surprise of my own over at Roundtree's."

Tommy wanted to say something, but the words stuck on a funny pain in his chest. *Don't do it. Do not compel me to find you and—*

What? Tommy shook his head to clear it out.

"I don't think I can make it." He got out of the car and began to walk up the sidewalk to get inside, alone. Light fell so bright in the morning. He liked it better now that his new job had him working indoors. Mr. Gorman had been very nice about the whole grade mix-up. Tommy had even found himself telling the older man about Peewee Coover's good advice. Really, Mr. Gorman had said, your friend sounds interesting. He sounds as if he has possibilities.

Anyway, Tommy thought as he strode toward the house, now he could stay inside most days until dusk came on.

"Hey!"

Tommy spun, puzzled. "What?" The gangly boy in the car looked familiar, but Tommy could not recall his name. It didn't matter. He turned away again; he wanted to be inside.

"You're fuckin' something, man," the boy yelled.

Pete, that was his name. Pete.

And something bad was going to happen to him.

"You're really a fuckin' treat," the boy yelled. "You don't wanna come, don't come. Nobody'll miss you, that's for sure, so just fuck off, man. You know? Just fuck off." With a shriek of tires and a billow of greyish exhaust, the big white car roared away.

Tommy watched it go with a distant feeling of regret. The pain in his chest faded. He shrugged and went into the house. Up in his room lay his calculus book.

Study. He would open the book, even though there would be no make-up test.

Calculus. He liked calculus. Somehow, it rested him.

Nicki Pialosta

Hours after laying the whole story out before Rifkind, Nicki still could hardly believe his response.

His exact words: "So what're ya tellin' me for? Write it down, Pialosta. We ain't talking-books, ya know, we gotta print the stuff. And by the way, I need that city council piece on my desk yesterday, so hustle it up. Ya got it?"

And that had been his entire reaction. "I want the whole nine yards on it. What the shelter means to you and your family, how it's affected your brother—you know, the whole sobby schmear. Get some other relatives in there too, awright? And some medical experts on how many bums woulda died this winter, and like that. Aw, hell, what am I tellin' you for? JFDI, kid, you know how."

And that was it. JFDI stood for "Just Fuckin' Do It," Rifkind's standard phrase to his reporters.

He hadn't even sounded surprised, almost as if he already knew about Rich. Which was ridiculous; if he'd known he surely would have called her on it long before this.

Nicki pulled the Toyota into the Meadbury Shelter driveway. What Rifkind did know was how to turn a potential disaster into an advantage. He knew the only way to handle her relationship to Rich was to make it look as if the paper already knew about it, and run with that. Too many resources committed now, too much of the paper's prestige at stake, not to mention the ad revenue for the extra pages. She could just hear Rifkind's answer if anybody dared to question him:

"Of course we assigned a reporter who gives a shit. This story is about giving a shit."

Later, maybe, he'd give her hell for it. But no pain, no gain—and for now she'd gotten away with it. Why he hadn't just fired her on the spot, she wasn't sure; someday, probably, she'd spell somebody's name wrong and he'd nail her for that instead.

Sometimes her job was like running through a mine field, and her after-work chore of visiting Rich was like a firefight. She angled the Toyota into the rough lot behind the shelter and forced herself to leave its protection for the icy twilight. At least the drive and the parking area were sanded and well-lit; Meadbury dealt as effectively with winter as with its other problems.

Better than she did with hers, she thought. Since the murders at the shelter site, she felt even more obsessive than before about checking on Rich. She still visited only once a day, but now had to restrain herself from telephoning between visits, just to make sure he was still alive, that no maniac had—

No. Don't think that way.

She strode between a cement mixer and a pile of sand, surprised as always that frozen ground felt so much harder than concrete. The sidewalks and landscaping would come in spring.

Not that these bums deserve it. Not that Rich deserves my concern. Bitter wind tore at her coat and stung her eyes with tears. Callous; she grew more callous even as the winter grew colder, and she hated it. She wanted to be able to reach out, to touch and to embrace, and yet she could not make these visits more than the ritual performance of an unwanted obligation.

Unwanted. Obligation. Two words, heavy and unyielding as cinder blocks. Sometimes she felt as if her skull were being pressed between them—her skull, and her heart, too.

Rich had not improved. If anything, he had degenerated, and wandered around drunk and mumbling most of his few waking hours. The shelter, whatever it claimed to have done for others, had not rehabilitated him. Still, she supposed, anything was better than letting him loll in the gutter, prey to nut and nature alike.

Anything but having him at home. Anything except taking care of him, spending time with him, doing the grubby salvage work the broken hulks of his mind and body required— It occurred to her suddenly that the personal angle story on the shelter would not be an easy one. Just having a personal angle on it wasn't easy.

"Hello, Miss Pialosta."

She stopped, blinking, just inside the door. "Tommy! I didn't realize you had— I mean, how nice you look in your uniform."

His smile came more deliberately, more confidently than before; it seemed less eager to please. He looked somehow bulkier, too; perhaps from the badge and gunbelt. With faint shame she realized that she had not even missed him, nor spared him a thought since she had seen him so worried about his test.

"Yeah. I'm a guard for Meadbury Guaranty, now. Mr. Gorman hired me and assigned me here himself." His hand stroked the butt of his automatic once and dropped back to his side. "He says I got a great future."

She hesitated, unnerved by a flicker of something nearly reptilian in the slow lowering of his eyelids, his air of listening to music she could not hear. "Have you seen my— Have you seen Rich Pialosta?"

Lazily he angled his head toward the lounge. "Oh, yeah, he's around here somewhere."

As if on cue, a hoarse scream arose from the room at which he had nodded. Tommy lifted his eyebrows once, and then, with the leisurely gait of one secure in his authority, ambled to investigate. His hand caressed his holster as he moved.

"You bastard!" Rich shrieked, and Nicki broke into a weary trot, dimly aware that she'd better reach the lounge before Tommy.

And that was odd; she'd never worried over Tommy. At least, not quite in this way. . . .

But she had no time to pursue the uneasy thought, for through the doors into the lobby burst a wiry black man, his toothless mouth twisted in fury. Colliding with her, he knocked her backward into a flailing stagger, then vanished through a door marked "Basement." Tommy swung around with oiled smoothness as another guard joined him in the chase.

Regaining her footing, Nicki hurried on. It could have been someone else, but of course it was not. Moaning theatrically, clutching his left temple, Rich lay sprawled on a brown vinyl couch. Center stage, just where he wanted to be.

"Sucker got my medal." Pouting, he rolled his eyes. Blood oozed from a jagged gash below the left one. "Tell 'er, Reg."

Forsten dabbed tenderly at the wound with a wet paper towel. For a moment she despised him; without the booze, he could have been so good.

Or was it because he was doing what she should have been doing?

Sarah shuffled in, carrying a cup of water and more wadded towels. "All right, all right— Oh. Hello." Blanking her face, she drew herself up. Since coming to the shelter she had transformed herself into a homey old charlady, decked out in flowered housecoat and fuzzy pink slippers, a purple silk scarf tied over her pincurls.

I miss the old Sarah, Nicki thought, then squelched the idea. If Sarah was less picturesque, less independent, surely she was still much better off.

Bending stiffly, Sarah elbowed Forsten aside. "Go on, Doc. This needs a woman's touch. There, now." Rich closed his eyes as she swabbed his cheek.

"My medal." Despite his whine, Nicki felt sorry for him. Their mother had given him the St. Christopher's medal on his confirmation; it was the only thing he owned that he had never pawned.

Through a door at the rear stalked Ned Gorman, eyes narrowed in displeasure. He wore a blue pinstripe suit of such careful tailoring that he looked sewn into it. "What is it this time?"

Forsten wobbled erect. "To depict the situation accurately would require a nonlinear approach, heavily dependent upon the Taoist con—"

"Save it, Forsten," said Gorman. "What I want to know is, who slugged who, and why?"

"Whom." Forsten's mutter earned him a dirty look.

Gorman stepped past him. "Okay, Pialosta, what's your problem now?"

Rich opened his eyes and looked at Gorman as if the shelter director had just kicked him. "It was my money —earned it shoveling snow. Wasn't giving none of it to that bastard Long Tom. He never— Anyway, he hit me. With a chain around his fist." He paused for the sympathy he clearly expected. "Then he grabbed my medal and ran downstairs. I want it back." His eyes filled with tears of pain and self-pity.

"The police will get it back, Rich," said Nicki.

Gorman stiffened. "Police? I'm sure there's no need for that. Our security men probably have him by now." He did a perfect about-face and walked away.

Reg Forsten's gaze followed him, flat and unfriendly. Then Forsten began strolling toward the stairwell door. Another guard started after him, then stopped and shrugged, as if to say, "Just don't come crying to me."

Nicki watched him go, and trailed Gorman into his office, a glass-walled affair in the far corner of the lobby.

"Using a bicycle chain," she said, "is assault with a deadly weapon."

Palms flat on his desk, Gorman swiveled his chair around. "Ms. Pialosta, last week your brother dented a metal pitcher on a man's head. That's ADW, too. If I called the police for every fight, our population would be even lower than it is. All our clients would be in jail."

She surveyed the red Oriental rug, the leather-topped desk, the framed prints on the wall behind his head. He did all right for himself, she thought. Then she took in what he had said. "Your population is dropping? In January?"

"Attrition." He gave his desk a brisk, impatient palm-wipe. "We're not merely warehousing people, you know. Granted, I'm only running this place until a permanent director can be found, but I do not believe we should create a dependency. We're counseling them, offering them drug rehab programs, AA, job training. We do everything we can to return them to productive life. That's our function, and we perform it well; in fact, the Meadbury Public Works Department has hired quite a few of them recently."

Which explained all the vacant-eyed, slack-jawed street-sweepers and litter collectors she'd seen around lately. Somehow the recollection unsettled her. Making them useful, in this case, seemed a little too close to making use of them. But that was unfair. Even Ned Gorman couldn't turn a bum into a banker.

"And the ones who don't respond? Like this Long Tom?" Or like Rich and Reg?

Gorman sighed. "Sometimes our best efforts, unfortunately, are wasted. The unreformed are a drain on our resources. We know too well the hopelessness of their cases. For them, I'm afraid, there's no—"

A guard, not Tommy, rapped on the glass as he came through the doorway, "Mr. Gorman, we lost him." Tall and broad-shouldered, he had a small paunch and scarred knuckles. The large letters of his ID tag read "Johansen."

Glancing at Nicki, Gorman frowned. "Lost him? How?"

Johansen looked uncomfortable, defensive, and puzzled. "Damned if I know, Mr. Gorman. Jefferson chased him down the front staircase. I went down the back. We figured we'd flush him up to Houley. He was waiting at the middle stairs. But the guy never came up. He's got to be down there, though. Riley'll get him." He scowled at his shoes.

"The laundry room? Did you check there, and the storage areas?"

Johansen squared his shoulders. "We know our business, Mr. Gorman. I'd like the keys to the locked rooms. If one of the doors was open, he might have slipped in."

Suddenly Rich wavered into the office. "He's gone, ain't he? Just like Kincaid, just like Rogers. Gone."

"Pialosta." Gorman's voice was tired. "Try not to be more ridiculous than you have to be."

"Gone." Rich spoke with the morose satisfaction of one who has predicted that his worst dreams will come true, and is seeing it happen. Then he trudged off, mumbling, alone.

Gorman adjusted his glasses. "Come on. Let's go find Long Tom." He arose with the air of noblesse oblige that he probably put on in the morning with his suit.

Nicki followed him toward the stairway. "Who were Kincaid and Rogers?"

"Punks," said Johansen. "Mr. Gorman, she can't come with us."

"Why, Johansen, you don't think your men can protect her?"

The guard glared and unsnapped his holster.

"Kincaid and Rogers," said Gorman, "were two of our

most unrewarding clients." They descended the cement stairs. The basement corridor stretched two hundred yards in a dazzle of polished floors reflecting white fluorescents. Several dozen doors opened off each side. "The way I see it, they stuck up a gas station or something, panicked, and skipped town without coming back for their belongings."

"Belongings," Johansen snorted. "Rags and trash is more like it."

Gorman shot a sharp look at the big uniformed man, but said nothing. Overhead, the fluorescents buzzed on the edge of audibility. Locks clicked open and shut as Johansen slid tigerishly from one room to another. They made slow, careful progress down the corridor.

(red) A flash at the back of Nicki's mind, like a highway flare.

Gorman hung back. "We're really quite proud of the job we're doing." His keys jingled softly. "Of course, there is some unpleasantness involved."

(red) Nicki shook her head to clear it, swallowed hard, her mouth all at once dry. Then she shook the feeling. *He's feeding me another line, wants to get in the paper again. As if he's not in it enough.*

She pointed to a door. "You missed one." A plain white door, it bore no number and no legend.

Gorman eyed her and smiled. "I think you're mistaken. Perhaps, though, you'd like to check it for yourself?" He chose a key and handed it to her.

I don't like this. But Gorman was watching, mild amusement on his face. Biting her lip, she slid the key into the lock.

The door swung open. She went in, fumbled for the light switch, and clicked it on. Something went *pop* in the middle of her mind and her vision blurred *(red)* for just an instant.

Then the thing on the floor lurched and sat up. Its head swiveled bonelessly to fix her with a dead stare. Flesh dripped as the jaw fell open.

A gush of blood boiled from the mouth-hole, shrouding the figure in clotting red sheets. But she recognized it, oh yes. And it knew her. A boggy, cavernous voice came out of the rotting throat: *"Daughter."*

She staggered back, scrabbling wildly for the door. But the door was gone. The thing on the floor hauled itself toward her, gagging and strangling on the blood which continued to spew from it, which splattered everywhere till the cell-like room was painted in it.

(redredredRedRED)

Cold sticky fingers closed on her ankles. She leaned on the seamless wall, hammering at it with her fists until the tiny black-and-white marble tiles of the floor roared up at her, smacking her into darkness.

And out of that darkness came the blood-choked voice: *"Yes, my darling daughter. . . ."*

Meadbury

Pete Cheney put the accelerator to the floor and let the big car's power push him into the seat. God, he loved power, that surging, flying feeling. But he backed off the gas as soon as he'd gotten the first rush; Locust Street was crawling with blue-and-whites this time of night, when all the kids were out looking for after-supper fun.

He pulled up against the curb in front of Roundtree's Market. The old fart was ringing up someone's groceries, his back turned to the street.

If only that sucker Riley wasn't turning into an old fart just like Roundtree. They could've had a blast tonight, and then Pete wouldn't be in such a foul, piss-ass mood. They could've all come down and sprayed the goddamn windows with words. Pete knew some choice words to spray on Roundtree's goddamn windows. He said a few of them to himself as he sat there.

But fuck it, just fuck it. He didn't need Riley for this, he didn't need anyone. This was between him and old man Roundtree.

He got out of the car and opened the back door and picked up the brick that lay on the floor among the beer cans and empty cigarette packs and hamburger wrappers. Looking around, he hefted the brick, liking the gritty weight of it in his hand. You could build with bricks like that—build a goddamn city—streets, and walls, and windows. . . . Windows? No, he thought, windows open. . . .

He stood motionless for a long moment while the hairs at

the back of his neck lifted. Someone was watching him, someone nearby. He looked around quickly, edgily. No cops in sight. Nobody paying attention to him. Just the usual evening traffic, cars going by, the drivers looking ahead, not at Pete Cheney. He could heave the brick and be off before the goddamn glass stopped crashing. Roundtree'd shit.

Pete ambled around the front of the car as if he were about to look under the hood. Then he whirled around and let the brick fly.

Go, sucker, go! It sailed through the air. He took two steps toward the open car door.

The brick stopped. Dead. It hung four feet off the ground, a foot from the big glass window. Pete stopped too, staring, then knowing that if he hurried he could see the glass exploding. See it real close, and in real slow motion.

Special effects, man. Pete Cheney began to walk forward, his eyes fixed on the distance between the rough-edged brick and the smooth, shiny glass. His legs moved stiffly. When he was two steps from the window, everything started again. Behind him the traffic sounds came back as if someone had turned up the volume. The brick lurched. Pete dropped to his knees.

The bottom half of the window collapsed. Glittery shards flew everywhere. Something struck him in the forehead. Warm wetness seeped around the thing sticking out of his skull, but it was okay, everything was fine, it really was. Harsh cement bit his knees as he crawled forward, reaching out toward the cave whose jagged edges shone, tantalizing, Inside, something wonderful waited, if only he could get there. He hauled himself to the window's narrow ledge.

Just inches away— Nearly blinded by the warm stream running into his eyes, he pulled himself up, forward, until he was almost inside. Any second now he would see it, the marvel that was waiting for him. Eagerly, he stuck his head through the wide, jagged gap in the glass. Here . . .

Above, something cracked; the glass quivered. He turned his head, craning his neck to peer up, just in time to glimpse the flash as the window's upper half slid down and guillotined him.

Nicki Pialosta

She lay on a tiled floor.

She sat on the couch in a Manhattan apartment. Her own old apartment.

A basement room wrapped her in clammy silence.

Down in the street, a taxi horn blared. A truck backfired.

Cold floor against her face.

Nubbly cotton upholstery beneath her hand.

No, that couldn't be right. She couldn't be in both places.

Could she?

Tried to move. No. Something . . . holding. She fell back —to where?

Tile. Couch. Which? She felt . . . both.

tilecouchtilecouchtilecouch.

Tile. . . .

Couch.

Flat on a floor, chilled and aching.

Upright, nausea threatening.

A whisper: Watch. Listen. My darling daughter. . . .

Rigid with fright in her old city apartment, thrust into her own past, Nicki Pialosta waited. Something was about to happen; something bad. Only she couldn't remember what it was. She couldn't remember. . . .

On a basement floor in Meadbury, one year later, she waited, too.

Then it began: a jittery horror show tap-dancing out of the dark at her; jerky, too-fast animation, bloody flailing limbs, broken mouth gaping, gobbling at—

No!

Gone. Stillness, Herself, on the couch.

Floor.

Someone chuckled.

Sorry.

Then the real show began, slowly: a curtain that tore down the middle. The world divided, split-screen. Then/now. Here/there.

Yes. No.

This was not happening. . . .

Oh, but it is. Watch.

A Manhattan foyer, pregnant with bloody disaster; her father approached it. Unaware . . .

In the other half of her sight, a street in downtown Meadbury: Victor Pialosta strolling along it, swinging his cane and stepping jauntily. Tipping his hat to the passers-by, he strode toward a bench on the green; under his arm he carried a sack of bread and a folded Meadbury *Bulletin*. He would feed the pigeons, sit in the sunshine, read the newspaper. His little girl worked for that newspaper, and he was proud of her; it showed in his face, the flesh of which looked firm and sweet as a winter apple. He snapped the newspaper open sharply, the bag of bread beside him on the bench.

No sound would come from her throat, which closed with love and grief as she watched him.

Because in Manhattan he was dying, bleeding and dying. The glassed-in foyer echoed with his bubbling shrieks. His hand shot up, clawing at the brass mailboxes, fingers straining, stiffening, sliding down. Trails of crimson streaked the marble wall. Victor Pialosta sat down hard in a widening pool of his own blood, fingers dabbling aimlessly in it as his life pumped out of him. On his face was a mystified look, as if he wondered why this had been done to him. Then it faded; his head fell sideways. A pink bubble grew on his lips. His fists clenched, and lay still.

Nicki Pialosta wept.

I'm sorry. Oh my God, please forgive me, I'm sorry.

Then she froze. He was looking at her.

Both of him: on the bench, in the foyer.

Both of her: on the couch, on the basement floor.

They spoke as one, the dead man's lips flopping like slabs of liver slapped wetly together, the living father's face stern, accusing.

Choose, Nicki. Which will it be? You must choose.

And then came the worst thing of all, as the living father rose calmly from his bench and vomited up a fist-thick gout of blood, spewing it straight at her.

Grinning.

Nicki screamed.

(red)

• • •

"Miss Pialosta?" A hand shook her arm roughly. Consternation edged Gorman's voice. "Johansen, get her some water."

"Dames." Johansen moved away.

Normal floor beneath her, normal voices above her, Nicki lay very still. Then she opened her eyes. Gorman was leaning over her. Something avid flickered out of his face. Then a look of concern came down like a mask.

Johansen returned with a paper cup of water, which he thrust at her. "You girls and your diets." He shook his head. "No wonder you're all the time faintin'."

She drank the water, shook off their offers of help as she got unsteadily up. "I'm perfectly fine. Really. I can't imagine why that should have happened."

But what had happened? She struggled to remember. Recollection came like a whiff of brimstone; *choose.* But nothing more; it was like trying to remember a dream. A bad dream. . . .

Gorman pursed his lips in an officious frown. "You realize the shelter can take no responsibility for injuries due to pre-existing illness or instability."

Nasty, unpleasant man. She stepped into the corridor. Her heart was pounding, sweat slicking her palms. "Of course not. Let's get this over with, shall we? I'd like to go home, or back downtown if we find something newsworthy." There. She had him where he lived.

"The man has probably slipped away by now." He strode past her.

She paused, then turned to stare once more into the tiny room, forcing herself to examine every detail of the smooth tile floor, the white wallboard, the mops lying in a stringy, greyish heap.

"See something interesting in there?"

She started and spun around. "Tommy!" He was smiling, sleepily, flatly, like a coat of cheap, thick paint slapped over something else. "No. Just looking."

He reached past her, brushing too close, and pulled the door closed. Its lock made a soft, secret snick. Then his hand came back, holding something glittery.

Her heart felt as if it might stop.

"Found this." He gazed down at it almost tenderly.

"Right outside this door." He looked at her through wide green eyes. "Guess Long Tom decided he didn't want it any more."

He held out Rich's medal, then dropped it into her open hand. The silver chain puddled around it on her palm.

She cleared her throat, unable to take her gaze from his. "Thank you."

He shrugged, still smiling, and ambled away down the long, white hall.

At the far stairway, Gorman waited. "He must be here somewhere if the guards are still up on the stairways." Despite his words, the urgency seemed to have left him.

"Yes, sir." Johansen blinked rapidly. "We're gonna go through this place again, Mr. Gorman, and I promise you we'll find that damn fool ni—" He glanced at Nicki. "I mean, the alleged perpetrator, sir."

"Yes. Well, we have recovered the stolen property, at any rate." He gave Tommy a quick, speculative look.

"Yes, sir. We have, sir." Tommy turned and gestured ahead of himself at the stairway.

She turned to eye him sharply, but the smile clung to his face as if installed there, a permanent fixture.

At the top of the stairwell she opened the door, then paused, looking into the lounge where Rich still sprawled. But it was not Rich, now, who commanded her attention; it was Reg Forsten sitting bolt upright on a bench, ignoring Rich completely.

Ignoring everything. His face was expressionless, his eyes deep holes. The lines of his face seemed oddly smoothed out, as if an eraser had passed over them.

Then Tommy reached past her, opening the door wider. "After you, Miss Pialosta. Don't trip, now—we wouldn't want you to hurt yourself."

Tommy Riley

Letting her get well ahead of him, he watched her legs as she went up the stairs. Jeez, slit skirts were neat. Was she looking over her shoulder? Did she feel his eyes on her calves? Blushing a little, trying to suppress a grin of pure delight as those nylon-clad legs scissored up the staircase, he—

Riley, take your responsibility to heart!

The flash faded; he blinked. But what was he doing? Where were these cement steps; why was he wearing this oddly heavy—uniform? With a weight dragging at his belt, a . . . gun? Riley? *Who— Oh. I am Riley.*

That was it. His gun. His job. His responsibilities.

He started up the steps, following the woman, whose name was . . . Miss Pialosta. Yes, Miss Pialosta. He put his hand on the rail and took one measured step after another. Fifteen times. With his eyes fixed on the risers.

At the top of the stairs she paused. He pushed the door wider. Now she was looking uncertainly at him, as if she wanted to ask him something. He smiled. *Get her moving.*

"After you, Miss Pialosta. Don't trip, now—we wouldn't want you to hurt yourself."

And it worked; she smiled back. He had reassured her. That was part of his job, of course, but the way she looked at him was not. All at once he felt light, as if the weight of the gun and uniform had dropped away. Nicki was smiling at him because he had made her feel better.

"I'll keep an eye on things here," he told her. "Don't worry."

It was wonderful to be able to say that to her.

She sighed, glancing back only once at Forsten. *That bum.*

"Thanks," she said. "Tommy, you've grown up. Seeing you in that uniform, the way you take charge—well. I have to admit you surprised me. I almost didn't recognize you."

He squared his shoulders, even as embarrassment made him laugh. "Still feels funny sometimes—all this." His gesture included the uniform, the gun, his polished shoes, and the haircut he had not at first wanted to get at all.

"You'll get used to it. You're doing just fine. Remember I used to tell you how you were going to do so well?"

"Yeah." The days in the parking lot seemed like years ago. "Listen, are you sure you're okay? To drive home and all?"

She nodded. "Sure. I just—maybe I've been working too

hard. It all hit me at once. Sorry if I gave you a scare."

She hitched her purse strap onto her shoulder. "Guess I'll go home, get some rest. Anyway, I want you to know how pleased I am that you're moving up. You won't stop here, will you? You'll keep working, keep advancing yourself?"

"Right. Like you always told me." He leaned back against the wall.

She smiled again, a tired smile that made his heart expand painfully. Then she reached out and laid her hand on his shoulder. It felt good, warm; it carried a whiff of her perfume, and if he hadn't been leaning against the wall he would probably have fallen over, his knees went so weak all of a sudden. He could only nod and smile and nod and hope he wasn't blushing too brightly.

He watched her stride away across the lobby, holding herself straight against the weight of her tiredness and all her problems. He wanted to tell her again that everything would be all right, not to worry. Jeez, she was pretty when she smiled, and she sure did have great legs. You could practically hear music when she walked. He really hoped she wouldn't think he was terrible if she knew how he liked to watch her move.

Riley!

A pain like the flick of a light whip snapped at the front of his brain. He winced and peered through the pain toward the front of the lobby, where he was supposed to be watching the doors.

A dark-haired woman was going out. She looked oddly familiar as she turned and waved. He waved back, a languid half-salute, because she seemed to expect it.

He couldn't place her, though. Not at all.

One more chore to take care of before he returned to his post in the lobby, he thought; Reg Forsten seemed to believe he could vegetate in the lounge forever.

Tommy thought he would just go over and correct that little notion.

Forsten. That bum.

Nicki Pialosta

Choose. Dimly puzzled by the faint memory, Nicki strode through the icy night toward the Toyota parked in the shelter lot.

But choose what?

MONDAY, JANUARY 14

Nicki Pialosta

"You mean he just disappeared? Vanished into thin air?" Ben Ibrani accepted another glass of burgundy and settled back onto Nicki's sofa. "You'll forgive me if I find that a little difficult to believe."

"I mean Long Tom's gone. And under the circumstances, I find that a little difficult to believe." She sat in the armchair across from him, beyond the direct rays of the single lit table lamp. In the past week she had slept at most three hours a night, had gained five pounds all in the face, and had chewed her nails down to the quick. She wished she did not have to deal with an Ibrani attired as perfectly as ever, behaving so politely and oh-so-reasonably.

For a moment she imagined Jimmy Conklin in Ibrani's place: leaning forward, not back. He would be proposing theories for the vagrant's disappearance, excitedly asking her opinion and offering his own.

But Conklin couldn't help her. He had no clout. Ibrani had, and would use it on her behalf. Besides, strictly speaking, the story she had in mind belonged to Jimmy Conklin; if she mentioned it to Rifkind, the Metro editor might just hand it to the crime desk.

And that mustn't happen, because the story was hers; never mind turf boundaries. Never mind the sort of reputation she was accumulating. Something had happened to Long Tom; something bad, she was sure of it.

She banished Conklin's inquisitive, freckled face from

her mind and tried to speak calmly. "What if he didn't just skip town?"

Ibrani's smile stopped an inch short of patronizing. "Exactly what are you suggesting? That Gorman buried him in quicklime somewhere?"

Unnerved, she stubbed out her cigarette. It wasn't what she'd meant, not exactly, yet the image disturbed her. It felt right, yet not exactly right.

"I mean it's odd. He never went back to the shelter. He's not in the hospital or the morgue. I checked. He's got no money, nowhere to go, no friends or relatives—I checked them, too. And he hardly hopped a freight in his shirt-sleeves, not in January. So where is he?" Her voice had gone shrill, and he was watching her carefully. She stopped.

"Listen, you're letting your imagination run away with you. You're seeing things that aren't there."

She stifled a sob of laughter. *If only you knew.*

"You wrote a great series, it did a lot of good, and it's up for an award. Don't get hooked on it. Go on to something else. That's my best advice."

"And if it's hooked on me?"

He raised his auburn eyebrows.

"Ben, I have a very strong feeling about this, and I don't understand your attitude. Why are you so intent on making me drop it? You're not even trying to get me to give it to someone else."

For the first time he squirmed. Slightly, but perceptibly. "Nicki, there's no story here."

"No, it's more than that. Priorities are getting skewed. The *Bulletin*'s supporting Gorman for mayor—" She raised a finger to keep him from interrupting. "Which, by the way, strikes me as trifle odd in itself. But now that we are on his side, it seems neither he nor the shelter can do any wrong—at least not in our pages. I thought you didn't trust the guy."

He spread his hands in mute appeal. "Look, I don't set editorial policy. But even if I did—so some bum disappears. I should blame that on Gorman? Rifkind's not going to run a piece on how funny you feel about the whole thing, which is all you've told me. That's all you've got. It's not a story, and for your own good I'm telling you—"

There it was. She snapped at it. "What? What exactly are you telling me for my own good?" It was in there, dammit, something was there. She could smell it. Smelled it now, in his whole manner, his voice and his face. So cultured and educated and experienced and hiding something he knew. Something that scared him. She looked at him again and saw that it was true.

A knock on the door made her start. She got up, cursing inwardly while forcing a smile. "Don't go away. I'm finding this very interesting."

She opened the door and Rich fell in, striking her knee a glancing blow with his cheekbone. "Don't— don't let 'em. Please don't."

"Boy, you really pick your moments, don't you? What the hell are you doing here?"

Ibrani touched her shoulder from behind. "Need somc help?"

"No. Dammit, Rich, you'd better have an explanation for this." She felt Ibrani's eyes on her back and imagined the comprehension welling in them. She gritted her teeth. Although Ibrani had never mentioned it to her, everyone knew from the personal-angle story that Rich was her brother. That didn't mean she wanted anyone reminded.

Here comes the real reason for all my concern, and there goes my credibility, right out the window again. Nancy Drew, girl reporter.

"Well?"

Rich grabbed the doorframe. "No one gave me an expla— explainsh—"

She had never seen him quite this bad: face hanging slack, drool in shiny lines from loose mouth to stubbled chin. He looked defective. Damaged in some vital way.

Then he spied Ibrani, who still held his half-filled glass. "Scared!" Rich raised his head like a baying dog and howled. "Oh God, oh Jesus, I'm sca—"

"Rich, shut up."

He stopped abruptly and turned a bleary, accusing gaze on her. "You promised. You promised Mom you'd take care of me." He cocked his head at Ibrani. "She killed my dad! D'you know that? D'you know she's just a—just a—" His eyes rolled up, showing the whites; he staggered back.

He's really afraid. He's afraid of—

"I think you should leave now." Ibrani moved toward Rich, who lunged out, swinging.

"Don't touch me, you bastard!" One wild fist caught Ibrani square on the nose; he lurched backward, blood gouting onto his baby-blue sweater.

Glaring, Rich wheeled around. "I'm gonna die. Die, you hear me? An' it's all your fault." He plunged his hands into his pockets. "Here." A deck of cards scattered to the floor; dice bounced and came up snake eyes. "Don't say I never gave you nothin'." Raking her with a last contemptuous glare, he staggered out.

Wait. Don't go back out there. The words reached her mouth but not her lips, not with Ibrani standing there. Besides, what good would they do? She closed the door and leaned against it, fighting sobs.

"I gather your brother's a difficult boy to handle." Removing the crimsoned handkerchief from his nose, Ibrani dabbed experimentally at his upper lip. The bleeding had stopped, but ugly red splotches stained the blue cashmere sweater.

"Let me soak that for you; it's going to be ruined."

He shook his head. "Thanks anyway." He wadded the handkerchief and tucked it into his pocket.

"I'm sorry you got hurt by my problem." She moved to the living room. "I don't know what to do with him. I thought the shelter would be a solution, but I guess for him there's no solution."

He was looking oddly at her. "Of course there's a solution. But he's not your responsibility any more. He's the city's problem now. Isn't that what your feature was all about—getting the city to solve its problems?"

"I guess so." The relief flooding through her shamed her. So he had not written her off as having lost her objectivity, her control.

"And none of it would have happened without you. Remember that. Meadbury must solve its problems, or we're all doomed." He opened the closet, put on his coat.

Something in his voice teased months-old memory.

Where had she heard it before, that tone of utter allegiance, absolute commitment, as if the phrases had been not merely memorized, but engraved on the mind? She had a sudden clear recollection of Harold Roundtree in his market, gazing at her over the counter as he poured coins into her hand. *Or we're all doomed.*

She stared at Ibrani, who paused, narrowed his eyes, and stooped. Then he turned to her. Something glittered on his palm. "These yours?"

Three keys clinked together, along with a clover charm.

Three?

Forcing her hand out, she took them. "Why, yes, I must have dropped them." She made her dry lips into a smile.

Rich had not had keys.

Ibrani had.

The apartment keys, the clover charm; so recognizable. Almost homey, in their familiar threat. Now a third: different, smaller, but familiar as well. Too familiar: the little brass key that fit her safety-deposit box.

Ibrani stood in the doorway, pity on his face. It was the look a predator gives its hopelessly wounded but still struggling prey. "You haven't been sleeping well," he said gently. "I could stay if you like. Or—" He made a little gesture, lifting his hand and letting it fall. "Or you could come with me."

Come, let us end this now, his look said.

"No." She shook her head. "No, thank you." An hour earlier she had thought his presence might change everything. She had been right. "I'd better stay here. I need to think."

He nodded regretfully. "As you wish." He seemed about to add something, thought better of it, and went out, closing the door behind him.

She fell against it, fumbling the chain into its slot, clutching the bunch of keys, whose sharp-edged teeth bit into her flesh.

She could call a cab to the train station, the bus depot. She could call an ambulance, or the police. Any one of them would arrive in two minutes, because Meadbury was efficient, well-run; it tolerated no waste. *And that is why I'm not going to call any of them.*

She sat down on the hall chair, wondering. If she picked up the phone, would she even have to dial? Perhaps she need only speak into it to be heard.

TUESDAY, JANUARY 15

Nicki Pialosta

Watching for cars on both sides as she maneuvered through downtown traffic, she heard the radio advising her not to go around tonight. If she did, something was bound to take her life; a bad moon was on the rise.

You're telling me. The music faded. ". . . eight fifty-five ayem on station KDOA in Meadbury, the town with a heart so big you could trip and fall right in. And that last one was for Miss Nicki Pialosta from 'a secret admirer.' Hmm. And now an oldie goldie, 'Mad Love,' from Linda—"

Her pulse skipped a beat. She snapped off the radio and wrenched the car into a space half a block from the bank. There were closer spots, but she had begun to tremble. Who was it? Why was he doing this to her?

But she was beginning to think she knew. Keys led to locks, and to doors; doors that someone wanted her to open.

Shutting off the engine, she lit a cigarette. A furtive glitter flashed from the bottom of her purse; she slapped it closed. Doors, some of which led into memory.

It had been so simple, even silly, but far worse than she had let Ibrani know. She had been dictating notes into a cassette recorder when the downstairs door buzzed. In Manhattan, one did not admit a visitor without checking. For a wonder, the intercom worked. "Hello?"

No one answered. She shrugged, and returned to the couch.

It buzzed again almost immediately. Kids, probably, still resentful about the article she had done on the local junior high. They had been harassing her for a week and a half already. Cursing, holding the small microphone, she had jumped and jabbed the speaker button. "Yes?"

"Nic-ki?" It was a deep voice, hollow and somewhat bubbly: an eerie effect ruined by teenage laughter in the background. "Please . . . help me."

"Dammit, would you just leave me alone?" She lifted her finger off the button, but before she could turn away, it buzzed again. She stabbed it. "Now listen, you—"

"Nick, it's Dad." A thick cough came wetly through the speaker. "I— please, come . . . now, I—" There was a scratching, sliding noise, and a click as the button downstairs was released.

"Dad?" Impossible—he'd never have come all the way from St. Louis without calling ahead. She started back for the couch, shaking her head. No way would she run downstairs at ten at night just to check the vestibule. Not with a street gang irked at her. That was called suicide.

She sat. The cassette recorder whirred softly; she shut it off. The voice had sounded like his. She reached for the phone, punched out the number of the house in Webster Grove.

Rich answered. "Nicki! Happy birthday! Helluva surprise, huh? Hope to hell the old man didn't catch you in bed with your boyf—"

She slammed down the receiver and tore out of the flat so quickly that the elevator had closed on her before she realized that she had left shoes and keys behind. She bounced on the balls of her feet. Muzak poured over her like acid. She should have called the cops. The car stopped, releasing her to dash across the lobby toward the locked glass doors which led into the vestibule.

The vestibule, which was empty except for a neighbor just leading her schnauzer in from the evening walk. A woman who stopped, whose mouth and eyes stretched into gaping circles, whose scream cut even through those heavy glass walls.

Her father lay in a slowly widening pool of blood beneath the directory; crimson smeared the wall where he had slid down. His outflung right hand spasmed once.

Nicki moved swimmingly toward the doors, through them without looking, as though she had less substance than her neighbor's shrieks, to him and down beside him but the hand was still and the eyes empty and nothing was ever the same after that.

She had fled Manhattan and been settled in Meadbury before she returned unthinkingly to the cassette recorder, clicked it unsuspectingly on, and heard him begging her again, as if from the grave.

She could not erase it, could not consign her father's last words to electronic oblivion.

Now, a block up the street, the bank doors flashed in the sun as a blue-uniformed guard unlocked and tested them.

She could not erase the tape, nor could she bear to keep it, yet she could not throw it away.

So she had locked it in a box, and locked that inside another, in a vault in the town where she was when she found her father's voice on the tape: Meadbury. There was—had been—a single key. In a final burst of absolutely ridiculous and macabre sentiment, she had cut a hole in the sod of his grave at Arlington, slipped the key into the moist earth, and left it there. She had told no one, and she had never gone back.

But the box still lay a few steps away from her, inside a vault, and now a new key had appeared, as if by magic.

No; no magic, no fantasy. This is real.

Clutching the key, letting its sharp point dig into her palm, she got out of the car, crossed the street in sunlight so pale it was like a skim of ice, and went into the bank.

"Thank you." Stepping into the small, fluorescent-lit cubicle, Nicki smiled at the clerk as he closed the door for her.

A plain metal safety-deposit box sat on the table: smug, silent, waiting. The clean, untarnished key fit smoothly; the box came open.

The cassette's box was there, but no tape lay inside. Instead, the box held a square of stiff white cardboard. Her fingers shook so badly it took her three tries to extract the thing.

You are cordially requested

to attend a

private reception

honoring

Nicolette Pialosta

for service to the town of

Meadbury

Tuesday, January 15 One P.M. Meadbury Shelter RSVP

She moved through the rest of the morning as if in a dream. At her desk: *I come in here and I sit down and make phone calls, and I write things, and then I go home. And then I come in the next day and I sit down—*

Ibrani's office door remained closed; Jimmy Conklin's chair, obstinately empty. She dropped her face into her hands, then sat up guiltily and looked around. No one had noticed.

Good. Can't have the ace reporter falling to pieces at her desk. Interrupts the steady functioning, the smooth, machinelike progress—

Stop that. Just stop that. The card lay on her desk, taunting. She picked up the morning edition of the paper, which she had not yet bothered to read, turning the pages as though they were blank.

It's simple. I can go out there, Or I can go see Ibrani. Or I can call the police, or check myself into a hospital. It doesn't really matter a damn which.

A boxed notice swam off the page and shimmered at her. The bold head was blunt, familiar. IN MEMORIAM. Beneath it stretched a list of perhaps a hundred names. A hundred? Scanning, she recognized several of them, began to frown, and stopped. She could not breathe. The print blurred, then clarified into three lines of type, etched sharp:

IN MEMORIAM
Reginald Harper Forsten III
Richard White Pialosta
James Patrick Conklin
free at last

The room blurred around her. On her feet, zipping her coat, scrawling a note to Jimmy because please God she had to trust someone. "At shelter, back soon. Wait for me here."

Striding out the door. *No.* Pushing the gas pedal, leaning hard on the horn as a woman jumped for the curb and shook her fist.

No. It's a joke, a sick joke. You can't believe everything you read in the papers. Please.

Except for the card on the seat beside her, she might have convinced herself by the time she reached the shelter. But then, swinging into the drive, she glimpsed Gorman's car: unmistakable, the silver Lincoln, moving slowly down the street beyond the shelter building and the wide raw plot of ground that would be lawn.

The Lincoln stopped; a tattered hitchhiker bent to look through the window, then climbed in. The car moved on.

Follow him, make him tell—what? Torn, she stared after the Lincoln. Wind cracked the flag chain against its pole like a bullwhip, snapping hard. There was no other movement anywhere on the grounds. She got out of the car.

"Rich?" The wind snatched her voice away, slapped her face. No bums lounged by the door, as they had in even the coldest weather.

No one sat at any of the chairs in the lobby. The TV hissed, flipping vacantly. Six breakfasts sat untouched in the dining room. She dipped a finger in a brown puddle of spilled coffee.

Cold.

"Hello?" Pots and pans hung silent on their hooks in the empty kitchen. Mechanically she turned off the burner under a sizzling pot of blackened oatmeal.

"Hello?"

Her footsteps echoed in the empty hall, past a coatrack on which no coats hung, and up the stairs to the second floor. "Rich?"

A bar of light lay across the corridor in front of his room. Electrified with relief, she ran toward it. "Rich!"

Stoop-shouldered, unshaven, he turned from stuffing T-shirts into a knapsack. His puffy eyes narrowed. "What do you want?" He was sober. Stone sober.

"Where is everyone? Where are you going?"

Silent, he shoved greying underpants into the pack.

"Rich, the whole place is deserted!"

"That's right." He rolled a pair of socks into a ball.

She stepped into his room. On the stripped bed lay Reg Forsten. Rich glanced at him, appearing to find nothing strange in the other man's blank appearance, his staring rigidity.

"Reg." Rich pointed at a pair of torn sneakers. "Those are yours. I'll fit them in my pack."

She pressed back against the dresser, not knowing which frightened her more: Rich's sober, nervous industry, or Reg's silence. Reg looked catatonic, as if he might stay forever in any position he was put; just stay, stiff and wordless, with that deep, dark expression in his eyes.

Scared stiff.

Ever since the basement, when he had seen . . . something.

Rich picked up Reg's sneakers along with a pair of his own, and looked at them; the old expression of mischief came onto his face. For an uncertain instant she believed he might drop them, or throw them at the wall.

Instead he tossed a sneaker up into the air. It rose, laces flying. Then he tossed a second. The third sneaker arched up, joining the first two, and then the last shoe rose, until all four were soaring and stooping in a whirling circle of flight as Rich juggled casually, effortlessly. To him it was as easy as breathing.

Remember this. Remember him—remember both of

them. Forcing back tears, she glanced at Reg, who stared, unseeing.

Rich blinked, then frowned at his hands. The sneakers clumped down one by one. "Shit." He stuffed all four of them into his pack.

"Listen." Hysteria lurked in Nicki's voice; she controlled it with difficulty. "Will one of you please tell me what is going on here?"

Rich's laugh was bitter. "Tell her, Reg."

Reg said nothing.

"Rich. . . ."

He turned. "I guess my good buddy here just doesn't feel like talking to you. Guess he thinks it never did him any good, so why bother now?"

"You tell me, then." She was begging, now, but did not care. "Please, I'll help you. I'll take you anywhere you want to go. Please, just tell me what is going on here!"

Rich nodded. "Okay. You asked for it. Let me try to put it in terms you will understand, as ol' Reg would say. Used to say.

"At eight this morning, thirty-five 'clients'—" He gave the word a sardonic twist. "—thirty-five clients got on a chartered bus to go to job interviews. At eight twenty-five, our friend Mr. Gorman fired all the shelter staff. That left twenty or so of us still here, all wondering what the hell was coming down. By quarter to nine, two of us were left: Reg and me."

"But that was—" She checked her watch. "That was almost four hours ago. What have you been doing? And where did everyone else go?"

Rich gave a short, despairing laugh. "I haven't got a clue. It's all foggy. Which is just okay with me, 'cause I don't want to know. There's a bus to Bridgeport in forty minutes. You driving us, or do we thumb it?"

An unpleasant picture of Gorman picking up the hitch-hiker rose in her memory. "I'll take you."

Rich nodded. "Reg, I'll get your other stuff." Digging in his pocket, he counted tattered bills. "And I got enough for two fares, so don't sweat it."

For answer, Reg began curling his knees up, pressing them to his chest. Huddled on himself, he slowly turned over to face the cubicle's wall. Except, Nicki thought with distant horror, "facing" wasn't really the right word. Reg's face was hidden now, his arms wrapped tight across it. It would take a crowbar to straighten him out again.

Rich crossed the room, crouched down. "Hey, buddy. Hey. Reg? Come on, boy, it's me. Remember? Come on, guy, we gotta get moving, huh? Come on." He shook Reg by the shoulder, gently.

Reg did not respond.

All that caretaking Reg did. All the watching out for Rich, hauling him out of trouble and big-brothering him and keeping an eye on him—it's coming back to him now, isn't it? With interest.

He would need it, too, because Reg Forsten didn't look like a man who would take care of himself ever again.

Rich's face glistened with tears. "I told you. Told him, too. Oh, shit, it's too late now. This is a waste of time." But he got up and strode from the room, down the hallway. "I'm gonna get his stuff."

Nicki followed him. "What about Sarah? Did she get on the bus?"

He shrugged. "Who cares?"

"She might still be here, then. Help me find her."

"Forget it. Wherever she's gone, I'm not going there."

There would be no persuading him, she saw. "All right. I'll go look by myself."

At that he turned and grabbed her arm. "No." But when she twisted away he shrugged sullenly again and released her. "Do what you want. You will anyway."

A stick-on label printed with Sarah's name identified her door, which swung open without a sound. Vacant room. Coats heaped on the unmade bed. A purple silk scarf with one bobby pin still dangling from its frayed edge hung limply over a chair. Shopping bags lined the window ledge like silent witnesses. A single fuzzy slipper lay on the floor.

Nicki backed out slowly.

The other rooms were the same: belongings tumbled from drawers and closets, their owners vanished. Nicki walked faster, her footsteps raising echoes that raced away to silence. Not a hinge squeaked; not a voice protested her intrusion.

Here an abandoned coffee cup, there a half-eaten sandwich. In the fifth room a game of whist abruptly suspended, two tricks taken. In the tenth, a neatly packed suitcase with two twenty-dollar bills atop the frayed shirts.

Without at all wanting to, she remembered Gorman's remarks, weeks ago, about the shelter's declining population. "Rehabilitated," he'd said. "Returned to the work force. We turn them around."

Sure, like a head turned around on its neck—all the way around. Trying hard to resist the oppressive silence, the strong desire to run, she checked her watch. 12:50. Rich and Forsten would be waiting for her, might even try to leave without her. She hurried back to Rich's room, pushed the door wide.

"Are you—"

Rich's pack perched on the bed, its flap hanging open.

"Rich? Hey, guys?"

Faint light through the blinds showed the room stripped bare; Rich had packed it all, down to the ashtray, in his canvas satchel, which bulged on the bare mattress.

Where Reg no longer huddled.

Panic congealed in her stomach, exploded.

Please. Please, I didn't mean it, I want them back— "Where are you?"

The silent walls hurled the words back in her face.

Plunging down the stairs to the first floor, breath coming now in short, painful sobs— *Out. I want to get out.*

On the floor by the door to the basement stairs lay something small, something shiny. She picked it up: Rich's medal, the stamped silver still faintly warm from his throat.

"Richard," she whispered to it, "you come back here right now. Please."

A door at the foot of the basement stairs slammed; she jumped, then let her breath out in a rush as relief washed over her. Their murmuring voices rose up toward her, probably from some sort of storage room.

Two voices, thank God. Somehow Rich had roused Forsten, coaxed him from his silence. She hurried down the steps toward the voices, which grew louder as she approached.

"Hey, guys? Come on, you're going to miss your—"

Her foot missed the bottom step and she fell, smacking

her cheek on the hard, shiny linoleum. Hands seized her shoulders.

She screamed.

"Nicki! Hey, easy!" Gasping, she turned to find Ben Ibrani crouched over her. Relief vanished as his mouth cracked into a dead smile.

"Hi, Miss Pialosta." Tommy Riley's voice came from behind her.

She let Ibrani help her to her feet, then took a step back. What was he doing here, anyway? "Where are they?"

"Forsten and your brother?" Ibrani pulled a huge key ring from his pocket, jangled it, and moved off down the hall. "Escort the lady, Tommy."

"Yes, sir." He gripped her arm so firmly that she had to follow.

Ibrani slipped a key into the lock of a plain white door that bore no number and no legend.

"No," she tried to say as the door snicked open, just a crack through which darkness flowed. She wanted to back away but Tommy held her.

"You know, Miss Pialosta," he said, his voice deep and somber, "if it weren't for you, I wouldn't be here today. I never would have passed the test." He propelled her toward the door.

She looked at Ibrani. "Ben, what's going on?"

"You wanted to see him," Ibrani said. "Now he wants to see you. Jason Goodmaster, in the flesh." He swung the door wide.

"No, I don't—" Tommy shifted his grip, placed his hand in the small of her back, and shoved her into the dark room.

Behind her, the door slammed shut.

Jimmy won't wait. He'll come to find me.

"Greetings, my dear." The voice, cultured and familiar, came out of the darkness. "How nice to meet you after all this time."

"Mr. Goodmaster." For a moment, understanding drove out fear: *This is the way it happens. You come to find somebody, or someone else—Gorman, perhaps—sends you here on an errand. Or a small voice whispers: Come. I'm here.*

She gulped, feeling behind her for the crack that marked the door, and finding none. "Where is my brother?"

"Ah. He is . . . how shall I put it? Making himself useful, let us say."

Rich? Useful? The room brightened slowly. Behind a squat desk sat a tall, thin figure whose features were not yet clear. Eyeing the figure, she eased a hand into her purse, biting her lip at the pain in her wrist. Her fingers found the pack of business cards the *Bulletin* had issued to her: Nicolette Pialosta, Reporter. She worked a card loose, slipped it out, and dropped it. Not lowering her gaze, she kicked at the card, trying to slide it backward through the slot at the bottom of the door.

The figure chuckled. "A nice maneuver. You are a resourceful, intelligent woman. Much too valuable to be wasted."

The room was larger than she remembered, and growing steadily lighter except for the pool of gloom in which he sat. "My brother, dammit! Where is he?"

"The problem with garbage," Goodmaster said softly, almost dreamily, "is not that it is useless, but that it is not properly used."

"What are you—"

"Once—many years before your time—the culvert of a long-defunct railroad became a serious nuisance. Vermin lived there, hoboes camped there, mosquitoes bred in its puddles; all of them emerged constantly to harass the good people of Meadbury. At approximately that same time, Meadbury's sanitary landfill reached its capacity. To me, a simultaneous solution to both problems seemed obvious, and I caused it to be implemented. That portion of the filled culvert which the city retained is now called Goodmaster Park. And do you know, its lawns and ornamentals are fertilized regularly with a compost made of sewage sludge? Why, the recycling capabilities of garbage are made finite only by the limits of the imagination."

She had to clench her jaws to keep her voice steady. "What. Are. You. Saying?"

"Miss Pialosta! Surely you recognized this truth, even if on a purely visceral level, when you turned the trash of your brother's life into a gem of a newspaper article."

"Mr. Good—"

"Call me Meadbury. I am, you know. I have been, for years."

And that was madness. He was mad.

"What do you want?"

"Your invaluable assistance. Help me and the city that cares." Eyes watched her out of the darkness. "A city is more than a clutter of buildings organized by random chance. It's a concentration of souls, of intelligences, that impinge and overlap and in their density create an overlife. Occasionally, that life may take residence in a single soul. As Meadbury has. In me."

"But you—"

"Ah, yes, but I was blind. Things were happening beyond my ken; you showed me my ignorance, and now I know I must take a more active hand."

"M-me?" Her knees trembled badly now.

"Of course. You provided information. I acted upon it."

"You killed them."

"Not all garbage need be dead to be of use. Why, in cancer research alone— The point, you see, is that I am sustained by the contributions of my member-residents. Those who do not contribute are, truly, cancers. I will not die from them."

"The memorial ads—you put them in."

"Of course. They helped draw you to me, did they not? Your newspaper is extensively computerized—so convenient for one who knows information is life. It was simple. And pleasurable." The figure emitted a dry cackle. "I want you, Miss Pialosta. And I shall have you. One way or another, you will contribute. The door will open—"

She found the knob, seized it.

"If you agree to continue providing your valuable service. You will be my eyes and ears, if you choose."

I'd never know what he used. Any word I wrote could be someone else's death sentence. I will walk straight away, get out to the highway, far enough so they can't get me back.

"All right. I'll do it. Let me out."

"Oh, no," Goodmaster said, his voice undeceived. "You mustn't dash off, not yet. We have a party arranged for you. A welcoming party, to show our enormous gratitude." He

chuckled again, and the light went out.
Her city began to express its gratitude.
Nicki Pialosta screamed. Once.

Ben Ibrani

I had to do it, he thought as he guided the silver BMW through crosstown traffic. I had to; I had no choice.

But it wouldn't wash, not this time. Usually he had a knack for justifying himself, for rationalizing and then forgetting certain deeds, events, decisions in his life—his early life, especially. Lately he hadn't had to use that talent so much, and he had begun to think things might be changing, even getting better. Maybe, he'd begun to think —had thought, until a couple of months ago—maybe it was over.

It wasn't over, though, and things weren't getting better. They were getting worse; much worse.

I pushed her into a basement room, and I left her there with him, because he made me.

No. He made me, but I let him.

Ibrani began sweating. This, he knew, was the kind of thinking he had to avoid at all costs, unless he wanted to—

Wash.

It won't wash. . . .

So simple, this morning, on the telephone. He'd nearly forgotten that it could happen so swiftly, so inescapably, with a single telephone call, a few words from the voice unmistakably accented with old Yankee money: "She is leaving. Follow her."

And he had done it, even as the clammy nightmare feeling dropped over him again, even as he knew without having to ask. Nicki.

He had followed her to the shelter, to the room. Pushed her in, and left her.

With Uncle Jason. An unwanted memory of Nicki's face rose up: You've seen him? You've actually seen Jason Goodmaster?

Yes, I have. Oh, God, have I seen him. And now you've seen him, too. And he's seen you.

And there he stopped thinking, for he did not want to imagine why Jason Goodmaster wanted to see Nicki Pialosta. Why he wanted to see her alone, in a tiny locked room in the empty basement of the deserted Meadbury Shelter. No, Ben Ibrani did not want to think about that at all.

Besides, he had already thought too much. Pausing for a red light, he lifted both hands from the steering wheel and wiped them on the front of his overcoat. Then, alarmed, he wiped them again.

But it didn't make them cleaner. In fact, it seemed to make them dirtier.

Not much dirtier, but enough.

Locked in the sanctuary of the BMW, he pursed his lips and whistled loudly, hollowly, off-key, as if passing a midnight graveyard. He stared at the car in front, scrutinizing the back of its driver's head, making up, as a distraction, a story about the red-lacquered nails that had tousled that razor-cut, blow-dried brown hair in the motel room at lunch.

Nicki Pialosta had red nails.

Uncle Jason had Nicki.

Ben Ibrani had filthy hands.

But they weren't, dammit; through his growing discomfort he had to keep telling himself that. The problem was mental, and nothing new; all too familiar, in fact.

In your head, boy. All in your head.

Like the voice at the shelter, the one that said, "Bring her here."

Stop thinking about it, he told himself.

But he couldn't.

He wrenched the wheel around, heading the car toward home. One in the afternoon, and he was knocking off. But he needed a shower: hot water pummeling, soap and a scrub brush, coal-tar shampoo.

A shower; yes. He wanted it badly. His hands closed hard on the steering wheel, slipping in the grease his fingers left there.

Didn't they? Didn't they?

No, they didn't. "No," he said aloud, and gagged. Shiny wet slugs as big as his thumb were humping up his throat, over his tongue and past his teeth—

Only they weren't. He knew it, even as he fought the strong urge to pull over, lean out of the car, and vomit.

Oh, come on, he'd said to himself as he drove away from the shelter; what's the worst the old guy could do? And this was the answer. This was the worst Jason Goodmaster could do: He could make a man, or a woman, feel like a festering heap of maggots.

At least, Ben Ibrani hoped it was the worst.

Abruptly, the slithering packed-throat sensation faded away.

He sank back in the driver's seat, gasping with relief. Now if he could just keep from thinking about Nicki.

The slugs returned; he almost gagged again. But he was moving, easing the BMW smoothly into a traffic circle, remembering without at all wanting to the first time he had seen Jason Goodmaster, really seen him for the first serious time. Of course, Goodmaster had known his parents for a long while, but being dandled on Goodmaster's knee as an infant or chucked beneath the chin by him as a toddler didn't count, as Ben found to his sorrow.

It didn't really teach him about Jason Goodmaster.

Ben had been sixteen in the early sixties, when Kennedy's vision had turned his parents' ambitions toward the Peace Corps. They'd been rejected; Ben's dad had a bad heart. But they were wealthy and had good connections, Goodmaster among them. The combination helped them locate a medical mission in Taiwan.

They joined it, and Ben couldn't go.

He begged to, arguing that it would broaden his horizons. They pointed out that it also would narrow his chances for college.

Ivy League college. Only the best for Jordan (né Giordano) Ibrani's son. And Jason Goodmaster was the best, a long-time family friend, although little seen of late. At Jordan Ibrani's request, Goodmaster welcomed young Ben into his house.

Not quite with open arms, though.

Simmons, the chauffeur, had deposited him outside Goodmaster's front door. The butler admitted him, murmuring that Mr. Goodmaster and his secretary were in the library.

Ben went alone down the long hall, tiptoeing almost. He had been there before but still felt in awe of the place, with its carved oak wainscoting, its red Oriental carpets, the black marble floor reflccting the high frescoed ceilings. Gilt-framed portraits frowned weightily down between tall arched doorways as if in judgment. His own home was big and well-kept, too, but this—

Well, he'd told himself, it would be okay. His parents never would have sent him here if it wouldn't. Shyly, he stuck his head in between the open oak doors of the library. "Hi, Uncle Jason, Miss Banester."

The old man broke off his conversation to fix Ben in a cold stare, and Ben realized at once that he had made a mistake.

Or someone had. But his parents were already on the plane.

"Boy," Goodmaster said icily, "there is a smudge on your forehead. And I can smell you from here. Were you an infant in diapers this would constitute permissible behavior. As you are not, it does not. Remedy the situation immediately."

Then the old man turned back to his paperwork.

Twenty years later, Ibrani reddened again at the memory of the words, his stammered apology. He'd fled the library, up the wide curving staircase to his new room and the bath adjoining it.

It was a room he would come to know very well; not the bedroom, but the bath: spartan, white-tiled, equipped with back brush, nail brush, rough loofah sponge, special shampoo. Later he learned the shampoo was the kind jails used on louse-ridden inmates. The soap provided was brown, harsh, impregnated with scouring grains of sand.

Later he would come to love the excoriation and loathe himself for it, to wonder how one could feel so supremely filthy in the act of getting clean.

Not then, though. Then he was just a boy taking a shower. The first of many.

Banishing the memory, Ibrani pulled the BMW into the narrow alley beside the Colchester. Home sweet home was the elegant penthouse atop Meadbury's most exclusive apartment building. The bright green-striped awning over the entryway's polished brass and glass made him feel dirty again, as if he didn't deserve to live here, as if anyone seeing him go inside must know it.

He struck the wheel with his fist. "What is this? Why is it every time I think of Nicki—"

Suddenly the skin on his feet crept, inside his shoes, as if he'd stepped barefoot into dog droppings. Anyone who got near him would smell it immediately.

Ibrani aimed the car toward the service entrance, hoping that Spinelli, the guy who accepted deliveries there, had taken a late lunch. God forbid anyone Ibrani knew should meet him smelling like this.

But no such luck. Three burly truckers lounged on the loading dock, drinking coffee out of styrofoam cups and listening to Spinelli spin yarns.

Disappointed, Ibrani kept going, took a right into the next alley, and went all the way around again, parking almost in front of the building. He nodded to Chomley, the uniformed doorman standing sentinel beneath the awning.

Itchier, now. Much itchier. As if Goodmaster knew Ibrani was thinking forbidden thoughts, and punishing him for it. Ibrani rejected that idea as old Chomley looked up expectantly, awaiting a greeting.

Ibrani didn't want to acknowledge him. It would be hard to talk while fighting back the rising nausea, but Chomley had not only become an institution at the Colchester, he had grown querulous with age, and took revenge for any slight, real or imagined, as only a doorman can.

At least Chomley wouldn't rag him, like Spinelli would: "Jeez, Ben, you step in dogshit or what? Man, you stink, you know that?"

"Lovely day today, sir?" murmured Chomley.

Ibrani kept his distance, rallied himself. He would rather chat with Chomley for a moment than have his parcels stamped Return To Sender, and his visitors told they must have made a mistake, no one by that name lived in the Colchester.

"Yes, they don't come this good often enough, do they?" He swallowed hard.

Chomley cast a cataract-clouded eye appraisingly skyward. "I do hope it holds, as I've promised my daughter to babysit the Star of the Show while Maggie does her shopping. She'll be three next week, you know. My little granddaughter."

"Already?" Ibrani choked back impatience, along with the bitter taste of bile. Through the pocket of his jacket, he scratched his ribs. "It seems like you were showing off the hospital pictures just last week."

"That'll be the weather, sir," said the old man, with infuriating slowness. "She was born in a January thaw much like this one, and it's easy to get confused."

"Yes, well." Ibrani made a point of looking at his watch. "I'm on deadline today." Ants nested between his watch and wrist. "Guess I'd better get to it."

"Of course, sir, of course." Chomley nodded, satisfied with the tithe of conversation Ibrani had offered.

Shuddering, Ibrani plucked off the watch and dropped it into his pocket. Hurrying in toward the elevators, he reached them just in time to watch one slide noiselessly, spitefully shut in his face.

He clenched his jaws, imagining the reeking cloud that must hang about him, hoping no one came in before the next elevator arrived. It would be okay if he were in running shoes and shorts; these days, half the residents of the building seemed to be training for the next marathon. But he wore his suit, and carried his briefcase, and no one in business clothes should look as grimy or smell as rancid as he did now.

No. No one will think you stink. No one but you.

Nonetheless he could not help eyeing the Exit sign that glowed discreetly red over the door to the fire stairs. Walking up would spare him the embarrassment of meeting a neighbor in his present mental condition. *That's right, dammit, mental. It's all in your head.*

But considering the stench rising now to his nostrils, this was small consolation. He glanced again at the door to the fire stairs. Home lay beyond it, just twenty-four flights up.

Grimly, he waited.

The elevator slid open without a sound, startling him with its abrupt invitation. Like a crocodile lying on its side, waiting for dinner to stroll in.

He went in anyway. Pressed "24." And hoped no one would burst panting into the lobby shouting "Hold the elevator, please!"

He thought if anyone were to do that, he would scream.

The lobby stayed quiet.

The elevator doors slithered shut.

Alone, he relaxed a little. Squelching a shudder, he scratched himself again, turning the gesture into a casual one as he remembered the closed-circuit TV camera staring down at him. Wouldn't do for the building's security staff to see a tenant ripping his skin off.

Spiders, big daddy longlegs scampered up and down his body. Just a few minutes more. As the car approached his floor, he prayed no one would be waiting to get in as he left. If someone stepped into this car right after he got off, that someone would smell the stink and know who had made it. And for weeks afterward that someone would look at him every time they passed in the corridor, eye him suspiciously and sniff the air for the lingering reek.

No, Ben, no, you don't stink; don't worry about it.

But he did worry, and he felt blessed when the door opened onto an empty hall. He sprinted down it to his apartment door, yanking his tie off on the way. Key in his right hand, he tore at the buttons of his shirt with his left; filthy hand, filthy shirt.

Filthy Ben. Inside, he stripped rapidly, letting his clothes fall to the carpet. Later, his hands safely rubber-gloved, he would stuff the clothes into a paper bag, drop them down the incinerator shaft where they belonged.

Now, into the shower. Ah, hurry—taps on all the way, too hot for comfort. Too hot for dirt, too, for germs and parasites, squirming infestations. Gasping in the steam, wincing under the scalding, cleansing assault of the thrumming water, he felt for the soap. His fingers closed in relief on its familiar, gritty abrasiveness.

Then he scrubbed himself. And scrubbed himself.

And scrubbed.

Himself.

Three hours later, the seizure had passed into memory —almost. He tried to tell himself he'd just felt a bit sweaty, had rinsed himself off, but his skin knew better. It was always that way afterward: telling himself everything was fine.

Knowing it wasn't.

The silk robe soothed him, but not enough. Walking bowlegged kept his thighs from rubbing together; nothing, though, could help his armpits, his crotch, or the insides of his buttocks. Cautiously, he raised himself from his bed and crossed to the dresser. His watch lay there, rescued from his pocket with a pair of kitchen tongs.

Waterproof, its face proclaimed. He wondered if it was proof against carbolic acid, too. *Takes a licking and keeps on—*

Something about that thought was dimly repulsive; Ibrani shut it off before he could find out what.

Four-thirty. God. The nap had helped only a little. He rubbed his eyes carefully. Might as well take the rest of the day off, although he would probably have to go into the office in the morning. The idea made him want to whimper; with his skin like this, his suit pants would torture him.

He glanced in the mirror above the dresser. The vee of chest showing between the lapels of his robe looked raw, and it hurt. Everything hurt, and from long experience he knew only work would distract him.

He limped into the living room, where his desk was. The room was long and wide, furnished in grey and silver, mauve and rose; it opened onto a paneled dining area at one end, a wall of ceiling-high sliding glass doors at the other.

The doors let onto the rooftop high above Meadbury, the rooftop he called "my back yard" when friends visited. Interestingly, most of his friends found the satellite dish more fascinating than the view, now a twinkling network of lights in the gathering winter dusk. Offices, apartments, the headlights of people hurrying on their way home—Ibrani stared out at them, then drew the heavy pewter-colored curtains shut, wondering why the sight made him feel so sad.

Maybe it was the satellite dish. Ground station, actually, because it held a transmitter as well as a receiver, and could draw enough power to send a signal to the relay twenty-two thousand miles overhead, blotting out any other broadcast on that frequency.

Another symbol of his acquiescence. He had bought it

because Jason Goodmaster had told him to, just as he had accepted the floppy disk from the bearded stranger on the street.

Just as he had used the floppy that one brief time, answering the two prompts—"HBO," he had typed, and "15 sec"—filling the screen of his computer with the single quotation:

> "I am the good shepherd, and know my sheep, and am known of mine."
>
> John 10:11

Four quick keystrokes had triggered the program on the floppy, and that program seized control of the dish, swiveled it, aimed it, and transmitted the image on Ibrani's screen to the television screens of every person in the area watching HBO at the time. For fifteen seconds a good percentage of Meadbury's population gaped at Jason Goodmaster's hubristic declaration and wondered what it had to do with the latest exploits of Sylvester Stallone. Then the disk drive *click*ed and the message disappeared from Meadbury's view, though not from the FCC's memory.

Sighing, depressed all over again by his helplessness to resist Jason Goodmaster's whims, Ben Ibrani turned away toward the big fieldstone fireplace. On either side of it, a pair of oiled-walnut gun cases held his collection of Winchesters, eight of the weapons racked behind each set of handmade leaded-glass doors.

He averted his eyes. On blackened andirons in the hearth, a trio of pine logs lay seasoned and ready, needing only the kerosene-soaked Cape Cod lighter and a match. But his gaze kept straying back to the gun case, and the guns, until he turned his back on them.

Wincing, he sat at his desk and switched his personal computer into terminal emulation mode so he could link up to the Meadbury *Bulletin*'s IBM mainframe. With his index fingers, he typed "Bull."

The program loaded swiftly, dialed the number of the *Bulletin*'s mainframe, and logged on with Ibrani's password. Ninety seconds later, he was checking the features slated for Wednesday morning's edition. One finger on the cursor key, he scrolled through the list of stories.

"Foggy Goes A-Courting." He shook his head, dubious. He liked this one, about a local firm that manufactured aeroponics equipment and had yet to show a profit, but he suspected its appeal might be too narrow.

Next. "Teens in Trouble." Ibrani scowled. Pieces on juvenile delinquency went over well, most of the time. But this allegedly in-depth analysis read like the outline of *West Side Story*. And how many times in his career had he seen that damn title?

Onward, then. "A Happy Hoofer." This one got a smile. Nice headline; give the copy editors "A" for effort. Too bad it couldn't run, even over a profile of a Meadbury High graduate who had gone on to become a leading dance instructor in San Francisco. Sorry about that, guys.

He scrolled up another screenful, to "Architects of God," and made a rude noise. An abysmal piece on the historic value of Meadbury's churches. He had tried as hard as he dared to kill it at the budget meeting, but no luck; the managing editor's wife, Lola, wanted landmark status for the First Congregational. And whatever Lola wanted, Lola got.

Win some, lose some, Ben thought, and scrolled up the next one.

"Council Votes Curfew."

He frowned. That sounded like a news article, fit for the first page of the local section, not the features. And it hadn't been raised at the budget meeting that had been held today. He skimmed the piece. Bylined "Nicolette Pialosta," it was indeed an account of a city council meeting. For a moment he felt relief: She was out of the shelter, then, away from Goodmaster.

But the council only met once a week, and its next meeting was not scheduled until—he checked his desk calendar—Thursday.

On top of which, how had Nicki found time to interview Goodmaster, cover a council meeting, get back to the office, and rap out this article all in one afternoon?

He scrolled back up, reread the lead sentence.

"At a meeting remarkable for civility of tone and unanimity of purpose, the city council voted Tuesday afternoon to impose a dusk-to-dawn curfew on all juveniles beneath the age of sixteen."

That didn't even sound like Nicki, or like a newspaper, either. Something was strange here. He reached for the phone and dialed her home number.

Fifteen rings later, he gave up. Damn, still at her desk? Probably. He reached for the phone again, drew his hand uncomfortably back. Why bother her, after all? It was the news he wanted, not the newsperson. Rummaging through his briefcase for his address book, he found another number, which rang once before a flat male voice answered.

"Yes."

"Is this Steve Wolverton?"

"Yes."

"Steve, this is Ben Ibrani, from the *Bulletin.*"

Waiting, Ibrani braced himself for a deluge of words; Wolverton wanted a seat in Congress and thought his own rhetoric would help him get it.

"Yes," Wolverton said after a long moment.

Ibrani held the receiver away from his head and stared at it. Then, perplexed, he spoke into it again. "Ah, Steve, am I calling at a bad time?"

"No."

No? The correct response was "Don't be silly, Ben, there's no such thing as a bad time to talk to the press."

Oh, well, Ibrani thought. Maybe it really was a bad time, and Wolverton didn't want to say so. In which case, tough cookies for Wolverton.

"I'm calling about this afternoon's council meeting."

"Yes," Wolverton said again.

Now, this really was strange; generally Wolverton's conversation made Ben wish for a crowbar, but to get in a word edgewise, not to pry words out. Maybe the guy had decided to give up politics and become a mortician? Now there would be a story.

"So there *was* a meeting this afternoon?"

"Yes."

"Uh-huh. An emergency meeting?"

"Yes."

"Who called it?" I mean, Ben thought, if you don't mind my asking, if it's not too much goddamn trouble.

"Chairman MacRoss."

"And what constituted the emergency?"

"Crime," Wolverton said.

Christ, Ibrani thought while waiting for Wolverton to say something more, it was like trying to jump start a cement truck. Given any excuse, Wolverton usually gabbed on and on about crime, its effects on civilization and American society. Surely he would rise to the occasion now, with an editor on the line?

Ibrani kept waiting.

Wolverton waited longer.

"Steve, are you feeling okay?" Ibrani said finally.

"Yes."

"Okay, good." Sure, and I'm the Dalai Lama. "So what did the council decide?"

"To impose a curfew." Wolverton paused. "On children." Another pause, maddening. Fifteen seconds passed. "Sixteen and under."

"A curfew?"

"Yes."

"Steve, you can't make that curfew stick and you know it. Freedom of Information says you have to announce a meeting forty-eight hours in advance for any ordinances adopted to be valid. So what's going on? How do you figure—" A click, then silence. "Steve?"

Dial tone. The bastard had hung up.

Muttering to himself, Ibrani flipped through his notebook to Caleb MacRoss's office number. It rang once.

"Yes."

"Caleb MacRoss, please."

"Yes."

Jesus. Had the council voted for monosyllables, too? "Mr. MacRoss, this is Ben Ibrani from the *Bulletin.*"

"Yes."

"Did the council meet in emergency session today?"

"Yes."

"And did you call that meeting, sir?"

"Yes."

"Why?" There; let the sucker answer that with one word.

"Necessity," MacRoss said.

Damn. "Did it vote to impose a dawn-to-dusk curfew on

youths under the age of sixteen?"

"Yes."

"Again sir, why?"

"To prevent delinquency."

"But why so abruptly? And why without the forty-eight-hour notice?"

Click-click; dial tone.

"Son of a—" One more try. Richard Reeves. The man had a good rep for fairness and resisting pressure. If anybody would say what was going on, Reeves would.

No one answered Reeves' office phone, so Ibrani tried him at home; the councilman's wife answered on the fourth ring.

"Hello?" She sounded angry.

He forced a breezy tone. "Hi, Deanna, Ben Ibrani from the *Bulletin*. Is Dick in?"

"Ben, you wretch, he just got here. He hasn't even kissed me hello yet."

"Deanna, I'm sorry, but I've got to confirm a story before we go to press, and—"

"Well, I'll make sure to keep you from unwinding some night. Here's Dick."

"Ben?"

"Hi, Dick. I'm sorry, but I didn't know you hadn't got your nightly necking session in yet."

Reeves chuckled. "I'll get you for this, you know that?"

"Deanna's already threatened me. But hey, that's what you two old fogies get for acting like newlyweds."

A laugh rippled out of the receiver. "Well, tell you what, Ben, since I want to get back to what I was about to get up to before you called, what's on your mind?"

"This afternoon's council meeting." He waited tensely for Reeves to go flat and robotic like Wolverton and Ross.

"This afternoon's what?"

Ibrani sighed, relieved. "Council meeting."

"The council met this afternoon?"

"That's what Wolverton and MacRoss told me."

"First I've heard of it." Reeves sounded almost disbelieving. "Did they say why?"

"An emergency meeting to impose a curfew on all juveniles beneath the age of sixteen, they said."

Reeves whistled. "Heavy stuff. You'd think somebody would have given me a call. Was the meeting posted?"

"Not to my knowledge. Somebody knew about it. The paper covered it. But usually they send us a flyer or something to announce it."

"Yeah," Reeves said, "I generally hear about 'em, too. Being a member and all. Gosh, do you suppose it's my breath?" His tone was humorous, but Ibrani could almost hear Reeves's brain working. "Listen, Ben, this is off the record, isn't it?"

Ibrani hesitated for only a moment. "Sure, Dick. If that's the way you want it."

"It is." Reeves sounded puzzled now as he doped out each possibility and found each one lacking. "I mean, Caleb MacRoss knows the law, and what the hell, it's just forty-eight hours. They could have waited; it's not like there's a rock concert tomorrow night or anything."

Ibrani made a noise of assent.

"You know what's going to happen here?" Reeves said. "Some kid'll get busted for being out, and his old man'll sue the city. First judge that gets a look at the ordinance tosses it on the grounds that the council didn't adhere to the law, so the city'll lose the lawsuit. We'll have to go through the whole thing again, and— What are the hours on this curfew, anyway?"

"Dusk to dawn."

Reeves snorted. "Well, in that case, it'll get tossed whether the meeting was posted or not. No court's going to let us put so much restraint on a juvenile's freedom, not without a damn good story about why we had to."

Deanna's voice interrupted before Ibrani could ask another question. "Ben, I want my husband back. Say good-night to him, now. And maybe, just maybe, I'll forgive you."

"Good night, Deanna."

Chuckling, Richard Reeves got back on the line. "Well, that's one decision I'm not going to appeal. Lunch tomorrow, though? I want to talk about this some more."

"Tang Gardens, twelve noon?"

"See you there and then." Reeves hung up.

Thoughtful, Ibrani replaced the receiver and turned back

to the story on the screen. A couple of points were glaringly absent from it: the fact, for example, that the meeting was an emergency session. And the fact that no announcement had been posted, although the Freedom of Information Act required one.

Odd, indeed: the facts, and Nicki's omission of them.

Well, nothing he could do about the maverick council, but he could at least fix the story. He pulled the keyboard nearer, then stopped.

Something to eat, first, maybe. It had been a long time since breakfast, and he had skipped lunch.

He went to the kitchen and washed his hands while he thought about dinner. His choices were limited: order a pizza, or microwave something out of the freezer. The thought of pizza was unappealing, so he dried his hands on a dish towel and examined his stock of frozen food. Both of the boxes remaining in the freezer held veal parmesan with peas and mashed potatoes.

Ibrani shrugged. What the hell, it would cook quick and clean up almost instantly. He washed his hands, unfastened the box, slid the tray into the microwave, and turned the thing on.

Then he washed his hands again.

Then he dried his hands again.

Then he turned on the water and picked up the soap and. . . .

A shiver ran up his spine. Staring at his wrinkled fingertips, he took a deep breath, and another, slowly. *Everything's fine, Ben. Your hands are clean.*

Then he rolled up his sleeves and cranked the hot water a little hotter. His hands were not clean. Slime coated them; greasy, fetid slime straight out of a sewer.

He shuddered, and reached for the dish detergent.

No!

With a violent jerk of his body, he twisted away from the sink and clutched a kitchen chair. He knew what was happening.

Goodmaster was torturing him again. How—and why now—Ibrani didn't know.

The feeling faded. Ibrani had a drink while he waited for his dinner. When it was ready, he ate it, then looked down at the empty tray. The taste of mediocre veal parmesan clung to his teeth. He got up, intending to wash the tray and dispose of it, but instead he left it on the cocktail table and went directly to his computer.

Nicki's story still glowed on the screen. It bothered him; he would feel better once he had fixed it.

"At a meeting remarkable for civility of tone and unanimity of purpose, the city council voted Tuesday afternoon to impose a dusk-to-dawn curfew on all juveniles beneath the age of sixteen."

He shook his head. His fingers stroked the keys. Abruptly, he began to feel very much worse.

"At an emergency meeting of the city council called by Chairman Caleb MacRoss in violation of the state's Freedom of Information laws—"

His fingertips skidded off the keys. He held them up, looked at them, rubbed them together.

Grease. Veal grease. Going rancid already. He sniffed; gone rancid. Putrefying, in fact.

He should wash.

Only a massive effort of will kept him from leaping to his feet and running to the sink. He understood; it was the same as all the other times, the same as this afternoon. Goodmaster wanted something, or didn't want something.

And when that happened, Ben Ibrani began to feel putrid, as if his own flesh were a piece of old meat that someone had left to rot in the hot sun.

He got up, caught the jamb of the door to the kitchen, and hung on as if resisting a hurricane. He was fine. He had eaten the damn dinner with knife and fork and he did not have grease on his fingers. It was all in his imagination. Goodmaster had put it there to keep him in line, had somehow triggered conditioning he had implanted years ago with the skill and ease of a scientist training a laboratory rat.

Ben was sure of that, though he didn't understand how Goodmaster did it. Over Christmas vacation of his senior year in high school, he had methodically searched his bedroom and bath in the mansion for tiny speakers, because he had concluded that Goodmaster must be drumming tape-recorded messages into his head while he slept.

He had found nothing. And slept poorly anyway.

Perhaps, he had thought then, it was the dreams he kept having, after all. So many mornings he had awakened mumbling, rubbing his hands one against the other, wondering at the vast quantities of blood, appalled at his own guilt, and knowing that while he could never, ever, expiate his sins, he could at least avoid punishment for them by washing. Thoroughly.

But even then he hadn't really believed any of it meant anything, because as soon as he had blinked a few times, taken a few deep breaths, the dreams had vanished. He had not accepted their importance until later, when he was in college.

He could have told someone, tried to get help. But by then he was too afraid to tell anyone. It was too crazy, too unbelievable—unless it was happening to you. Besides, he knew if he did tell anyone, he would be . . . punished.

The lesson had been drummed in, late in his freshman year, while he was trying to choose his major. The telephone rang in his dorm room: Goodmaster.

"Journalism." The familiar voice, like slivers of dry ice. Even so, Ben tried to reason with it.

"I was thinking more pre-med, Uncle Jason."

"Journalism."

"But I like science a lot, and—"

"Journalism, boy."

He had gotten angry, then. "Now wait a minute, Uncle Jason. It's not like you're going to be paying for this. I know the situation; the trust fund my folks set up."

Goodmaster sniffed.

"What?"

Silence. A deep, unyielding silence, full of the time Ben needed to perceive his greasy hair, his filthy skin. He'd held the receiver in his left hand and scratched the nape of his neck, where the small hairs prickled as if rabid ants marched between them. The air grew rank and his scratching more desperate, until at last he screamed.

"Yes, I'll do it, please Uncle Jason, I'll do it just stop, please—"

Click-click; dial tone.

His roommate found him later, passed out in a pink froth

on the shower floor, a can of Ajax on its side by his hand.

When he came to in the infirmary, he finally understood. Jason Goodmaster controlled the Ibrani family trusts. (And who made it possible for Helen and Jordan Ibrani to join that mission?) He controlled the capital. (And how did Jordan Ibrani, angina sufferer, come to be driving a car on a badly maintained mountain road miles from nowhere?) And he controlled the interest. He would control it all for years to come, while doling out a liberal allowance, the carrot to go with the stick.

After a few weeks of counseling—stress, they'd said; acute anxiety reaction, they'd said—Ben had returned to college, where without any hesitation he finally chose his major: journalism.

Ibrani shuddered now, still clutching the doorjamb. Goodmaster, wanting or not wanting something, was pressuring, warning him.

That much he knew.

But why?

Shakily Ben released his hold on the woodwork and went back to his desk, telling himself that he was fine. He reached for the keyboard.

"—laws, those council members attending voted Tuesday afternoon to impose a dusk-to-dawn curfew on all juveniles beneath the age of sixteen. The ordinance is not expected to survive its first court—"

Ibrani stiffened. Things lived in grease. Invisible things. They especially liked veal grease because they could fatten on it, then swarm up fingers to wrists, elbows, armpits.

Into his eyes. Into his nose, and his mouth.

A whine came from his taut throat. He cast an agonized glance at the shotgun cases, his collection.

Perhaps also his salvation.

Hemingway had done it. Barrel in his mouth, work the trigger with his toes. Messy, but quick. Why so many cops ate their guns: efficient. Thorough.

He could do it, too.

But first he had to wash.

No. He shivered, reached for the keyboard again.

Something tickled in his nose hairs. He drew his hands back from the keyboard; the tickling faded.

Ibrani blinked, then reached for the keyboard again. Whatever had been in his nose came back, squirmed wetly up into the space behind his eyeball, and started laying eggs there.

Ibrani screamed.

So that was what Uncle Jason didn't want. Helpless, knowing full well now what he would do to himself if he continued revising the article attributed to Nicki Pialosta, Ibrani canceled everything, sent the piece on just as Nicki had written it. If she had written it.

Then he shoved back his chair and ran to the kitchen sink.

When he returned, finally, his hands and face tingling, his fingers spongy, a new story had appeared on the VDT screen: "Councilman Reeves Dies."

Numbly, Ibrani read the article. Dick Reeves had suffered a heart attack and died before the paramedics could reach him.

Ibrani could believe that part, all right. Deanna had sounded pretty hot to trot, and Reeves was no youngster.

I hope that's how you went, old buddy.

It was the story's next line that scared him; the line that said Reeves died "shortly after returning from a meeting of the city council, at which he had voted to impose a dawn-to-dusk curfew on juveniles under the age of sixteen."

Either Dick Reeves had lied to him, or the *Bulletin* was lying to Meadbury.

Ibrani thought he knew which. Something was happening in Meadbury: on the city council, at the *Bulletin*, and everywhere.

Something Jason Goodmaster had something to do with. Otherwise, why stop Ben from revising Nicki's story?

Of course, he simply could have stopped Ben from reading it. But he hadn't, which told Ben something else: It was all right for him to know that something was happening.

He just couldn't do anything about it.

Because I'm filthy.

With trembling fingers he shut off the machine and got out of his chair. His knees shook so badly it took him two tries to get to his feet.

Then he gave a low moan and headed upstairs to the

shower, trying not to think of the wire brush in the trunk of his BMW, the one he used to scrape paint on his boat.

Only he couldn't stop thinking about it, because this time Jason Goodmaster didn't want Ben Ibrani to forget.

No.

This time Goodmaster wanted him to remember.

WEDNESDAY, JANUARY 16

Jimmy Conklin

Brutal buzzing knifed through the soft, warm darkness. The clock's red numerals glared mercilessly: six A.M. Groaning, he fumbled for the snooze button, pressed it, and closed his eyes again.

Silence. Ah, blessed silence. He pulled the covers back over his shoulders and burrowed in, torturing himself with the sweet temptation of just staying here all morning, warm and comfortable. Meanwhile his brain was steadily counting down, as he had long ago trained it to: *three, two . . . one.*

He kicked off the covers and hit the floor before he had time to think. Which was the whole point; if he thought about it, he would never do what he was going to do now; no, not on a bet.

Crossing barefoot to the window, he drew the curtain aside. Darkness still held the morning in its icy clutches, as if the night were reluctant to let go. The corner streetlight shone bluely through the tracery of frost ferns growing on the windowpane.

Ain't you poetic. Shivering, he sighed and plodded to the bathroom, where he emptied his bladder, rinsed his mouth, and eyed the cynical choirboy who stared blearily out of the mirror at him. He splashed cold water on the fair, freckled face. *Take that, you ugly mug.*

Three minutes later, in sneakers and sweatsuit, Conklin pushed himself out the front door and broke into a grudging trot. His breath chuffed out in ghostly plumes; the hairs in his nostrils prickled frozenly. His feet smacked the sidewalk and the chill rose through them, not retreating until his circulation sped up.

Up ahead lay a tiny park, postage-stamp-sized, with a couple of trees. *Just my size.* Willing his legs to work automatically at a slow, steady warm-up pace, he jogged toward his private morning miracle.

If he tried to tell anyone about it, they'd probably think he was nuts. "Yeah, Conklin, that's what happens in the morning. It gets light."

Only it didn't just get light. One moment, blackness. No trees, no sky. Just inky night. Then, in an instant, night dissolved and trees materialized before a background of deep blue-grey, naked sharp branches coming up crisply as light rose behind them, like a photograph being developed. After that, pinkish streamers across the sky; pretty, but he did not care quite as much for them.

He'd had his moment, the instant when day came. Thanking who- or whatever arranged for there to be moments like that, even just once a day, he lengthened his stride. His muscles griped, but went along.

Criminy, it's cold. Running was one thing; you could stay warm if you kept moving. But sooner or later you had to stop, and then your sweat turned to icy crystals; you chilled down and froze, froze solid like a side of beef, solid as iron. He tried to imagine it: no apartment to go back to. Just a doorway, or an alley. No steaming shower, no hot coffee.

He was, he realized, thinking of Nicki and her homeless folks, loonies and losers. After a night as cold as last night it was a wonder she had anybody left to write about, except for the shelter, of course.

But the homeless people in lots of other towns, most other towns, didn't have shelters. And how the hell, he wondered, did those other towns' homeless survive at all? Because he knew damned well one winter would do for him, cut him down with the first bitter stroke of its scythe.

Or maybe not. Before Europeans came, the Tierra del Fuegans were supposed to have slept naked on bare earth all year round, and it got plenty cold down there, too. The human animal could survive quite a bit if it had to. And that, of course, was the key: animal.

Because that's what it would turn you into. All your

humanity, or most of it, would freeze and fall off. Along with a few fingers and toes, probably.

Thinking of this, he kicked into the second mile of his run. No matter what history books tried to say, he wasn't sure he believed any Tierra del Fuegans really slept naked on the bare earth. Not in this kind of winter; not any that woke up next morning, anyway. It was just too damned cold.

He slowed at the boulevard, glancing both ways because the traffic light was against him. A blue Dodge Charger pulled up to the intersection at the same instant —consoling Conklin with the knowledge that other people had to get up early, too—but instead of gunning on through, the Charger stopped and the driver waved him across.

Nodding his thanks, Conklin ran through the fog of his breath, passing the little park where the trees were now clearly visible, no longer skeletal black cutouts pasted against a lighter sky. The buildings along his route were real now, also: mostly brick, a few stucco, here and there a clapboarded veteran that the bulldozers somehow had missed. Now that gentrification had set in, those old frame houses were getting valuable, gleaming with fresh paint even in the thin dawn light.

Probably the Tierra del Fuegans didn't sleep out. Probably some seventeenth-century journalist just needed a grabber headline and came up with that one. In those days, when the whole world wasn't a phone call away, editors didn't confirm stories so relentlessly.

Which probably meant that journalism was a lot more fun back then.

Cripes, it was cold.

A garbage truck rumbled up the street behind him, interrupting his thought, slowing as it came alongside.

"Attaway to go, champ! Keep it up!" The driver grinned, flashing a victory sign.

Conklin grinned back and waved. "Hey, what's shakin'? Anything?"

"Just my nuts, keep 'em warm. Yours gotta be freezin' off."

Conklin laughed, concealing mild disappointment. This same driver had once tipped him to an arson-for-profit operation; the five-part series he'd gotten out of it came close to winning an award.

He shrugged off the memory. What the hell, maybe next year. Hey, you couldn't get good tips off a garbage truck every single morning; if it were that easy, everybody would be doing it.

Conklin tossed the driver a salute. "Gotta roll."

"Right on." With a dieselly roar the truck trundled away. Conklin stopped jogging in place and began once more to put one foot in front of the other. Even warmed up, running never got easy, just less agonizing.

Not much longer, J. Patrick, ol' boy, just another mile and a half. Ten minutes and we're done. Now his feet slapped the cold concrete with a steady rhythm. He never tried much for speed, and especially not on cold mornings like this. When the mercury shivered down near zero, being out here at all was virtuous enough.

Today no one else even got that far; he'd seen no other joggers at all. Not that he could blame them; it was frigid. Warmer mornings, especially in late spring, he got to feeling like a herd animal, thundering along with the rest in their shorts and T-shirts. A lot of people were into fitness. Sometimes it seemed like half of Meadbury was out there with him.

Not that he minded. One spring morning, those shorts and T-shirts were wrapped around a magnificent blond with a bottom like two peach halves and breasts like cupcakes, and running turned all at once into a real good way to wake up. Of course, when she proved to be a marathoner and he found himself doing twelve miles instead of three, it was sort of embarrassing, especially at the end when his breath came in painful, audible gasps. He'd had shin splints for a week, and never saw her again.

He smiled at the recollection. Company did make running easier; on the other hand, even now he wasn't really lonely. Like the Charger, slowing down for him, and the garbage truck driver stopping just to say good morning, shoot him the V sign. Any other town, Chargers ran you over and garbage truck guys shot you the finger—when they took any notice at all. Who gave a shit if some dumb joker wanted to bust a gut, freeze his nuts off—that was the way it was everywhere else.

Everywhere but Meadbury, where people were more than tolerant. Here, they actively approved. Here, when he forced himself out to puff his way down a chilly predawn street, he got the feeling that even people still inside were silently applauding him. They liked his keeping himself in shape even though it wouldn't help them personally one bit.

Now there was a story. He rounded the corner and headed home. "Why Meadbury Likes Joggers." Feature, though. Not his department. He could probably talk his way into it, get time off if no major crimes were going down, then get Ibrani to okay it—nah, get Ibrani's okay first—

Or maybe just give it to Nicki, he thought as his first enthusiasm cooled. Because it might be a good idea, but the story had no glitter in it for him, no muggings or murder, no drug busts or bank stickups to hold his interest, which was already waning.

Because—he had to face it—he was a crime writer, just a little fish in the great big ghoul pool. Who the cops busted, who got dead—and be honest, the gorier the better. Not just for the great unwashed readership, because it made them buy papers. For him. Because it excited him, and he could communicate that excitement. It was why he was good.

For a moment he wished running poured less oxygen into his brain; David Halberstam he wasn't, and he didn't need to know it quite so clearly. Most of the time it was good enough to be what he was, but sometimes. . . .

Cripes, it was cold. Only another eight blocks. He ran them, maintaining radio silence in his mind which had gone surly on him. At last he quickstepped up his own front walk and into his building, where the vestibule greeted him with warmth. Damn near too much warmth; it was like jogging into an oven. He gave a last violent shiver, glanced at the stairs, and pressed the button for the elevator.

Up in his apartment, the hot shower reached into his bones, pulling out warmth that had gone into hiding; no longer feeling like Frosty the Snowman (and a grouchy one at that), he shaved, scrubbed his teeth, and ran a comb through his hair. His bad moods never lasted very long before the mirror.

How could a guy who looked like that stay bummed out?

Freckles dotted the peculiarly translucent skin so common to redheads, skin crinkled at the corners of his green eyes and stretched around a rueful smile. In his worst moments he thought he looked like Howdy Doody; on better days he resembled Jimmy Olsen of the *Daily Planet*. And that was bad enough. He often thought that if one more person made a Clark Kent crack, or asked him if he knew where Superman was, he'd punch that person out.

But they did, and he didn't. Maybe that was why he'd gotten into crime writing: just to contradict his Mom-and-apple-pie wholesome looks, without having to get run in on a drunk-and-disorderly, or worse. Lord knew he didn't always feel that wholesome.

Pulling on his blue suit, he frowned at a stain on the cuff, but let it ride. He was going to work, not to a dinner dance. Besides—he glanced at the clock—he was already late. Then it hit him: dinner dance.

Hurriedly he rummaged through the pile of papers on his dresser. Laundry bill, credit card carbons, ticket stubs, why did he never get around to sorting it out? He just emptied his pockets every night and let it all mound up. Money might be at the bottom of that pile; a stray twenty he'd forgotten, or a paycheck lying there undeposited. It could happen; his checkbook was in the same disarray as his dresser top.

At last his fingers closed on the invitation to the Thomas Aquinas School Benefit Dinner Dance. It was more like a demand for his appearance; his cousin Bobbi would kill him if he begged off. His glance fell on the family photograph tucked into the edge of the dresser's mirror, with Bobbi's face, freckled and round like his own, smiling out of it. Behind her stood Dom, her husband, round and balding, smiling too but also looking just a little bit worried, as if any minute his wife might say she was pregnant again.

Bobbi, gimme a break. You already got eight kids paying fees at Saint Tom's—your reproductive system is a fund-raising committee all by itself.

But Bobbi's face just kept radiating energy, like a sun-lamp that would burn you if you didn't move. Which was why this year, like every year, the whole Conklin clan was shelling out fifty bucks a head for a bad dinner, worse music, and another speech from Father Aloysius. Oh, well, at least it kept Bobbi from giving a speech of her own. Bobbi was a pretty, pleasant woman, but when she got hot on a subject you could mount her on a squad car and use her voice for riot control.

And this year again she was bugging him to bring a date. Time he got serious, she kept telling him, and wasn't there anybody special he could bring to a lovely event like the Saint Tom's School Benefit Dinner Dance? There would be prizes for best waltz and fox-trot, Sister Millicent was leading the first- and second-graders in a choral presentation, and the Rosary Society was putting on a religious playlet that Mary-Margaret Weston had written.

Snorting with laughter at the memory of last year's playlet, he grabbed his topcoat, flipped a scarf around his throat, and went out the door, shaking his head as he caught sight of the clock. 7:07. Seven minutes late already, and the sun just barely into the sky. He had a horrible premonition that by the time it went down, he'd be so far behind that he would never catch up.

If last year's dramatic offering was any hint, the dinner dance wouldn't be so bad. It was worth fifty bucks to see Mary-Margaret Weston's fractured Bible stories. Her last one had featured Mary Magdalene in a flowered housecoat, pincurls, and blue satin mules with pom-poms on the toes. Cigarette dangling from her red lips, she'd pulled off Christ's Frye boots and dunked his feet in a galvanized pail.

By some miscalculation, the water in the pail had come directly from a tub of slushy ice where, moments before, beer for the thirsty dinner dancers had been cooling. Gentle Jesus had nearly ascended into heaven on the spot, meanwhile adding several choice, heartfelt lines of vernacular to the script and reminding Jimmy, who had needed it, that true religion really was funny as hell.

Cheered by this memory, he went out once more through the vestibule, down the street, and into the coffee shop on the corner. At the sight of him, the waitress reached for a cup and saucer.

"You're late," she said.

He made a face at her. Marge Margate was fat, fair, and forty, with a tongue like a scorpion's stinger. She was an honest, hardworking, straight-ahead woman whose luck had been lousy. Conklin liked her.

"The usual, please." He stepped back as she clattered a full cup of coffee onto the formica in front of him.

"Tell me, Jimmy." Folding her arms, she leaned on the counter, pushing her open, honest, plug-ugly face at him. "You see 'the usual' onna board anywhere? Huh? I see twelve kinds of doughnuts, six kinds of danish, three kinds of coffee cake, but I don't see no 'usual.' Do you? Huh?"

"C'mon, Marge, gimme a break. It's early."

"Hey, I know it's early. It's early for me, too. Early for me to have to remember what you have for breakfast 'cause you're embarrassed, people hear you say how many donuts Mr. Marathon scarfs down, he's had his morning run."

She turned away, fiddled with the malted milk machine, and said in a mutter, "Yeah, some people give me morning runs."

He sipped his coffee. "You in a bad mood today, Marge?"

"Might say I am." She grabbed a plate and stomped to the donut rack. Without asking she piled eight donuts on the plate: two raspberry jelly, two chocolate cream, two honeydip, two powdered sugar. Then she slid the loaded plate down the counter and did not look up to see if he caught it.

He did—barely. The woman had an arm on her, all right. Jimmy figured she wanted to use that arm, and the fist clenched at the end of it, on something bigger than a plate of donuts.

A couple of other men at the counter glanced at each other, obviously assuming the same thing and keeping their mouths shut about it. After all, they were bigger than a plate of donuts and Marge didn't look as if she'd be discriminating in her possible choice of targets.

Jimmy ate. After a while Marge came back, slapping down a fistful of paper napkins.

"Get up at four, you know?" she said. "Because I have to be here at five, deliveries and set-up, open at six? Get dressed in the dark, use the john downstairs, don't wake Alf, right? Because Alf hates getting woke up, says it screws up his routine, whatever that is, right? So I get all that done, I'm out on the porch, I close the door, and my hands like to fall off, that's how cold."

Conklin mumbled agreement through fragments of chocolate cream doughnut. He always ate one of them first, and saved the other for the very last. He loved chocolate cream. For a while he'd eaten no other donuts, but that got boring after a year or so. He took a sip of coffee. "So you're in a bad mood because your hands were cold?"

"No!" She thwacked his shoulder with her clean-up towel. "I went back in for my gloves, you know? And I heard a noise in the kitchen, so I grabbed Daddy's cane from the umbrella stand, the one with the brass head?"

It took him a moment to put the cane together with the brass head. "Oh! Oh, yeah. Right. So somebody was breaking in."

"Somebody was sneaking in. Somebody named Alfred William Margate. Who was supposedly sound asleep in the bed upstairs. Now don't that beat all?" She moved down the counter and began wiping up after a long-departed diner.

Conklin had never met Marge Margate's husband, but he had heard enough to know him through and through. "So did you lay the cane upside his head? Beat a little tattoo on his ribs? C'mon, Marge, you can't leave me hanging. How am I gonna concentrate today if I don't know what you did to him?"

She drifted back toward him, shooing crumbs off the formica. "Well. . . ." A smile played about the corners of her lips. "I got to the swinging door between the kitchen and the dining room? Just as he was opening the back door, right? An' he stuck his head in, peeked all around, but I only pushed the swinging door in just a crack, so he didn't see me. And he comes in, right, with his jacket over his left arm, and his shoes in his left hand? And I wait for him to get most of the way in? And I leap!"

In demonstration, Marge pushed off from the rubber mat that covered the floor behind the counter; Conklin stared as she seemed to hang for a golden moment in the air, between the big hooded grill and the stacks of fluted glass ice-cream-sundae dishes on the shelf. Then she came down a good eight feet from where she'd started, rattling his cup in its saucer and provoking alarmed stares from the other men eating breakfast.

"I give this yell," she went on, "it'd do a banshee proud, and I tell you, I am Errol Flynn with the cane." She whirled herself sideways and struck a pose: plump left arm curled back above her head; right arm outthrust like a demented fencer.

Conklin took a quick gulp of coffee so he would not choke on the mix of laughter, amazement, and chocolate-cream donut all battling for space in his throat.

"And I pounce! Yee-ah!" She bounced forward on her toes, lunged, and thrust at the imaginary Alf with her imaginary sword. "And again! And again and again and again!"

"So did you run him through, or did the seconds call it off?"

She looked at him, puzzled. "Seconds? It hardly took that long. But I run him off is what I did, Jimmy. And the beauty part is, when I jumped out at him, he got so scared he pitched his coat and shoes and keys straight up in the air. And before they came down he was out the door, with me inside lockin' an' boltin' it tight? And the grates on the first floor windows, and the front door too? So Mister Sneaky-pants Alfred William Margate is out there somewhere right now, no shoes or coat or keys. Which to my way of thinking is just good enough for him."

Jimmy considered. It was awfully cold. But then, Alf deserved it. This wasn't his first stunt, nor his worst; there was the time he talked Marge's brother out of five hundred dollars for an absolutely surefire investment, then lost it all upstate at the racetrack. Or the time he disappeared for three months in the dead of winter, came back with a tan, and tried to persuade Marge that he'd been in a VA hospital suffering from amnesia.

"Well, I can't blame you for being in a bad mood if Alf stayed out all night," he said.

"Hell, no, Jimmy. I'm just mad I didn't get the sucker's wallet, too." She sniffed, and carried his cup back to the urn for a refill. "Tell you something else."

"What's that?" There was more? How could there be?

"This'll sound funny, but I don't think Alf's got any girlfriend. He hasn't stayed up late for sex all the twenty-two years we been married." She smothered a giggle. "Hell, he has trouble staying up for sex when he's getting it."

Conklin decided not to comment on that. "Uh-huh?"

"Only two things keep Alf awake." Marge counted on her fingers: "Liquor and cards. I think he's found himself some place he can get 'em both all night long. Like an after-hours club. You know any of 'em around here?"

"Marge, I know this is going to play hell with my dashing image, but I've never been in an after-hours club in my life. I run in the mornings, remember? I need my beauty sleep."

"Beauty sleep, hunh?" She regarded him. "Hate to say, but it isn't working."

"Thanks, pal." He chewed the last of the last chocolate cream.

"Any time. But you haven't heard anything? I mean, you talk to cops an' all. Don't they say?"

He shook his head. "But maybe—" He paused to wash down the final chunk of the donut with the last of the coffee. "Maybe if I ask around, somebody will mention something."

She patted him on the shoulder with one rough, reddened hand, her pale lumpy face all at once—no, not pretty. Kind, though, and grateful. And those were tears brimming in her slightly bulging eyes. "Appreciate it, Jimmy."

"Oh, hey." He fumbled in his pocket for change to disguise the sudden sadness she had roused in him. "Hey, it's as much for me as for you. There might be a front page story in it." Which was a lie, he was pretty sure. But. . . .

"That'd be good." Then she spoke again, half to him and half to herself. "I don't mind the drinking so much. But Alf is a lousy poker player. Just lousy, you know?"

Heck. Heck, she still loves the bum.

Conklin thought ol' Alf was lucky his wife did still love him, instead of deciding to put a hit man on his slimy trail. Because Marge Margate had a genuine way of making you want to do things for her, things you wouldn't ordinarily do, like nail somebody's kneecaps. That'd crimp Alf's style some.

He got up and ambled toward the door. "See you tomorrow, Marge."

"Take care of yourself, Jimmy."

He checked his watch as he crossed the street to the parking lot. 7:39. Nine minutes behind, now. Maybe he should find a coffee shop with a waitress who didn't talk?

Nah. Marge was too much fun to give up, most days. And too sad the rest. . . .

He got behind the wheel of his ancient Nash Rambler

and turned the key. It started right up; he blinked in surprise.

"Well, all right, guy," he said to the dashboard, "it's high time you worked the way you're supposed to. Is this a sign? Am I going to get through the winter without another major repair bill?"

In answer the engine settled into a smooth and sensuous idle, as if it only wanted to get onto the highway and show him what it could do.

Swinging his right arm up onto the passenger-seat back, he glanced over his right shoulder and put the car in reverse. He pressed the gas pedal very gently, no sense tempting fate, and let out the clutch.

The Rambler backed fluidly out of the parking lot into the street. Humming, Conklin shifted into first, pressed the gas again. Yes sir, the Nash was a good little buggy; he didn't care what people said about it.

At which moment the engine clattered, gave a morbid, terminal shudder, and stalled hopelessly.

By nine he was downtown and into the *Bulletin* building, his hands now reasonably clean, although black circles of engine grease still showed beneath his nails. He didn't even want to think about the condition of his bathroom sink, or the towel he'd used.

Damn, but that Rambler's a vicious little heap. He cut the idea off superstitiously, in case the car could hear him, and headed on into city room. Five after nine already. Heck. He hated getting to work late. Aside from the practical problems it caused him, it also made him feel as if he'd be given demerits and kept in after school.

Which was silly. Nobody cared, as long as he got his stuff in on time. Thinking this, he walked down the aisle of scuffed linoleum to his desk, pulled out the chair, and found a wildly-scrawled note stuck to his blotter:

"At shelter, back soon. Wait for me here. Nicki."

He frowned at it for a moment, then turned around in his chair. Nicki sat where she always sat, gaze fixed on her VDT, very clearly not at the shelter.

She looked a little pale, maybe, but hey, it was winter. Spring would pink her up again. So would a good laugh, if he could remember any jokes.

Aw, heck. Even if he could remember a joke, he'd forget the damn punch line if he tried to tell it to her.

Aware of the note in his hand and his own work waiting, Conklin leaned back in his chair and kept on watching her. He told himself he was practicing unobtrusive observation —yeah, that sounded good—but in truth he knew he simply couldn't tear his gaze away from her.

Truth is, I'm about sixty percent in love with her and the other forty percent is catching up fast. He watched her hands move toward the VDT's keyboard. She had this unconscious gesture that for some stupid reason always put a stutter in his heartbeat. It was a silly thing, just the way she'd brush back the hair over her right ear with her smooth white hand. Then she'd toss her head a bit, impatiently, like a high-spirited racehorse.

Nicki's nails flashed red as she swept back her hair.

He swallowed hard, forcing his mind back to— The note. Yes. The note. He looked at it again. Nicki's writing, though more scribbled-looking than usual, so if the thing was a prank, then she was the prankster.

Only one way to find out. He would have to go talk to her. He grinned to himself as he strolled to her desk.

Reaching over her shoulder, he dropped the note on her keyboard. "What's with this?" Fighting back the temptation to touch her hair, whose faint sweet scent rose up intoxicatingly. . . .

She swiveled her chair around, forcing him to step back. "Oh, that?"

Her expression was odd. Kind of dreamy, as if he'd brought her back from woolgathering.

"Uh, yeah," he said, suddenly uncertain. "That. What's it all about?"

Her look focused on him, now, level, unblinking. He felt as if his eyes really were the windows to his soul, and she saw through them to his thoughts as they scrolled through his consciousness.

"I thought the box in yesterday's paper might have upset you," she said quietly. "I wanted to reassure you."

"Another box? Heck, I thought that was—"

Still studying his face, she reached for a folded-open newspaper. "Here."

"—all over," he finished, taking the newspaper and

wishing at once that he hadn't. Because it very clearly wasn't all over. Not at all.

IN MEMORIAM
Reginald Harper Forsten III
Richard White Pialosta
James Patrick Conklin
free at last

Knees suddenly shaky, he sat on the edge of the neighboring desk, took a deep breath. *Still here. Heart beating, lungs pumping—so far.*

He found his voice. "I feel like somebody just dumped a tub of ice water on my head."

"I know. That's how I felt when I saw Rich's name. And that's why I left you the note before I went out to the shelter."

"And?"

She blinked, smiling. "And? And what?"

He looked closely at her. "What did you find?" He made the words distinct. "Is your brother okay?"

The question seemed to surprise her. "Yes, of course," she said. "In fact, he's been discharged. Reg, too."

"What?" Conklin got off the desk, not quite believing his ears.

"Discharged," she said, her voice mild. Too mild. "Let go? Released? It's English, Jimmy; you can look it up. He found a job down at the television station, so he's not at the shelter anymore. It's that simple."

For a moment he wondered if maybe he was still in bed, dreaming. It was just as likely as Rich Pialosta's having got a job. More likely, in fact. He frowned. But no, he was wide awake, he was sure of it, and something stranger than a dream was going on.

"Uh, Nick? Are you by any chance laboring under a big dose of Vitamin V this morning?" That would account for the smoothed face, the wide, dark pupils.

"Pardon?" Her eyebrows went up a dreamy fraction.

"Valium, Nick. Are you on tranquilizers right now?"

"Goodness, no." She looked faintly amused. "Why

would you think that? I'm simply telling you everything's fine, you shouldn't worry. I feel so much better." She sighed, turned her chair halfway back toward her desk and gazed at it, as if trying to remember what she had been doing.

Not hard, though; not as if it mattered.

He held up his hands. She was tranked, all right, but if she didn't want to admit it that was her business. "Okay, skip it. Everything's fine at the shelter, and I shouldn't worry about the memorial box. The one with my name in it."

"That's right." Her head bobbed up and down. "That's it exactly."

"Uh-huh." He stifled his irritation. "Well gee, that's just great. I'm real happy to hear it. Only, one more thing still worries me."

She glanced at him in inquiry.

"See, along with your name in this box, you get a prize, and the prize is a casket. At least that's the way it's worked up till now. In one box, then into another box."

"Mmm," she said agreeably.

"So—" He fought to keep his voice from rising. "Now I'm in line for the prize. My name is in here. And since you clearly don't think I ought to be concerned, or that Rich should be, either, I'd like to know why. If you can energize yourself enough to tell me."

She shook her head, sighed again. "Sorry. Can't."

He stared, stunned at the refusal. "Nick, we're talking my life here!"

"Sorry," she said again. "This is my story. I dug it up; I get to break it." Then she smiled, a real smile this time, with the accustomed hint of mischief. "You'll find out. I promise. Don't worry."

Smile's too wide. More trank effect. But even a glimpse of the normal Nicki reassured him. And she did sound as if she knew what she was talking about, and Rich's name in the box didn't worry her.

Which meant she had something new on the boxes, and by extension something new on the Meadbury Slasher, which was by rights Conklin's story, no matter what she said.

He swallowed hard. Okay. She'd been stepping on a lot of toes lately; dumb of him to think she'd avoid his. Ambitious, she was reaching for something, that was clear; she had some kind of deal going with Ibrani, Rifkind, maybe even Old Prickly.

And she wasn't going to tell him what it was. Which, he realized suddenly, was fine with him, because he was perfectly capable of finding out for himself. She didn't have all of it, because if she did she'd be typing madly, shooing him away. And that meant. . . .

A wicked grin spread over his face. *Love ya, Nick. But I'm gonna scoop you anyway. Just wait.*

"Uh, not to change the subject," he said, deliberately doing just that, "but what do you know about after-hours clubs around here?"

She cocked her head and stared at him. "What's an after-hours club?"

"Are you kidding me?"

"No, I'm not. What—"

"And here I thought you were a yuppie. It's where you go when the bars close. Private clubs are allowed to serve liquor after the statutory closing time, see, so these places pretend to be private clubs. Usually you can buy a membership at the door, though, which means they're really not all that private. Are you following all this? I know it's complicated."

Jeez, Conklin, you'll really win her affections with sarcasm. Why don't you insult her taste, too?

Nicki shrugged. "I guess I haven't hung out with the right young urban professionals. The ones I know have always had to get up in the morning."

He chuckled, then cut himself off because she was looking at him curiously. Once again he felt uncomfortable. Cripes, this was not his day.

"Okay," he said, "thanks anyway. I'd better get back to my desk."

As he stood, she caught the sleeve of his jacket. "Wait. Did you want to go to one of those clubs?"

"No, I just thought there might be an article in it. A friend of mine thinks that's where her husband's spending his time and their money."

"Are the drinks expensive?"

The question seemed almost a *non sequitur,* and for a moment he just goggled. "Uh, I don't know, really. I imagine in some places they are. I suppose it'd vary from place to place, you know? But see, that's not what's bothering her. She thinks he's gambling there. And losing."

"Oh." She looked troubled. "But that's illegal."

"Losing?"

"No. Gambling."

He closed his eyes. This conversation could not be happening.

"Nicki," he said gently, "lots of people gamble lots of money every day. I thought you lived in New York."

She waved a hand dismissively. "I know they break the law in New York. I just didn't know they did it here, too."

Again he couldn't quite believe she'd said it. "Why wouldn't they?"

"Because this is Meadbury."

"Ah. Yes." He laughed, because come to think of it, he saw what she meant, even if she did sound childishly naive. Meadbury did have an air of rectitude about it. Not self-righteousness, though. At least, not often enough to be obnoxious.

"But look, Nicki. I mean, human nature. Some people are going to break the law, that's just the way it is, I mean, why else pay for cops, or courts, or jails? Or even crime reporters, for that matter."

She looked at him for a long moment, seeming to digest what he'd said. "I see. That's right." Then her gaze drifted from his face to a point on the far wall. "So are you going to be investigating these clubs?"

"Among other things, yeah."

"If you learn anything interesting, let me know, okay?"

He had to smile. "Why? You want to hit a few of these joints, check 'em out before the cops close them?"

Surprised delight lit up her face. "What a wonderful idea!"

Yeah, there was the Nicki he knew. His heart thumped with pleasure. Of course, she might not think it was wonderful once she found out he meant to snatch his territory back from her.

Then again, maybe she would; she wasn't the type who always wanted things easy. And neither was he. Which made them a perfect match. . . .

"So what else are you working on?" she said suddenly.

Her inquisitiveness struck a note of caution in him. But heck, if he told her he was already working on a story, she'd keep her hands off it. Anything else would be dirty pool, and she wasn't like that.

"I've been poking around Ned Gorman," he admitted. "Not really as a crime thing, at least I don't think so. But jeez, the guy's such a cipher. I don't know. Makes me uneasy. You've talked to him a few times, haven't you? Did he give you anything on his background?"

She put her hands up in a gesture of ignorance. "Shelter, Chevys, and the PTA. That's about it. His bio's on file here somewhere, though. Not much memorable in it, as I recall."

"That's for sure. High school debater, 440 on the track team."

"So? Sounds like a typical bio to me. What's the problem?"

"Nick, what's memorable about that bio is what's not in it. It doesn't say what high school, or even what city. It says he got a B.A. in history from State University, but what state? There's nothing about his service record, or about any jobs he held before he went to work for that Chevrolet dealership on Eighth Avenue."

Then he stopped, that note of caution seizing him once more as he saw the interest in her eyes. He had more about Gorman, things that hadn't been in the bio. But he wasn't going to tell her. Uh-uh.

"So he's a man of mystery," she said, smiling.

"Uh-huh. Or no mystery. I want to know which."

"Is it safe to assume," she asked, "that you are going to unravel that mystery? Or lack of it?"

He hesitated again before answering. "I'm gonna give it a go. If the guy's covering up something criminal, that makes it my department. If he's not, no story. But at least I'll know." He stood. "So. Let me go cover my assignments."

"Okay," she said. "If you hear anything, you'll let me know?"

"It's a two-way street, right?"

"Of course," she said, smiling again.

Of course. He walked away, more uneasy than ever. Two-way street, hell. Something was going on. A bio with nothing checkable in it should have set all Nicki's bells ringing; either it hadn't, or it had and she hadn't reacted. Either way, something funny. Could Nicki and Gorman be—

He shook himself mentally. Not a chance. Nicki might be tight with Ibrani. He had money and polish, and wasn't a bad guy, really. But Gorman—no way. All Gorman had was a connection with Jason Goodmaster.

But Jesus sweet Christ, what a connection. What hadn't been in Gorman's bio had been in other, harder-to-get-at references.

Like, for example, Bill Wallace's head. Wallace, by day, was the president of the Meadbury-Colonial Savings Bank. By night he was father to an adorable seven-year-old girl named Amy. Wallace had somehow gotten the idea that Conklin had helped save his Amy's life, a couple of years ago when that pretty blond toddler was in the hands of some nasty fellows.

The nasty fellows had thought Bill Wallace would give them big money for one small girl. They had been right. But a guy named Weasel Bodine had come to Conklin with a sniff of what was going on.

Conklin had paid him for the sniff, then gone to Wallace. He'd stuck with Wallace for thirty-six hours, getting the story. All of it. And holding it.

Until a small blond girl named Amy was back in her own four-poster canopied bed. By that time, of course, it was old news. Wallace owed Conklin a favor, a favor Conklin had finally thought it was time to call in.

Jason Goodmaster had not only given Gorman personal references, enabling him to get the Chevy sales job that established Gorman in Meadbury, he'd also given Gorman substantial loans.

Jason Goodmaster lending money to someone without a Dun & Bradstreet rating was like . . . heck, it was like a palm tree at the North Pole. It just didn't happen.

But it had. Why? There had to be some connection between the two men.

Now Conklin wondered just how intimate the connection was. The coincidence of the first letter of the last name . . . because it had to be coincidence. Conklin, more curious than ever after his talk with Bill Wallace, had gone to the trouble of checking out the pertinent blood types.

Easy enough: Gorman was a recent blood donor—part of his public relations campaign, no doubt—and Goodmaster had once been admitted for a dental procedure. That meant Meadbury Hospital's mountain of records held their blood types, and Conklin had always made it a point to be friendly with all the right clerks, at the hospital and everywhere else.

Result: The older man could not have fathered the younger. The reverse, of course, being clearly impossible. . . .

But if it wasn't blood, then what was it? Extortion?

Could Ned Gorman be blackmailing Meadbury's foremost citizen?

Again, he thought not.

But he thought also that he would find out.

And what the hell was the matter with Nicki, anyway?

Tommy Riley

Red satin bows noosed the poodle-numerals jumping through hoops beneath the big top. At center ring stood the robed, hooded ringmaster, hands up his sleeves, his eyes in shadow. The crowd roared approval. Ground coffee shifted in inches-high drifts on the tent floor, its aroma sweet, though bitter-tinged and somehow threatening. Up on the high wire a countdown clock balanced, swaying, heart-stoppingly precarious.

Hissing, popping flames ran riot around the hoops the number-dogs leapt through. The numerals cringed, each dropping the tail of the one before it, whimpering cravenly.

Hush in the audience. The ringmaster clapped his hands —once.

And the show went on. Red bow ties blazed up, smelling like burnt toast. Tossing back his cowl, the ringmaster shouted, "Tommy Riley! Get up! You're late for work!"

His eyes snapped open like a camera's shutter. Above him, light from the hall threw a blocky yellow swatch on the ceiling. He lifted his head. His mother's round figure stood silhouetted in the doorway.

Own room. Own bed. Yes.

His eyes fell shut. He tossed back his hood, the sweet smell of coffee rising around him, his eyes on the high wire. The countdown clock read:

2:57
(blink)
2:56
(blink)
2:55
(blink)
2:54

His mouth moved.

"It says I have almost three minutes, Ma."

"What?" His mother came into the room. "Get up, you're dreaming. And you're late for work. Come on now, breakfast is waiting. Tommy. Up."

He surrendered. Sat up. "I'm on a new shift, Ma. Eleven to seven."

"It's dark then," she said. "Why that shift? I thought Mr. Gorman liked you."

He folded his legs up, hands on his knees. He could give his mother a thousand reasons why he had taken the shift. The simplest came first: "I didn't have a choice, Ma."

She made a noise of exasperation. "Of course you had a choice. You could have said, 'No, I won't do that.' If they really value you like you say, they'll be reasonable. If they won't, it means they don't value you, and you don't want to work for them if they feel that way. Simple."

Yeah. Easy for her to say.

His alarm buzzed, saving him the problem of replying.

"I got to get up now, Ma."

"All right." Backing out of the room, she pulled the door almost shut, then pushed it open again. "But don't go back to sleep."

"I won't, I won't."

The door shut again and he fell back in bed. Mothers. What was it with them? They buy you an alarm clock and then never trust it to wake you up. Probably if there were robots that carried you from the bed into the shower and turned the water on you, mothers would still come in to make sure you got good and wet.

He hauled himself up again, calculating as he stumbled down the hall into the bathroom. Let's say you lose two minutes fifty— No, she was early today, try an average of two thirty.

Crank on the hot spray, step underneath it . . . two minutes and thirty seconds of sleep, that's 150 seconds a day times 7 equals 1050 seconds a week more'n fifty-two thousand seconds a year fifty-four? fifty-five? And somewhere in there is the soap, ninety-nine and forty-four percent pure divided by 3600 seconds an hour, five forty divided by thirty-six, aw, round it off to forty and throw in the towel, fifty-four divided by four is thirteen and a half, jeez, a night and a half's sleep you lose just 'cause your mother doesn't trust the alarm.

At which point, somewhat to his surprise, he found himself standing before the mirror adjusting his tie. His hair had been combed wet. Had he slept through a whole shower? And got dressed, too? The idea unnerved him, but his appearance provided distraction.

You look sharp, Riley. Just like she said.

He patted the gun belted on his hip. Ma was cool about some things. Like the revolver. Some mothers would get seriously hysterical having a loaded piece in the house. Not her, though. Uh-uh. She not only accepted it as part of his job, she tried but failed to disguise her pride in a son she'd raised to be responsible enough to be trusted with something so dangerous.

Funny how she still worried about him coming home after dark, though. He fiddled with the tie a final time. Probably mothers never got over worrying that their darlings would get beat up by the big kids.

Well, Ma— He smiled at himself in the mirror, then grimaced. That was a little boy's smile, not a cop's. Come on, try again, a little less excitable, a little more, uh, Clint Eastwood, yeah, and a little less goddamn eager. Yeah.

Ma, your darling is *one of the big kids now.*

But even at the advanced age of nineteen he was not too big to read the comics over breakfast. He did not laugh as hard as he used to, especially at Beetle Bailey, but Peanuts still made him chuckle, and he liked Bloom County when it was not making fun of the government.

Then he gave his mother a peck on the cheek, peered into the sparkling windowpanes of the back door to adjust his hat, and headed out.

The car started right up, pleasing him immensely. He had spent a good deal of time lately cleaning and adjusting the engine. It ran like a charm, now.

He slipped into traffic and settled back. Jeez, he loved driving. Horsepower throbbing, the rules so plain and simple, the other drivers not obstacles or competitors but partners in the most complexly choreographed dance he knew. One mistake could cost half a dozen innocent lives.

He liked that part almost best of all.

Still, it wasn't hard, not if he relaxed. Sitting back, seat belt snug across his waist and shoulder, he looked at the other drivers and at once understood them. Anticipated them. Like there was a little voice in his head telling him all about the other folks on the road, what they did, where they were going, what they were about to do next. He liked that, too.

Because he certainly didn't want to hurt anybody. Not by accident anyway.

The guy to his left, in the grey Mercedes: a lawyer driving down to the courthouse. He would not budge from the middle lane for thirty blocks, Tommy knew. But he would go faster than he ought to because the hearing would start in fifteen minutes, with him or without him.

Now, the den mother driving the blue Celica directly ahead would not speed up because she wanted to go right at the next light. In another twenty feet her turn signal would come on— There. Just as predicted.

But the den mother wouldn't go around the corner; she would stop. Because an old lady was going to be crossing the other street by then. Tommy lifted his foot off the gas and coasted until the Celica's brake lights flashed. By that time the Mercedes had eased on by toward the lawyer's appointment with fate, leaving a gap between the Mercedes and the plumbers in the pickup just behind.

Tommy touched his indicator and nudged his car one lane to the left, smooth and gentle and very satisfying. He only wished the shelter lay on the other side of town instead of smack-dab in the middle, because no matter where he started from, it never took him more than a couple of minutes to get there.

In fact, reaching the parking lot was the only part of the job he didn't like; then he had to put the car keys back in his pocket, not to be used till the end of the shift.

He did just that, and checked that the car's door was locked. Yeah. He stretched, then shivered as the chill wind grabbed at his leather uniform jacket, tugged at his hat brim.

Hand on his hat, he ran for the door. Wallace Wallabee, another guard, motioned him in with an envious grimace. "Say, hotshot, the office just called for you."

"Yeah?" Tommy glanced around the lobby. Pretty quiet this morning.

"Yeah," Wallabee said. "They're reassigning you; they want you down for a briefing ay-sap."

"'Aysap'?"

"A.S.A.P., Riley, A.S.A.P. As soon as possible, that's what ay-sap means." Wallabee shook his balding head, clearly wondering what the office wanted with someone as ignorant as Riley.

"Oh, sure," Tommy said. "Uh, but did they say why? I mean, who's replacing me here?" He scratched uneasily at his memory, wondering if he had done something wrong. Mr. Gorman had said he was doing okay, but that was last week.

"Replacing? Nobody." Wallabee snapped his fingers. "Say, I'll bet you didn't hear."

"Hear what?" Tommy glanced around again. In fact, he didn't hear anything. Or see anybody, either. No one but Wallabee. "Hey! The place is empty."

"No shit, Sherlock." Wallabee grinned in sarcastic appreciation of Tommy's powers of observation. But he went on to explain, mostly because he liked explaining things to people he thought were dumber than him.

"Gorman, he worked some kind of deal with uh, I guess it must be the shirt factory, 'cause they're the only ones I know putting on a new shift. Anyway, everybody who was here got a job and left."

"So they closed the shelter?"

"Well, they got nobody who needs it any more, you know? What I hear is, they're gonna wait a couple months, see if they missed anybody out on the streets, right? And then if they can't find any more winos or bag ladies, this is gonna be like a dorm or something for the university."

Gee, that was fast, Tommy thought. Then he slapped the thought away. Of course it was fast. Mr. Gorman was efficient. "Wow, that's great," he said.

"Yeah." Wallabee leaned back against the front desk and hooked his thumbs through his pistol belt, looking as thoughtful as he was able. "Yeah, it's great, all right. You don't know how great."

"Sure I do!"

"Nah, you're still a kid, you know? What're you, maybe nineteen? Wait'll you pay city taxes, you'll know how I feel. Relieved, that's how. Say, there was the city, pissin' away my money on a lotta winos, though I gotta be honest, I needed the work myself. Yeah, I thought this was gonna be just another hole to pour my money down." He shook his head in admiration. "That Ned Gorman, though, he's really something. Made it work the way he said, can you beat that? Yeah, he's got my vote."

"For what?" Tommy frowned.

Wallabee shrugged. "Anything he wants it for." The older man chuckled at Tommy's expression. "You'll learn, Riley. Just a kid yet, you think it's all a cakewalk. But guys like Ned Gorman, they're always running for something or other. Sometimes it's an election, sometimes it's an appointment. Either way I'm for him. He did a real good job here, and in this day and age, that's something. He don't have to pretend he done it for his health, not to me." He glanced at his wristwatch. "Say, you better get going."

"Oh, right! Thanks. And hey! I'll see you around, huh?"

"That you will, friend." Wallabee hitched up his belt, which promptly slid back down the underside of his paunch. "Good luck."

"Thanks. And you, too." Wallabee was like that; started out sour every morning, then talked himself friendly. Tommy threw him a salute and strode back to his car.

Great! He got to drive down to Meadbury Guaranty, and then (he would not let himself consider the awful alternative) out to his new job site. He wondered where it would be. The shirt factory would probably need some guards, especially if they'd just hired all those losers.

He made a face at himself. *Riley, Riley, have charity, like they teach you in church. "There but for the grace of God," huh? Those bums—*

No. Those people didn't want to be that way. They had problems, problems they could solve if only they would work at them. And if they all found jobs at the shirt factory, it meant they were working at their problems, didn't it? And so the factory wouldn't necessarily need more guards, would it? 'Course not.

But cruising down Oak Street, relaxed behind the wheel, he suddenly burst out laughing. No, of course it wouldn't need more guards. Considering the way those winos were housebroken, what that factory needed was janitors, a whole new shift of them. And about a billion mops.

Still grinning, he pulled into the parking lot behind the Meadbury Guaranty building and sprinted up the outside staircase.

Old Mrs. Hegelios' black eyes flashed behind her bifocals as he went in and closed the door behind him. "Thomas Riley?" she said dubiously, though he had told her his name a thousand times and by now she ought to know it.

"Yes, ma'am," he said.

She picked up a pencil and reached for a piece of paper on the corner of her desk. "Do you know where 681 Main Street is?"

He shrugged. "I can find it. What's up?"

"You're to go see Mr. Ned Gorman at that address, Suite B-30, right away." Brushing aside a thin lock of white hair, she printed the address for him.

"Okay." He kept his expression bland, but inside he was elated. More driving! After a while he would know Meadbury like the cracks in his bedroom ceiling. And what a great opportunity it would be if he got to work for Mr. Gorman again.

"Will I be assigned there, or what?"

"Young man." Mrs. Hegelios peered over the top of her glasses at him and rapped the side of her typewriter with the pencil. Her expression said that she might next rap his knuckles. "I have told you everything I know. Just report to Mr. Gorman at that address. Perhaps he will tell you more."

"Yes, ma'am." He touched the brim of his cap with the tip of his right index finger. An Air-Force-ace kind of gesture, he'd seen it on the late movie the other night. Respectful familiarity, breezy and relaxed, everything he wanted to show. And be. "I'm on my way, ma'am."

She sniffed, but smiled grudgingly.

He grinned all the way back down to his car.

681 Main. Easy to find. Cruise up the street, one eye on the numbers. Not on blond secretaries in wind-whipped coats that flew apart to flash stunning swathes of sheer nylon, not on the red-cheeked high school girls whose pleated skirt hems didn't come within shouting distance of their knee-sock tops, not even on the gorgeous reporter from the Meadbury *Bulletin*, who was just now leaving the office building emblazoned with the brassy numerals 681, but—

Six eighty-one? Right. Okay. He pulled into an empty space and looked over his shoulder, but Miss Pialosta had disappeared around the corner. Oh, well. Sooner or later he would see her again.

A frigid wind numbed his chest as he dropped a coin into the meter and crossed the wide sidewalk, making him wish he had listened to his mother just this once and zipped his jacket. But that would hide his badge, his uniform shirt, and at least part of his service revolver. Besides, the admiring look from the cute little redhead just inside the building melted the frost off his ribs, and then some.

Unfortunately, she disappeared into a ground-floor door, so he did not get a chance to talk to her on the elevator. *Yeah, and what would you say to her, anyway, smart guy? Stick the gun in her ribs and tell her to lie down, maybe?*

The thought shocked him; he banished it at once. Suite B-30 turned out to be the northwest corner office on the second floor. Outside it, a guy Tommy vaguely remembered from shop class was painting letters on the door's frosted glass. The letters, black and shiny-wet, spelled "Ned Gor."

The guy looked up, his freckled face brightening. "Riley, my man!"

The guy's name came back in a rush. "Yo, Brockway!"

They high-fived in the deserted hallway. "Hey," Tommy said, feeling daring and nostalgic, "Hey, looks like you took ol' Brush Head's teachings to heart, man."

Bob Brockway rubbed his crew-cut scalp self-consciously. "Hey, I, uh, needed a job, you know? Sooz hadda quit the café when the kid came, and, y'know, like, this is what there was." He stepped back and ran his gaze up and down Tommy's uniform. "Whoo! A rent-a-cop, huh? You breaking hearts with the uniform, or what?"

Tommy shrugged, meaning to make a relaxed, breezy comment. But the comment went out of his head as he realized he'd been told to report to Mr. Gorman immediately, besides which he was on company time. Standing in the hallway, wasting that time, just to shoot the bull with an old high school buddy—that was wrong.

Not that Brockway had ever been a buddy. An acquaintance. A face you said hello to. Nothing more.

He hitched up his gunbelt, nodded to the door. "The man wants me," he said shortly.

Brockway's smile faded; he swept an arm toward the frosted glass. "Well, excu-u-u-u-se me."

Without acknowledging the insolence, for that would be lowering himself, Tommy stepped past the painter, whose name was almost on the tip of his tongue, and went on into the office.

Inside, Ned Gorman sat at a large metal desk whose top was covered with papers. "Riley." He gestured to a chair in front of the desk.

"Hi, Mr. Gorman." He sat in the chair and folded his hands in his lap. "They told me—"

"In a minute, Riley." Gorman bent his head over the papers and frowned at them. He took a gold mechanical pencil from his pocket, made a show of twisting it to advance the lead, then scratched a tiny note on a sheet of paper. Finally, with a sound of satisfaction, he leaned back in his leather swivel chair and squinted at Riley.

"So," he said.

Tommy nodded, not sure now what was expected of him. "Yes, sir?"

"You were born here, weren't you, Riley?"

"In Meadbury? Yes, sir, I was."

"Ever lived anywhere else?"

"No, sir." He shrugged. "The only time I've even spent the night anywhere else was Boy Scout camp up in Maine." He glanced up, then quickly shut up. From the look on Mr. Gorman's face, it was clear he didn't want to hear about that.

Mr. Gorman touched the pencil to the paper again, leaving another comment in microscopic handwriting. "Tell me, Riley, would you be willing to relocate?"

Tommy's guts tightened. The thought of leaving Meadbury set off an unexpected, panicky kind of feeling, as though he could not quite get enough air. Still he tried to keep his face placid.

"Where, sir? If it's all right for me to ask," he added at Gorman's quick frown.

"Boston. I'll be needing someone there."

"Wh-why—" Tommy's voice cracked; cursing silently he clenched his teeth and started over. "Why not just hire somebody from one of the Boston agencies? Sir."

"I am looking for someone I can trust, Riley." Gorman spoke slowly, patiently, but he did not look patient at all. He looked like someone about to pounce on the wrong answer. Or on the wrong guy.

Don't be a wrong guy, Riley.

"Well, sir, I—"

"Never mind talk. You've been recommended. Will you take the job or not?"

"Boston?"

"Yes, Riley. Boston."

Tommy licked his suddenly dry lips. His mother's words came back to him: "You could have said, 'No.'"

This, he felt sure, was what people meant when they talked about crossroads in life, only they never said you could hit the crossroads so fast. The decision he was about to make would affect him until the day he died, he was certain of it. He wished to God he knew what the right answer was.

In the end, he flipped a mental coin. Imagined it, tossed it, and in a split second made himself say how he wanted it to come down.

Then he sat up straight. "No, sir."

Gorman blinked. "Pardon?"

"I don't want the job, sir."

"Why not? We pay all expenses involved in relocation. And Boston's a fine, cosmopolitan city."

Tommy moved uncomfortably in the chair. "It's not that, sir."

"What, then?"

He groped for an explanation that a man like Mr. Gorman would understand. "It's just, I know it sounds silly, but it's just that my life is here, sir." Then he wanted to sink right through the floor. *What a sap answer.*

But to Tommy's surprise, Gorman smiled warmly. "You really think so, Riley?"

"Yes, sir." He had made the right choice. Gorman's expression and his own feelings said so.

"All right, then. In that case, I have a different job for you. One right here in Meadbury."

Relief flooded through him. He would not be fired after all. He'd done what he wanted, and kept his job. "What is it, sir?"

Gorman leaned forward again, lifting aside a stack of papers to uncover what looked like the remote control unit for a television set. He picked it up and began to fiddle with it. "Well, Riley—"

The door at the back of the office banged open; Tommy flung himself around in the chair. A short, skinny man with a nylon stocking pulled over his face had slammed into the room, a long knife glittering in his hand.

Holy cripes, it's Weasel— from the shelter. Even through the stocking, his pointy rodent face was unmistakable. *Yeah, he found work all right, and not at any shirt factory.* Either this was a stickup of some kind or Weasel had finally flipped what was left of his lid.

But even as he thought this, Tommy was moving: on his feet, legs braced apart, left hand steadying his right as it aimed the heavy revolver at Weasel.

"Freeze!" The order left his mouth effortlessly, echoing off the bare walls. How, he wondered, had he moved so quickly, so surely? And why the hell didn't the worthless little bastard make a move, too, so Tommy could blow his brains out right here and now? *Ah, the hell with it—* His finger began to pull back the trigger in an easy, gentle squeeze.

Gorman, too, was on his feet, and now Tommy became aware that Gorman was applauding. "Well done, Riley, well done indeed!" Then he turned to the intruder. "Thank you, Mr. Bodine, that'll be all for now."

Weasel didn't move. Through the sheer nylon his dark eyes stared down the barrel of Tommy's gun. "Uh, boss—?" he said shakily.

"Oh, of course." Gorman chuckled. "Riley? You can let him go, Riley."

Tommy looked at Mr. Gorman out of the corner of his eyes, still pinning Weasel, who appeared to have wet his pants. "Sir?"

"I said it's okay, son. This was a test. You can put the gun away."

"Oh. Yes, sir." He tried to conceal his disappointment, but Weasel saw even if Gorman did not. Relaxing, pointing the pistol at the ceiling, Tommy thumbed the safety back into position and returned the weapon to its holster.

"Sorry," he said insincerely to Weasel. "I didn't know."

"You weren't supposed to, Riley," Gorman told him. "As I said, this was a test. Of your reflexes."

Very quietly, Weasel went out.

"Yes, sir," Tommy said. His anger fading, now, he wondered what had made him so mad at stupid Weasel, a guy who'd do anything for twenty bucks.

Meanwhile, a part of him—a small, nearly voiceless part—was speaking quietly. *My gun was loaded. I almost shot him. What kind of person would stage that kind of test? And what would Mr. Gorman want with the kind of person who could pass it?*

Aloud, though, he said nothing more, merely waited.

"Flying colors, Riley, just flying colors." Gorman clapped him on the shoulder. "I knew you had it in you."

"Thank you, sir," Tommy said, knowing Gorman had meant that last part as a compliment.

"I believe you'll do just fine for the spot I've got in mind."

"And what's that, sir?" Hijacker? Assassin?

"Personal bodyguard," said Gorman, "to Mr. Jason Goodmaster."

Gravel crunched under the car's tires as Tommy made his way up the long driveway, toward Goodmaster Mansion.

He clutched the wheel in something like shock, still hardly believing: He was guarding Jason Goodmaster, the most important person in Meadbury. Maybe the most important person in the whole state.

No wonder they gave hard tests. Ma was going to die when she heard about this.

His hands shook on the steering wheel. He brought the car to a halt by a patch of looming evergreens, put it in park, and spoke sternly to himself.

Jeez, Riley, chill out. It's not like you're in the Secret Service or anything. Jason Goodmaster doesn't have crazies coming at him all day and all night. That Weasel stuff, that was just in case. Sure, it's a big responsibility, but not too big. Not for you. Mr. Gorman wouldn't have appointed you if he didn't think you could do it. So chill out, huh?

Along with a few deep breaths, that steadied him; enough, anyway, so that he could put the car back in gear and roll on up toward the massive house.

A hundred yards more and the drive diverged; without thinking, he took the right fork, the one that led to the back entrance of the mansion. A liveried chauffeur eyed him haughtily, then pointed to a spot beneath a bare-limbed maple.

Tommy parked there and got out, hitching up his belt and tugging his cap down. Then he zipped his jacket almost to the collar, leaving it open just enough to show the knot of his dark tie.

A gravel path led to the back door, which a balding, stiff-spined butler opened as Tommy reached it.

Now what do I say, "Hi, I'm your hired gun"? But the butler saved him the trouble.

"Riley?" The little man's pursed lips barely moved.

"Yes."

"Throtway." He twitched his head. "In."

Tommy stepped past the rigid old servant, his heart beating fast again all of a sudden. Now he was in a hallway;

linoleum, wallpaper. White-painted woodwork, semigloss. On the floor, along the wall, some sheets of newspaper; work boots and galoshes lined up there. Far down the hall a door stood ajar; beyond it he glimpsed a washer and dryer.

So far, so good. He took a deep breath, trying to hide his nerves. Throtway's glance flickered at him; he thought he caught a gleam of malicious amusement.

But that, of course, was his imagination.

"Coat goes there." The old man jerked his chin toward a row of hooks on the wall; two raincoats, one cloth coat with a tattered fur collar, and a brace of umbrellas already hung there.

Tommy slipped out of his jacket and hung it on the last hook.

"Wipe your feet."

He did.

"Follow me, then." Throtway turned, not toward the laundry room but down another high-ceilinged passageway. It made a sharp left turn and opened into a large room tiled with black marble. Six straight-backed chairs with red cushions stood against the walls, three on a side.

The butler's shoes made no noise on the tile. Tommy's did. His toes cringed, as he tried to be quiet, but it was no use.

Throtway stopped at a pair of wooden doors at least twelve feet high. Their panels, gleamingly varnished, showed scenes from life in Puritan New England: a man in stocks, girls and women spinning and weaving, another man driving a pair of oxen. The final panel depicted men, women, and children carrying stones. Their faces looked strange, eager and scared all at once.

Like me.

"Wait here." The butler opened the right-hand door with a fingertip and slipped noiselessly into the room beyond.

Tommy waited, not looking at the doors again. The pictures made him feel funny.

A few minutes later Throtway returned, passing Tommy without a single glance, disappearing back down the long passageway.

Another man stepped through the doors. Perhaps an inch taller than Riley, a bit more stooped at the shoulders, but more imposing . . . lots more. He wore a white silk dress shirt with a brown silk scarf knotted at the throat, brown velvet jacket, dark slacks, and soft-looking patent-leather slippers. His hair was pure white, as were his thick eyebrows, and his eyes were blue, paintbox blue, a blue that just kept coming at you.

In the one quick glance Tommy allowed himself, he felt his whole idea of proper male grooming and dress change forever. Suddenly his badge and gun seemed tacky, like part of a Keystone Kops costume; his blue uniform shirt, already wrinkled and moist with nervous perspiration, clung grossly at his armpits and across his back.

The old man kept looking Tommy up and down. Finally he spoke. "Thomas Riley?"

"Yes, sir." Tommy stared straight ahead.

"I am Jason Goodmaster."

"Yes, sir."

"You are here to protect me."

"Yes, sir."

"With your life, if it comes to that?"

"Yes, sir," Tommy said, hoping it wouldn't.

The old man eyed him, then nodded almost imperceptibly. "Carry on, then." He turned back toward the room behind the painted doors, then stopped, eyeing Tommy a final time.

Just for a moment, but long enough. Long enough to wrinkle his nose and sniff. Meaningfully. In repugnance.

Standing there ramrod-straight, Tommy thought he might just drop dead of pure shame. Jeez, his very first minute on the job and what did he have to go and do but stink?

First chance he got, he would go home and shower. Absolutely. Use more deodorant, too. Lots more.

And wasn't there something . . . something called bay rum?

Yeah. He'd try some of that.

Ben Ibrani

From where he stood, naked and quivering with pain in the middle of his bedroom, Ben Ibrani could see the shotguns racked in their glass case a few feet away. Not far, really, not unreachable. Just out in the living room, maybe a dozen steps or so.

Clutching the back of a chair for support, Ibrani whimpered at the thought of taking those steps. His hands throbbed from gripping the chairback's top rail; he'd been in one position for nearly ten hours, now. He didn't dare move, for moving would make it worse.

More of the mewing sounds escaped him. But noises like that were all right here, weren't they? Here in his own apartment he could cry. Of course, it wasn't manly of him; still, it was necessary. And discreet. So that was all right, then, he thought through a haze of pain.

The guns, though. He stared dully at them, at the oiled-walnut case toward which, if he mastered the anguish long enough, he might manage to stagger. Or crawl. Then he could put himself out of his misery.

Because this was the worst, worse even than the night back in college when Uncle Jason had made him change his major. That time he had given in almost immediately, as Uncle Jason must have known he would.

That time he had passed out. Last night, he hadn't. Scrubbing and scrubbing until he ought to have been unconscious ten times over, longing and begging for release from the awful pain his own hands dealt him, still he stood under the steaming spray. Upright, wide awake. Weeping.

And scrubbing himself. Rubbing and scrubbing. Abrading. Scraping. He couldn't pass out; something wouldn't let him. And he couldn't stop, because if he stopped an infinitely worse thing would happen: The filth would rise up and ooze down his throat, plug his nostrils, stop his breath.

God, he belonged in a hospital—or on a marble slab. The idea of the smooth, cool stone sent a spasm of yearning through him, followed by more pain as his hopeless wish for relief set him helplessly shivering again.

Every blink and shudder, every shift of his stiff, cramped

muscles ripped sizzling flames through his raw skin. Sweat dripped from the few dime-sized patches the wire brush had somehow missed; it trickled, stung, seared.

What the hell was wrong with his body, he wondered with the little part of his mind still capable of coherent thought, that it refused to short-circuit and plunge him into the dark?

And what was wrong with Uncle Jason, that he would force Ibrani to do this to himself?

His neck hairs prickled suddenly. Something unseen but all too real stood behind him, glowering at his naked back.

I didn't mean that! Honest, I didn't. Whatever you want, that's okay, I'll do it. Just, please, don't ever make this happen again.

As if in response, the hateful thing hovering behind him softened, mellowed. Cracklings of malice flickered and winked out. Whatever it was regarded him fondly. Approvingly.

That scared him even more than its anger, but fear washed away on a sudden tide of relief, as, incredibly, the pain eased.

He almost wept again. He didn't care why he felt better. Shock, or the thing in the room, rewarding him—nothing mattered except that he could breathe without torment. For the first time since he had staggered out of the pink froth in the shower stall, he was not on fire. Sore, stiff, stinging, yes; but not in anguish.

The telephone on his bedside table rang.

Ibrani groaned. *No way.*

It rang again. Then two more things happened: The pain vanished utterly, and slime began spreading, mucous tendrils inchworming horridly on his cheeks, invading his nostrils.

Filthy slime, germ-ridden slime. Slime that had to be scraped off, now, at once, with a stiff wire brush—

The phone rang a third time.

Pain returned; filth fled.

And now he understood. *Carrot and stick. Answer the phone. Or . . . rub-a-dub-dub, blood in the tub. Slime and punishment.*

Gritting his teeth, he reached for the receiver, forcing back bitter laughter harsh as a scream. Movement now did not hurt at all. That did not surprise him any more. Uncle Jason had won. He lifted the receiver. "Ibrani here."

"Ben? Bill Lessopa from the *Daily Investigator.* We met last year at the awards banquet?"

Oh, God. Sick resentment seized him: The whole damn world going on as usual. Never mind that he'd just nearly flayed himself alive. . . . But he forced cordiality into his voice. "Sure, I remember, Bill. How have you been?"

"Just fine, just fine, listen, I'm sorry to bother you at home, but we caught the wire story on the curfew you people have set up, up there. It looks like our kind of story, but my tightwad publisher wanted me to make a few calls before I sent a guy, check it out."

"Uh-huh," Ibrani said carefully, his mind racing. Now he did remember Lessopa, and the *Daily Investigator.* In his opinion Lessopa's paper was good for just one thing: lining the bottom of a birdcage, where it could soak up the same sort of material it published. That rag didn't cover stories, it excreted them, then smeared the result over every supermarket checkout counter in America. "Uh, so what can I do for you, Bill?" His mind's eye already saw Lessopa's garish headline: "Meadbury: The Town That Hates Kids!"

"For openers, this: Is it worth the plane fare?"

"Mmm. . . ." Ibrani stalled for time, as if pondering the question. He had never in his life lied to a colleague, and he found it difficult to do so for the first time. Almost as difficult as thinking of Lessopa as a colleague. . . . "I don't mean to insult you, Bill, but I don't think your guy would get a *DI* kind of story out of this."

"How do you mean?"

"Well, there's certainly no controversy about it."

"You mean the kids aren't screaming?" Lessopa snorted his skepticism.

Ibrani thought fast. "Oh, some of them are grumbling, sure, but even they know that homework has to come first."

"Homework?" Now frank disbelief rose in Lessopa's voice. "What the hell do you mean, 'homework'? Your own article talked about juvenile crime, Ben. You telling me you sit the little punks down, make 'em do their ABCs?"

"That was just our gal trying to sell papers," said Ibrani swiftly. "And remember, I'm the features editor, not the city editor. I'm not responsible for what they print, even though I sometimes feel like I am. The fact is, we've got a very good situation here. The curfew is simply the town's move to keep it that way."

"So tell me about homework, Ben," said Lessopa, his tone challenging.

"Our kids've always scored in the top quartile on all the standardized tests—Iowa, PSATs, SATs, the works. But that's not good enough any more, Bill. It's a new world out there. Our kids compete fine with other American kids, but they're not at the level of, say, the Japanese. They know it. And they don't like it."

Ibrani took a deep breath. "So. The PTA, and the school board, and the student council petitioned city council for a curfew during the school year, so kids would stay at home and study instead of hanging out and generally wasting time. And that's it. That's all there is to it."

"The student council supported this?"

"Why, yes," said Ibrani. "In fact I believe they first suggested it." Lying through his teeth, now, but what the hell. What Lessopa wanted to do was worse.

"Who paid 'em off, that's what I want to know." Lessopa chuckled. "Ben, this sounds really dull."

"What can I say, Bill?" Ibrani tried to keep relief from his voice. "Around here, academic standards are a vital issue." Then, worried but wanting to hammer his point home, he took a calculated risk:

"Listen, why don't you send somebody in, assign him to, oh, a week in the high school? Let him go to class, do the homework, take the tests. You'll get an upbeat piece, but hell, why not run an upbeat article for once? You know? Show a city that really works, instead of focusing on the fuck-ups. We're proud of Meadbury; you'll get some great quotes."

Ibrani waited, but all he heard was the hum of a silent line. It made him want to cheer. "Bill?"

"Uh, yeah, Ben. Thanks for the offer, but listen, I think you were right in the first place. There really isn't a *DI* story here. Only nice towns our readers want are ones with ax murderers loose in 'em. So thanks again. Catch you at the conference next year, eh? Bye."

The phone clicked in Ibrani's ear, and after a moment the dial tone droned.

With a sigh of relief, he put down the receiver.

Something pulsed gratitude at him.

He stiffened. *No. It's me, something's wrong with me. Nothing's here, it's all in my mind. I'm doing these things to myself, mutilating myself.*

Because he'd much rather be insane than have the thing be real, the thing standing behind him. . . .

Swiftly, it enveloped him in a mantle of searing anguish.

He screamed, and it drew back, his nerve endings fluttering in terrified anticipation of the next bolt. But instead, the pain dropped away with each thudding beat of his heart, until it was gone.

Convinced?

His shoulders sagged. *Please don't hurt me again.* Oh yes, he was convinced even as his brain said that what he now knew could not be true.

The thing was real, all right, not a psychosis. He wasn't insane.

But it was. And it had him.

Weariness hit him like a brickbat, fatigue so crushing it took all his will not to drop where he stood. His eyelids felt weighted down, closing in spite of him. Distantly he felt his legs moving, carrying him to his bed.

He clawed back the blankets, yanked blindly at the sheets, wrapped his arms around the long-awaited heaven of his pillow.

He shivered once as the thing in the room smiled down on him, patting him gently.

And he went to sleep thinking it was over.

But it wasn't over. Midafternoon: He woke in the room's curtained darkness to the sound of heels clicking across the parquet floor of the living room. A woman's step, coming nearer.

He lifted his head, and a bolt of pain shocked him breathless, paralyzing him.

A warning. He understood.

I won't move. The pain vanished.

Trembling relief did not count as motion, apparently.

A whiff of perfume reached his nostrils, the scent spicy-sweet and familiar. And very desirable.

May I speak?

A burning brand sizzled into his forehead.

All right, I won't, please, just don't hurt me any more!

Again the pain subsided. So he would not move or speak. He would just lie there, spread-eagled and motionless, and it would not hurt him. He hoped.

Behind his closed eyelids, Ben Ibrani waited in a misery of fright, acutely aware that every inch of his body lay naked and exposed to someone moving toward him. A female someone. . . .

Apprehension turned to icy slush in the pit of his stomach as he realized, with sudden bleak clarity, who that someone was.

And what she was about to do.

Rather, what she would be made to do. . . .

"Don't open your eyes, Ben." Nicki's voice, expressionless.

He heard shoes drop to the carpet, the rasp of a zipper. Cloth whispering, falling. Her scent was stronger now, carried on waves of heat from her body, very near him.

He gasped with the sudden shock of her touch, rose to the firm manipulation of her soft hands. It was as if all the pain he had suffered now concentrated itself, transformed itself to a fiery core of pleasure at his very center.

Warmth rippled liquidly down the sinews of his thighs, her nails raking lightly. Her hair brushed his belly like warm perfumed feathers. Her hands grazed his hips, then slipped underneath, her fingers probing, insisting.

Invading. He moaned with the pleasure of it, then bit his lip to keep from crying out again. Helplessly he lifted himself to her searching mouth. Delight spread in coursing waves, urging him. God, he had known she would be like this. Nicki. . . .

Nicki. The thought knifed coldly through a maelstrom of sensation; he shrank and grew chill. This wasn't Nicki; at least, not the Nicki he knew. He'd been right in his apprehension, but for a few moments she had made him forget. Or something had.

Because nothing he knew of her made him think she

would ever come here like this of her own accord. She had never even been in his apartment before.

As she waited, hovering over him questioningly, he wondered if she knew she was here.

A few hours ago, he'd been wondering why he was the only one to whimper and cringe beneath the crack of a spectre's whip.

Now he knew he wasn't the only one. For if the thing that Uncle Jason sent to torture him was real and not a product of his disordered mind, then it was not necessarily confined to him, was it? It could find others, tempt them and hurt them.

It could bring Nicki here.

He could send her away. He could lift his head, tell Nicki to go, throw her out if he had to. And fight his demon to the death once she had gone. At least he knew it was real, now, acknowledged it and knew it by its name: Uncle Jason.

The other choice was to obey. Give up; give in. Whatever Nicki knew or thought, her body was here right now, waiting for him. He'd wanted her all along. Why not take her?

Take, and be taken. Like a good little puppet.

She shifted impatiently over him, and he wondered how it had been done to her. He had always wondered—he realized it, now that he permitted himself to acknowledge it—how Uncle Jason controlled the others. And what those others thought, if they thought at all, while they submitted to Uncle Jason's control. Performed for him, as Ben was about to perform. Because no matter how he might try to deny it, he knew that eventually he would give in.

He was so afraid.

"Ben," she said.

Still he hesitated for another instant. In that moment rancid grease oozed from the pores of his belly; it spread up and down his body in a flash; he must clean it off right away, scour it off now, scrub it off—

He made a small noise in his throat, a noise halfway between sobbing and laughter, because no matter how it looked, no matter what anyone thought, he was suffering even as he obeyed.

"Don't talk," she said, and although her voice was dead

and lifeless her hands were alive, her hands and her mouth and her long, slim legs. . . .

With a despairing internal groan he seized her, mounted and entered her with a brutal thrust. Her thighs clasped him hard as her heels rose, urging him, forcing him deeper.

Okay, Uncle Jason. You want me to fuck her? Fine, I'll fuck her. See? I'm fucking her.

But as her arms slipped around him, as her nails dug into his shoulders and she sighed, her lips at the hollow of his neck, he forgot Uncle Jason. He forgot everything in the liquid, bubbling chuckle of pleasure she made, the taste of her sweat, her slipperiness and strength. All his fears went away with the things she whispered to him, her shuddery moan as she clutched him and he felt his climax begin, a bright prickling star at the base of his spine.

Her hands urged him wonderfully; he was losing control. When he came, a million bright sparklers exploded in his mind.

And inside every one of those flashing sparklers was a cold eye. Unblinking. Watching.

Laughing at him.

Beneath him, Nicki lay motionless.

Only it wasn't Nicki, not really. In a cold rush of reality, he remembered it again. All the sounds and the movements, the whispering and touching: not hers. Not at all. All of that had been planned, prerecorded—if in fact she had really been doing any of those things at all.

Feeling her beneath him now, chilly and limp, unresisting, Ben thought she hadn't. Maybe, he thought, she'd just been lying there all along. Maybe that was all she'd done, all the time she'd been here.

Because Uncle Jason could make him hurt himself. Uncle Jason could make him cry or laugh. Feel pain, or pleasure. Anything.

Anything at all.

So that, however he'd deluded himself for a few glorious moments, he hadn't been making love to Nicki Pialosta. Oh, no, not at all. Instead—

Instead, he'd been fucking Uncle Jason's monster.

"Get off," she said. He obeyed, fell back blindly in the bed, and listened as she dressed and left without another word. The apartment door clicked shut.

He was alone. Except for the thing still hovering all around him, the thing that had watched, laughing, while he—

Sleep, the thing said. He knew he would obey. And he did.

Only later, when he woke again, was he truly alone. Still only afternoon, but the change in the room was palpable, like a sudden drop in humidity.

Beneath his cheek, his pillowcase was wet with tears.

Ibrani opened his eyes. In the faint light his gaze found the bedroom doorway, and the shotgun case in the living room beyond. Then in a small, quiet corner of his mind that he hoped belonged to only himself, he vowed that somehow, soon, he would use the thirty ought six on Jason Goodmaster.

Or he would use it on himself.

Looking down at his pillowcase, he traced the tear stain on it with his finger, knowing he had made it while he slept.

Wondering if somewhere, right now, Nicki Pialosta was crying, too.

Jimmy Conklin

"Right," Conklin said into the phone, plugging his free ear to block the commotion of the newsroom. "Sure, he'll get back to me. Like last time? Look, I've been trying to get through to him since—"

The phone clicked. Dial tone.

"Jesus sweet Christ!" He slammed the receiver down, thinking of all the tortures fit for people who never returned calls. People like Jason Goodmaster, for example.

Beyond the Plexiglas divider that marked off the city editor's square of office space, Will Rifkind hung up his own phone and got up casually, scanning the newsroom.

Jimmy straightened abruptly and began smacking his typewriter keys, slogging any old words down in any old order. It was look-busy time: Rifkind was hunting for a reporter to send out on a story that had just been phoned in.

Conklin did not want to go. He didn't even care what the story was. He already had enough work to hold him till Labor Day, and every bit of it took time away from the important thing: Gorman and Goodmaster. Together and separately, dammit, because something stank here, something made the kind of sense he could smell a mile away.

"Conklin!" Rifkind, a vulture under glass, crooked his finger dangerously. "Get in here, Conklin."

"Damn." He sighed, ambling over.

"Hey, Jimmy!" called a voice from behind him as he crossed the room. It was Joe Malone, sports writer and newsroom wit, or so Malone thought. "Hey, ain't you supposed to be dead? I saw your obit."

"Blow it out your ear, Malone," Jimmy called back, shaking his head. With or without reassurance from Nicki, he still didn't think a death box with his name in it was funny. Then he went on into Rifkind's cubicle.

"At y'r service, m'lord," he said with a low, sweeping bow.

"Not funny, Conklin."

Conklin straightened. Some days, the court jester routine would have gotten him off the hook. A man of many moods, Will Rifkind. None of them easy to anticipate or endure. "What's up?"

"What are you working on right now?"

"Half a dozen things." He began ticking them off on the fingers of his left hand. "The school levy, the liquor store fire, why the gas company took a week to fix that broken main, the lousy plumbing system at the projects—"

No crime stories, because with the exception of the Meadbury Slasher there had been oddly little crime in the city lately. Conklin thought he'd better not mention his Gorman-and-Goodmaster ideas. They hadn't been assigned.

"Good," Rifkind said. "Nothing important, so here's one more. Take Trinh for photos." He thrust a folded, coffee-stained sheet at Conklin.

"Will—"

Narrowing his eyes, Rifkind rattled the paper impatiently.

"Okay, okay." Conklin took it, skimmed it, and looked

up at Rifkind. "Chlorine tankers?"

"That's right. Down at the railyard."

"I don't get it. We've all known about them for a week—they leaking, or what?"

"Go find out," Rifkind said. "Then write it up. Your job, remember?"

Conklin scowled. "C'mon, Will. Are we talking potential safety hazard, bankrupt carrier, interstate violations, what? What's changed?"

"Work stoppage in Boston," Rifkind said. "Tankers're gonna sit here until somebody up there can deal with 'em. They're safe, they're paid for, and as far as we know all the paperwork's complete." Rifkind made shooing motions.

"Then why bother?"

"I'm not sure."

"Come again?" Conklin peered up into Rifkind's face, searching it for signs of borderline lunacy or excessive drug use. He found none. "You're sending me out to cover nothing and you're not sure why?"

"Oh, I know why I'm sending you, Jimmy. I may not know why I'm sending anyone, but I know why I'm sending you." He pointed to the phone on his desk. "I been told to. Hizzoner the managing editor says you're running up the phone bill around here."

Conklin stared, comprehending, furious and trying hard to suppress it. "So all those garbage assignments this morning—"

Rifkind just kept looking down at him, waiting.

"The Golden Agers' bingo, a lexicographer's convention —what the hell's going on here, the Peter Principle Workout Tape? Since when do you sidetrack me on that jerk's say-so? He wouldn't know a story if it bit him in the ass, dammit."

Rifkind's chin came up. "Cool off, boy. I'm telling you, now, you want to shut up."

Only he didn't. He didn't want to cool off, or shut up. Because suddenly it all made too much sense, too much damned ugly sense. They wanted him to get off Goodmaster and Gorman. "What's the matter, Will?" he said softly. "Am I making someone nervous?"

Rifkin stonewalled. "My boss gives me an order, I do

what he says. Your boss orders you, you do what he says. That clear? You got it?"

Conklin shook his head. "Oh, yeah. I got it, Will. What thc fuck's happened to you? Bought off, or scared off? And if you were bought, you mind telling me the price? 'Cause I've got some money in the bank, I'd pay you to kiss my ass."

Rifkind went white. "You're out of here, you fucking midget. Clean out your desk. We'll mail you a check." He turned his back.

Conklin stood there. "I'm going to grieve this one, Will, and the union'll back me. I'll get reinstatement, back pay, damages, and one hell of a satisfaction, 'cause there's a real juicy story somewhere in all of this." He took a step closer to Rifkind's stiffened shoulders. "The wires'll carry it, Will. 'The Paper That Sold Its Soul;' all about the *Bulletin*. Because I'm going to write it. Starting now."

He spun toward the doorway, then turned back. "Oh, and by the way—shove those chlorine tankers up your butt."

He stalked out, his heartbeat booming in his ears. Jesus, he couldn't remember ever being so mad, so goddamn mad. Yanking an empty cardboard box from the storeroom, he wrestled it back to his desk and began dumping papers and objects into it.

Then he stopped. The newsroom was curiously silent. He looked up.

Nothing. Desk after desk, and face after glazed, cartoon-blank face. Pretending not to have heard; pretending not to know, or to care.

Or really not caring. Nicki's chair was empty.

Abruptly, anger fled. Sighing, he tossed a black iron paperweight shaped like a locomotive onto the heap of files and papers, dropped a Donald Duck combination calendar and message holder on top of that. And that was it. The sum total of his career at the illustrious Meadbury *Bulletin*.

S-s-s-so long, folks.

He wasn't sorry, though. It was this, or cut himself shaving every day, because he wouldn't be able to look at himself in the mirror.

Jeez. He folded the box flaps shut, hoisted it under his arm, and stood. No one looked up as he walked down the aisle between the desks.

At the door he paused, turned, and scanned the room he was leaving. Opened his mouth, and spoke in loud, clear, ringing tones:

"Frankly," he said, though no one was listening, "frankly, I gotta tell you I don't give a damn."

Then, hoping it was true, he walked out.

Rage returned as he drove aimlessly, going over and over the head-on with Rifkind. Midget!? The guy had a helluva nerve, a helluva goddamn nerve. He wanted a liar, he should've hired a liar in the first place. *Ah, but Jimmy me boyo, they paid you to get the goods on everyone else, didn't they? Not on them.*

Yeah, well that's where they'd made their mistake.

He would file the grievance, but he didn't want the job back. Not on a bet. In three weeks he'd bust their stones for every penny and benefit he could squeeze out of their black hearts, then turn around and throw the job back in their faces. Meanwhile. . . .

Meanwhile, he would make good on his threat. Experimentally, he uncurled his fingers from the steering wheel. His hand no longer clenched reflexively into a fist.

He could talk straight, too. And straight talk was just what the doctor ordered. Time for the phone call.

Because it wasn't just a threat. It was what anybody with a shred of journalistic ethics, or any kind of ethics, would do. It was making things right, before they got so wrong no one could stop it. His mind careened back to the Saint Tom's Dinner Dance.

Yeah, well, maybe Saint Tom's ran a little too heavy on beer and bingo parties, but he'd soaked up the major message. Do the right thing, and the devil take the hindmost.

He swung the Nash into a shopping center, pulled up in front of a bank of pay phones, and jumped out, digging a fistful of coins from his pants pocket. Boston was far enough. And big enough.

The Boston *Beacon* switchboard picked up on the first ring. At least he thought it was the *Beacon;* a truck rumbled by at the critical moment.

"Pardon? I can't hear you."

". . . connect you?" Static blurred the voice at the other end.

Conklin scowled at the mouthpiece. This was getting off to a marvelous start. "State desk, please!"

". . . moment. . . ." Scratchy Muzak filled the line until a gruff, middle-aged voice came on. Music cut off; static didn't.

"State, Mather."

Conklin tried to project through snap, crackle, and pop without breaking the other man's eardrum. "Mr. Mather, this is J. Patrick Conklin."

He hesitated, giving Mather a chance to remember him, or to ask him to speak up. "I interviewed with you a few years ago for a position on your paper?"

"Yes?" No recognition.

Conklin waited till a teenager in a battered Subaru finished beeping at a blond girl nearly bursting out of her Burger King uniform. "I've been at the Meadbury *Bulletin* for the last few years, and, uh, Mr. Mather, do you remember me at all?"

Voice hissing down the line on a burst of electronic sputter and ping, Mr. Mather seemed to say that he did.

Conklin bolstered himself. "Well, I got fired today." It wasn't what he'd meant to say.

"Mr. Conklin, we're not hiring right—"

"No, sir," he cut in hastily, "that's not why I called. You see, I was investigating a prominent member of the community, and it appears as though he, ah, has more influence with my publisher than I suspected."

"I'm not sure I'm hearing you clearly, Mr. Conklin. You're calling me about a friend of your publisher's?"

"No, sir." He took a deep breath. This approach might make Mather sit up and take notice, or blow up in Conklin's face. "I think my publisher's been bribed or blackmailed. I've got facts, sources, and I want to write the story for you."

Mather did not reply at once, and just as he did begin speaking an ambulance screamed by Conklin's booth.

"What was that, sir?"

"I said, on speculation," Mather shouted.

"Yes, sir. On spec. If you use it, you can pay me whatever you think it's worth. If not, well, you're not out anything but a little time."

"I hardly have an abundance of that, either." Mather chuckled, his voice coming through more clearly now. "Can you give me some more details, Mr. Conklin? Names, dates, events?"

"The subject is Ned Gorman, age and background as yet unverifiable. . . ."

"Can you speak up, please? This is a terrible connection." Mather's voice trailed to a whisper.

Conklin opened his mouth to repeat himself, then yanked the earpiece away from his head as static roared out of it.

"Mr. Mather?"

". . . something . . ."

Conklin couldn't make it out. "Mr. Mather?"

The line spat and whistled.

Conklin hit his forehead with his fist. "I can't hear you! If you can hear me, I'll call you back later on a better line." Then he hung up, feeling victimized and not liking what the feeling implied.

It was as if the call had been jammed. Scrambled.

Which was absurd. But then, this morning he'd have said the *Bulletin* couldn't be bought, and that had turned out to be wrong. Still, you could buy a city desk, maybe even a managing editor. But you couldn't buy the phone company; it was too big. Besides, to judge from the bill he paid every month, they already had all the money in the world.

No. It took too many people to screw up a phone call; dozens, maybe hundreds of people, all of whom would have to know which mall he'd impulsively pulled into, which phone he'd chosen from the bank of booths. . . .

Paranoid, Jimmy. We don't need a worldwide conspiracy to explain a fritz in the phone lines. He picked the phone up again, called the operator, and complained heatedly about the connection. Five minutes later, he had the operator's promise of a refund.

And a persistent, chilly wiggle of suspicion in his stomach.

Go home; call Mather from there. Too much noise here, anyway. Too many distractions. He swung away from the bank of phones, turned, and nearly thrust his face into the looming bosoms of the blond girl in the too-tight Burger King outfit.

"Oops! Gee, mister, sorry!" She giggled, a high, silly-ass whinny. Her eyes weren't giggling, though, as she backed away. They weren't even smiling.

They weren't silly-ass, either, and he felt them watching him as he got back into the Rambler and drove away toward the mall's exit. He waited for a bakery truck to clear the lane, and pulled out into traffic. As he did so he glanced up into his rearview. The Burger King girl was gone.

Paranoid. Or was he? Either way, in five minutes he'd be talking to Mather from the privacy of his own apartment. A much wiser idea, that, in all respects. Then another idea seized him as, off to the right, black speartips of wrought-iron fencing presented arms to the winter sky.

Conklin, you old dog. He eased into the right-hand lane. He hadn't meant to come here, or at least hadn't known he'd meant to. He'd just been driving, trying to cool off, think what to do.

Yet here he was, as if some interior compass had brought him to confront the devil in his lair. He signaled to turn right, slowed as he approached the wide gravel driveway. The gates stood open.

What the hell. Maybe the old bastard's home.

Gravel pinged the Nash's underside as Conklin swung past the sign marked "Goodmaster Mansion," and headed on up the drive.

The door opened at his ring. He handed his card to the butler, who looked as if he'd come out of a box marked "Contents: One Butler."

"J. Patrick Conklin. I'd like to see Mr. Goodmaster."

The butler held the card out between his thumb and index finger, as if something nasty might leap off of it. "Mr. Goodmaster is not at home to you. Furthermore, it is my understanding that you have been discharged from the Meadbury *Bulletin.* Hence, your use of this card is fraud." The butler's pinched mouth made the word sound like "frewd." "I am going to close this door. If your car does not leave these premises within one minute, I shall call the police and have you arrested at once."

"But—"

The door slammed sharply.

"Jesus sweet Christ!" Conklin stomped down the granite steps, teeth clenched and face pushed out into the stiff, chill wind that had sprung up. The wind caught his scarf and flipped its end back over his shoulder. He half turned, reaching to yank it back.

From the corner of his eye, he caught a flicker of movement at one of the mansion's high windows. He stared; the figure was familiar.

Nicki?

He couldn't be certain, and now the shape was gone. Still, it had looked like Nicki. Similar height and build, similar shape of dark hair against a white, indistinct profile.

Nah, couldn't be. He got into the Nash, turned the ignition on, and threw it into reverse. Then, deciding, he popped it straight into first and splattered gravel visibly and loudly across the walkway, so that anyone inside would know he was leaving.

Outside the gates, he drove another block until he found a parking place. He parked in it, got out of the car, looked around once, and quickly hotfooted it over Jason Goodmaster's candy-ass wrought-iron fence, dropping to the frozen grass inside.

Nothing like a good fence for keeping out the riffraff. Glancing around once more, he dusted his hands on the seat of his pants and ducked into some evergreens, keeping to the hedges as he made his way back toward the house.

Because if Nicki wasn't here, that was fine; that was all well and good.

But if she was, then he damned well wanted to know why.

Besides, that butler had been very rude, and rudeness always piqued his curiosity. It made him want to know what people were being so rude about. And a fellow couldn't be blamed for indulging his curiosity.

Could he?

Tommy Riley

Inside the big house, Tommy Riley stood by the library door, shifting from one foot to the other and trying to stay awake. So far, that was the whole job of guarding Mr. Goodmaster: standing, and boredom. Just sitting down for a minute would be heaven, only then he would fall asleep for sure. Besides, the straight-backed chairs along the wall looked like they belonged in a museum. Probably if he sat in one, it would collapse.

He imagined himself on the polished floor, the chair just a nest of broken sticks around him, skinny old Throtway looking at him as if he were a bug. The thought made him almost want to do it; hey, it would break the monotony, anyway. This place needed some shaking up, and so did Throtway, who looked like he belonged in a museum, too.

Tommy hoped he wasn't starting to look like that: old, and overly preserved. The upholstery on the chairs was frayed and faded, although spotless. What good was a chair if no one sat in it? Above the chairs, big gloomy paintings of Pilgrims and Founding Fathers hung in thick, ornate dull-gold frames. Overhead vaulted the twenty-foot-high ceiling —jeez, you could play basketball in here, except nobody would ever dare.

Still, it beat herding winos at the shelter.

"Follow me." Tommy jumped as the butler doddered around the corner at him. Heck, he wished the old guy would put cleats on his slippers. He kept popping up like a shriveled jack-in-the-box. And that voice, like wind whispering in a dried-out snake skin. . . .

Already, Tommy didn't like the butler, and he was pretty sure the butler returned the feeling. Jerking his head toward the library doors, he began, "I'm supposed to—"

"The master would not be pleased to hear you arguing with me."

Pretty bossy for such a little guy. "I thought I was supposed to stay here until I was relieved."

The butler's eyebrows lifted a fraction. "Questions have been raised concerning your fitness, young man. You might be wise to answer them before insisting upon the prerogatives of your duty. Now, come along."

"All right," Tommy said finally. "But I don't like leaving my post."

"I shall be certain to mention that," Throtway said dryly. "This way." He turned and headed for the wide, curving staircase.

Tommy followed, not touching the banister for fear of leaving a smudge on it, climbing the marble treads on tiptoe so as not to scuff them. Ahead, the butler seemed to be gliding up, the gold threads in his black house-slippers twinkling. He had good wind for an old guy. Tommy wanted to pause at the top to catch his own breath, but Throtway was already moving swiftly down the hall, past more oil portraits of old Puritans whose narrowed eyes seemed to follow Tommy as he hurried to catch up.

The ceilings here were not quite as high, and the corridor was a bit narrower than those on the ground floor. Still, the lavishness impressed him. Persian rugs, their pile soft and deep enough to trip the unwary, lay at meticulous intervals on the immaculate marble floor. Small figurines, alabaster and jade, stood on narrow carved-ebony tables. And cut into the oaken wainscoting, a running design of vines, peacocks, and pineapples twined down both sides of the hall and up into the heavy lintels.

There was more, but Tommy stepped along too quickly to catch anything but a blur of door after closed, silent door. *So many rooms. What the heck does Mr. Goodmaster do with all of them?*

Stopping suddenly, the butler twisted an oval brass doorknob and inclined his head toward the room. "Go in."

Uneasily, Tommy tried to glance inside, but the old man had only unlatched the door, not opened it. Tommy glanced at him in suspicion. "Are you sure I'm not going to get in trouble for leaving my post?"

"Quite." Faint impatience underlined the syllable.

Shaking his head doubtfully, Tommy pushed the door open, expecting more grim paintings, more rugs and paneling and priceless knickknacks. Instead, a gymnasium spread out before him. Well, not gymnasium-sized; even Goodmaster Mansion wasn't that big. But all the equipment—Tommy goggled at the row of Nautilus machines, the computerized LifeCycle and treadmill, the rack of free weights beside the tumbling mat. A tennis ball throwing machine squatted in front of a floor-to-ceiling cage of netting. Beside it stood a Ping-Pong table, two paddles and one ball lying together on it. The air here was warm and humid, and from beyond the door at the room's right-hand end came the unmistakable churning whoosh of a whirlpool.

"Riley?"

Tommy jerked and swung around, his hand moving reflexively toward his hip. A man in a white lab coat was moving toward him, stiffly, as if his body didn't like him much. The man carried a clipboard in one hand, and a cheap ball-point pen in the other. The pen, Tommy noticed, had leaked black ink onto the tip of the man's index finger.

Feeling a little foolish, Tommy let his hand fall away from his gun. That was the other thing about this job: When he wasn't bored, he was spooked. Plenty spooked, although he didn't like to admit it. Heck, the mansion was a spooky place. "Yes," he said, "what—"

"Go into the examining room." The man in the white coat spoke without looking up, his voice without accent or emphasis. "Strip to your shorts and get on the scales."

Tommy backed up a step. "Hey, wait just a minute, buddy—"

"Riley." Now the man in the white coat did look up, fixing Tommy in the invisible cross-hairs of his gaze.

Something like a tack hammer seemed to deliver a sharp blow just above his eyebrows. When it faded, he realized: The doctor wanted to examine him. Therefore he must walk past the doctor and over to the bench and the row of lockers behind the LifeCycle.

There he stopped, his unbuckled gunbelt heavy in his two hands. He stared at it an instant, trying to remember why he had taken it off, why he was standing here, and why the white-coated man was staring at him.

Then he remembered again, or at least it felt like remembering. The doctor was going to give him a physical examination. Of course. And Tommy would cooperate. Which was why he must hang up the gunbelt, kick off his shoes, and take his clothes off before stepping onto the scale.

Which he did. He wanted to cooperate. Certainly he

wanted to. It felt funny, though. The scale's platform chilled his feet, right through his white sweatsocks. He frowned at the calibrated crosspiece.

But the doctor wanted to check him, and Tommy Riley really did want to be checked. To be pronounced fit. Didn't he? Of course he did. And so he straightened, inhaled, turned his head, and coughed—once, twice—on command. Fingers tapped his chest, probed at his neck and his armpits, prodded behind his ears and deeply into his belly.

Meanwhile Tommy bemusedly pondered the sensation of being a step behind; instead of directing things his brain seemed to be just following along, noticing his actions but not . . . not initiating them.

It wasn't an unpleasant sensation. Just . . . funny. Not ha-ha funny. Forget about it, he thought. Or someone did.

Tommy forgot about it.

Some time passed. He frowned, glancing back at the pile of free weights. His fists felt cramped, and his arms hurt. His back, too. He felt as if he'd missed something important. The doctor was leading him across the hardwood gymnasium floor toward the treadmill. A little woozily, he stepped on.

"Hold on to this." The doctor took Tommy's hands and wrapped them around the handlebar. "Run until you drop."

Tommy nodded, relaxing, a smile spreading over his face. This was easy, more his kind of event. He'd never been great on the flashy stuff; no high jumps for him, no hundred-yard dashes. But now the treadmill's rubber belt turned at a steady, even pace under his stockinged feet, and this he could do forever. Endurance was his strong point.

Gradually, the treadmill began turning faster. But not much faster; it was still almost relaxing. The muscles in his thighs and back began loosening, calves stretching as he leaned into it. He filled his chest with air and grinned as sweat trickled down over his forehead, snorted and tossed his head to fling droplets of it off the end of his nose.

Faster. He gripped the handlebar, fixed his eyes on the end of the room where the doctor stood. Heck, he could do this. His lips curled back in a grimace.

It was getting harder now, but he wouldn't give up, ever.

He'd never given up in his life. And he sure as heck wasn't about to start here, not even with his legs on fire and his breath coming in huge tearing sobs, his heart trip-hammering. Not here, not now, when his whole life depended on it.

Because . . . endurance . . . was his strong point.

Faster.

Then, hair sweat-sodden and T-shirt clammy, he lay flat on his back, the acoustic ceiling hovering like the top slice of bread in a sandwich. The doctor stood over him, making a note on his clipboard.

"Showers through that door," the doctor said. "Soap, towels, deodorant. Use them."

"Yes, sir." He rolled onto his stomach and slowly, slowly pushed himself to his knees. "How far?"

The doctor was walking away on rubber-soled shoes that made faint squeegee sounds on the hardwood floor.

Tommy got halfway to his feet and crouched there. His legs felt watery. "How far'd I run?" he called.

No answer.

He grabbed the vertical bar of the treadmill and pulled himself up the rest of the way. A gauge like an odometer was fastened there; he hadn't paid much attention to it but knew the counter had read 000,000 when he began. Now the digits stood at 025,236.

As he staggered toward the shower, he puzzled over that number. Twenty-five thousand two hundred thirty-six whats? Not miles or kilometers, that was for sure; he'd be dead, instead of just nearly dead. So what was the counter counting?

It was not until the hot water needled into his chest that he got it: steps. Something under the treadmill's belt counted the impacts of his feet. And let's see, he thought as he rubbed shampoo into his wet hair, maybe four feet a stride when he was jogging easy, like at the start, anyway. So that gives, oh, call it a hundred thousand feet, divided by call it five thousand feet just for convenience and that made it— Tommy stopped lathering. Twenty miles?

He'd have had to run all afternoon.

Quickly rinsing, he looked for a window to see if it was still light out. But—no windows; exhaust fans instead. He shrugged and began toweling off. His watch was with his clothes; he would check it when he got dressed.

He couldn't have run twenty miles, though. He'd read the gauge wrong, or miscalculated. Slowly, he dried his hair. Whatever he'd run, it was pretty far; his thighs had the tingly, too-alive feeling they always had when he'd overdone it, and his knees and ankles were beginning to ache. Jeez, he was really going to hurt in the morning.

Out on the gym floor the doctor was waiting for him with another man who wore a loud checked suit. Both men eyed Tommy incuriously as he dressed, registering his appearance as if it were just another datum to be noted.

"Go with him, Riley," the doctor said.

Tommy nodded, too tired to speak, and followed the man in the checked suit out the door. Not the one he'd originally come in, though; this door led to another, and another just like the first. Feeling punch-drunk, he just kept going through them, behind the bright orange-and-brown houndstooth check that was the stranger's back. The final door opened onto an ordinary room: two easy chairs, a couch, a coffee table, two floor lamps, and a metronome.

A metronome? Yeah, sure. Nothing could surprise him now. He looked around for the piano. Or the ragtime band. What the heck.

Mr. Bright Suit waved at the couch. "Sit."

Tommy sat, adjusting his holstered gun so it wouldn't dig into him. Dully, he wondered if he could lift it. Maybe he had run twenty miles. Maybe twenty thousand. He didn't care.

The man in the suit set the metronome ticking. "Close your eyes."

No problem, Tommy thought.

"Now count back from one hundred."

"A hundred, ninety-nine, ninetyeightnin'seven . . ."

"Slowly."

"Ninety-six. Ninety-five. Ninety-four."

He opened his eyes, frowning. Mr. Bright's plaid tie was loosened, and he was opening a briefcase Tommy had not seen before.

"Catch," Mr. Bright said.

Something sailed through the air. Tommy's hand went up

before he thought, snatching. It wiggled; he flung it away. "Snake!" He leapt up. The creature S-turned smoothly across the carpet and vanished beneath an easy chair.

"Catch it." Mr. Bright's voice was expressionless, his flat eyes watchful.

Tommy stood gaping, then realized: All this was a test. Goodmaster's voice came back: "With your life, if need be?"

Snake, right. He dropped to his belly, reached under the easy chair in the corner and grabbed the damn snake. Then, sighing with soreness, he hoisted himself back up, turned, and dropped it into Mr. Bright's lap. What the heck. He already felt pretty snake-bit.

"Thank you." Deftly, Mr. Bright snagged the reptile, slipped it into a canvas bag, and dropped the bag back into his briefcase.

Tommy watched in disappointment. He'd hoped for some reaction, at least.

All he got was, "One more." Bright's pudgy hands went into the briefcase again.

Now Tommy stepped back; he was beginning to understand this test. "Another snake?"

"Nope." From the briefcase came a clear plastic box.

Tommy took it. And shivered. Snakes were one thing; he'd never minded snakes. But this—

Inside the transparent cube there hunkered the biggest, the hairiest, the meanest- and hungriest-looking spider he'd ever seen in his life. Legs as thick as cigarettes jutted off a body the size of a salad plate. Red eyes waving on stalks as thick as his own thumbs tracked him purposefully. In his hands, the box itself shivered with the creature's clicking mandibles, long and sharp as a pair of nail scissors.

"Take the top off the box."

He didn't want to. That damned spider was as big as his whole face. Nevertheless, this was a test. And it wouldn't do them any good to have their star guard devoured by this thing, would it? Heck, if that happened what would they tell his mother? "Gee, Missus Riley, we're awful sorry but your boy got et up by our spider. . . ." Suppressing a giggle of near hysteria, he lifted the box's lid.

"Reach in."

"Oh, sure," he snorted.

"Put your hand in, Riley."

His jaws clenched. Bright's face was as fat and pudgy as his fingers, and as expressionless.

Tommy was pretty damned sure this jerk had never stuck so much as his pinkie in with Tarantuloid, King of the Spiders. Now he realized how easy the first tests had been; running twenty miles wasn't bad if you didn't have to think about it till later. This, though. This he had to think about now.

Or did he? "Fuck it," he heard himself say very clearly, his hand already inside the box. Crouching, the beast wedged itself back as far from him as possible. Good, it was as afraid as he was.

"Now pick it up."

"You know," Tommy said, "I had an awful feeling you were going to say that." He eyed the spider, which was eyeing him, then he glanced once more at the man in the ugly houndstooth suit.

The man was watching with bored disinterest, clearly not caring. No skin off his nose if Tommy picked the spider up, or if he didn't. Yes or no. Win or lose. Pass or fail. It was all the same to the man in the suit.

Still, the man in the suit couldn't pick up the spider. Tommy knew it. Not wouldn't; couldn't.

I'm better than you. The thought felt good. He wanted to keep it. Biting his lower lip, he eased his hand very slowly toward the creature. In a flashing instant it sprang to the back of his hand, scrabbling up his wrist with its horrid, prickly legs, scrambling the length of his shirt-sleeve to dangle from his armpit. Tommy froze as it hauled itself to his shoulder where it perched weightily, ominously, an inch or so from his right ear.

He strained his eyes sideways to where it sat hovering fat and dark at the edge of his vision. Its eyes waved around, and he wondered what it was looking at. Most of all he wondered what it ate, and if those jaws were as strong as they looked. Probably they were. From what little he knew, animals weren't into a lot of flashy, useless decoration; they used what they had. Depending on this thing's diet, he might walk out of here minus an ear.

"Good," Mr. Bright said carelessly. "Now put it back in the box."

All at once, Tommy felt immensely irritated. And tired.

"Put it back in thc box, Rilcy."

"Right." He jerked his shoulder sharply.

The spider flipped off, fell on its back, struggled to right itself.

Tommy stepped on it, a soft, yielding crunch. Legs stuck out all around the sides of his shoe. He crouched beside the mess, scraped up the parts of it he could get off the carpet with the plastic lid, dumped the result in the box. "Here." He handed the box to the man in the bright, ugly suit.

The man nodded silently, looking down at the remains of the spider.

Tommy went to the door and opened it. *The hell with this.*

Throtway waited outside the room.

Somehow this did not surprise him. He made a face, but said nothing.

The old man's eyes were no longer as contemptuous as they had been.

Tommy wasn't sure he liked the new look any better, though. It was . . . satisfied.

"One last test of your fitness to serve," said Throtway. His voice quavered more than Tommy remembered, as if in a few hours he had grown weaker. Or Tommy had grown stronger. "Pass this test, and your place here is secured. For the rest of your life, perhaps longer."

Funny. He wasn't even sure he wanted the job anymore, not if it meant running twenty miles, or catching snakes, or scooping giant spiders out of boxes. So he could do those things; big deal.

He moved down the hall past the butler and found himself standing before a carved wooden door. Puzzled, he turned his head and looked back the way he must have come. The corridor behind him was not the one he remembered: no carpets, no wainscoting. No small glittering trinkets on carved tables. Blank white walls, instead, and grey linoleum, and fluorescent lights set into acoustical tiles in the ceiling.

More tricks. Leave me alone, I'm tired.

The butler jogged his elbow. "Go in, boy."

"What now?"

A most unpleasant smile creased Throtway's face. "Just what comes naturally, boy. Just what comes naturally."

"What the heck is that supposed to mean?"

The butler executed a perfect about-face and padded away.

Whatever this is, it better be good. Tommy turned the doorknob. Inside, a single small lamp glowed dimly beyond the half-drawn curtains of an enormous four-poster bed. After a few moments, his eyes adjusted to the low light.

A woman lay in the bed: Miss Pialosta. Asleep.

He blinked, not believing.

Under the sheer gauzy sheet, she was naked.

The old man's instructions echoed in his head: "Do what comes naturally, boy."

All of a sudden, he didn't feel like a boy. Not at all. He stared at the shadows of her nipples, the darkness between her legs. He wasn't tired any more, either.

What comes naturally. No problem. He moved nearer, while the most insistent erection he'd ever had sprang to throbbing life. Whatever this tested, he liked it.

A beautiful woman, and not just any woman. Nicki Pialosta. He'd dreamed about her, fantasized about her. And now she was his. He yanked at his tie, still staring at her, his eyes going over and over every part of her. He pulled off his shirt, and dropped it. Fumbled with the buckle of his gunbelt. And stopped.

Riley, what the heck are you doing?

Oh, no. Oh, no, come on. Don't go all good-guy on me now, damn it. Don't you see what we've got here? This is a dream, man, this is—

Yeah. This is Miss Pialosta.

So?

I can't believe this. I'm standing here having an argument with my own hard-on.

Yeah! Come on, man, hop on her. You're gonna love it. And so will she.

But—

She shifted dreamily, lips parting. Her breasts rose and fell softly with her sleeping breath. A sly suspicion struck him: She wouldn't even know it was him. She wouldn't even wake up, not all the way, anyway. Only enough to. . . .

Go for it, man. Come on, you can do it.

Tommy swallowed, dry-mouthed. Yeah, he could do it. That's what she'd always told him. Go for it, try, work for what you want. You'll make it.

"I believe in you." That's what she'd always said.

Only, she'd been wearing her clothes when she said it.

A sob of disappointment rose up in his throat, not only because he couldn't have her, but because he couldn't do it. This was it, the end of the test. And he was failing it, because he loved her.

Tears prickled in his eyes as he realized it was true. He could make love to her; oh, easily. No problem there.

But he wasn't going to rape her, not for anything. Or anyone. Because she'd believed in him, and that was simply, unavoidably, more important than all the jobs and all the hard-ons in the whole damn world.

And even a jerk like Tommy Riley knew that. Miserably, he picked his tie up off the floor. He finished buttoning his shirt and went out, closing the door quietly behind him.

Throtway stood waiting, arms folded, implacable. As Tommy pushed past him the old man muttered something, but Tommy, depressed, missed it. "What?" He strode toward the stairs, impatient now to go down and face Goodmaster, get himself fired and get on out of here.

The servant scuttled ahead of him, turned and faced him at the top of the staircase, blocking his way.

"I said," the old man quavered, "you pass."

Ben Ibrani

Sly late-afternoon shadows lapped the living-room chair where Ben Ibrani sat, a set of stereo headphones over his ears. Eyeing the soft grey pools of twilight that grew even as he watched, he reached for the lamp.

Then he pulled his hand back. No; the shadows wouldn't hurt him. It hadn't gotten into the shadows. Yet. At least, he hoped it hadn't. Deliberately, he turned his attention back to the racket shrieking through the headphones. Mick

Jagger was yelling about how pleased he was to meet someone, and how he hoped that someone guessed his name, and how puzzled he thought that someone must be.

Nope. Not puzzled any more.

Behind the music pounded his headache, a simpler, even more primitive rhythm of pain that made him yearn for silence. Yes, that was it: silence, and a good, brisk walk outdoors. A few gulps of fresh air, before night settled in like a deep-freeze, except that he had to keep wearing the headphones, had to keep listening to Mick Jagger's harangue. The singer's voice shook Ibrani's skull like a dentist's drill.

Ibrani didn't like it. It wasn't his sort of music, not at all.

But it was exactly what he needed: arrogant, insistent. Impossible to ignore. Impossible to hear through, too, in case anyone was trying to talk to him. Anyone, for example, who might want to tell Ben Ibrani how dirty he was, how he needed a shower. And how the wire brush would make him clean again.

It had known before, that voice, just how hard to make him scrub: hard enough to torture, not hard enough to kill. The antiseptic soap had helped, too, and the hours of standing when he could bear no touch. Otherwise, he would be dead now, of infection if not of pain.

Mick said he had no expectations to pass through here again.

Ibrani hadn't any either, because the next time would kill him.

This was it, he realized: Knuckle under, or die.

But he didn't want to knuckle under, not any more. Nor did he want to die. But how long could he live with Mick Jagger howling and moaning between his ears?

Because the music, the clamor, was saving him. Without it, his probable life span might be a few minutes; hours, perhaps, if Uncle Jason's monster decided really to torture him. Now, though, he could not hear it, or perhaps it could not hear him.

But that line of speculation was meaningless; the why of it didn't matter. The thing was, it worked. He wasn't sure how he'd gotten the idea, but it had done the trick. Somehow, the noise protected him.

So now, beneath the din, he could concentrate on his plan. He could think of his next step, and cobble together a defense against his fear of taking it.

Mick yodeled and groaned. Today, he said, was the day of the plunge.

You got it, buddy. It was today, all right, and if it didn't work . . . well, if it didn't work, Ibrani wouldn't be worrying tomorrow, because he would be dead.

Through the evening shadows he looked across the room at a pale rectangle on his desk, against the wall: the screen of his personal computer. With it, he would destroy Jason Goodmaster.

He hoped.

But it would work, it had to. Surely, he argued with himself, if the citizens of Meadbury knew the truth—

What truth? That kindhearted old Jason Goodmaster was actually a power-mad monster? That he controlled some kind of—well, some kind of psychic power?

But they would believe it, he'd make them believe it, and then they would—

What?

Impeach the old man?

Run him out of town on a rail?

Drive a stake through his heart and bury him at a crossroads?

Between Ibrani's ears, Mick Jagger threatened howlingly to kill the king and rail at all his servants.

And what would the servants do, then? Ibrani wondered. Revolt? Or silence the traitor?

"Know the truth," he said softly to himself, "and the truth shall set ye free."

He still clung to the journalistic superstition that knowledge was power. In fact, he was about to bet his life on it. Still, it struck him that the truth hadn't helped him much lately, hadn't given him any freedom. Without the Rolling Stones stomping and blaring in his head, he'd be in the shower right this minute, tearing himself to shreds. He shuddered at the thought. And sat up straight, his mind suddenly churning.

Why did the headphones protect him? It was not, as he had first thought, a meaningless question. Did the music jam some sort of transmission, either from the monster to him or the other way around? Or did it, somehow, put him entirely beyond the monster's reach?

Think about that, now, Ben. Is it the volume, the beat, the melody, the lyrics? What is it and what does it do?

Could it be, he thought, more excited now as professional instincts suggested he must be closing in, could it be that none of those was the answer? Because he'd just happened to pluck that album off his shelf, out of all the dozens of records there; it was too coincidental to suppose he'd chanced on the only one that could do it.

All right, then: many records. He was the constant. The answer was in something the music did to him.

So what was it doing?

He slumped back into the chair, closing his eyes, letting the full force of it wash over him.

Defiance. That was it. That was what it evoked in him. Hand stuck straight up, middle finger to the world. . . . Fuck you, Jack, the music said, I don't care. I do what I want. And Ibrani, listening, said it too.

But there had to be more. Defiance wasn't enough; he'd raged often enough while scrubbing himself raw.

Distraction? Pain had distracted him, never saving him.

The music, though; it didn't really distract him. It attracted him. But to what? Or did that really matter?

Yes. He cudgeled his brain. It did matter. The music attracted him to . . . well, to itself. The more he listened, the more he got past the superficial, deliberate ugliness of it, toward the mind behind the music.

Mick suggested a drink to the hardworking people. In spite of himself, Ibrani agreed. He felt himself beginning to draw toward Jagger's nakedly expressed emotion, the singer's unvarnished, unprettified honesty.

Was it the drawing toward that mattered?

Or was it that the drawing toward drew him away from something else?

Could that be protecting him? Was it by feeling (not thinking, feeling, down in the gut by the base of the soul) that he rose above or fell below any wavelength on which Goodmaster's monster could touch him?

It seemed right, felt right. Something in the music told him to stay on this track; something in the music, in fact, was cheering him, telling him he was finally starting to catch on.

But where did that leave him? Wearing headphones for the rest of his natural born days, that's where, unless he found a way not just to resist or to hide, but to fight back. Uncle Jason had something, some power: a force he could control, and that Ben Ibrani couldn't even imagine. What the hell was it?

Ben didn't know. Hunched forward in the darkness, he lowered his face into his open hands. God, did he have to figure it all out at once? Why couldn't he just write the damn article, tell the truth as far as he knew it, and let it go at that?

Because it won't work, that's why. Not without all of it.

All of it, that's what they'd want before the *Bulletin*'s readers would believe, before there was even a chance of their believing him. And he couldn't give it to them because he had no chance at all of figuring it out himself.

All right. All right, there was another way: Get right down to it, down and dirty.

He groaned. It would be shabby, manipulative, against everything he stood for. Also, this kind of thing was delicate; when you started ringing people's chimes with a piece like the one he contemplated, you had to hit just the right notes, or the whole thing fell apart.

As if understanding the situation completely, Mick Jagger began urging Ibrani to use all his well-learned politesse, or have his soul laid to waste.

Ibrani thought, this Jagger guy was actually pretty astute. You had to take all your goodness and turn it inside out; take all your skill and hand it over to a prancing entertainer, a gabbling fool. A liar. Only you weren't doing the lying; no, not even that. You had to let that wickedly practiced gabbler do your talking for you, and then, then once you'd deceived them in all these ways, they might believe you.

And that hurt him more than anything, that he could not simply tell people what they needed to know most of all: the truth. Because who in his or her right mind would believe it?

Fellow residents of Meadbury, Jason Goodmaster can read your minds.

Yeah, sure. That would go over real well.

All right, then, he would lie, for the simplest reason in the world: It would work. He'd do it fast, and he'd do it now. And to make sure no one saw it too soon, he'd write it here on the terminal before he went on-line, then bump it across quick. Onto the front page.

But at the terminal, he hesitated. There would be hell to pay for this. He would lose his job, his reputation.

Maybe his life.

The hell with it. He flipped the record and cranked up the volume.

". . . no expectation," Mick Jagger crooned roughly.

But I do. I do, and that's why I'm going to destroy Jason Goodmaster. Ibrani sat down in front of the terminal, snapped it on, and began to type.

An hour later, he stood straight up and screamed.

Until that very moment, it had not occurred to him —perhaps because he had been afraid to think about it at any length—that he could not possibly slip an article defaming Jason Goodmaster into the *Bulletin.* Yes, he could link directly into the mainframe; yes, he could bump a scheduled article and insert his own; yes, the computer made the printing plates; yes, but—

But from then on people took over. People who could read. People who, he had to presume, would dance to Jason Goodmaster's tune. People who could break the plates, stop the presses, refuse to load the trucks—

People who could thwart Ben Ibrani with very little effort.

So all his work had gone for naught. He touched a few keys and the operating system deleted the file.

Jason Goodmaster had won again.

Another hour later: God, he hated Mick Jagger's raunchy voice. He crossed the room to the racks of shelving that supported all the entertaining electronics a status-minded young man-about-town can acquire in a decade and a half. He had other records. Surely one of them could replace the Rolling Stones.

He passed in front of the giant color television—and stopped dead in his tracks.

TV. Satellite dish. A 5¼-inch floppy diskette in a Lucite box.

"Gotcha," he said in a whisper.

He raced back to the computer, tangling his feet in the headphones' cord but catching himself just before he fell.

No cunning journalistic tricks on this one. One screenful of information, he knew he could send that much, and wasn't sure he could transmit more. But with it he could get their attention, make 'em sit up and wonder out loud.

And the way to do that was to take advantage of things the public was already hysterical about.

Using the graphics package, he wrote in oversized letters:

NEWS UPDATE

JASON GOODMASTER TO BE INDICTED
FOR CHILD MOLESTATION

WEALTHY RECLUSE DYING OF AIDS
SECRET ORGIES AT MANSION REVEALED

—FILM AT ELEVEN—

So quick.

So dirty.

So powerful.

He adjusted the colors for maximum visual impact, stored the file, and inserted the other diskette into the drive. Holding his breath, he loaded the program.

>TARGET? it asked.

His fingers trembled as they typed "HBO" and pressed <ENTER>.

>DURATION OF PREEMPTION (nn sec/min/hr) ?

How long was long enough? A minute? Two? Too long and the FCC could triangulate on him; too short, and the audience could miss it. "1 min." His finger hovered over the <ENTER> key, then stabbed down.

>READY.

He took a breath, a deep one, and let it out with a "Yes!" Four quick keystrokes: r u n <ENTER>

At the last instant he spun around in his chair, grabbed the remote control, and flicked his own television on.

Bam. There it was. In vivid color on his own screen. Now, how long before the cable company disavowed it? Or would that matter?

Not if Ibrani knew the public as well as he hoped he did. Where there's smoke. . . . And he'd just blown more smoke than Meadbury had seen since the tire recycling plant caught fire.

He leaned back gingerly, wishing he could have figured out a way to reach the reading public as well as the couch potatoes.

Then he smiled, because although he could not directly reach the city's readers, he did not have to. Every paper in the cable company's service area would report his act of piracy; most of them would phrase their articles in such a way as to repeat the text of the message without risking a libel suit. But the suggestion would still be there.

Ah, the lawyers would be busy tonight.

And he, Ben Ibrani, had just struck the first blow against Goodmaster. Mister Goodmaster. Uncle Jason.

His face twisted in mingled satisfaction and fear; he glanced at his shotgun rack.

The first blow, he thought. But not the last.

Jason Goodmaster

Nearly evening. Beyond the flames leaping and crackling over the logs in the massive fireplace, beneath the andirons, shadows lurked. Jason Goodmaster watched them. Hands in his lap, he sat in another, deeper shadow, just outside the pool of firelight. Impassively, he stared past the flickering play of red and orange to the shadows below, and within.

Odd, he thought, how a fire might crackle and leap, yet leave such pools of darkness. Not even the brightest fire could illuminate everything.

Around him rose the high, silent shelves of his library, felt now rather than seen. Goodmaster liked the shadows here, the darkness. Worldly light was no light at all, he thought, in the eye of the soul. A distraction, something to be managed. A drain on his energy, his attention, just when he needed to concentrate his attention—inward? or outward? He wondered still. Which?

He chuckled dryly. He never had been able to settle on the direction. Certainly at moments like these he looked inward. What he saw, though, lay outside himself. No maddened figment, this; not summoned from himself. No. The truth made more monstrous sense. Monstrous, just because it was the truth, though many denied it for the sake of their sanity.

Jason Goodmaster no longer felt he had any sanity to save. It was not that he thought he was mad, only that the feebleness of such imaginary constructs, such useless definitions, did not interest him. He had more important things to do, and the thought of how others might describe him no longer troubled him. Faintly sometimes, they amused him.

Because madness—ah, madness was a short-term thing. A word for narrow ideas, nearsighted visions: of people and their meaningless doings. A word for children and the things that ruled them: money, religion, governments.

Jason Goodmaster preferred the long view. A view through the eye of the soul. Swathed in shadow, alone by the fireside, he looked:

Behind the hiss and flicker of the fire, a swarming tension, like heat lines, but shimmering with more than heat.

A jittering jiggle of diamond gnatlike particles.

Hovering, and aware. Structured, purposeful, and chiming, ringing together like a tapped crystal.

Thinking. And quite energetically, too.

The life of the mind—the life of this mind—was the life and the soul of Meadbury. And only Jason Goodmaster saw it: a life transcendent. The glittering motes, the dancing crystalline dots: each the life-force of someone, somewhere near. The ebb and flow of the dancing bits formed patterns invisible to most individuals, but not to Jason Goodmaster. Not to the watcher in darkness, who took the long view.

When he called it anything, he called it the oversoul.

More often, though, it called him.

He had seen it first, quite by accident, when he was thirteen. Late at night he lay awake in darkness, dreaming of the great things he would do and wanting desperately to touch himself. He didn't, though; he didn't, because if he did hairy warts would grow on the palms of his hands, and everyone would know.

And even if no person knew, Jesus would. Jesus bled on the cross for boys like him: wicked, filthy little boys, boys whose minds fevered with shameful things. Boys who peeked at magazines; boys who recited dirty rhymes. Boys who played with themselves.

The eyes of Jesus cruised through the night, beaming like X-ray machines, hunting for boys playing with themselves. Lying in darkness, Jason cringed under that ever-present, supernatural voyeurism; Jesus wanted to find boys doing those things, didn't He? Otherwise, why would He look for them?

Even at thirteen, Jason Goodmaster wasn't going to give Jesus any satisfaction. So, although every night the desire grew sharper, the temptation stronger, Jason resisted. Jesus, naturally, responded by making it worse, until the very thought of going to bed caused Jason's little member to spring up painfully, in anticipation.

Jason began to blank his mind out around eight-thirty every night. By ten, he was under the covers, ignoring the tightness in his groin, spinning his mind to a sharp, tightly-focused kernel of concentration. Focusing it, and directing it . . . elsewhere.

One night, he had looked into that elsewhere and found something in it: the dancing, whirling dots. Shimmering, ringing . . . what?

Jason didn't know what it was. But, being a thirteen-year-old boy, he at once tried to do something with it anyway. The result gratified him immensely.

Some unfairness at school; he hardly remembered, now, but the new teacher had blamed him for something. He'd protested; she'd doubled his punishment. Not because she really thought he was guilty; she knew better. But because he was a Goodmaster, and in Meadbury it was well-known that Goodmasters did no wrong. Goodmasters were different.

"It's not fair," he said when she assigned him to memorize the parable of the talents; tomorrow, he would recite it before the class, some of whom already snickered with satisfaction. He knew the lesson she meant to teach was not for him, but for them: that she could punish a Goodmaster.

Still, he memorized the parable that evening. Afterward, as usual, he got into bed and went . . . elsewhere. From the shining whirlwind of dust motes, he picked out the one that was hers. How did he know? He wasn't sure. It felt as if the whirlwind itself were showing him, helping him zero in. It showed him how to identify each mote by its special, secret traits, to identify it as he would a person, by walk, posture, shape. It taught him how to punish, how to push.

The crystal grain faltered, wobbled in the matrix-place, dropped out. He giggled as it spun away.

The next morning found her paralyzed, drooling. A massive stroke, he heard the other teachers whisper. He knew better, of course, but kept his knowledge to himself as he recited the parable for the substitute teacher, who naturally gave him an A. Which, all things considered, he thought he deserved; he had, after all, just made the most of his talents.

Now as he remembered the rashness of his youth, a smile dusted his lips. Foolish boy. He returned to the more subtle problems of the present: his successor, for example. Jason Goodmaster was a youth no longer, and soon must settle his responsibilities on another.

Goodmaster searched the oversoul's hot patterns for Ibrani. Harshness, regrettably, was needed here; Ibrani was stubborn. And yet that was always the way of the fit ones. Ibrani would see reason. He would see the oversoul; Goodmaster would teach him the long view. In good time. Still smiling, he located—less easily than usual; the city thrilled to an unsettling vibration tonight—the miniature jewel of intelligence that would succeed him, in knowledge, and in power.

But young Ibrani spun tonight on a mad solitary path, battering himself against the darkness like a moth beating itself to death on a lampshade.

Foolish boy, foolish foolish boy. Goodmaster's smile crumbled. His vision lunged forward; Meadbury's jittery mote-pattern enlarged until its edges spread out of view.

Sternly, Goodmaster homed in on the youngster, knowing from years of experience just where to touch to push the boy back into line.

His own mind bounced back at him.

Goodmaster stared, incredulous. What had he hit, and how? The young pup was rebellious, that he knew. But he'd never managed completely to reject Goodmaster before.

Now, though; now he had. What shield had the rascal found?

The long view offered no insight.

Well, even the stoutest of arms tired finally; the wariest rebel lowered his guard sooner or later. And when he did. . . . Goodmaster's smile was grim. Young Ben would find that fending off the good advice of his elders, of his betters, was hard work. Sweaty work. Dirty work, in fact. And when the dirty work was over, when all this rebellious nonsense had ended, little Ben would need to bathe.

Most thoroughly.

With long-practiced ease, Goodmaster assigned a shred of himself to watching Ibrani. The rest of him drifted: up, down, around, browsing through a Meadbury that, most intriguingly, burned a bit brighter than usual.

A solitary diamond whirled in eccentric ellipse, struck the city's already-agitated pattern, and broke it. Discordance rippled.

Goodmaster sat up, greatly pleased. So much of life merely restated, recapitulated. But here was something new—which, *ipso facto,* merited investigation. Squinting at lives in the vicinity, he recognized one immediately: the woman, the news reporter whom he had selected for her nugget of independence. This one, like Ibrani, would need a great deal of riding before she welcomed the saddle.

Spinning into a fine, thin needle of coherent energy, as strong and as swift as a beam of laser light, he stabbed his thoughts into her, stopped, and expanded. The part of her that controlled the rest fell away, tumbling into blackness, there to remain until he vacated the premises. When he had finished, and departed, natural vacuum would draw her back in.

Slowly, the world appeared to Goodmaster through her eyes:

The Meadbury High School gymnasium. Long tables

lined the basketball court, tables loaded with cakes, pies, cookies. People milled near them, their chatter and smell in the air along with the sweet reek of sugar. From somewhere, a ringing sound: a cash register.

Of course. The PTA Bake Sale.

Stealthily, Goodmaster eased more into the body he had borrowed. It was easy, for he had moved this body earlier today: first, in the afternoon, to Ibrani; later to the mansion, to test young Tom. In each instance she had performed admirably, and afterward remembered nothing.

Now, moving her hand, he touched the small gold cross at her throat, then discreetly unfastened the top two buttons of the crisp white blouse. The girl had lovely breasts, but never used them.

Now he turned her head, scanning with her eyes the sea of smiling faces. Faces of fools.

There, for example: his target. The disturbance he'd spotted arose from a sharp-nosed teenage boy by the door, who waved his hands theatrically while he addressed two husky youths in varsity jackets.

Jason Goodmaster walked Nicki Pialosta across the crowded floor, nodded her head toward the school's principal, waved her hand at the president of the PTA. Then he stopped her beside the teenager, who was saying, "—on HBO twenty minutes ago! If the whole team went up and knocked on the old pervert's door—"

"Hello," her voice said. "What pervert?"

The boy twitched. His startled brown eyes focused on her face, dipped to measure her from toe to head, then relaxed slightly. "Hi."

Goodmaster adjusted the pattern; the football players nodded and left. Then he nudged Pialosta half a step closer, so that her shoulder pressed against the side of the boy's biceps. "I'm Nicki."

"So?"

"So, what pervert?"

"Oh, uh—" He shifted his weight from one foot to the other, shrugging her fingers off his shoulder in the process. His gaze dropped to the opened buttons, though, and lingered for a moment. "Goodmaster. Jason Goodmaster himself."

"Really!" Goodmaster softened her voice, lowered it. "I

hope you'll tell me more. Is your car outside?"

The boy stared at her for a good five beats, unbelieving.

Goodmaster laughed to himself. *You should live so long.*

The juvenile's mouth opened and closed again like the mouth of a fish, a hooked fish. "Yeah," the boy said, "uh, yeah. Are you, I mean do you want—"

"Let's go." Goodmaster sent her toward the doorway, knowing the boy would follow, and once more divided his awareness. Leaving the smaller part within Nicki, maintaining possession of her, he withdrew the rest of himself to a point just outside the two and studied the boy minutely.

Yes, it was working. A sudden burst of sex hormone seldom failed to bring a maverick into the pattern; since the oversoul survived through the population that made it, procreation was an important stimulus.

Nicki Pialosta paused just outside the gym doors, unfolding her coat.

Swiftly the boy stepped behind her, took the coat, and helped her into it. Then he pressed close, hands on her hips, pushing his face into the hair over her right ear. "It was on HBO just a little while ago. I taped it if you want to see—"

Leaning her back into the boy's arms, Goodmaster left her and scrutinized the results.

Yes, the boy's path ran parallel now to one of the patterns in the larger shape of things. Only the fool had no control, no purpose or direction. He tumbled along in the oversoul's current like a flimsy canoe on a river. A fast-moving river, with many dangers: rapids, and whirlpools. Just one quick little swirl. There.

The canoe overturned.

The current gobbled the boy in a blink, stretched him, flattened him, pummeled him. No more quirky rough edges now. He was Meadbury's.

So easy; hardly a challenge at all. Certainly not very interesting. Not, for example, like Pialosta. While the boy stood paralyzed by the process of absorption and synchronization, Goodmaster slipped back and sent Pialosta to her car. Home, it was time to go home. Then he withdrew completely, knowing that momentum would carry her until consciousness returned.

It might have been amusing to let the boy take her in the

back seat of his car, but despite her stubbornness, she was delicate. And she would prove useful later, he thought; best not to ruin her if he could help it.

Moving back now, he rested his soul's eye on the clear, perfect pattern; yes, the oversoul, luminous, complex beyond belief, and, perhaps, a bit more . . . Brownian than usual tonight.

Jason Goodmaster looked; and saw that it was good.

Then his gaze narrowed, suspicious and questioning. Had he looked closely enough after all? Was that not another, larger pattern, whirling outside and incorporating the first? The pattern of. . . .

No. Goodmaster relaxed. The darting diamonds that were human souls composed Meadbury's soul: the oversoul. Once more he gazed upon its hot glitter, reveling in it like a miser with his gems.

Yes, it was good, and all his. And it was . . . all. All there was; the ultimate power. No greater one existed. No greater one could.

When Jason Goodmaster looked, nothing looked back.

Or so he thought.

Something did look back at Jason Goodmaster, though, something larger than he ever saw. Something that was beginning to be angry. The town of Meadbury did indeed have a soul, and that soul knew a greater power—and rebelled against it.

Unamused, the greatersoul was not inclined to be merciful; just the reverse, in fact.

Exactly the reverse.

Jimmy Conklin

The iciness of winter earth seeped into his bones as he lay flat on his stomach in the rose garden of Goodmaster Mansion. Around him, cut-back rose canes raised knobby arms to the twilight sky. Beneath him, the trimmings jabbed their thorns through his gloves, his slacks, and sometimes even his coat. Under each bush, rotted manure had been heaped high; now it was frozen solid. With his nose two inches from it, Jimmy hoped he would smell better when he was frozen solid, which would be any minute now.

But there was a story inside that house, and he wanted it; more, even than he wanted a cup of hot coffee. Whatever it was, it was going to blow the lid off this town. All he needed was the match to light the fuse. And it was there, inside.

After that, he could write his own ticket. Whoever broke this story would get on the network news, probably *Nightline,* too. And then the job of his dreams, *The New York Times* or *The Wall Street Journal.* Some big daily where a million people would see his name, read his stuff. Heck, maybe he'd even do an American Express commercial.

He grunted, and carefully lifted his head. *Dream on, Jimmy me boyo. Even if you nail this one down tight, you won't get more than a couple of awards, and maybe a job offer on the* Beacon. *Unless, of course, ol' Goodmaster's henchmen decide to blow up your car with you in it, in which case you'll get all the attention you ever wanted. Posthumous of course. Ah, the carefree life of a newsman.*

He peered upward. Behind drawn shades, lights glowed in a dozen windows of the the big house. Occasionally someone moved in there, throwing a lumpy shadow he could not recognize. Once he'd thought he heard a car pull out of the side drive at the other side of the house, but by the time he could see it, it was disappearing down the front drive. The car had looked like Nicki's, but he couldn't be sure.

Wriggling nearer the house, Conklin paused every few feet to free his elbows and knees from the vicious rose thorns, and to listen for voices. Voices, or footsteps . . . or dogs. He shuddered inwardly at the thought, then forced himself forward a few more inches. He didn't think Goodmaster owned any dogs. He raised his head again, listening.

Nothing. Only wind, whispering frozenly in the canes of the rose bushes.

Then he ducked. Forty feet away a pair of French doors opened; two men stepped onto the patio. Holding his breath, he strained to listen, but heard only windblown scraps of their voices, no words.

Squinting through the shadows, he tried to make out their features. Suddenly the patio light went on. Delighted, he held himself rock still. So, who were these men who slipped outdoors to talk in quiet voices, heads ducked confidentially?

As if responding to his silent plea, they shifted. Conklin recognized Ned Gorman at once. But who was the other one? Gorman stepped to one side; now Conklin saw that the other man was just a security guard. Gorman was only giving the guy his orders; no confidential conference, after all.

The guard turned. Conklin's interest pricked again at the sight of his face. *Tommy Riley?*

Abruptly, Gorman's voice rose, and the porch light went out.

Conklin crawled forward as quickly and soundlessly as he could. Ten feet from the porch he realized: Someone might turn the light back on again. And the gun on the kid's hip looked damned big. . . . Wriggling into the relative shelter of an ancient rhododendron, Conklin began listening again.

"Oh, no, sir," Riley said. "It's just that— Well, I don't want to sound like a kid or anything, but I really ought to let my mother know. Just so she doesn't worry about me."

Then Gorman's voice, richly self-important. "Of course, Thomas. It's a good sign that someone so young should be so aware of his responsibilities, so sensitive to the needs of the important people in his life." Gorman's hand moved to Riley's shoulder. "Maintain that attitude, Thomas, and you'll go far in life."

Embarrassed shrug from the kid. "Well, thank you, Mr. Gorman."

Christ, Conklin thought, Gorman must have the kid brainwashed or something, get him to thank him for that crap.

"Again, I apologize again for imposing on you like this. I can't imagine why Purney hasn't shown up to relieve you. Unless he got into an accident on his way over, wound up unconscious in the emergency room." He let out a nasty laugh. "For his sake, he'd better be half-dead."

Riley clasped his hands behind his back, shifted his weight from one foot to the other, and said nothing.

"All right, then? You'll carry on?"

"Yes, sir." The kid sounded subdued now.

"Fine. Tell your mother. . . ." Gorman shook his head; suddenly the half-light made his shape ghastly, like the shadow of some bloated insect.

Conklin shivered, and scolded himself.

"I'm afraid," Gorman said in that fruity, unpleasant voice, "it will be at least four hours, possibly five. You will get time-and-a-half, though, as well as the premium for working the night shift."

"Thank you, sir." Riley looked like he wanted to end this talk. Sure; probably his mom was already frantic. "Uh, could you tell me what phone I can use?"

The two of them moved toward the French doors. ". . . alcove by the front entrance," Gorman was saying. Then they went in and Riley pulled the door shut, cutting off all sound.

Swiftly, Conklin scrambled out of the rhododendron and across the patio, hoping to glimpse what locks the kid threw on the door. A chain? Bolts into the floor and ceiling? If there were, he'd just call it a night and go home.

But if it was only the standard latch, well, a little breaking and entering now and then was good for the soul. And for the career, too, as long as you didn't get caught.

Conklin peered through the glass. No servants in sight. The kid had his back to the doors, heading across the front hall. To the phone, no doubt. And there was Gorman, just starting up the wide, curving stairs. Going to talk to Jason Goodmaster. Conklin was willing to bet on it. And he wanted to hear that conversation.

He squinted at the hardware inside the doors, and grinned to himself. Heck, it was practically an invitation.

Tommy Riley

"And just how am I supposed to sleep," Mrs. Riley demanded, "knowing you're out there till all hours doing who knows what with who knows who?"

Good thing, he thought, she doesn't know about the tests I took this afternoon. "Mom, I won't be out. I'll be right here—"

"—won't even give me a number where I can reach you—"

"Mom, this phone doesn't have a number. I mean, it has a number, but I don't know it. The little card's blank."

"And there's nobody there you can ask?" Her tone rendered her opinion of that.

Tommy sighed helplessly. "You don't expect me to disturb Mr. Goodmaster, do you? And if there was anybody else here, they wouldn't need a security guard, would they?" As soon as the words were out of his mouth, he wished he could call them back.

"What do you mean, nobody else there? You mean you're all alone in that place? What are those people thinking of, assigning a boy to—"

"Mom. Hey, Mom? Listen. Just listen a minute. Everything's fine, there's absolutely no danger; it's just a big house. They're worried about kids, you know? Vandals, spray-painters, window-breakers, like that. Mom?"

Long silence while she decided whether to believe it. Then, "So when will you be home?"

He forced himself to be patient. "Mom, I promise I'll be home twenty minutes after my relief gets here. When that's going to be, I'm not sure. But I'll be all right, okay? Look, don't wait up."

She made an exasperated sound. "You know I won't get a wink of sleep until you're safe in your own bed."

Tommy sighed again. "Yeah. Yeah, I know, Mom. Listen, I'll call you again right before I leave, okay? So you'll know I'm on my way. Will that make you feel better?"

"I suppose so." Doubt filled her voice, but so did an acknowledgment: There wasn't much she could do about it.

Except give him the lecture. "Now Tommy—"

Quickly he interrupted. "Mom, I gotta go. Talk to you later. 'Bye."

"—and watch out for—"

Feeling mean, he hung up. But once she got going, she would never finish. Shaking his head, he replaced the telephone in its alcove ledge, wire tucked neatly behind it as before. Mothers. He turned just in time to glimpse motion on the stairs. Stunned, Tommy recognized Jimmy Conklin as the reporter tiptoed around the curve of the staircase and vanished.

Hardly believing, Tommy surveyed all the things he had done: doors, windows, all locked, he was sure of it. And no glass had shattered, not audibly. But that didn't matter now; Conklin was inside. Upstairs.

And Mr. Gorman was up there.

Damn you, you idiot. You'll ruin everything for me. If it were just Mr. Goodmaster here tonight, Tommy would have a chance. He could hustle Conklin out before anybody else spotted them, and then no one would have to know. But Mr. Gorman had ears like a dog. He'd hear for sure if Tommy or Conklin raised so much as a whisper.

And that would be the end of this job, because Conklin wasn't supposed to have gotten in here in the first place. It was—had been—Tommy's job to keep him out.

Now Conklin must be moving silently along the upstairs hall. What the heck was he doing here, anyway? Other than losing Tommy the best job and the best future he'd ever dreamed of. . . .

I passed all the tests. I'm good enough, smart enough, strong enough. I've got this job, and I'm keeping it—no matter what.

In silence, he started up the stairs. Because whatever Conklin thought he was doing, in a minute he wasn't going to be doing it. As he climbed, he put one hand on the butt of his gun. That's how he would do it; guns didn't make noise if all you did was point them. And that would be enough.

He reached the top of the stairs. The hall was dark. Conklin would get the idea, wouldn't he? Just . . . leave. No one would hear a thing.

That was it. That was what he would do. Point the gun at Conklin. March him out the back way. Way out back. And pull the trigger. His finger tightened reflexively; a slow smile spread on his face. Yeah. That would do it.

Then he shook himself like a dog coming out of the rain. *Shoot Jimmy Conklin? Murder him?*

But the thought persisted. It would be murder. That was true, that was definitely true. But it would solve a lot of problems. Save a lot of trouble. And Conklin, after all, was making trouble for Mr. Goodmaster and Mr. Gorman, wasn't he?

What would Mr. Goodmaster and Mr. Gorman want Tommy to do about that? It was his job, after all; that was why they'd given him all those tests in the first place. To make sure he could do, would do . . . what they wanted him to do.

Downstairs, all the lights went out. But never mind; whatever it was, he would deal with it later. Easing into the hall, he listened left and right. Which way had Conklin gone? He held his breath, alert for the slightest sound. All he could hear was the frantic thumping of his own heart.

Then, from his right, in the dark by the library, came the faint scrape of shoe leather. Tommy moved toward it, quiet as fog. That's what he was, he thought: a silent presence. A thinking presence.

What would they want him to do?

Maybe . . . maybe they would want him to take responsibility. Remove the burden of decision from them. Just . . . do it.

On the other hand, Mr. Goodmaster had been permitting Jimmy Conklin to live and work in Meadbury for years. Mr. Gorman could have had Jimmy Conklin removed, like a wart, any time he'd wanted. And he hadn't, had he?

Still, things had changed. Jimmy Conklin had broken in and was sneaking around. Surely that would alter Mr. Gorman's attitude toward Jimmy Conklin. Mr. Goodmaster's, too. A lot, probably. Maybe completely, once and for all.

Thinking this, Tommy silently unsnapped his holster.

And took another step.

Ben Ibrani

One more round of "Jumpin' Jack Flash" would drive him mad. Or deaf. Or both. Meanwhile, the stereo headphones grated on his ears and Mick Jagger insisted yet again that everything was a gas. Ben pulled another heavy cardboard box from his front hall closet. He cut through the tape that held it shut and wondered why he had never gotten around to organizing his things.

His old records, for example, were here somewhere, in a carton. Of course, if he had ever imagined just how vital finding them might be, he would have labeled it. But he hadn't. Because this whole situation, this whole thing, was unimaginable.

He wrenched the carton open, and cursed. Old science fiction magazines; great. He shoved them aside, then grabbed another box. Somewhere, he knew, he had those records; he'd stuffed them away instead of putting them on the shelves when he moved here, because they embarrassed him. Sixties stuff; he still had it, and some rock from the early seventies.

Loud, angry music. The kind that did not fit with his good yuppie image. The kind that would save his foolish life, if he could only find it. It had to be here somewhere. Absolutely had to be. But where?

Dust clung to his body, glued with sweat. His back ached, and his head, too, and his shoulders. . . . Still, they were normal pains. Just the kind of creaks and groans a normal, nearly-middle-aged guy would get from hauling out boxes, shoving them aside, and hauling out more. Not the kind of pains he could be having. Would be having, if he let his mind get vacant for just one instant.

He needed music, and not just any music. And unless he wanted to listen to the Rolling Stones for the rest of the night—or the rest of his life—he would have to find more. Or go out and buy more.

Could he get away with that? Here in the apartment was one thing. With the music in his head, nothing else could invade him. Crazy, but it worked. Out on the street, though;

would it work there? Especially after the HBO thing?

It looked as if he was going to find out. He could not find those old albums. And he couldn't stay in his apartment forever, either, records or no records. Okay. He had copied The Stones record onto a cassette. He would simply pop it into his Walkman. Thus armored, he could go anywhere.

He hoped.

So. Cassette in the Walkman. Walkman turned on. Prepare to switch headphones. Ready, set— Wait. Batteries. Fresh batteries.

Okay. Batteries on bedroom dresser. Pulling more slack in the headphone cord with his right hand, he went to get them, meanwhile trying to figure out where he should go once he got outside.

Kmart, maybe? They were open late, but he didn't know how late. And he had no idea what their record selection was like. He wasn't quite sure who else sold records, either; not the kind he needed, anyway.

Hell, maybe he should check the yellow pages; he wanted this to be a fast run, not a leisurely shopping tour. The phone book was on the nightstand, next to his bed.

Yeah, good idea. Good thing he had a long cord on these headphones, too. He looped it around the bedpost at the foot of the bed so he wouldn't yank it loose from the stereo by accident. Then he sat, pulled the book into his lap, and opened it.

For perhaps the hundredth time, Mick Jagger begged to introduce himself.

Yeah, Mick. Ibrani licked his index finger.

Mick bragged: He'd been around for a long, long time.

You sure as hell have, buddy. Ibrani ran his finger down a page.

Mick was pleased to meet Ibrani.

Right. Likewise.

Then Ibrani blinked in total darkness as Mick Jagger's voice died and his own body grew a sudden coating of slime.

Because the power, the goddamn electricity had gone off.

But . . . the Walkman. The batteries. Ibrani leaped to his feet.

No, Ben. No . . . music. No, none of that. Soap. Dirty Ben did something nasty tonight. Filthy Ben needs to take a shower right now. The voice sounded inside his head, where Mick Jagger had been.

Gritting his teeth, he turned in darkness toward the dresser where the batteries were; this time he would resist. And he did, too, until from out of that darkness something touched him.

Something . . . unspeakable. Something obscene.

Something dead.

His bowels and bladder emptied in a hot, shaming rush as fright seized him and held him.

The touch lingered, caressingly. Then it faded, and he stood there alone. Except for the voice in his head.

Time to shower, Ben, it said, gently amused.

And it had him. He knew it had him. A single sob of anguished defeat tore out of his throat. Then he turned and stumbled in darkness, toward the shower. *Hot water. Soap, cleanser, bleach. And the brush. Yes, especially the brush.*

The thought sent him lunging blindly, heedless of the headphone cord still looped around the bedpost, and now around his ankles.

The next moment, his feet went out from under him while his upper body continued rushing forward.

The moment after that, his forehead slammed into the corner of the dresser.

The pain astonished him. It occupied all his attention. Through it, he had one instant more to wonder at how clean he suddenly felt again, and to decide that, as a distraction, he preferred Mick Jagger to a broken head.

Then his own lights went out, and he thought nothing.

Jimmy Conklin

He crouched in the dark upstairs hall of Goodmaster Mansion, ear pressed to the polished wood of the library's closed double doors. Inside, a peevish old voice said, "Hell and damnation. I've lost him again." A cane thumped the floor; a chair creaked.

Conklin frowned. *Lost who?*

"Yes, I see that." Another voice, younger, sounding

excited but puzzled. "But how exactly did you have him at all? And what happened just now?"

Yeah, what did happen just now?

"He fainted, I believe," the older voice answered. "From fright. I had to . . . motivate him a bit."

"About the HBO thing. It's libel, you know; we can—" The younger voice grew anxious.

An unpleasant chuckle interrupted. "Children throw mud. Ignore it."

Holding his breath, Conklin reached out, unlatched one of the doors, and eased it open a crack. Then he slipped his camera from his pocket. Inside: Goodmaster and Gorman, firelit.

Goodmaster snorted. "Best get the power back on, boy."

"Coming up."

And what the hell did that mean? Wanting to hear some more questions—and more answers—Conklin nudged the door again, giving thanks for the kind of wealth that did not endure squeaky hinges.

Obscured by darkness, Jason Goodmaster and Ned Gorman sat in wingback armchairs before the fireplace, their backs to the door. On the table between them stood snifters that trapped and twisted dancing firelight. The man on the right picked up his snifter, stared through it into the flames, and intoned, "Done." Gorman.

Conklin flinched as lamps sprang to low, glowing light in the corners of the room. The power had been off. And Gorman had just turned it on again.

By . . . *looking? Now that is spooky.*

"Very good," Goodmaster said.

Yeah. Now let's see you pull a rabbit out of a hat.

"You see, Ned. It's not the thought that counts. It's the action that counts. You need not understand; you need only . . . do."

Gorman shifted uncomfortably. "My campaign is going well," he said, as if to change the subject. "Too well, I think."

Goodmaster chuckled again. "Surely you're not serious. How can anything ever go too well?"

"The early stages of a political campaign should be full of glitches, sir. Small problems, of course, you wouldn't want anything major, but . . . oh, double bookings or inane press releases or anything on that order would be helpful. To condition the staff, you see, so that when a major crisis really does break—well. A few small training exercises, if you will. Call it conditioning."

"Yes, of course." Goodmaster's voice was richly approving. "How good you are, Ned. Perhaps—" He cocked his head, held up his right hand, raised his index finger, and fell silent.

Gorman, sipping his brandy, waited for his mentor to continue.

Conklin frowned again. What the hell was going on now? Goodmaster's lips seemed to be twitching, but no words came out. A trick of the shadows?

More than a minute later, Goodmaster lowered his hand and took up where he had left off as if nothing had happened.

Something had, though. Conklin was sure of it.

"What if we were to arrange something ourselves?" Goodmaster said. "The fire department sets buildings on fire to train their men."

Gorman looked into his snifter. Then, slowly, he shook his head. "I don't think so, sir. They'll turn to me for guidance, you see, and in a genuine crisis, I would provide it." His small laugh pretended to modesty. "Which means, you see, that I need the training quite as much as they do. So—"

"Of course," said Goodmaster. "I shall arrange something."

Gorman's head jerked up. He half rose, apparently to protest. Then he stopped, settled back, and nodded. "Thank you, sir."

The old man waved his hand in dismissal. "My pleasure, boy."

"Would you, ah, care to give me a hint as to your plans?"

"Well—" Again Goodmaster froze in mid-sentence. His head twitched once, twice; a low moan escaped his lips. His jaw worked hard for—Conklin couldn't quite believe it—almost two minutes. Then the old man's armchair shuddered and he spoke again. "No. No, I don't believe I would. As you say, you need the training, too."

Gorman rose. "Of course. And now I really should be going."

Conklin gripped his Nikon. Time for a few quick shots of the plotters, though he still didn't know what they were plotting. He brought the camera to his eye, squinted through the viewfinder. Fast, now, before Gorman came out and caught him. *Just a little to your right, Ned, smile and watch the birdie—*

A hand clamped itself to the top of his head. Another snatched the camera.

Conklin broke left, thrust his elbow back—

And froze as the small cold thing pressed against his ear.

That loud sound was the pistol's safety catch, clicking off.

"Don't." The voice was Tommy Riley's.

"What's going on here?" Lamplight washed out of the library as the doors opened.

Riley spoke tensely. "I caught him snooping, Mr. Gorman. And he had this camera."

"The ace ex-reporter, eh?" Gorman stepped into the hall, looking Conklin up and down. "Good work, Riley."

Goodmaster spoke from inside the room. "Bring him in."

Riley grabbed Conklin's collar. "On your feet."

Okay, okay. Never apologize, never explain. He clambered up, brushing imaginary dust from his coat. It gave his hands an excuse for moving, so no one would see that they were shaking. Funny how easy it had all seemed, back when he was still standing outside. Now, though: caught.

He thought fast. No signs of forced entry; they couldn't get him for breaking and entering. Trespassing? Maybe. There was that fence.

Old Prickly would have had his ass for this, if he were still working for Old Prickly. Only he wasn't. Not anymore. Which meant Old Prickly wouldn't be going to bat for him, either. No *Bulletin* behind him. Just Gorman, in front of him.

So kid the kidder. He tried an ironic smile. "Isn't this convenient?" He offered his hand. "I've been looking for you."

Gorman ignored the attempted handshake. "You seem to have found me." Then, seizing Conklin's arm, he hauled him into the library. Riley followed.

Wing it. Just fucking wing it, and get out of here. "Just where I wanted to be. I have a lot of questions for the two of you." He reached into his pocket for notepad and pen. "To begin with—"

Goodmaster looked bored. "Shoot him, Riley."

Conklin stiffened. "Hey. That's not funny." He took a step back. Because it wasn't, it wasn't funny at all. None of it. Especially the expression on Tommy Riley's face. Nothing. Vacancy. Porch lights on, but nobody home.

Riley dropped his gaze to the gun in his hand.

Shit. Oh, shit. "Look," said Conklin, vamping for time now because this kid Riley, here, this kid was not right, this kid was bonkers and he had a fucking gun in his hand, "look, I realize I've intruded, but there's really no reason for—"

Riley's arm came up. His eyes looked like Orphan Annie's: two circles. Blank.

Conklin put his hands out. "Hey, listen, dammit! You can't just shoot a man. You can't just—"

Riley's finger twitched.

Muzzle flash exploded in Conklin's face.

Shit, he thought again, and died.

Tommy Riley

The pistol's recoil jolted his arm all the way to the shoulder. His hand tingled. His nose wrinkled at the sudden stink of gunpowder. It smelled like firecrackers. Only it wasn't. Numbly, he looked down at the corpse he had just made.

Jimmy Conklin lay on the carpet, his arms flung at crazy angles, one leg twisted awkwardly beneath him. Death had surprised him, wrenching his lips into a startled grimace and snapping his eyes wide open. The hole in his forehead was about the size of a dime, blackish-red. A small runnel of blood trickled out of it, down into the corner of Conklin's left eye and then along the side of his nose.

Tommy's ears still rang from the shot, but he knew that in fact everything was very quiet. He felt his arm lowering the gun, felt it as if from a distance, and wondered for a moment if he would drop the weapon. Then his hand tightened around the grip. He needed something to cling to, and this would serve.

Mr. Gorman and Mr. Goodmaster were staring at him. Everything else in the room kept stretching and shrinking, the floor rippling, too, as if they were all trapped inside some kind of funhouse mirror. Tommy heard himself moan. He kept clutching the gun, though. *Don't let go of it.*

All of this took no more than five or ten seconds. When the seconds had passed, Conklin was still dead.

Because I killed him. Tommy wondered at the finality of it. His mind kept trying to play the last minute backward like videotape, scoot the blood and the bone fragments back into Jimmy Conklin's forehead and scramble him jerkily up off the floor again.

Ha, ha, guys. All a joke. Special effects. No problem, see?

But the minute wouldn't run in reverse, and Conklin wouldn't scramble anywhere ever again. Beneath the reporter's head a soggy mush of thick dark blood was spreading rapidly. Tommy felt a sudden, strong temptation to freak out, go nuts and lose himself. Run around, scream and cry and laugh. Nutso. Flip city, only something wouldn't let him.

And that was a relief, because it meant he could let go. Calmness washed over him. After all, he'd only been doing his job. This guy at his feet was an intruder—

A friend.

—the kind of person who might do something bad to Mr. Goodmaster—

A friend who'd always been decent to you.

—the kind you shot when Mr. Goodmaster said, "Shoot him."

But you murdered him because someone told you to.

Tommy opened his mouth to speak. A whimper came out instead. There seemed to be two of himself, in his head, and they were arguing. He wanted to tell them to stop. That, however, was not how things worked. He didn't tell them things.

They told him things.

One of them was telling him he was a slimebag asshole murderer who had just blown a hole in Jimmy Conklin's forehead.

The other one was calmly directing him to take Conklin's body to the carbarn, back to the old disused grease pit, and dump it in. And cover it with quicklime from the bags he would find there.

That wasn't the worst part, though. The worst part was that, in this detached and horribly clear, crystal-clear moment, he recognized the voice telling him to do those things. It was not his own. It was the same peevish old voice that had told him to shoot Jimmy Conklin in the first place.

Stunned, Tommy stared at Jason Goodmaster.

Goodmaster smiled.

Tommy shivered like a little kid afraid to go into the cellar because the boogeyman lived there. He trembled even though he was almost a man, too old to believe in the boogeyman.

The trouble was that the boogeyman believed in him. The boogeyman lived here in this big rich house. He wore a maroon velvet smoking jacket. He sat a few feet away, smiling at Tommy, and at what was left of Jimmy Conklin. He was Tommy Riley's boss, and somehow he had gotten into Tommy Riley's head. Weeks ago.

Tommy retreated unthinkingly, bumping his shoulder hard against the doorframe.

Mr. Goodmaster's look turned suspicious. He got to his feet and stepped close to Tommy. "What's the matter, boy? Follow your path. Dispose of the body, then come back here."

Tommy put his hand out, flattened it against the old man's chest, and shoved. "No!"

Goodmaster flailed backward, almost tripping over Conklin's body, but Gorman caught him before he went down. The two men stared at Tommy.

"No!" He brought up the gun. Hardly believing what he was doing, he braced his right hand with his left the way he'd learned on the pistol range, holding both men at bay and wondering what in the world he was going to do next. They'd taught him a lot at that pistol range, but not about situations like this. Heck, they'd have locked him up if he'd even asked about drawing on Jason Goodmaster.

His mind searched desperately for possible actions, anything to get him out of here. But the butler would come running in any second, the police would be all over the place in a couple of minutes, and here he stood, murder weapon in hand, menacing two of the town's most prominent citizens. He'd be lucky to even get a chance to tell his story. Not that anyone was going to believe him, anyway.

Sure, kid. The devil made you do it. And the devil is Jason Goodmaster? Yeah, sure he is. Now just stick your arms right into this here straitjacket, and step into this cozy padded cell. . . .

Meanwhile they kept staring at him, and that was driving him nuts. He couldn't get enough air. The gun dragged at his arms. Gravity. Thirty-two feet per second. Pulling on a two-ton revolver—

He tipped the barrel up a fraction and fired a round just over their heads.

Startled, they jerked as one and turned to each other, their faces questioning.

Tommy nearly laughed. *Nope. Neither one of you made me do it that time. That time* I *made me do it.* Something —*the equation; I was thinking about the equation*—had somehow freed him, never mind how. He flung himself around and ran like hell.

The butler hustled down the hall at him, trotting stiffly but looking determined. "Stop!" The old geezer's voice cracked.

Tommy charged. He had only played football at the playground level, but he had watched a lot of games on TV. *Fake inside, cut left, and spin. Clip the old fart in the head if you have to—*

Or even if you don't have to. No penalties here, except for not getting away.

But to his immense disappointment, he reached the stairs two steps ahead of Throtway and clattered on down. No chance for a nose punch, even. Elation seized him as he sprinted across the hall. He would make it. Throwing open the door, he hurtled onto the wide, dark porch.

And stopped.

His car was out back, under the lights. He would never get to it. By now Gorman would be there for sure. Elation turned to panic; he was all alone, with no idea what to do, or how to do it.

And he had killed Jimmy Conklin.

Get away!

Frantically, he stared around. Should he run? Down the driveway? A zillion miles from here to the street. And the driveway stretched arrow-straight between walls of thick, thorny hedges. If he ran a four-minute mile, a car traveling at sixty miles per hour would—

Wheels, he needed wheels. A car, or— A bicycle?

There had been one, just this afternoon, leaning against the side of the garage. He vaulted over the porch rail and ran toward it, still clutching the impossibly heavy gun but afraid to throw it away. Because he might need it yet. Terrible as the idea of using it again was, the gun was here and the bicycle might not be.

It was, though: old and rusty and balloon-tired. He holstered the gun and jumped on the ancient Schwinn as a car started up out front.

So much for the driveway. He headed through the bushes, toward the far backyard. Back there somewhere, if he could only find it in the darkness, curled an old footpath that went through a hole in the chain link fence. Kids used it, not so much as a shortcut but to dare each other. Walking that path was a test, like going into a haunted house. Yeah, only the kids didn't know *how* haunted.

Pedaling ninety pumps a minute now, he bounced through the gardens, over clumps of frozen earth that threatened to spill him with every turn of his wheels. Ghastly bushes reached for him with thorny arms, snagging at him as he sucked in great whooping gulps of the freezing night air. Ahead sprawled a wide, flat patch that had been grass, and was now white. Beyond lay more shrubbery, with the path somewhere in it, but how could he find the entrance in the snow?

As he wondered this, the path found him. The sunken spot where it opened up had melted and frozen a dozen times. Now ice covered it, and it waited treacherously under a skim of snow. The bike's front tire hit, slid across, and caught a rough patch; the handlebars lurched and the rear tire came skiddingly around.

Tommy flew. The bike clattered down. He landed with a *whump* that knocked the breath out of him. As he clambered unsteadily to his feet, he saw it: the path, a faint line twisting away through the bushes.

Clenching his teeth to keep from whimpering, he grabbed

the bike up again and ran with it until he reached the protective cover of frozen azaleas and rhododendrons. Then he swung back onto the seat and pedaled away as fast as he could.

Behind a hemlock, he found the hole in the chain link. Probably no one had even noticed it; it was only the size of a little kid. Tommy forced his way through, tearing his shirt in the process. He didn't care. The bicycle, though; the bike wouldn't fit. He wrestled with it for a few moments, then abandoned it. He hated leaving it; it had gotten him this far. But he was going to need something more than a bicycle, anyway. He might as well start getting it now.

Two hundred yards away—less than thirty seconds—a phone booth glowed outside the 7-Eleven store, kindling hope in him. With a quick, hunted glance up and down the street, he set off. As he ran, he counted strides, and wondered who he could possibly call.

He needed help desperately. Not from one of his friends; from someone reliable. From a full-grown one-hundred-percent adult, in fact. But not his mother.

Or the cops.

Or Miss Pialosta. What had she been doing, anyway, nearly naked in a bed in Goodmaster Mansion? Whose side was she on? He didn't know. And he didn't have time to find out, either. So, not Miss Pialosta.

And not Jimmy Conklin, because Jimmy Conklin was dead. Murdered. *By me.* He shuddered, realizing his crime once more.

Which left . . . who? He was suddenly aware of how few reliable, friendly adults he had in his life. Maybe that's why he'd been so anxious to be a man—so he'd have one when he needed one. Then another thought struck him with the force of inspiration: *Mr. Ibrani!*

Glancing around again, seeing no one who looked as if they were looking for him, he grabbed the phone with shaking hands and punched the number of the Meadbury *Bulletin* switchboard.

"I'm sorry." The switchboard operator did not sound sorry at all. "He went home hours ago. May I take a message?"

"Do you have his home number?"

"I'm-sorry-I-cannot-give-out-that-information."

And that was what finally broke him, hearing her say it that way just because it was a rule, and hadn't he tried to follow the rules? Hadn't he always tried so goddamn hard, so hard. And look what it had got him—

"Please," he said, begging, hearing his voice break and not trying to stop it. "Please, I have got to talk to a grown-up person and he's the only one I know. Please." He was crying, now, tears freezing on his cheeks. "He is. Please tell me."

A pause. Then she did. "But you didn't get it from me, understand? It's in the book, you could have looked it up, so you didn't—"

"Right," he said, "right, I didn't, oh, thank you—" He hung up, found another dime, thank Christ he had another, punched the buttons—

And hung up again. What if Ibrani told him not to come over? Or just hung up on him? And if he was in the book, his address was there, too.

Gasping with fright because somebody might drive along at any instant, spy him, and catch him, Tommy fumbled with the thick telephone book. Thank Christ too for no vandals in Meadbury; phone books stayed put, and— Yes! Here it was. The address: only thirteen blocks away.

Mr. Ibrani might not want to be disturbed at this time of night. To someone on the telephone he could easily say, "Don't come." No matter how desperate that someone on the phone might sound, he could say it. But he wouldn't slam his door in a friend's face, would he?

Only one way to find out. Tommy turned into the night, into the dark streets full of who knew what.

Or whom.

Ibrani's place lay . . . that way.

Shivering, Tommy Riley began to run, counting his steps because counting helped, numbers helped, he didn't know why.

Nicki Pialosta

Nicki Pialosta opened her eyes. Moonlight glowed through the curtains. A square of familiar carpet showed, and a familiar bedspread. She was in her own bed. The knowledge brought vague relief. Just as vaguely, she wondered why it should.

Garish red numerals on the nightstand clock: 9:47.

She sat up, fully dressed, even to her shoes. Again the question, so muted it could have come from the next building: *Why?*

Because.

She made her way through shadows to the bathroom, closed the door. In darkness, she ran her fingers through her hair, then used the toilet. *Sore. I'm sore there?*

Never mind.

The question vanished.

Standing, she pulled off her rumpled suit, slip, stockings. Panties and bra dropped. Then she pulled the shower curtain back, reached for the faucet, and paused.

Puzzled momentarily, she riffled through memories like cards in a Rolodex. *The doorbell. If it rings while I shower, will I hear it?* No. The running water would drown out the chimes. Which meant the shower could wait. Until afterward.

Stepping back into her shoes, she pulled the short, terry cloth robe from the bathroom door hook. Tying its sash, she went into the living room. *My living room,* she thought mildly. *My chair.*

Smiling, she sat. The curtains blocked any glimmer of moonlight. Still, she needed no lamp. Sitting quietly, hands in her lap, she waited. Perfect silence filled the room, filled her head.

Until the single, familiar, very clear voice said, once and once only: "Tommy Riley will come to you. When he does, kill him."

Nicki Pialosta stiffened at the sound of the voice.

"Yes," she said. "Yes."

Tommy Riley

One thousand six hundred ninety-seven— Another hundred— His breath came in frightened, exhausted puffs. *Ninety-eight— Ninety-nine— 1700* (1700 strides x 6 feet/stride = 10,200 feet ÷ 5280 feet/mile = 1.9 miles, hummed his brain). He could do it, he could! Slamming the heel of his hand onto the bell marked "Ibrani, B." he gasped in harsh, ragged sobs. The buzz came. He shoved open the door and nearly fell into the deserted lobby.

Upstairs, Ibrani opened his door little more than a crack, and peered out suspiciously. Bandage on his forehead, Walkman headphones on his ears, he leaned on the wall, looking wiped out.

Which was no wonder: Music from the cassette deck clipped to Ibrani's belt spilled out of the headphones and throbbed in the corridor. Stones. Loud; really loud.

"What do you want?" Ibrani shouted over the sound.

God, it must be scrambling his brains. Tommy spluttered senselessly for a moment, out of breath and taken aback by Ibrani's appearance and behavior. Then he forced his lips to frame words, forming them very clearly because Ibrani could not hear him: "I need to talk to you."

"Go away."

"Please, Mr. Ibrani, please, it's important."

Ibrani's eyes half closed. His head sagged. Alarmed, Tommy stepped forward, supporting Ibrani, who slumped hard against him. Then Ibrani stepped back. "All right. Come in." His tone suggested surrender.

Tommy looked up and down the corridor a final time, then went inside. Because Ibrani seemed incapable of purposeful movement, he closed the door himself.

Ibrani shuffled around to trudge across the dark vestibule. Tommy followed.

Suddenly Ibrani spun. Before Tommy could react, Ibrani seized his collar, turned his body, and jammed his face into the wall. Something hard and cold jabbed him in the small of the back. "Spread 'em!" Ibrani kicked Tommy's feet apart. "G'wan, get your hands up there where I can see them."

Tommy complied. He was learning fast about paranoia, and he thought he understood it. Slapping his palms wide apart against the cool plaster, he shouted so Ibrani could hear. "Okay, okay. I swear, though—"

Ibrani's hands slapped Tommy's kidneys, skimmed his body from top to bottom, front and back. He found the gun, removed it from its holster. Then Ibrani stood back. "What the fuck are you doing here?"

Tommy craned his neck cautiously and began slowly to push away from the wall. Then he stopped at a flash of light glinting off blued steel: not his pistol. His pistol was jammed into Ibrani's waistband. A shotgun glared instead at Riley through dark, double-barreled eyes.

"Don't do anything quick," Ibrani said.

"Yes, sir." *You bet, sir. Whatever you say.*

Ibrani slapped the shotgun into his other hand. Eyes still on Riley, he moved back toward the apartment door, tested the knob, threw the dead bolt, and snapped the chain up. Jerking his head toward the lighted room at the end of the hallway, he spoke again. "Go ahead."

Tommy went, fear drying his tongue into stiff leather. Suddenly it occurred to him why Ibrani was being so careful: Tommy Riley was a murderer, wasn't he? "Did they call you? You won't need that gun, honest, Mr. Ibrani. I mean, it wasn't my idea to shoot him, it was Mr. Goodmaster, he made me do it, and Mr. Gorman just stood there nodding. I—"

Ibrani moved around where he could see Tommy's lips move. "Shut up."

Tommy nodded.

Ibrani peered at him through bloodshot eyes. "Who sent you?"

"Nobody, I—"

"The truth, Tommy, the whole truth and nothing but—or else." Ibrani's voice rang too loud. He patted the stock of the shotgun. "The truth. I mean it, now." He hoisted the gun to his shoulder and sighted down it at Tommy's head.

So. Now it was his turn. He was going to die. Right there in Mr. Ibrani's living room, Tommy Riley was going to die. Just like Conklin. And just like Conklin, he could not do a damn thing about it.

That terrified him. But terror had become familiar enough to numb his perceptions of it, his reactions. So he was scared. Big deal. He'd been scared for an hour now. Goodmaster hadn't killed him; neither had Gorman. The damned doddering butler hadn't even come close.

Now, though, Ibrani was going to kill him. And that infuriated him. Which meant he didn't have a hell of a lot to lose any more, did he? Abruptly, without asking permission, he sat down in one of Ibrani's overstuffed chairs and crossed his legs. On the end table beside the chair stood a glass of amber liquid. Scotch, probably. Again without asking, Tommy took it and swallowed down a long, solid belt.

Then he nearly coughed it all back up. His eyes watered; his throat burned. His belly burned, too. But he felt better. He was still scared, all right. More than that, though, he was pissed. "I didn't ask for this," he said, not caring if Ibrani could hear through those idiot headphones. Screw it. "And I am telling you the truth."

Ibrani watched carefully. In his eyes, Tommy saw the beginnings of a new thought, as if Tommy had impressed him.

With the scotch, maybe. Tommy knew the stuff sure as hell had impressed him. He hefted the glass for a moment. Then, without stopping, he drank down the rest of it. "Okay. I gotta tell you, I don't really know where it started." He stopped, looked up.

Ibrani nodded, watching his lips carefully.

"Maybe it started in night school, that crazy test. Maybe when I went to work for the guard company and they assigned me to the shelter. Remember that day—" He stopped again. "God, it was yesterday! Only yesterday? When Miss Pialosta went through that door in the basement?"

Ibrani grimaced, and nodded.

"Well, the thing is, that wasn't me! I mean it was, but it's like there's two of me. The person I've always been, and this— this robot that every once in a while takes over and does things. Things I'd never do. Like tonight." Okay, he'd said it. And so far, Ibrani hadn't told him he was nuts, and hadn't shot him. He laced his fingers together and stared at them as he told the rest of his story: Conklin's invasion of

Goodmaster Mansion, Conklin's death on the library floor.

"Honest to God, Mr. Ibrani, it was Mr. Goodmaster. I don't know how he did it, but it was like he pulled the trigger. With my finger. I know it sounds crazy, but—"

"No."

Tommy looked up, knowing Ibrani couldn't believe this part. "But that's how it happened. I'm telling the truth. Only—"

"I know." Ibrani studied the shotgun in his hands, then laid it on the coffee table, barrels aimed away. He went to the armchair across from Tommy's, moving slowly, stiffly, as though pain wracked his every joint. "I know you're telling the truth, Tommy. In fact, I think I know just what you mean."

"You do?"

"Only too well. I wish I didn't. But I've been there."

"The mansion?"

Ibrani shook his head.

He was, Tommy realized, still listening to that blaring tape of the Rolling Stones. But that didn't matter now. "Then, if you understand, will you go with me to the police and help explain it? If I try to tell them, they'll never believe me."

"No." The answer was flat.

"But—"

"You're not going to the police, Tommy." A sad smile moved the corners of Ibrani's mouth. With a grunt, he pushed himself from the chair, crossed the room, and poured each of them another drink.

"But I have to," Tommy said. "I have to explain about Mr. Conklin!"

Ibrani handed him a glass. "You think they'll believe you?"

"If you come along and back me up, they will."

Ibrani looked pityingly at him. "Tommy, who do you think controls the Meadbury Police Department?"

"Well—" Tommy stopped as a very bad feeling passed through him. "Mr. Goodmaster."

"That's right." Ibrani sipped at his drink and nodded. "He does. Just the way he controls about everything else in town. The way he controlled you. And the way he's trying —right now, even—to control me."

Suddenly Tommy understood the possible usefulness of music. Very loud music; louder, even, than voices in your head. Like calculating gravity at just the right moment, or counting steps. He gazed at Mr. Ibrani and the headphones with new, comprehending admiration.

"And how do you think the police will treat you," Ibrani went on, "if you walk in and accuse Goodmaster of murder? Hmm?"

Tommy sagged in the armchair. Not to be able to go to the police; God, it was worse than being afraid they would catch you. "So what do I do?"

"You wait."

"Huh? For what?"

"For word to get around. See, I've been working on this, too."

"Pardon?" Tommy poured some of the fresh scotch down his throat. It burned, but it stayed down without any back talk, this time. He sipped at it again, more cautiously.

"I broke onto HBO, Tommy." Ibrani's voice, still too loud, had regained some of its normal fluency. He no longer sounded paranoid, or maniacal, just scared. Tommy could understand that. But he sounded hopeful, too. And to that, Tommy Riley clung with all his might.

"I inserted a fake news bulletin," Ibrani went on, "that claimed Jason Goodmaster has AIDS, and is about to be indicted for child molestation. By morning, everybody in Meadbury will have heard all about it. They might not believe it, but they'll know somebody said it."

"Uh-huh. So what happens then?"

Ibrani shrugged. "I don't know. Not for sure. I think what will happen is that it will shake things up. Folks who believed in Jason Goodmaster all their lives will start to wonder. A lot will mutter about the garbage on TV these days. But they'll think about it, won't they? And some of them will say, 'Where there's smoke, there's fire.' And after that, because there really is something bad, their suspicions will carry them. They'll want to know more, and they'll find out more. And finally all the suspicion, all the hostility, and all the truth—"

Ibrani dropped his hands, which had been clenched together in front of him. "If there is a God," he said quietly, "if there is any justice at all, when they find out the truth, they'll tear Jason Goodmaster and his monster into little pieces, and let us live free."

"Or die," Tommy said. "Like on the license plate."

"Yeah. Or die. But that happens anyway." Ibrani's smile broadened quirkily, as if talking to Tommy had made him feel better. "Like the man says, getting there is half the fun."

THURSDAY, JANUARY 17

Meadbury

Wanting only his newspaper and some black coffee, Mike Schantz walked wearily from predawn gloom into Roundtree's Market. The clock above the cash register said five o'clock. Yesterday had been the longest day he could remember.

Damn all baby-sitters to hell, anyway. Mike still could not believe the silly little putz had tried to flush a cloth diaper. And then called her boyfriend to fix it. And he, in turn, had somehow broken not only the toilet itself but the drainpipe as well. And the both of them arguing about some HBO news bulletin the whole time.

On the other hand, that silly little putz and her boyfriend had earned him seven hours of work at night rates. *Thank God for amateurs. Weren't for them, I'd have to find a job somewhere.*

Not a pleasant thought. Working for himself, he grossed in the neighborhood of a hundred thousand a year. He could probably do better if he went fishing only four weeks a year, instead of eight.

But what the hell, he was thirty-five, living alone in the house his folks left him; he had no reason to make a few extra bucks. Especially when the Feds took sixty cents out of each of those extra bucks, and the state stood right behind them with its hand out.

Yeah, sure he'd need a job. . . . He had reached the coffee urn before he noticed the chill wind that blew through the open back door of the market, and the acrid smoke that swirled in on that wind.

Fatigue fell away. He hesitated. Call 911 and then check the source of the smoke? Or investigate first, and then call? Look first, probably. The smoke wasn't thick, and it did come from outside.

He chugged across the back of the store, his belly bouncing above his belt, his breath already coming in quick, winded pants. What the hell, he was a plumber, now, not a wide receiver like in high school. And the weight wasn't all bad; he had fought pipes that demanded every pound of leverage he could muster.

Puffing, he burst out into the loading zone behind the market, then stopped. Good thing he hadn't called the fire department. There was no fire. No accidental one, anyway. Only Harold Roundtree, burning newspapers.

Then the incongruity of it struck him: Harold Roundtree, burning papers? Harold Roundtree, the most fanatic recycler Mike knew? The man who demanded a ten cent deposit on every glass bottle he sold, then turned around and paid twelve cents for every one he got back?

This man was burning newspapers outdoors on a cold January dawn?

"Hey, Harold!" He walked over to the fire. "Hey, what'sa matter, the columnists didn't make enough of an ash of themselves, you have to help them out?"

Roundtree lifted his head and stared into Schantz's eyes. "Filth!" he mumbled. "Blasphemy!" He wadded more of the pages and threw them on the flames.

"What? Where? Lemme see that." Frowning, Mike reached for a *Globe.*

Roundtree's stiffened hand chopped down into his wrist.

"Jesus, Harold!" He drew his arm back, shook it. "You coulda fucking broke my arm, man, what the hell's the matter with you?"

"This—this is an invitation to sin and I shall not permit anyone to be served that invitation! It is my duty to provide wholesome goods, not filth. Filth, do you hear me?" Roundtree put himself between Schantz and the stack of papers. "I shall not sell the *Globe* today. Or ever, if they persist in this abomination!"

Schantz shook his head. Harold sure had a bug up his ass. What kind of blasphemy could be in the *Globe*? "Shit, it's been a long day and a longer night, you know? I was looking forward to the comics. What other—"

"Go!"

"Huh?"

Roundtree took a menacing step toward him. "Go thou and sin no more!"

Uh-oh. This man has wigged out. I think I had better leave the premises and when I get home make a call to the gents in the white coats. Schantz backed away. "Hokay, Harold. Whatever you say." He patted the grocer on the arm. "Listen, man, as one individual proprietor to another, I'm gonna tell you straight: You've been working too hard."

"Go!"

Mike Schantz went. Poor Harold.

Out on the street, he looked around in discouragement. He wanted his paper, he wanted his coffee, and he didn't want to have to walk far for them. He could get the paper at the newsstand on the corner, but the coffee— Ah, yes. Halfway down the block, a diner's lights glowed neon-red. Mike headed for the newsstand first.

He entered the store, skimmed the rack, and frowned. "Hey, Timmy, where've you got this morning's *Globe*?"

Timothy McGillicuddy stuck his skinny Irish face out over the counter. "Michael. They've not delivered them yet, more's the pity, for I've had a dozen early customers walk out me door, cash still hot in their own hands. Try a *Bulletin.* And have you got a moment, then?"

"Timmm-mmmieee," Mike wailed, mocking McGillicuddy's accent because it was a thing they did, "Timmm-mmmieee, sure and begorrah, how is it ye haven't a real paper for a news-starved man, now?"

"Oy, vey, Michael!" Tim slapped his forehead. "It's a turrible t'ing—"

"Funny, you don't sound Jewish."

McGillicuddy shrugged. "It's that I don't get enough practice, Michael, you being the only one of my Jewish customers who doesn't object to it. Not, in faith, that I have that many Jewish customers, you'll be understanding, but th' ithers, Michael, narrow-minded to the marrow. Sure and they t'ink it's fun I'm making of them, when all's I'm doing is having a bit of fun wit' 'em."

"Timmy." Mike Schantz had had enough.

"Yes, Michael?" Tim gazed at him innocently.

"Where—" Mike put his fists on the counter, "—where is this morning's *Globe*?"

"It's as I was telling you, Michael, they haven't delivered it yet."

"Timmy." He sighed. "Timmy, the last twenty-four hours, you wouldn't believe. Two hours on a steam pipe so corroded that it didn't matter where I put the wrench, the metal crumpled, nu? Three hours— But if I didn't deserve to live it, you don't deserve to hear it. So let me just say this. It is either very late, Timmy, or it is very early, and I am tired. Oy, am I tired. All I want, me foine darlin' boy, is me paper and enough coffee to get me through till noon, but me usual purveyor, one Master Harold Roundtree, has gone t'oroughly and truly 'round the bend, so I'm looking for 'em elsewhere, and Timmy, me friend, ye doon't have the fucking *Globe* on your fucking rack!"

"It's as I said, Michael—"

He leaned across the counter. "They delivered the little asswipers to Harold, and Harold is half a block away from you, so they delivered them to you, too. Now gimme a paper, Timmy, before I reach over and grab you by the Adam's apple and slowly make you stop breathing."

Tim McGillicuddy blinked. "Oh, Michael, and here I thought we were friends 'n' all. 'Tis a sad, sad t'ing when a man doesn't know his own friends. Sure and it's loyalty we're speaking of here, Michael, loyalty and order and good citizenship."

"Good citizenship?" He stood up straight. "Timmy—"

"Sure and there's damn all else that matters, Michael."

Disgusted, Mike began to turn away.

"Nah, nah," McGillicuddy said, his voice coaxing. "Don't ye be trying to leave, now, Michael, for I've not finished speaking to you."

Mike stopped, turned back to the counter. Tim McGillicuddy's eyes fixed him in a feverish stare. Suddenly all Mike wanted was to get the hell out of the newsstand.

He didn't, though. He stayed where he was. Not because he wanted to. But because he had to: The soles of his shoes seemed to be stuck fast to the floor.

"Oh, it's a sad, sad t'ing, Michael, me foine friend,"

McGillicuddy said. "When a city turns to bite the very selfsame hand that has fed it all these many years—"

Mike could not tear his gaze from McGillicuddy's. He could not, in fact, move at all. An odd calm swept over him at the realization. And something funny was happening, in his head. Like somebody was moving furniture around up there.

Furniture, or . . . thoughts?

Now there was a crazy idea. Still, Mike Schantz could not do a thing about it. He could only stand there in front of Tim McGillicuddy's cash register, listening and listening as McGillicuddy raved on.

Listening, and eventually agreeing.

Before very much longer, in fact, Michael Schantz was entirely of one mind with Tim McGillicuddy.

Entirely of one mind.

Tommy Riley

He blinked. Just hours ago, he had ripped the cellophane off a new yellow legal-sized pad of paper. Now, every single sheet was covered with algebraic equations backward and forward in every combination known to man, and some he had invented on the spot.

Tommy Riley, math robot. Jeez, it was almost funny. But he'd had to have something, sitting awake through the night in the armchair in Ben Ibrani's apartment. Because the thing might try to get back into his head, and Tommy knew Ibrani's Stones album real well. Sometimes he even used to study while it played.

And if calculus could get through Mick Jagger, anything might.

Algebra and calculus themselves, though, x's and y's; $f(x)$'s and Σ's—stare at them long enough, and they began to look like the crosshatched wires of a cage. A cage to keep things in. Or . . . out. His studies, as it turned out, were good for something, after all.

In the bedroom, springs creaked.

The poor guy had needed sleep. Tommy set his pencil aside. And the poor guy had gotten it, too, hadn't he? Sort of. Well, Ibrani had told him what to do, and Tommy had done his best.

Now he hoped Ibrani hadn't gone wacko in there. Probably he ought to get some coffee going before he went in to find out. Because this was all insane, but he thought he might be starting to get the hang of it. The name of the game was don't freak out until you have to.

Yeah. Keep everything nice and normal as long as you can.

Which might be another day, or another second. He stretched, yawned, stumbled to the kitchen, his head still full of equal signs and parentheses, timeses and divided-bys. He found coffee and Ibrani's dripmatic gadgets, and got them together, sniffing in anticipation as thc good aroma began drifting steamily up.

Then he went into Ibrani's bedroom, where the man lay moaning, just the way Tommy had left him: spread-eagled, wrists and ankles bound to the bedframe with silk neckties. A fifth tie served as a gag; Ibrani's lips worked wildly beneath it.

He had, Tommy saw unhappily, chewed it nearly through. The fact drove all thoughts mathematical out of his head.

"Good morning." Keeping his voice calm, Tommy knelt on the edge of the bed and wrapped his hands casually about Ibrani's throat. With his index fingers touching at the back of Ibrani's head, his thumbs overlapped by about an inch. As they began to squeeze, he worked it out:

Eight inches from thumbtip to index fingertip, times two is sixteen, minus one is fifteen inches in circumference, which is equal to two-pi-r, so r equals fifteen divided by two-pi, and that's about six point two eight, so the radius of Mr. Ibrani's neck is roughly fifteen divided by six, which is two and a half but—

Then he yanked his hands back. *What. The. Hell. Am. I. Doing?*

Swiftly he turned the Walkman on and slid its headphones over Ibrani's head, then ripped the gag out of the other man's mouth. "Jesus, I'm sorry, Mr. Ibrani, I—"

" 'Sokay." Ibrani drew a deep, shuddering breath, let it out slowly, did it again. "It's okay, Tommy. You stopped. You stopped yourself, and that's important to know."

"I nearly killed you!" Frantic, he began to worry at the necktie fastened around Ibrani's right wrist. "Damn it, I nearly did it again, I'm going nuts, and I don't know how to stop. The only thing that helps is numbers, and even then—"

"Tommy—" With one hand freed now, Ibrani rolled over and worked on his other wrist. "Get my feet, all right?"

"Yes, sir. Once I get you loose, maybe you better tie me up." Glumly, he set to work on Ibrani's right ankle. Blood oozed from beneath the binding. "Tell me if it hurts," he said through gritted teeth, tugging at the knot which Ibrani's nightlong struggles had tightened.

"How about if I tell you when it doesn't hurt?" Ibrani answered faintly. "Save a lot of useless conversation."

"Right." Tommy did not speak again until he had freed Ibrani, they were seated in the living room, and Tommy had poured two cups of coffee. "I don't even know it's happening. It's just, one minute I'm normal, and the next minute, I'm doing something— something I'd never do. When you're wasted or something, you know, you feel different and you know you can't trust your own judgment. But this—I don't feel any different—I just—" He stopped, blinking back tears.

"Please. Tommy, I understand."

Ibrani seemed to have gotten the hang of reading his lips pretty well. He probably did understand, too. Only that didn't make Tommy feel any better, because right now he wasn't worried about understanding. He was worried about killing people. "But I don't. I don't understand what I need to—how to stop." Jeez, he was going to bawl again. He sank his teeth hard into his lip until his voice stopped quavering. Because Mr. Ibrani needed him, and how could anyone depend on someone who cried?

Or . . . killed? "What's wrong with me? Why is this happening to me? Am I insane, or what?"

Ibrani touched his shoulder. "Tommy, listen. It's not your fault. You didn't do it, or cause it. This happened to you because . . . because you were here, that's all. In Meadbury, at a moment when an evil old man needed another warm body to do his bidding. That's all."

He looked up into Ibrani's face. "But why did he pick on me?"

"Tommy, he—" The older man stopped abruptly. His gaze seemed to focus on a point a hundred miles beyond Riley's shoulder. "Do you know," he said slowly, "I've been asking myself that same question for years. At first —no. Until very recently, I thought I was the only one, too. Then I started wondering, but I didn't want to think too hard about it because—" Ibrani frowned. "Because I was afraid. But it's not just you, Tommy, and it's not just me. We're just a couple of guys who found out, and who found each other. But he has more like us. Lots more. Unfortunately."

Tommy blinked back more tears. Suddenly they didn't seem so bad. Mr. Ibrani was scared, too, and that made Tommy's fears seem normal. Well, not exactly normal, but like a person could deal with them. "You're sure there are more?"

"Oh, yes." Ibrani's head bobbed up and down, but his thoughts seemed a million miles away.

"Who?" Tommy asked, though he was pretty sure he knew at least one of the names. "Mr. Gorman?"

Ibrani's shoulders rose and fell. He sighed. "Yes, Ned Gorman, for one."

Tommy's lips trembled as the next name came to them. "And Miss Pialosta?"

Ibrani's eyebrows went up. "What makes you say that?"

Tommy squirmed. He'd seen them together, Mr. Ibrani and Miss Pialosta. They'd been walking out of the *Bulletin* building together, real close. Laughing. She was probably Mr. Ibrani's girlfriend. And she probably thought he, Tommy Riley, was just a little idiot. With pimples. And then he'd nearly raped her. He couldn't tell Mr. Ibrani that. "I just think so," he mumbled miserably.

Ibrani nodded. "I think you're right." Sadness shadowed his eyes. He cleared his throat harshly, then jumped up from the chair. "Breakfast!" He clapped his hands. "Can you cook?"

Tommy laughed. It would be okay. Somehow. "I think I can cook, but Ma says I'm wrong."

"Hmm." Ibrani stared down through narrowed, measuring eyes. "Well, my mother thinks I'm really a Borgia in disguise, too."

"Huh?"

"Lucrezia Borgia?"

Blushing, he hated himself for his ignorance. "I don't know who that is."

But Ben Ibrani seemed more amused than disappointed. "She liked to cook people's last meals for them," he said. "Go thou, buddy, and do almost likewise."

Tommy grinned. "Uh, gotcha. I think. What's in the fridge?"

"Eggs. Bacon. And there's a loaf of raisin bread."

Suddenly Tommy felt enormously hungry. "You want the whole loaf all at once, or should I only toast half of it? I mean, to start?"

Ibrani grinned back at him. "I like your attitude, kid. But I also like my toast real fresh, so don't get more than two pieces ahead of us."

"Will do," Tommy said with a mock salute. "Is there jelly, too?"

"I'm liking you more and more. Yes. Peach preserves. Top shelf, all the way to the back, on the left. And hop to it, while I take a quick shower—"

Terror flung Tommy across the room. "No!" Feet planted, arms spread wide, he blocked Ibrani's way. "No," he said again, ready to tackle if he needed to. "Don't do that, Mr. Ibrani, please don't. Just . . . keep the headphones on, okay? Really, I think you'd really better . . ."

And now Ibrani did laugh, a big, gut-shaking laugh that Tommy felt in the marrow of his bones.

Just the sound of it, oh, jeez, the wonderfully normal, ordinary sound of it made him nearly burst out crying again. Laughing. Oh, God, laughing. Would he ever be able to do that, ever again? Would he ever be able to forget that Jimmy Conklin was done doing it?

"Hey." Ibrani stepped forward, made a gentle fist, and regarded Tommy. Then he punched him, softly, on the shoulder. "Riley. Hey, guy. It's okay. Because. . . ." He tapped his headphones, looking sly. "This little job is absolutely waterproof."

Surprise and relief made Tommy say the first thing that

came into his head. "Mr. Ibrani, are you *sure* you're a grown-up?"

Ibrani grinned wickedly. "Only when I have to be, Tommy. From now on, only when I absolutely have to be." He chortled in delight, then danced off into the bedroom.

"You know," Tommy heard him say from in there, almost as if to himself, "you know, I think I'm actually getting to like this music."

Later, having surrounded four eggs, half a pound of bacon, and eight slices of peach-preserve-spread toast, Tommy sat at the kitchen table in a haze of contentment. Mr. Ibrani looked reasonably satisfied, too, and that made him feel even better. "I'll start on the dishes."

"Just throw 'em in the dishwasher, while I make a phone call."

From the living room: "Give me Rifkind . . . Will? Ben. Whatever this is, I've still got it. Just no way I'm going to make it in today. Can you cover for me? Thanks. Oh, is Nicki Pialosta there? Yeah, I'll wait."

Tommy dumped the silverware into the dishwasher's wire holder and listened to Ibrani humming a little tune, then speaking again.

"She isn't? Okay, I'll call her at home. Thanks, Will. See you tomorrow." Then Ibrani came back to the kitchen. "Enough of that, Tommy, it's time to head out. We're going to go see Nicki. You are, that is. And you're not going to let her know I'm there too, got it?"

"Uh, yeah. If that's what you want."

Ibrani nodded firmly. "That's what I want."

Tommy wiped his hands on a dish towel. He didn't really want to go outside at all. It felt safe here; safe and good. Outside, who knew?

He pulled on his jacket, wondering. Mr. Ibrani had been good to him, and seemed trustworthy. But now the nice moments were over, weren't they? And Mr. Ibrani wanted him to do something. Just like certain other people had wanted him to do things. Some of those things he had even done.

And they hadn't turned out so good, had they?

No. They hadn't. Waiting at the apartment door for

Ibrani, he decided to go along with whatever the older man wanted, as long as it seemed okay. So far, the guy had been straight-ahead.

Still, Tommy didn't know what was going to happen. He felt doubts.

Doubts were for grown-ups. Still, he thought, they might sometimes save your teenaged ass for you. Heading out the door behind Ibrani, Tommy decided to keep his.

His doubts, and his ass.

Tommy raised his hand to knock, then glanced to his right, where Ben Ibrani, flattened against the wall of the corridor, mouthed the words "Good luck."

Riley flashed the V sign, and rapped on the door.

It swung inward at once.

Then Miss Pialosta appeared, wearing high, spiked heels and a very short, loosely-belted terry robe.

Tommy's heart suddenly felt as if it were using his tonsils for a punching bag.

"Tommy!" Miss Pialosta smiled. Turning in toward the room, she shot a sideways, flirtish look at him. "Won't you come in?"

Gulping, he did.

She helped him off with his jacket, standing very close behind him, brushing the backs of his arms with her knuckles. He had never known knuckles could feel so good.

"I'll just hang this in here." She reached around him to open the closet door.

"Oh, I can do that."

"It's no trouble." She hung his jacket, closed the door, and led him into the living room. "Here," she said, switching on a lamp. "Make yourself comfortable. I'll get some coffee."

"Thank you." Tommy sat on the edge of the chair and pressed the palms of his hands hard on the tops of his thighs.

When she came back, she carried cups of steaming coffee on a tray. She bent to place the tray on a low table. As she did so, her robe fell away, exposing her breasts. Lamplight fell on them, making them look like—

Jeez, he didn't know what it made them look like. Breasts was what they looked like.

He forced himself to look away.
"Oh, I forgot the cream and sugar." She straightened, touched her forehead. "Silly me." Her robe gaped open nearly to her navel; the belt hung loose and ready to fall. "I'll be right back." She smiled warmly at him.
He let his breath out as she left the room.

Nicki Pialosta

In the kitchen, she opened a drawer. Removed a Sabatier carving knife.
Thc bladc glintcd sharply, approvingly.
Turning to the doorway, she put one hand behind her back.
One hand. And one knife.
She opened the robe, let the belt fall. Smiled to herself a final time. And called: "Tommy? Tommy, could you come here a minute, please? I need . . . a man's help. Silly me again, I'm afraid."
Then she waited.

Tommy Riley

Something in Miss Pialosta's voice made him jump up from the chair. She sure had great legs. And the way she was acting—well, he guessed he'd been wrong about her, and that was great too. The way she was acting didn't remind him of Mr. Goodmaster.
No, not at all. He ran a hand down the front of his shirt in a vain attempt to smooth some of the wrinkles. He hitched up his pants. He took a step toward the kitchen, where she was waiting for him.
And he stopped, as Ben Ibrani slipped noiselessly into the room. Ibrani put a finger to his lips, and shook his head.
Tommy frowned, spread his hands.
Ibrani tapped himself on the chest, pointed to the kitchen, then held up one finger. He did it again. Me. Kitchen. First.
Tommy nodded reluctantly. Okay. Heck, this was going to make Miss Pialosta mad. Then, hoping he could still

explain it to her, he followed as Ibrani crept forward on tiptoe.

At the kitchen door, Ibrani paused, stepped through fast, then stopped suddenly. Behind him, Tommy pulled up short.

Beyond Ibrani, in the small kitchen by the formica-covered counter, stood Nicki Pialosta. Her terry robe hung completely open. A small lascivious smile wavered on her lips. It faded as she saw Ibrani.

"Hello, Nicki." Tension throbbed in Ibrani's voice.

She blinked once, twice. "Ben. Good morning." Her left hand rose to the collar of her robe and dragged it open wider, baring her left shoulder and breast.

"Nicki," Ibrani said, "cover yourself up."

Her right hand swung wildly. Light flashed on the blade she brought around, flashed in a swift, savage arc that was meant to end in Ibrani's heart.

The knife, Tommy realized sickeningly, had been intended for him.

Ibrani chopped up fast with his left hand, swatting her wrist. The knife fell, clattering.

She howled. She threw back her head and bayed like a wolf in fury, fear, and frustration. She dove for the knife.

Ibrani threw himself onto her back, pinning her. "Nicki?" he said uncertainly.

She grunted, her forearms bulging with strain. She pushed herself up off the kitchen floor, straight-arming it, carrying Ibrani. Then, so fast Tommy couldn't believc it, she whipped one arm around to snatch at Ibrani's hair.

He cried out in pain and surprise.

She ducked her shoulder and yanked his hair again, hard, somersaulting him over her.

Tommy heard Ibrani's head hit the linoleum, and looked around for something to hit her with. Because this wasn't Miss Pialosta. Oh, no. This was something else entirely. And he was very much afraid he knew what.

Panting, she scrabbled for the knife. Tommy leapt at her, slugging her shoulders. She sprawled, the knife skittering and sliding away underneath the refrigerator.

He couldn't let her get it, but even now her hand snaked out. Ibrani was out for the count. What to do? Tommy looked around wildly, but there was no help for it. He straddled her, lowered his weight hard down onto the bare-naked small of her back, and immediately became aware of just how very bare-naked it was.

But it wasn't that easy. God, she was strong, bucking madly and flailing until one wild clenched fist caught him solidly, square in the crotch. She squirmed from beneath him as pain exploded, turning his muscles to water and bleaching out his vision.

Lying there, helpless, he wanted intensely to vomit. He wanted to die.

Also, he wanted to kill the little bitch.

Only it would be the other way around if she got to the knife first.

Reaching out blindly, he found a fistful of her hair and slammed her head down murderously. *That ought to hold her.*

It didn't. A flurry of fists and feet came at him, and then her nails, red-lacquered and clawlike.

Okay, you asked for it. Holding her off with enormous effort, he thumped her head on the floor twice more. Thunk. Thunk!

And that did it: Abruptly, she went limp. Her mouth fell open. Drool ran down her cheek. She looked disgusting.

Almost as disgusting as he felt.

Ibrani shifted, groaning.

"Please. Mr. Ibrani? I knocked her out, but I don't know when she's gonna come to, and if it's soon I'm dead, so please, wake up. Help."

Ibrani flopped onto his stomach and pushed himself to his hands and knees. Head hanging straight down, he made a feeble attempt to get up, then crawled over instead. "You okay?"

"She got me in the balls." Tommy winced. It wasn't just a memory, and by the feel of things it wouldn't be for quite a while. "How about you?"

"I'm gonna die, but not from what she did. Damn Goodmaster to hell."

"So what do we do now?" Cautiously, Tommy let go of Nicki's hair and tried to close the robe over her, but too much of it was bunched underneath her. Finally he gave up.

"Let's get her into the bedroom," Ibrani said.

Hand on the nearest countertop, Tommy levered himself

to his feet, and at once doubled over. "Oh, jeez, that hurts!"

"It'll fade." Ibrani gave a very small laugh, and grimaced. "I think."

Hands over his kidneys, Tommy forced himself straight. He helped Ibrani up, both of them groaning. Then he looked down at Miss Pialosta and immediately glanced away, not from modesty, but because a punch in the balls could keep a guy's thoughts clean for a long, long time. Still— "Should I go find, like, clothes or something for her?"

Ibrani made a face. "And risk having her wake up before you get back? Just get her wrists, and I'll get her ankles."

In a minute they had her on her bed, a pillow behind her head, her robe at last tucked neatly around her.

"Go through her dresser drawers, find some nylon stockings or pantyhose."

Tommy stared. "Now you're going to get her dressed?"

"Sure, maybe take her out to lunch, too." Ibrani touched his auburn hair and looked at his fingertips suspiciously. "No, now I'm going to tie her up."

"Tie her up? Why?"

Ibrani sighed. "Because," he said patiently, "if she's immobilized, then she won't try to attack anyone else, will she? Like maybe someone who's not as gentlemanly as us. Go on. Find the nylons. It's as much for her own good as everyone else's."

Unhappily, Tommy found a bunch of them, and handed them over.

"Good," said Ibrani. "Pantyhose, right. Now, we take one pair—" he matched actions to words "—and knot one foot around the leg of the bed, bring the rest up the side, pull it taut, bring the wrist to the corner of the bed, and very securely tie that wrist. See? You don't want to cut the circulation, but you don't want it so loose she can pull her hand through the knot, either. Here." He tossed a pair over to Tommy. "You get her right wrist, I'll start in on her ankles."

"Hey." Tommy frowned. "Listen, you're not going to—" Heck. "You're not going to tie her with her legs spread, are you?"

Ibrani looked up. "Tommy, if I could, I'd lash her ankles to her shoulders, all right? I don't want her getting away, here. Why? Is it important?"

"Well, yeah. Yeah, it is, because it's, like, it's pornographic, okay? I mean, can't you maybe tie her ankles together first, and then tie them both to the foot of the bed?"

Ibrani shrugged. "Yeah, sure. Christ, and they say the older generation's the puritanical one. Get that wrist, all right? Unless you think that's pornographic, too."

He did, sort of, but he did it anyway. When Ibrani had finished binding her ankles, they covered her up.

At least this way she doesn't look like a picture in one of those dirty magazines. Yeah, this way's much better. This way, she looks crucified. "So now what?"

Ibrani held up the last pair of pantyhose. "Gag."

Tommy put his face in his hands.

"Tommy." Ibrani's voice was reasonable. "If we don't, she wakes up, she shouts. Somebody breaks in and lets her loose, Goodmaster gets hold of her. Next thing you know, she'll be trying to kill us all over again. Except this time the cops will also be after both of us for aggravated assault, illegal restraint, and, probably, rape."

"But she could choke to death."

"In which case," Ibrani replied, "they'll also be after us for murder." Swiftly he looped the pantyhose around her mouth and tied it tight. "Okay, we're out of here." He led the way to the door, but stopped. "No, wait. Turn around."

Tommy's shoulders sagged. "Mr. Ibrani, I gotta tell you. I like you, I trust you, and I appreciate what you did for me. But this, what we're doing here, it's making me feel pretty sick. So if you don't mind—"

"I know, Tommy. I feel just the way you do about it. So turn around, now, and look. Take a good, long look at what we've done to her. And remember it."

Tommy did. The sight made him want to puke.

"Right," Ibrani said. "You're absolutely correct. It's as bad as you think it is, maybe worse. So remember, and remember the reason." He looked once more at Nicki, and his face filled with pain.

"Remember it well," he said again softly. "Because now we are going to kill Jason Goodmaster. And this is why."

Meadbury

"Tsk, tsk," said Mrs. Stanhope, executive secretary to the commonwealth assistant district attorney. She had held that position since before the Revolution, or so it seemed to her boss, whose feet, in defiance of etiquette and tradition, rested atop the polished cherrywood of his desk.

Smiling at Mrs. Stanhope, Assistant District Attorney Thurmon Gordon settled himself more comfortably into his red leather chair, and rattled his newspaper to indicate that she ought to let a man have his morning read in peace, for heaven's sake. After all, he was the boss.

Mrs. Stanhope bustled about, trailing the scent of lavender talc as she opened blinds, straightened folders, and plucked a dead leaf off the philodendron. "Feet on the desk." She shook her head at the unsuitableness of it. "What if the schoolchildren came through and saw you now?"

Gordon gave a small sigh. Schoolchildren—runny noses and dirty faces and bright little minds—what an irritating prospect. "They're not due yet, are they?"

"Not till ten." Mrs. Stanhope, sworn enemy of dust, ran a finger over the windowsill and frowned at it suspiciously.

He glanced at his watch, then back at the newspaper. "Good. Then I have time to read the— Hey!" He sat up straight; his feet hit the floor with a thump.

"Thank you," she said, narrowly inspecting his blotter for traces of shoe grit.

"Did you see this?" He stared at the front page.

"Since I have no idea what 'this' refers to—"

"Here, in this morning's *Bulletin.* Somebody hijacked HBO last night to slander Jason Goodmaster."

Frowning, she raised her lorgnette and peered over his shoulder. "My, my," she said, reading.

He craned his neck to look into her wrinkled face. "That's all you have to say? 'My, my'?"

"Well," she said primly, "it's hardly my place to comment."

Gordon grimaced. That hadn't been her policy as long as

he'd known her. "Try stepping out of your place a moment, Mrs. Stanhope, and venturing a guess. According to the *Bulletin,* some airwaves pirate has accused Jason Goodmaster of a rather nasty crime."

She scanned the article again. "Do you honestly wish my opinion, Mr. Gordon?"

"Yes, Mrs. Stanhope," he said with exaggerated patience, "I do. That's why I invited it. I'm funny that way, you see. If I don't want to know what someone's thinking about a particular article in the paper, why, I don't wave it at them and say, 'Hey, did you see this?' That way, maybe ten percent of the time, I don't have to listen to their opinion. Do you understand what I'm saying to you, Mrs. Stanhope?"

"Yes, Mr. Gordon," she said imperturbably. "I understand. Here is my opinion: I was born and raised in Meadbury, and the Stanhopes and the Goodmasters have been two of the town's leading families since, oh my, early Colonial times, at least. So naturally we're all acquainted and, well, to put it tactfully, we keep ourselves informed of each other's activities."

Gordon had to laugh. She was a sketch, she was. "You're telling me the Stanhopes gossip about the Goodmasters? My word, Mrs. Stanhope. I'm shocked, I really am."

She raised her aristocratic eyebrows a fraction. "Would you rather we discussed our social inferiors?"

A political animal to the core, he knew when he was beat. "Heaven forfend, Mrs. Stanhope."

She inclined her head by exactly the same amount she had lifted her eyebrows. "At any rate. To be blunt, Mr. Gordon, the Stanhopes know the Goodmasters, and the Goodmasters know the Stanhopes. More to the point, the servants know each other." Her lips tightened meaningfully. "And, Mr. Gordon, you know how servants are."

Of course he did; he'd seen them in the movies. Still, she sounded sure of herself. "So you don't think Goodmaster, ah, likes 'em young?"

"Jason? Oh, Mr. Gordon, if Jason were involved in anything like that, he'd have been the mainstay of Stanhope dining-room conversation for lo, these many years. And he hasn't been, I do assure you."

"So what's all this about, then?" He rapped the article with his knuckles. "Who would risk a federal rap to libel Goodmaster?"

She thought a moment. "Someone with a grudge, I presume."

He leaned back in his chair, pondered the reasonableness of her suggestion, then snapped his fingers. He had it. "We'll empanel a grand jury."

She shook her head. "But Mr. Gordon, I just finished telling you—"

"No, no, we're not going to investigate Goodmaster." He waved his hand dismissingly.

"But—"

"Listen." He planted his elbows on his blotter, folded his hands, and rested his chin on his knuckles, smiling with anticipation. Oh, this was going to be good. "Now, I'll confess, I am probably not the brightest guy in the commonwealth, and probably I won't ever run for governor, and probably I'll never have more than a competent legal career, private or public. . . ."

Mrs. Stanhope blinked at all these admissions, most of which he knew she privately agreed with.

"But," he went on, "sooner or later I would like to be district attorney, and maybe even a judge after that, and what we have here, Mrs. Stanhope, what we are studying here on the front page of this morning's newspaper is what's called a golden opportunity for an ambitious ADA to make himself a rep. The grand jury will keep my name headlined on this front page for weeks, and then the trial itself, examining Goodmaster and—" He slapped his desktop as a new thought struck. "Politics!"

"Pardon?"

"Nobody libels Jason Goodmaster just for fun. It's not him they're after, it's that errand boy of his, Ned Gorman."

"May I infer from your smug expression," Mrs. Stanhope inquired, "that you do not care for Mr. Gorman?"

The question was very unlike her, but Gordon was feeling pleased enough to answer it anyway. He swung his feet back onto his desk, leaned back in his chair, and grinned at her. Oh, this was going to be a turkey shoot, and what a slimy turkey he had for the main attraction. "Mrs. Stanhope, dah-ling, in deference to your ever-so-refined sensibilities, I will limit my reply to this: If I were a vice cop, and if in the course of my official duties I found Ned Gorman in a hotel room with a lady of the evening, I would arrest the lady. For bestiality. Now, infer to your heart's content."

"I see." Ice edged her tone. "What are you going to do now?"

He shrugged. Shouldn't have made that dah-ling crack, he supposed. Oh, well, she'd get over it.

"Get that grand jury going. There's a hundred forms to fill out and sign, so you start filling them out, and I'll start signing them. Maybe by the end of the day, if we've dotted all our *i*'s and crossed all our *t*'s, why, we'll be able to serve Mr. Ned Gorman with a subpoena demanding his testimony. If that's amenable to you, Mrs. Stanhope. Oh, and cancel those schoolkids. We're going to be too busy."

"Very well, Mr. Gordon. I'll get started on it right away."

"Thank you, Mrs. Stanhope." He turned his attention back to the newspaper. Just a sneak peek at the sports section, he thought, and he'd get started on his end of things. He flipped the pages, casually looking for the basketball scores.

Without warning, something looped around his neck and tightened. *What the—?*

Gordon lunged forward, choking, clawing as the slick twisted plastic of a telephone cord compressed his windpipe. From close behind him came a whiff of lavender talc.

Mrs. Stanhope. My God, she's got strong hands. Then the oxygen stopped flowing to his brain, and he stopped thinking entirely.

Nicki Pialosta

She did not struggle. She did not cry out. She blinked occasionally, and she breathed, and she lay limp on her bed while the makeshift bonds chafed her faintly.

She waited.

Eventually a door opened and closed, as she had known it would. A man's measured footsteps approached. The bedroom door opened.

She stared at the ceiling.

Reg Forsten moved to the side of the bed and gazed down

at her. Clean-shaven, hair neatly trimmed, he wore a dark wool suit, white shirt, and a burgundy tie: the uniform of a banker, or a lawyer. No one would have thought twice at seeing him in a building full of young professionals.

He pulled off the sheet that covered her, and dropped it to the floor. From the pocket of his tailored pants, he drew a long folding knife. Wordlessly he opened it, slipped its gleaming blade between her ankles, and sliced through the nylon binding. He freed her wrists, then put a thumb on her right temple and turned her face toward the wall, laying the back of the blade against her jawbone and slicing upward to sever the gag. Finally he pulled the sodden mass of nylon from her mouth. Folding the knife and returning it to his pocket, he dropped the gag on the bedroom floor, then crossed the room and stopped before her dresser.

Nicki sat up slowly. She swung her feet over the edge of the bed, and stood. Eyes focused on nothing, she untied her robe and let it fall.

Forsten watched her in the dresser mirror. His face remained expressionless. He opened dresser drawers methodically until he had what he wanted: underwear, sweater, stockings. He handed them to her; as she pulled them on, he riffled through her closet, found a skirt, and brought it also.

Nicki drew the skirt on, and stepped into a pair of low-heeled pumps. Then, pausing briefly to brush her hair, she followed Forsten from the room.

At the hall closet he paused, handed her coat to her, and gestured at the front door.

Nicki put on the coat. Then she opened the door, stepped out into the corridor, and waited while Forsten came out, closed the door, and locked it with his own set of keys.

Together they walked in silence out of the building and got into Nicki's car.

With distant approval she saw he had keys for that, too.

Tommy Riley

Back at Ibrani's apartment, hc stared into his cup of fresh coffee as if he might find an answer in it. But there was no answer, nothing he could have done to make things come out differently.

Miss Pialosta wasn't herself anymore, and that was that. He was lucky she hadn't put that carving knife into his liver. She would have if Mr. Ibrani hadn't suspected something. She would have called him out to the kitchen in that sweet, seductive voice of hers, then gutted him like a fish.

Tears stung his eyelids.

Behind him, Ibrani bustled around making sandwiches, keeping his mouth shut and letting Tommy alone.

Tommy guessed he didn't feel too good, either.

The older man set a plate of ham and cheese on pumpernickel on the table.

Tommy sighed. "Uh, listen, I don't think I want any—"

"Eat," Ibrani said flatly. "It's cold outside. You're going to need the calories."

Tommy frowned. He didn't want to go outside again today. He wasn't sure he wanted to go outside ever again. What he really wanted, more than anything in the world, was to go home, put his arms around his mother, and cry. Then go upstairs to his own familiar room, get in his own little bed, and fall asleep. Maybe forever. The way he felt right now, that would be a relief.

He couldn't do any of that, though. He couldn't see his mother, or even call her, because it was too late. Too much had happened, and was still happening.

Sickly, he realized it was up to him to stop it, because his mother lived in Meadbury, too.

Shuddering, he thrust away a sudden, unwelcome picture of her: plump and pleasant in her flowered apron, humming a little tune as she put the final touches on her famous pot roast. Slicing warm rich slabs of it onto his plate, then calling him in to eat. Waiting for him, with the carving knife behind her back. . . .

The sandwich tasted like spun plaster. He washed the bite

down with bitter coffee. "I guess it didn't work, huh?"

"What?"

"The HBO thing."

Ibrani shrugged. "Anything tried to get into your head lately?"

"No," he said, realizing it all at once. "No, it hasn't, but—"

"It used to run you like a cart horse, though, didn't it? And it wants you, you know it does. It wants both of us. But it hasn't come after us, not since dawn. Why?"

Tommy nodded. "Well, maybe—maybe that news flash did do something. But then why was Miss Pialosta still—"

Ibrani leaned across the table. "Look, Tommy. Whatever it is, it isn't limitless. It has rules, things it can and can't do. It could get at us before, because it already had us. It had weaseled its way into our heads, and it counted on us not even noticing, or being too afraid to fight." He looked very earnest. "But then we broke free, and my 'bulletin' hit the air and disorganized things, got a lot of people wondering and thinking instead of just laying back. Now the . . . the monster's just got too much on its plate; it's got all of Meadbury to try to whip back into line. It's too busy, or too disorganized, or too something, to find us. That's what I think, anyway. But Nicki hadn't broken free."

Ibrani laid out his right hand, palm up, and slowly curled his fingers into a fist. "It had her so damn tight that—" He shook his head. "Anyway, I think that's how it's going to be. I think anyone whose mind was free when I hijacked HBO—well, he's still free. Anybody else—" His hand fell open.

Tommy understood. Anybody else was probably dead meat, or soon would be. He reached for his sandwich and saw with surprise and relief that it was gone. He must have eaten it automatically while listening. "So what are we going to do?"

In answer, Ibrani got up from his chair and left the room, returning with a tablet of paper and two pencils. "I've told you what we're going to do, Tommy," he said. "And it's very simple: just three easy steps. The first we've already done: gotten our heads straight. In fact I think it would even be safe to take off these—" His hands went to the headphones he still wore.

"Don't!" Tommy lurched from his chair.

Ibrani smiled. His hands dropped. "Maybe you're right at that."

Tommy sighed and sat back down. "What are the other two steps?"

Ibrani tore a sheet from the tablet and picked up one of the pencils, gesturing for Tommy to do the same. "Like I said, Tommy: simple. First, we plan exactly how to kill Jason Goodmaster. And then—"

Ibrani's face went suddenly cold and still. "Then we do it."

Meadbury

Zenna Allard peered through the observation window into room 722 of Meadbury General Hospital's pediatric ward, then turned to her companion. "Isn't she a darling, Paula? Such a cute little smock."

Paula Groenler nodded, saying nothing. Paula's own presence ruled out the child's being a darling, cute smock or no. For transporting darlings, the State Social Welfare Department didn't call Paula. Still, the kid was cute. Too bad she was getting shipped off to an orphanage, and a nutso orphanage at that. Cuteness wouldn't buy her much there. At least, not much that she wanted. Shaking her head, Paula shrugged off her own bitter memories and assessed the child again.

Inside room 722, six-year-old Emily Polk sat cross-legged on the hospital bed, an expression of listening inquiry on her smooth, babyish face. Her hair had been washed and brushed, and put up into pigtails. Their soft blondness gleamed in the light from the room's single, wire-reinforced window to the outside. Her eyes were blue and heavily-lashed; her cheeks pink; her lips a small, perfect red rosebud.

The only hint of trouble in the room, in fact, was Emily Polk's rag doll: Its head lay on the linoleum floor. The rest of it—a small pile of rags and stuffing—peeked out from under the bed.

Silently, Groenler took the child's clipboard from Zenna,

who said, "I wonder why they assigned two of us?"

Paula's eyes moved over the sheets on the clipboard. "Honey, you know they don't send me just to keep you company. When they put me on a case, it means they need muscle." And Paula Groenler, who stood five feet, weighed a hundred and sixty-five, and maintained eight percent body fat, could provide it. She wasn't queen of the weight room for nothing. "But this little shrimp won't make much trouble."

Zenna nodded. "Mmm. Still, she is pretty disturbed, supposedly. I mean, small wonder, when you think of what she's been through."

Paula frowned, rereading three paragraphs in the psychiatrist's note. Then she looked thoughtfully at Emily Polk. "Yeah." Suddenly, the child wasn't cute any more. What was left of the doll wasn't cute, either. "Yeah, any kid who watches TV for ten, twelve days while her ma's corpse rots in the next room, I guess you might say she's disturbed. Or something. Come on, let's get this show on the road."

Zenna opened the door to room 722, smiling brightly and putting on her nice-nice voice. "Hello, Emily, we're the ladies from the Social Welfare Department. Did the nurses tell you we were coming?"

The little girl's sea-blue eyes darkened stormily. "I'm not going with you, and you can't make me."

Zenna hesitated, then continued explaining about the trip and the orphanage.

Paula thought that was a mistake. But she let Zenna finish her pitch anyway. What the hell; you couldn't just bundle the kid up like a sack of feed and haul her out. Although that was probably what it would take.

If there was one thing Paula Groenler didn't like, it was a mouthy brat. Generally, this dislike made her job much easier; most of the violent or disturbed kids she dealt with had major league mouths, and so she hardly minded dumping them into the grim institutions they got sent to.

This Emily Polk, however, was different. Paula didn't want to dump her anywhere. All of a sudden what she really wanted was to jog on down to the gym, and work out —hard.

Two or three hours of sweat, a long sauna, and a hot shower, she thought; that might just begin to wash away the hot stench of madness that seemed to come off this child in waves, cloaking Paula in its slimy repulsiveness, clinging and stinking. . . .

Paula Groenler had been a welfare worker for fifteen years. She knew a Wrong Kid on sight. A kid you never trusted, never turned your back on, never gave an inch to, because if you did, the kid would make you very, very sorry.

This was a Wrong Kid.

As if Paula had spoken, Emily turned to her, smiled beatifically. Then she winked.

Paula swallowed. The kid knew, she knew what Paula was thinking— No. That was ridiculous. Clasping her hands behind her back, she let Zenna try again.

"Now, Emily, you have to go, dear, someone has to take care of you—"

Emily's bright, smiling face snapped shut. She slid off the bed, folded her arms, and scowled. "I am not going."

"You'll like Fredda Mountain, dear, it's a lovely place."

"It's an orphanage. It's far miles away. And I. Am. Not. Going." She stamped her small foot for emphasis.

Zenna glanced over her shoulder for help. With a nod, Paula stepped forward. Hands on her hips, she glared down into the defiant young face. "Listen, half-pint, let's get something straight. You're the kid, we're the grown-ups, and the point is this: Our boss said to take you to the Mountain, so we're going to. You can go quiet, or you can go noisy, but either way, you're going to go, so get used to it."

Emily kicked Paula hard in the shin and shot for the door. Paula's arm went out, her fingers snagging Emily's collar and yanking. Emily's arms pinwheeled; her legs pumped in futile desperation.

"I think," Paula said, "we need some medication here. That, or a brickbat."

Zenna nodded and headed for the door.

Emily whirled, half strangling herself in her smock collar but not seeming to care. Paula had time to notice that the child was missing two front teeth before Emily sank her still-intact canines into the flesh of Paula's wrist.

"Why, you little—!" She shook her arm, but Emily hung on like a dog, growling and wrenching her head back and forth. Blood oozed from between her clenched teeth, spattering her face and the floor.

Through her pain, Paula reminded herself with an effort: This was a child. A minor. A person who by law was not fully responsible for her own actions. A sharp-fanged little bitch whose teeth were grating on Groenler's radius, but she must not lift her arm, swing it, and smash the brat full-length into the bright yellow cinder-block wall— "Uh, Zenna. Wait a sec."

The other woman turned, gasped, and lunged to help.

Paula waved her off with her free hand. "No, just wait till I check, see if she hit any—" Quickly she reached around and pinched Emily's nose shut. The child had to open her mouth. At once, Paula flung her face-first onto the bed, twisted her small arms back, and pinned them with one hand while she examined the other.

Blood ran freely; good. Not spurting, though; good, too. "Missed the artery." On the bed, Emily hissed. "Tell the doc to bring a bandage, though." *And a goddamn sharpened stake.*

White-faced, Zenna nodded and set off at a dead run.

"Let me go, you fat-assed tub of lard," came the child's voice. One heel kicked back, barely missing Paula's jaw.

In response, Paula pulled upward and neckward on the child's arms. Not much. Just enough.

Emily lay still.

"Now, listen," Paula said sweetly, tugging again on her arms for emphasis. "We've got to make a deal, here, you and I. The deal is, you lie still, and I don't break both your shoulders and then wring your little neck. Got it?"

Emily continued to lie still, except for her mouth. "You fucking hoor! You don't know who you're dealing with! Lemme go, you overmuscled, underbrained fucking hoor!"

Paula blinked. The kid sure had a vocabulary. "Hoor" was one thing; lots of little kids knew that word. But "overmuscled" and "underbrained"?

A few minutes later—more minutes than Paula would have wished—a young black man in a white coat and stethoscope hurried in with Zenna on his heels. Quickly he opened his satchel. "Sorry I took so long."

"That's okay." Groenler giggled. She was mildly dizzy, partly from watching her own blood leak onto the sheets and partly from what she had been hearing. "I've learned six new words, and seven new facts about my family. Miss Foulmouth here thought she told me eight new facts, but I already knew about Aunt Letty and the delivery boy." Then it hit her: She'd known, but how had Emily?

Meanwhile the doctor produced a glass syringe and a small vial. "Okay, now," he said, "let's just—"

"Wait a minute." Paula flipped Emily over and pulled her up, ignoring frowns from Zenna and the doc. The child grinned. "How the fuck did you know about Aunt Letty?"

Emily laughed, a high, innocent sound that made Paula's blood run chilly. "I know a lot more'n that. I know about the Coke bottles, and last Tuesday in the locker room with—" Her childish forehead creased in thought. "Alison! The equipment manager. Paula loves Alison," she taunted in a wicked singsong, "Paula loves Alison, but Alison loves—"

Paula flipped the child back onto her face with a brusque movement.

". . . Larry!" came the muffled, taunting voice.

Then Paula turned to the doc. "You about ready, or you wanna stand here some more?"

His look was level. "I'm ready." He stepped up to the table. "Hold her still, now."

Yeah. Not as still as I'd like to hold her. But I'm good at restraining myself. Just not quite good enough. A picture of Alison rose in her mind; she banished it, finally and completely, as a stinger-sized needle found a vein in Emily Polk's arm and the plunger pushed home.

On his way out, the young doctor turned to Paula once more. "Coke bottles?" he said with the hint of a grin.

She met his gaze without flinching. "Tell me. Do they give you guys a good dental plan here? I mean a real good dental plan?"

Consideringly, he eyed her: shoulders and biceps, pecs, torso. The whole shebang. Then, to his credit, he managed a real smile. "Forget I asked, okay?"

Half an hour later they were on their way: Zenna driving, Paula riding shotgun, and Emily Polk in the back seat, trussed up in what the manuals referred to as "security restraint."

About the only thing the kid could move was her mouth,

and she was doing a helluva job with that. "Police! Help! Lemme go!"

"Zenna," Paula shouted over the din, "if we don't gag her, I'm gonna go nuts."

Zenna shook her head abstractedly. Snowflakes whipped straight at the windshield; the wipers could barely keep up. "We can't do that without a court order."

"Goddamn right, you hoors!"

"So who's gonna know?"

"The whole fucking world!"

"We will," Zenna said. "And so will she, I'm afraid." She squinted at the windshield. "Besides, the gag would leave marks on her cheeks and the corners of her lips, and the examining physician at Fredda Mountain would report them."

"Come on, he won't write us up on a little thing like—"

"He'll do whatever I tell 'im to!"

"Paula," Zenna said in a voice that suggested patience sorely strained, "you and I cannot get away with one single teeny-tiny infraction, and you know it. And frankly, I can't afford to lose this job. Or go to prison, either."

"Bullshit, you'd love it, you dyke!"

Paula stared. "You? You're in trouble? I mean, I knew I was headed for it when I whacked that Zielinski kid, but what did you do?"

Zenna shrugged, gripping the steering wheel. "Just what you're suggesting. Stopped up a little line of back talk. That's how I know it'll show."

"You gagged a kid?" Paula felt disbelief. "Miz Go-By-the-Book stuffed a sock in a brat's mouth?"

"That's not all she stuffed!"

"I did not stuff a sock." Zenna's voice was thin. Outside, snow kept piling up; the road crews were getting behind. "If you must know, I tied a wool scarf. But that's why I go by the book from here on out. They took me to court, civil and criminal."

They both paused in anticipation of Emily's next shriek, but it did not come. "So what happened?" Paula said finally.

"Lemme go lemme go lemme go!"

Zenna sighed. "Well, they tried the criminal case first, and I might have been convicted if the prosecutor hadn't put the child on the stand. But she did, and in the midst of his testimony this seven-year-old boy with the face of an angel let out a string of remarks about my eating habits."

"You do eat shit, you old biddy!"

Zenna pursed her lips, then went on. "In his summation, my lawyer emphasized that I'd had to listen to that kind of stuff for most of the drive to the Mountain. I guess the jury thought I'd gagged the right kid, and that weakened the parents' civil suit against me, and finally they settled out of court with the insurance company."

"Hahahahahaha!"

Groenler blinked. "Wait a minute. Parents? And the kid was going to Fredda?"

"Kidnapper! Help! Lemme go!"

Zenna nodded. "They had deserted him. Then they heard a suit might produce some money."

"Police!"

"What did they settle for?"

"Not very much." Zenna shrugged. "Ten thousand, I think. But they never got it because the insurance company made sure it went into a trust fund they couldn't touch. So they took off again. And that was that, except I've got to watch my back now." A small frown creased her forehead; she glanced in the rearview. "Hey, you hear that?"

"What?"

"Silence." Zenna peered through the windshield again, into the thickening swirls of white.

Paula looked into the back seat. Emily's eyes bulged, her cheeks puffed with stubborn fury. "I think the kid's holding her breath till she turns blue."

"Wonderful." Zenna bit her lip as the car tried to skid, then straightened. "Jesus." She glanced in the mirror again. "I wonder why the sedative wore off so fast."

Paula turned to the front. "Ah, those guys, you know how scared they are of malpractice. Probably they don't even put you under when you go on the operating table these days. You see all those damn papers they made me sign? I'll bet what they gave her wasn't much stronger than two aspirin."

"Ladies," Emily said hoarsely, "I beg of you, release me at once. I am needed in Meadbury."

Zenna blinked. "Emily?"

"If you prefer." It was not Emily's voice, though.

The sudden chill in Paula's spine had nothing to do with the snowstorm. Not a kid's voice, not a kid's words, or a kid's way of phrasing. And not a kid's memories. She shivered, remembering the things Emily had said earlier.

All at once she really did want to throttle the kid, and if Zenna hadn't been here she might have. Because who knew what else the brat was going to blab? Maybe all kinds of things that even a good pal like Zenna didn't need to hear.

"Please." Not a kid's voice. Too tired; too gravelly, too . . . old. "There's an interchange a quarter mile ahead; I beseech you, turn around and take me home. It is vitally important, I assure you. And I do have someone to take care of me."

Zenna glanced questioningly at Paula, who shrugged and forced herself to turn toward the back seat. Something funny, here; something very funny. Big as she was, Paula was glad the kid was wrapped up in restraints. "So who'll take you in, Emily?"

"Jason Goodmaster," the child said at once in that oddly adult voice.

Despite her unease, Paula laughed. "Old Man Goodmaster? You?"

"I am not fantasizing, I assure you. You've already passed the interchange, but if you take the next one, stop at the booth by the gas station, and place a phone call to Mr. Goodmaster, I promise you he will accept responsibility for me."

Paula let her breath out slowly. "Emily, how come you didn't mention any of this before, huh? I mean, why'd you wait till it was too late?"

"I was . . . distracted." The child closed her eyes. "What do you mean, 'too late'?"

"Just what I said. All the paperwork's done. We take you anywhere but the Mountain, they nail us for dereliction of duty, jeopardizing the safety of a minor, kidnapping, the whole ball of wax, you know? But if what you say is true—"

"It is," said Emily flatly.

"Then when we get to the Mountain, we'll give Old Man Goodmaster a call for you—"

"You need not inform him of my whereabouts; he already knows."

"Uh-huh." Paula made a face. The kid was not only weird, she was also a stone liar. "Then why didn't he bail you out, huh?" *Keep her talking about this. Not about anything else. Half an hour, we'll be rid of her.*

"As I've already said, he was distracted by events."

"So, now his lawyers will take care of everything and the court will appoint him your guardian and off you'll go."

"You don't understand. Meadbury needs me today."

"Sorry. We're not going to take you back now."

"You must!" Emily's small forehead creased in fury. It gave her the face of a little old man. "I'll kill myself if you don't."

"Right." Paula faced front again. "Okay. Whatever you say. Only do me a favor, will you? While you die, keep your mouth shut." *Christ, the brat had me going there, for a while. A couple lucky, random cracks and she had me thinking she was psychic, or something.*

Like Alison? said a sly voice in her mind. Was that just lucky? Random?

Shut up. The little voice was of course just the voice of her own doubt, niggling at her, but she didn't care what it was, as long as it shut up.

Surprisingly, the little voice did. Outside, through swirling snow, a sign flashed by: "Meadbury City Limit. Buckle Up—And Come Back Soon!"

In the back seat, Emily was blessedly still. Probably she'd fallen asleep; that much screaming would tire anybody out. In the sudden silence, Zenna cleared her throat. "What do you figure, ten more minutes?"

"Fifteen, I think. Maybe longer, if they haven't plowed lately."

"No, they're good about that. The hospital's right there, they keep the road open for the ambulances." Then Zenna, too, sank back into silence.

A quarter of an hour later they pulled into the plowed, sanded lot at Fredda Mountain Youth Home. Zenna switched off the ignition with a long sigh of relief.

Now all they had to do was get the kid inside, and that was the last they'd ever see of her, which was just all right by Paula. "Hey, kiddo," she said to Emily, "rise and shine. We're here."

No answer. Turning, Paula saw why.

Emily lay in her straitjacket, stretched out full-length on the back seat, her swollen face purplish, her puffed tongue protruding like some grotesque mushroom. Her cracked, blue lips stretched into a horrid rictus, as if her mouth had been wrenched open by a brutal hand. Her blue eyes were wide open, too, and as Paula stared in that first stunned, speechless instant, something flickered in them.

bargain i told you so please i dont want to mommy

Then it was gone, and what remained was one small female child, strapped as per regulation into pediatric security restraint. Also, she was dead.

Not secure enough. Hysterical laughter rose in Paula. Because something was funny here, something was very, very funny; she did not know what, or how, or why. But it was.

She had seen it. With her own eyes. And that, decided what still remained of her fatally shocked mind, had been a mistake. Oh, yes.

Hoarsely, Paula began to laugh.

She was still laughing when the burly attendants' arms wrapped around her, when they trundled her inside and into a soft room.

Security restraint. Paula laughed harder still.

Tommy Riley

Late afternoon, and still snowing hard.

"Uh, Mr. Ibrani?"

The older man pulled the Walkman headphone away from his right ear, spilling Mick Jagger's voice into the passenger compartment of the BMW. He drove very slowly, keeping to the back streets, bulling the car's powerful engine in low gear through drifts which accumulated faster than the city plows could clear them. "Yeah?"

"Uh, have you thought this out? I mean, all the way through?"

Ibrani grinned. "Deftly phrased. And the answer is, no."

Tommy Riley's heart sank.

"I've just decided," Ibrani went on, "the only way to stop Goodmaster is to kill him."

"Yeah, but—"

Ibrani jerked his thumb over his shoulder. "The two shotguns in the trunk are all we need. And you don't even have to pull the trigger. Just keep anybody else at the mansion from getting in my way. I'll take care of Uncle Jason." His jaw muscles bulged as he gritted his teeth. "Oh, yes, I'll take care of him."

Tommy silently turned his face to the window. Off to the right Goodmaster Mansion loomed, its roof and gables topped with a thick layer of snow. He wished he were anywhere else in the universe. Except maybe inside the mansion. . . .

Ibrani slipped the car around the corner and parked near the hole in the fence through which Tommy had escaped the night before. "Over by that hemlock, right?"

Unable to trust his voice, Tommy nodded.

"That hole's been there since I was in high school. I can't imagine Uncle Jason doesn't know about it. Which means he wants it there." They got out of the car, and the wind slammed the doors for them.

"I'll bet good old Uncle Jason has been picking and choosing all these years," Ibrani went on. "Kids go scampering through the back lot." He popped the trunk open. "Kids like you, even." He pulled out two double-barreled shotguns in canvas cases, handed one to Riley, and pocketed an extra box of shells. "And then, later, some of you wind up in guard's uniforms, or working down at City Hall, or even better, teaching in the high school." He thunked the trunk shut. "Or editing the features section at the daily paper. . . ."

His voice trailed off as he looked toward the mansion, whose gable peaks just showed above the trees. "Ah, hell. Let's go."

Tommy followed, nearly doubled over against the wind. It seemed to be hurling shovelfuls of snow straight into his face, gleefully stuffing it in fistfuls down his collar.

Hunkering down, they squeezed through the break in the chain link, then made their way through the evergreens to the edge of an abandoned orchard. The ancient trees clawed upward with twisted, deformed limbs that were naked and scarred. Wind rattled the branches vengefully, cracking and snapping them, howling in triumph.

They moved out, heads down, trudging. Wind like a

highballing freight train battered them. Snow slapped and punched at their faces, confusing them with shades of white on white. Somewhere behind that pale, flaky wall lay the mansion. Somewhere. . . .

A shed rose up ghostlike, vanished, and finally rematerialized in front of them: grey, rotted wood, frosted with driven snow. The potting shed, Tommy remembered. Ibrani hauled on the door. Shuddering against gusts, it opened at last and the older man went in.

Tommy hesitated, trying to see, but it was useless. Then Ibrani's arm—at least, he hoped it was Ibrani's—yanked him inside, too.

Nicki Pialosta

Crooking his finger urgently, Will Rifkind beckoned Nicki Pialosta across the *Bulletin* newsroom. "I'm glad somebody around here has snow tires," the city editor grumbled as she approached his desk. Behind him, the police band radio crackled and spat news of yet another fender bender.

"All-weather radials," she said cheerfully, then stopped, realizing with a tickle of anxiety that she did not remember the drive at all. This wasn't the first time, either. . . .

Then she noticed Rifkind's expression.

Dropping his gaze, he tapped the eraser end of a pencil on his blotter. "Nicki—" He stopped and struggled to compose himself. "Nicki, Jimmy Conklin's dead. Someone shot him out in the parking lot last night."

The world fuzzed over. Now she remembered struggling through the blizzard, felt it as if she were still out there. Cold. The rest of the newsroom faded to a murmur. *No. Not Jimmy. Jimmy's too . . . too alive to die.*

Only he must have, because those were tears sliding down Will Rifkind's knobby potato-face.

Static from the police radio fizzed in her ears, bringing her back to focus. "What happened? Dammit, Will, how?"

"Shot in the head at point-blank range. The snowplow turned him up this morning. His watch, wallet, keys, and car were gone. The cops think somebody blew him away just as he was leaving. I don't know what the hell he was doing here—I'd just fired him." He laughed wanly through his tears, hauled a handkerchief from his back pocket, and blew without shame.

"You know, Nicki, sometimes I think I need a vacation." Rifkind's voice seemed to come from far away. He looked odd; shrunken. As if he had gotten old overnight.

She pressed her fingertips to her temples.

"You ever feel that way?" Seeming not to need or want an answer, he went on. "Like—hell, I don't know. Like the good times are gone, good stories are gone. Like you're gonna open up the obits some morning and find your own name? Or maybe it's happened already, and you didn't even notice. . . ." His voice trailed off; he chuckled hollowly.

Nicki stared. This wasn't the Rifkind she knew. Then a snatch of something from the police band radio needled her eardrum. Her hand darted past the city editor and spun the radio's volume control to high.

"—Ibrani, Benedetto, male Caucasian, thirty-seven, six-one, one-eighty, hair auburn, eyes blue, no facial, no distinguishing. In company of suspect Riley, Thomas, male Caucasian, nineteen, five-nine, one-thirty-five, hair brown, eyes green, no facial and no distinguishing. Suspects armed, considered very dangerous, radio backup before attempt apprehending. Repeat radio backup before apprehending."

Nicki looked for a chair to collapse into, but there weren't any.

Rifkind, by contrast, reacted as if he'd been slapped awake. "Jesus!" He jumped to his feet. "Ben Ibrani. Holy shit. What is this world coming to, muggers after my reporters and cops after our editors? An' who the hell's this Riley kid, you got anything on him?" He yanked a pad of paper toward himself, grabbed a pencil with one hand, and scrabbled in a desk drawer with the other. The hand came out clutching a cigar, which he swiftly unwrapped and stuck into his mouth without lighting.

For all the world as if he wants me to forget that he was acting like a human being. Or as if he's forgotten it. . . . As if someone had reminded him who he is, and what he's supposed to do.

"Tommy used to work here," she said automatically. "And if he's dangerous, I'm the man in the moon. He was an attendant out in the lot, and then he went to work for

Ned Gorman's rent-a-cop outfit—Meadbury Guaranty—and got posted to the shelter. They closed the shelter Tuesday morning, though, and I don't know where his next assignment is."

"He a friend of yours?" Rifkind scowled up at her. "I mean, your information's pretty good, seein' as he was just a lot attendant."

"Tommy?" she said, incredulous. Then she paused, turning it over in her mind. God, the recent past just seemed to run together. There was so much she couldn't remember. Maybe she was the one who needed a vacation. "Yes, yes, I suppose he is a friend, come to think of it."

"In that case—" He pulled open another drawer and removed something from it. "Your 'friend' might come around looking for help, and you might need this when he finds out you're going to turn him in." He held out a pistol: small, nickel-plated, and ugly as a viper.

"Will, I don't need that. I don't even know how to load it—"

Rifkind, watching through alert and measuring eyes, was a different person from the weeping man of a few moments ago. Nicki kept trying to make sense of that, and couldn't.

"It's already loaded," he said. "To use it, you aim it. Then pull the trigger. You can do that, can't you? You sure you haven't seen Riley lately?" Now faint suspicion tinged his scowl, as if he might like to catch her in something. A lie, maybe.

Memory nudged her. Tommy. She had seen Tommy recently. But where? When? She'd had a message for him. . . . No, not a message. A package. A gift. And now—she looked down at the gun.

Now she had another one.

Rifkind waved the pistol at her. "Take it, Nicki."

After a moment, she did.

He touched her arm, a little reminder that propelled her gently toward her desk. "Go on, now. Go do your job."

After another moment, she did that, too.

Tommy Riley

"Fifteen minutes to sunset," Ibrani said, crouched by the door of the potting shed behind the big house.

"Great." Tommy was trying like hell not to sound sullen, but then, he was trying like hell not to freeze to death, too, and look how far that was getting him. The shed had broken the wind, but now the wind had died down. The snow had stopped, too. There remained only the cold: numbing cold, aching, hammering cold.

Killing cold.

He wished he could stamp around slapping his hands, but in the still, frigid dusk, sound would travel crisply. And that, as Ibrani had pointed out, would be disastrous. By now Jason Goodmaster surely would have traced the source of the HBO newsflash.

And, Ibrani said, Jason Goodmaster would understand that it meant war. Which meant the old monster would be getting ready to defend himself.

Success could come only if the nature and timing of the attack took Goodmaster by surprise, because he would be on guard. But even he might not be ready for his carefully nurtured ward and protégé, the son of his dead friend, to jump out of a potting shed and blow him to smithereens with a twelve-gauge.

Therefore, the plan might work. So Tommy kept quiet, but by God he was cold. He tiptoed to the door, where Ibrani was peering through a crack. "Getting dark."

Ibrani nodded. "A minute longer. I can just barely see the rhododendrons by the patio, which means anyone at the French doors might still be able to see the shed."

Tommy peered out. Ibrani was right. "I guess I just want to get it over with."

"You're not alone." They stood a few minutes in silence, waiting. Then another thought struck Tommy.

"You think they might've spotted your car?"

Ibrani shook his head. "Covered with snow. Footprints filled in too. Okay. It's dark enough now, let's do it." He turned from the door. "Get your gun."

Tommy snatched up the shotgun, which Ibrani had

shown him how to handle. His teeth began chattering. When he clenched them together, his shoulders shuddered.

Ibrani turned. "You ready?" His smile was sympathetic.

Tommy couldn't speak. He was about to go help murder a guy, another guy, and for an instant he couldn't quite believe the hellhole his life had so suddenly become.

"Tommy," Ibrani said. "Tommy, if I hadn't given in the way I did when I was your age, you wouldn't be here with me now, doing this. So I'm sorry, Tommy. But I do have to do it. Now." He turned and pushed on the door. It didn't budge.

"Shit. Oh, shit." Ibrani put his shoulder against the slab of rough grey wood. "Snow's blocked it. Dammit." Then he reared back and readied himself to kick hard.

And stopped. Shotgun held parallel to the ground, he took a deep breath, then another, and shook his head. "Nope, not a kick, after all."

"You mean because they'll hear it?"

"They're going to hear us no matter what, now. Change of plan. We don't try to sneak up. Charge as soon as the door's clear. Top speed. Head for the patio doors. Put both barrels into the lock from about five feet. Reload immediately. By the time you're reloaded I ought to be there, but even if I'm not, don't go in. I go in first. Got all that?"

"Yes, sir."

"Okay. Stand clear." Ibrani paced to the other end of the shed, inhaled hugely, and ran. An instant before impact, he leaped into the air, twisting as he rose. His right shoulder slammed into the top half of the door. The hinges popped loudly, and the top half of the door sank down onto the drifted snow outside.

The bottom half swept up inside the shed and missed breaking Tommy's knee by an inch.

"Let's go!" Ibrani hissed, and was gone.

Tommy clambered over the edge of the door and into a nightmare. His feet disappeared into snow to his knees; it was crusted just enough so that he sank heavily into it with each step, and had to flounder out for the next.

Jeeringly, the mansion stayed miles away. His breath came in great painful gasps that the cold cut off. The gun gained weight by the second. His pulse began screeching in his ears. The mansion came an inch nearer. Lights danced in front of his eyes. His pulse screeched louder. The lights flashed now, whirling red and blue: cop cars. He stumbled to a halt.

Up ahead, Ibrani stopped too. Past the corner of the big house, in the front drive, uniformed police spilled from half a dozen cruisers and began to fan out. Their badges and buttons flashed as they stalked past the mansion's lighted windows. Their silhouettes showed behind upstairs curtains. At one window, they lifted an awkward shape to the sill.

Tommy frowned, trying to identify it, but failing until it began to glow.

"Sodium-vapor lamps," Ibrani muttered. "Couple of minutes, this whole back lot's lit up like a Hollywood stage."

The yellow-orange glimmer on the window flickered twice, then brightened steadily. At the next window, a second lamp was warming up. "He knows," Tommy said. "He's going to have guys by the hole in the fence."

Ibrani shook his head. "No. He's playing with us. He could have those guys on top of us now if he wanted. He could have called more of them." He turned. "There won't be anyone by the fence."

There wasn't.

"But how did you know for sure?" Tommy said, once they had gotten Ibrani's car cleared off and started, and were driving away.

Ibrani's smile, in the golden glow of the dashboard lights, was mildly serene.

That smile frightened Tommy almost more than anything that had happened so far.

"Because," Ibrani said, "I know my uncle Jason. I know he plays hardball. But he likes to tease. And what he doesn't know—" He eased the big silver car around a corner. "What he doesn't know, see, is that I can play hardball, too." Slowly, they moved down the quiet street. The car's tires crunched and squeaked sounds on the cold snow. "After all, I had a great teacher. We'll try something else."

Tommy sagged back in his seat. As long as heat kept coming out of that dashboard, he wasn't sure he cared.

"You know," he said, "I had a feeling you were going to say that."

Ibrani just smiled some more.

Jason Goodmaster

He sat by the fire in the darkened second-floor library. Outside it, officers thumped on the staircase, tramped up and down in the hallway, searching. Searching for nothing. The random visits were Gorman's idea, and Goodmaster thought it had been a good one. In case anyone should pay you an uninvited call, Gorman had said; in case someone should be watching.

Plotting, Gorman meant, and Jason Goodmaster supposed it might be so. He didn't think young Ben really had the backbone for it, but the boy's television piracy had shown surprising bite. Under other circumstances Goodmaster might even have approved.

Perhaps I underestimated the boy after all. Stranger things have happened.

Now Jason Goodmaster turned his eye—his inner eye—to one of them.

Where is he? On the hearth, flames writhed. Through them, Goodmaster watched the city: chaos, confusion, and disarray. Tidy, elegant patterns tending now toward formlessness, yearning for order.

Jason Goodmaster might have laughed, but he was not a laughing man. Instead, he gloated. *See? See what you are without me?* There, there was one of the town's good citizens. . . .

/I b'lieve I'll have me another piece of pie, Martha./

/Now, Elvin, you know you gots to watch your weight./

/Never mind that, woman, just cut me another piece./

Goodmaster smiled, and gave a faint push.

/On second thought, give me the whole pie./

/Elvin!/

/And get me the ice cream—all of it. And the cookies. And the rest of that pound cake from last night, and the butter, and the chocolate sauce, and—/

So easy, really. And a trip to the emergency room would do Elvin good. Afterward, he would be glad of a little control, would cleave to the source of that control with even more energy—

And so would all the rest. And then Meadbury would be perfect. Forever. A city with one mind, one conscience, one soul.

So let them spin randomly for a while. Let them wallow in whatever freedom they think they desire. Only a few really needed his attention. The Pialosta woman required brief touches, and so did one or two others, at the newspaper and in politics. Gorman, of course, being groomed to wield power rather than to be wielded by it, spun independently. And meanwhile the Roundtrees and the McGillicuddys of the city would go on, out of habit, in routines Goodmaster had set for them.

So he would let the rest sin.

The better to repent.

And now. . . . Where was the boy? He stared searchingly into the flames. He no longer needed Ben Ibrani. After all, Ned Gorman was heir apparent now. In good time, Gorman would learn to do all that Goodmaster had done. Gorman understood power, and he liked it. He would serve well.

But Ibrani had rebelled. Somehow he had slipped the leash that had noosed him. He was hiding, evading the punishment he so richly deserved. And that could not be tolerated. No, not at all.

Some might fail. Some might die. That was acceptable; that was part of the plan. But no one escaped. No one.

Patiently, Goodmaster searched the leaping, licking flares of yellow and orange, minutely examining each whirling world therein, each small soul dancing to the momentary delusion that it was free.

Where was the boy?

Tommy Riley

Riding back toward Ibrani's apartment, Tommy Riley began to relax. He still couldn't believe the cops hadn't caught them sneaking out through the fence, but so far, so fine. If you could call this fine.

Ibrani drove slowly, partly because of the snow in the

streets and partly to avoid attracting any unnecessary attention. They hadn't passed any police cars yet, but that was probably just dumb luck.

And they could use plenty of that. "Hey, Mr. Ibrani. How can you hear me? You've got that Walkman on so loud I can hear it myself."

Ibrani shrugged without taking his hands from the steering wheel. "I've been listening to this for so long, I know exactly what's coming next, and I'm sort of listening to everything else around the edges, if you know what I mean."

"Sort of. I guess." Tommy frowned. "But isn't that dangerous?"

Again the older man shrugged. He sure seemed to be taking everything sort of mellow. Tommy thought that was just as well; he himself had been close to freaking out back there, and if they both did. . . .

"I don't know," Ibrani said. "If I park in front of the police station, you might want to bug out on your own."

"Yeah." Tommy squirmed at the thought. It could happen. He hoped it wasn't going to. "Hey, would you mind if I turned on the radio?"

"What, Mick Jagger doesn't do it for you?" He jerked his chin at the dashboard. "Go ahead."

The car's quad speakers came to life: "—Riley and Benedetto Ibrani. Police are combing the area for the suspects now, and according to department spokespersons an arrest is expected very shortly. In other news—"

Riley slapped the radio silent. "Did you hear that?"

"Yes." Ibrani's lips tightened.

"What are we going to do?"

"I don't know. We can't go home, that's for sure. Not only that, we've got to dump the car. Let me pull over, we'll think about it."

"Pull over? Are you crazy? Keep moving!"

"To where? We're getting low on gasoline here. And heading into the nearest service station might not be such a hot idea, either. An APB means they've probably notified the gas stations."

"Yeah, but. . . ." Tommy groaned inwardly. "Mr. Ibrani, this sucks."

"Tell me about it. We've got to find a place to go, and I'm

not sure I can think of any. Sure as hell we'll never make it out of town."

"How about Miss Pialosta's? Jeez," he said with a sudden jolt of guilt, "we gotta go there anyway, she's been tied up now for over. . . ."

Ibrani was shaking his head. "How do you suppose they know we're together?"

"Oh," Tommy said. "Somebody found her, huh?"

Ibrani's laugh was grim. "Yeah, I think somebody did."

Slumping down, Tommy jammed his hands dejectedly into his pockets. The fingers of his right hand touched a set of keys, and so did the fingers of his left.

Wait a minute. Keys? "Hey! Mr. Ibrani! I got it—a place for us to go!"

"Where?" The relief on Ibrani's face made it all ghastly real again: They had fallen into deep shit, here, and Ibrani hadn't been going to get them out. Grown-up or not, he had been stuck. But now—

"The shelter," Tommy said, gabbling with relief. "It's all shut down now, but I never gave the keys back, I forgot to, and I'll bet there's still food, even, and no one would ever look for us there. Would they? Do you think?"

By way of answer, Ibrani swung the car around a corner, heading with all deliberate speed for the one place in town where no one would ever think to look for them.

Or almost no one.

The shelter keys worked, as Tommy had known they would. He swung the small service door open and held it.

With a shrug of resignation, Ibrani stepped inside. "I guess the car can't be helped. They'd have to come all the way around back to see it, anyway." He touched the switchplate on the wall. "And it's still snowing, that'll cover—"

The overhead lights flickered, then came on coldly fluorescent behind diffusion strips of pebbled plastic. Frowning, Ibrani took two quick steps back. "The power's still on. And so is the heat." The barrel of the shotgun tilted up, drawing a bead on Tommy's heart. "You said this place was deserted."

Tommy took a deep breath and spoke quickly. "Mr. Ibrani, honest, nobody's here. It's the weather. Don't you see, they left the heat on so the pipes won't freeze, and stuff won't get mildewed."

Ibrani frowned. He'd gotten progressively twitchier during the drive over, Tommy had noticed, as if he didn't completely trust any ideas except his own.

Tommy could understand that. He wasn't feeling real trusting about things, himself. But neither was he feeling particularly tolerant, and Ibrani's fast-growing paranoia was a pain in the ass.

"To hell with it. I'm not setting you up, but if you think I am, blow me the fuck away, all right? And while you're thinking about it, I'm going to see what's left in the pantry. I'm starving." He strode down the hall, pushing past Ibrani without so much as a glance at the shotgun.

Ibrani blinked, let him pass without comment, and fell in behind him.

Now fear prickled at the base of Riley's spine, right where the buckshot would hit if Ibrani pulled the trigger. He kept walking, waiting for the click that would mean his life was over, but heard only Ibrani's footsteps behind him.

After a moment, Ibrani spoke again. "You think they left any coffee?"

Tommy shrugged. "What am I, a mind reader?" He stomped on into the big institutional kitchen, began yanking open cabinets and drawers. Macaroni, big cans of soup, tightly-lidded canisters of rice, flour, sugar. . . .

"Tommy."

"What?" He slammed a drawer shut and jerked open another one.

Ibrani lowered the shotgun. "I'm sorry."

Tommy turned, and what he saw sent his anger abruptly away. Ibrani's shoulders slumped in exhaustion. He'd been wearing the Walkman headphones so long that his ears were swollen and red. His bloodshot eyes searched Tommy's. Fright, desperation, and miserable apology played over his drawn face.

"Forget it," Tommy said.

The walk-in refrigerator belched a rotten stench. Ibrani slammed the door quickly. "Looks like we stick to the canned stuff."

"I guess so." Tommy opened another cabinet. "Pay dirt."

Ibrani's expression lightened at the sight of coffee. "My

hero." He pulled a big saucepan from a shelf and began filling it at the sink.

Tommy continued to explore. He'd found his way to the walk-in freezer and was poking at a wrapped package labeled "ground chuck" when he heard his name being called.

"Over here!" Jeez, Ibrani was really antsy, couldn't leave him alone for a minute. . . .

"Where?"

"In the freezer!" he yelled in exasperation. If they could find a big knife or a cleaver, they could carve off enough meat for hamburgers.

"Where?"

Jeez. He strode out into the kitchen. "Don't get so nervous, will you? I'm right here."

Ibrani looked up. "Huh?"

"I was just back there in the freezer."

Ibrani shrugged, and spooned more coffee into the saucepan. "So? I knew that."

Tommy sighed. "Then why did you ask me where I was?"

"I didn't."

"Come on, you kept asking me—" Tommy stopped as Ibrani stared at him. It hit him like a punch in the stomach: Ibrani hadn't been calling him at all.

Jason Goodmaster had.

Ibrani grabbed the shotgun. "What did you tell him?"

Where are you? "Nothing. The freezer. I said I was right there, in the freezer. Jeez, find me a paper and pencil or something. . . ." He pressed the heels of his hands to his temples.

Where are you?

Ibrani patted his shirt pocket, found a felt-tip, and shoved it at Tommy, who seized it and began scribbling on a formica countertop.

$4x^2 + 12xy + 9y^2 = 529$ *Where are you?*

It didn't help, he'd done that problem too many damned times; the answers were obvious. He prayed for a problem.

$4x^2 +$ (*where*)$12xy + 9y^2 = 3600$

$(2x + 3y)^2 = 3600$

$2x$(*are*) $+ 3y = 60$

$x + 3/2y = 30$

$x = 30 - 3/2y$(*ou?*)

Which only proved zero equaled zero and that hardly strained the brain at all.

Where are you where where. . . . The ink beaded on the formica, thinning as it dried, vanishing into an illegible smear. Ibrani's hand slipped a piece of cardboard under the pen's tip. Tommy nodded thanks but did not look up, desperate to keep the numbers in front of his eyes.

Where are you?

A *real* problem. Okay, say you want to buy a small house that sells for $80,000. He scribbled the price on the cardboard.

At once, the 8 began swelling, changing, until its shape was a woman's shape bulging up at him. Scolding him. His mother. "Tommy, you tell your mother this instant—"

He blinked and squinted her back to an 8 again. Bank says put 20% down—

The percent sign flapped itself batlike away from the numerals and flew at him, clawing. *Sixteen thousand!* he yelled at it mentally, writing as fast as he could. The bat tumbled backward, shriveling.

You take out a thirty-year mortgage at 9.875%, oh, God, what was the formula? He froze for a horrid instant before he realized he didn't have to get it perfect. Nobody was grading him. All he had to do was try, dammit, try— The pen began scratching out the long, complicated equation. Which, he realized, was exactly what he needed; something challenging, something really hard. . . .

"Tommy?" Ibrani's voice.

He ignored it, squeezing the pen till the tip of his finger turned white because the damned equation was trying now to wiggle away from him, turning into—

"Tommy, are you all right?"

Parentheses: scissor blades snapping. He nailed them to the page with thick, broad strokes of ink.

Ibrani's hand rested on his shoulder. "Tommy?"

"They're not going to get me." The words escaped his clenched jaw. Fraction marks slashing, equals signs chewing cruelly at him. . . .

"Answer me, please." Ibrani sounded very nervous now.

"I won't let them take me back."

"Tommy, I'm getting worried here. Come on, talk to me, now!"

Ibrani's dismay battered Tommy's concentration, but he had to hold firm. Hang onto the numbers, stay sharp as a pencil point, solid and sure as the simplest addition.

$2 + 2 = 4$.

"Tommy!"

"I'm pushing them back." Did he say that? Or only imagine saying it? It didn't matter, did it? Because it was true, true. . . .

$2 * 2 = 4$. Another eternal truth. $2 + 2 = 2 * 2$.

All four 2's lunged at him, yowling and snarling and trying to rip the nose off his face. He beat them back with a quick division.

$1 = 1$.

That's what it comes down to. One. Unos.

E pluribus unum, something whispered slyly.

No. He felt his own lips curling back, snarling, heard as if from a distance the soft click of hammers cocking. Shotgun. Ibrani, getting ready to solve the equation once and for all in case he had to. . . .

No, no manys. Just me. One. Myself. He scribbled madly. One one one $(1 + i\%)^n$. . . .

Behind him, finger on the trigger, Ibrani hesitated a moment, and then another, and another.

Jason Goodmaster

Where?

Intent on his search, he did not notice that he was himself being scrutinized. He did not notice the growing anger that was gathering with him as its focus.

Still, it was there.

For, although he did not realize it, Jason Goodmaster had made two mistakes. The first was believing himself to have power. He did not, and he should have known that; he himself called it "the oversoul." Meadbury was not a sun throwing off power for a burning glass to focus. Meadbury was a living entity, an organism, and had merely followed his lead for a time. Goodmaster had forgotten that the overriding rule of life is self-preservation.

Distracted by a mistaken belief in his own power, he had begun to endanger the oversoul's survival, or so it had decided. That anyone but its chosen few should be aware of it—that its existence should be hinted at by the publication of "death boxes," for example—was anathema to it. And that—endangerment of itself—it would not permit.

Goodmaster's second mistake stemmed directly from the first. He had known from nearly the beginning that the lives of the people in town had coalesced into a single larger life: the oversoul. But in his arrogance he had never contemplated the inevitable ramification of that fact: that the lives of the towns in the region could themselves coalesce to compose a still greater being.

Meadbury. Boston. Hartford. Springfield. New Haven. New York. Newark. Young cities compared to a Rome or an Athens; barely teenagers on that scale. But quite old enough, some of them, to have gone thoroughly mad, and thus to pollute the judgment of the greatersoul they comprised.

Once before, an individual human had proved so capable of manipulating his oversoul that he had gained control not only of his greatersoul, but of the macrosoul beyond that. Thousands of New Englanders had given their lives to shatter that man's demonic hold on the spirit of his nation. Now a new manipulator had arisen, and he was training an apprentice.

Greater New England was sane enough that it could recoil from the notion of being perverted into a new Nazi Germany, but demented enough to see its salvation in the liquidation of the tainted oversoul: Meadbury.

It gathered its forces.

FRIDAY, JANUARY 18

Meadbury

Unaware of the forces gathering against Jason Goodmaster and thus against himself, Ned Gorman ushered Charlie Yee into his office. The Ibrani problem still simmered on the back burner of his mind, but he did not care to give it serious attention. He was sure that Ben Ibrani, Goodmaster's erstwhile ward and protégé, was merely playing a role in thc command-post exercise Goodmaster had promised to arrange as practice for Gorman and his campaign staff.

So, he thought, Ibrani could wait, at least until he had interviewed this Yee fellow, the man he wanted as an election consultant. Thinking of this, Gorman allowed himself a small smile.

Interview—what an appropriate word. Since I do plan to look deep into Charlie's cynical soul. And make a few changes, if necessary.

Briefly, he reviewed his priorities and found himself satisfied: campaign first, cranks second. After all, if it were really important, Goodmaster would handle it himself.

Charles Yee took Gorman's spartan office in with a glance.

So far, so good. No affectations, no opulence. Just straight-backed chairs, clean beige indoor-outdoor carpeting, a pair of Zenith microcomputers, new metal filing cabinets, and lots of light. Yee thought his potential client might be on a power trip—most candidates were—but at least his campaign headquarters projected an air of no-nonsense efficiency.

"So, Mr. Gorman—"

"Call me Ned." Gorman guided Yee to a chair, then headed for the urn on a table in the corner. "Coffee?"

"Tea, please." Yee took his glasses off and polished them lightly with his handkerchief. He did not have to think about how to phrase what he was about to say; he had said it many times before. "Mr. Gorman, I never call clients by their first names. I have no desire to become your friend. I am a media consultant, and I wish only to bring you victory in this and subsequent campaigns, if I accept you as a client."

Styrofoam cup in hand, Gorman turned. "That's the way you do it all the time?"

"Yes." Yee replaced his glasses and smiled. A business smile.

Gorman shrugged. "Is this your first visit to Meadbury?"

Yee nodded. It made no difference, Meadbury or Anytown. But now Gorman was going to say why it did, and that Yee must not take offense at the use of his own first name, or some diminishment of it.

"We're very friendly here in Meadbury," Gorman said. "For all that it's an old New England town, there aren't too many starched shirts. Call me, and anybody else in the campaign, whatever you like. Just don't take it wrong when folks call you 'Charlie.' "

Yee accepted the cup of steeping tea. "Thank you." He dunked the bag a few times before speaking again. "Mr. Gorman, I'm a professional. I honestly do not care what anyone calls me while I am working." This was not quite true, but no matter. "My only concern is that when I call, you listen."

Gorman nodded vigorously. "Since I'm paying you an exorbitant fee to give advice, you can bet I'll listen."

Yee went on. This next part was generally the sticking point. "Should I accept you as a client, you will pay me my entire fee in advance."

Gorman's eyebrows went up. "Is that customary?"

"Only for me, Mr. Gorman." He watched Gorman absorb the implications. Gorman was not stupid. He understood that Charles Yee could set what conditions he wished.

"And if I lose," Gorman said slowly, playing the canny businessman, "do I get a refund?"

Yee shook his head. "No, Mr. Gorman. No refunds. You know quite well that of the forty-three campaigns I have assisted, only one resulted in defeat. I could have salvaged even that if the FBI's man had not been wearing a microphone at the time my client accepted the proffered bribe."

Gorman grinned. "I read about it. As I recall, you almost won anyway."

Yee nodded. "That is true. After two recounts, a total of one hundred thirty-one votes separated my client from the victor."

Gorman laughed. "Mr. Yee, you are amazing. One question, though. Why is a man of your talent willing to help with a run-of-the-mill municipal election? Couldn't you be working on something more important? The gubernatorial election in New York, or the senatorial race out in California?"

Yee nodded once more. "Conditions again, Mr. Gorman. My talent, as you put it, enables me to set them, to arrange my life as I wish. I don't fly, and I don't drive more than ninety minutes to a client's campaign headquarters."

Gorman accepted this with a shrug. "Well, from all I've heard, your quirks are my good fortune. You're on the team the minute you're ready to go. Which I hope will be soon."

Yee threw back his head and chuckled deeply. These candidates were all the same. "My dear Mr. Gorman, I have not yet offered to join your team. That is, after all, the purpose of this visit: to ascertain whether or not you meet my standards."

Gorman raised his hands in a sign of surrender. "Okay, Mr. Yee, I see you're captain of your own fate. What do I have to do to get you to sign on?"

Yee leaned back in his chair. "Tell me who you are, Mr. Gorman."

Gorman looked surprised and a little unsettled.

Yee kept pressing. "I research potential clients before I visit them, you see. And your background is, shall we say, obscure?"

Gorman smiled ruefully. He braced his elbows on his desk top, rested his chin atop his clasped hands, and stared deep into Yee's eyes. "Well, you know, before I moved to

Meadbury, I didn't amount to much. Nothing scandalous in my background, of course, but nothing that would leave much of an impression anywhere. School, the service, a few sales jobs—"

Yee listened. The man was an astonishingly good liar. Charles Yee had worked for many such liars; this one had real possibilities. The eye contact did it, of course. That blue gaze became a warm, still lake that lured the audience in deeper and deeper.

Gorman stopped abruptly. His head jerked up; he frowned at the door.

The interruption made the lake water go ice-cold. Annoyed, Yee thought he would have to teach Gorman not to break off like that; annoyed, Yee glanced over his shoulder. The door was closed; Yee turned back to Gorman, whose eyes now widened slowly, his lips pulling back into a snarl.

This, Yee decided, would be a more difficult campaign than he had thought. A madman's money was as good as anyone else's, but voters had an antipathy to madmen. Such a handicap could be overcome, but still. . . .

Hissing, Gorman jumped to his feet and clenched his hands into fists.

Yee made his decision: It wasn't worth it. Gorman's psychiatric history would pop up at the worst possible time, and Yee's own record would drop to forty-two and two.

Gorman threw a punch at nothing, but his fist stopped in midair as though it had connected. A wild smile spread across his face.

Yee set his Styrofoam cup on the table and stood up. "Well, Mr. Gorman," he said as smoothly as he could, "I think I've learned all I need to, so I'll be—"

Gorman screamed, vaulted his desk, and headed for the door at a dead run. Halfway there, he tripped over something Charles Yee could not see, and fell flat on his face.

"I'm going now," Yee said hurriedly.

"Let go of me, you bastards!"

"Is there anyone I should call?" Yee stuck his head out of the office, but no one sat at the desk in the reception area.

Gorman did not answer. Instead, he writhed on the floor, struggling with half a dozen invisible assailants. Veins stood out on his reddened forehead; his arms stiffened as if they had been seized. Then both wrists jerked around to the middle of his back, met, and crossed. There he lay, his face pressed into the carpet, his shoulders still heaving but his body immobile.

Then he gave a grunt. With one swift motion he went from a prone to a kneeling position, like an athlete doing an exuberant push-up, except that his hands stayed in the middle of his back. He grunted again and rose smoothly to his feet.

Thoroughly unnerved, Charles Yee decided to find a telephone some distance from Gorman's headquarters and call the police. He was considering what to say to them, so as not to be institutionalized himself, when Gorman screamed "You fuckers!" and lunged forward.

He snapped right back into an erect position, as if he had been tied with invisible bonds to an invisible pole. His jaws opened wide, and a string of gibberish emerged from his yawning throat.

Now Charles Yee wanted to run, but he could not tear his eyes from the spectacle. Plunging his hands into his pockets, he gripped whatever he found there as if it might help him hold onto his sanity in the face of what he was seeing.

Gorman's neck muscles strained with a terrible effort but his head did not move. Drool ran down his chin; his right foot drew back to kick— And abruptly returned to position beside the left foot. Ankle bones met with an audible click. Gorman moaned.

Charles Yee almost did, too. He squeezed the disposable lighter in his pocket so hard he feared its plastic shell would crack. He neither understood what he was seeing, nor wanted to. The police. Yes, he would call the police from the pay phone at the corner and they would send someone. He edged toward the door.

Then black dizziness hit him, cold and clammy like tendrils of seaweed drawn across his brain. He lost control of his senses, but not of his consciousness, as though someone had shoved him headlong into a sensory deprivation tank. He had the impression of stumbling about for a moment, but knew for certain only this: that when vision returned like a TV clicking on, he was holding the door open, his lighter in his hand, thoughts of flight foremost in his mind.

Gorman's strangled howl of anguish made him glance back. Immediately, he wished he hadn't.

Small yellow flames licked up the legs of Ned Gorman's pants. Another flame, bigger and brighter, chewed the tip of Gorman's necktie. Smoke wisped off the surface of his vest.

Gorman shrieked. He squirmed. But he did not run. He wriggled, jerked, and strained, but remained immobile, for all the world like a man being burned at an invisible stake.

Charles Yee looked down at the lighter in his hand, and again at Gorman. Then he stuffed the lighter back into his pocket. Finally, he stepped out of the office and closed the door behind him. From inside came another muffled scream, more terrible than before.

Charles Yee hurried through the reception area. No, not the police. The fire department. Anonymously, of course.

Nicki Pialosta

She sat in the *Bulletin* newsroom, listening to the latest radio report on the manhunt for Ibrani and Riley, and wondering what to do.

She knew where they had gone, of course, knew it with the perfect certainty of unwanted revelation.

They had gone where she would go if she were hiding and wanted a place nobody would think of: the shelter. Silent and forgotten now, it held no interest for anyone because nothing was happening there.

Her hand moved toward the telephone, detoured instead to her pack of cigarettes. As recently as yesterday, she would have known exactly what to do, and then done it. The trouble was, she couldn't remember yesterday. Great swatches of the recent past, in fact, were simply gone: flat, white, and featureless, as if last night's blizzard had covered them over along with everything else.

She lit a cigarette. She ought to call the police. She really ought to. But—

Ben Ibrani is no more a dangerous criminal than I am. Oddly, the thought frightened her. It provoked an overwhelming sensation of guilt, as if believing in Ben's innocence was itself a criminal act.

Any minute now, she felt, she would remember why faith

in Ben Ibrani, and especially in Tommy Riley, seemed so forbidden. And that frightened her most of all, because she was suddenly, intensely certain that she did not want to recall whatever it was she had forgotten.

The shelter: a perfect hiding place. So quiet, so empty. So like a trap. She stubbed out the cigarette, then rose, crossed the room, and pulled on her coat. Saying nothing to anyone, she left the building, got into her car, and headed toward the center of town, to Meadbury Shelter. She did not quite know what she was going to do when she got there. She only knew that she had very little time before she began to remember.

She wanted to let sleeping memories lie, but she knew that they would stir, and then waken. When they did, her time would be up. Time for what? She didn't know. A sob of fright escaped her.

Either I'm crazy, or someone has been doing something to my head. Her knees shook so that her foot kept slipping off the accelerator.

To calm herself, she began to sing a little song, an old one her father had taught her her a long time ago, about the ants that go marching one by one, and then two by two, and then three by three. . . .

Oddly, it seemed to help.

Meanwhile, a small, distant part of her mind looked on with detached amusement. Yep, you've gone 'round the bend, old girl. Driving and crying and singing and shaking.

Nevertheless and without knowing why, she was absolutely certain that she ought to go on doing all of these things, except for crying and shaking, which she tried to stop.

The ants were marching thirty by thirty when she succeeded.

Tommy Riley

Give up.

Tommy Riley woke with a shudder, breath rattling in his throat. Drenched in sweat from a night-long series of dream-battles, he nearly whimpered when he realized they had not ended, but just begun. Though still at the shelter and still free, he had not won the war, only the opening skirmish. Others would follow, day after day, night after night.

Give up now, before you exhaust yourself.

Not his own mind talking. No way. And he was not going to listen to that crap. He would get up and fix breakfast for Mr. Ibrani and himself. Ibrani was a good guy, for all his gun-pointing paranoia; being around him, even sitting silently at a table with him, did more to harden Tommy Riley's resolve than anything else, because he was a grown man, like Tommy could be. He hoped.

He sat up. Searing pain tore at his throat. Somehow it didn't surprise him. He flopped back down, almost used to insanity by now. When it wasn't one thing, it was another. "What the hell?" he said to the ceiling.

The ceiling did not reply.

Gingerly, he put his fingers to his throat and touched the cold metal links of a chain. Relief pulsed through him. Of course. Ibrani had chained him to the bed late last night, when it looked as if he, Tommy, would finally give way.

Ibrani had stood watching, first with suspicion and fear, then with admiration as Tommy scribbled furiously. Tommy's jaw hurt now from clenching it for hours. But he had not given in, and at last Ibrani had wrapped the chain around his throat and laid him down here, so that if something happened, Tommy would not be able to hurt him.

He shivered as the memory of one dream flooded back. He turned his mind forcefully away from the bloody image of it.

Goodmaster, he knew, had spent the night inside his head, soaking up information and leaving suggestions, putrid dream-traces that set Tommy to gagging. Goodmaster must have learned where they were hiding, too.

But Ibrani must have figured that out already. He was probably somewhere nearby right this minute, thinking up another plan.

"Mr. Ibrani! I'm awake. Let me up."

Mr. Ibrani did not answer.

Tommy called again, a little louder.

Still no answer.

The third time he shrieked at the top of his lungs.

Nothing. Only the echoing silence of the shelter, wrapped around him like a clammy blanket.

Tommy tried to think. If Mr. Ibrani had left him this way, he must have meant him to stay this way. But he was hungry, and he had to go to the bathroom. Worse, he felt rattly; he was beginning to recognize the start of an attack, now, like a bad smell seeping up his mental nostrils. He needed a pencil and a piece of paper.

He rolled on his side, tracing the chain with trembling fingers. A weak link, maybe, or something he could unscrew. Or snap off. Anything, just to get free.

That's right, Tommy. Just get free.

At the voice in his head, Tommy Riley began to shake. Noises of fear came out of his throat, and he thought he might wet himself in his awful fright.

It was coming. The thing was coming. And it wanted him.

He lurched upward with all his might and fell solidly back again, thrumming with pain and knowing he'd nearly murdered himself. Another ounce of effort and the chain would have crushed his larynx.

Give in to me, boy. Or strangle on your own blood.

Eat shit, you perverted son of a bitch. The pain, the blessed pain had earned him one instant of mental silence. He sank his teeth fiercely into the flesh of his own hand. Blood seeped between his teeth, its taste bright and coppery sweet. For a moment he thought he might faint, and then all would be lost.

No. *Son of a bitch.* Through his anguish, he forced thought. Padlock around his neck. Loose enough to breathe. Other end round the bedframe, padlocked again. Steel bedframe. He flung himself onto his other side, scanning his surroundings for anything that might help.

A memo pad and pencil lay there. He snatched them up.

"Tommy," the pad read, "the key to the lock at your throat is in the hall. The combination to the other lock is 3 turns to the right to x, left past x to y, right to z. Good luck and I'll see you later."

Below the note were three equations:

$3x + 4y + z = 98$

$2x + 5y + 3z = 168$

$8x + y + 2z = 178$

With a joyful thrill of pain, he pulled his teeth from his

hand. Genius. Ibrani was a genius; the phrase made a little song in his heart. Ibrani had chained him to the bed, but in such a way that Tommy had to be himself to calculate the combination. And the act of calculating it would raise his shield against Goodmaster.

Graphite dust flew as he worked through the equations. In just a few minutes he was dialing three turns right to 12, left past 12 to 6, right to 38.

The padlock fell open. He unwound the chain, stood, and stretched. Chain clanking at his feet, he went to the hall, found the key taped there, and unlocked his neck. Then, letting the chain fall, he headed for the bathroom.

Ibrani had left, though. The parking lot was empty. Maybe he was moving the car; he'd been nervous about it.

But why hadn't he come back? Maybe he'd gone to kill Jason Goodmaster by himself.

Tommy shivered over his coffee. If Goodmaster's people caught Ibrani, they would have no trouble catching Tommy, too. Alone, he just didn't have a chance, and neither did Ibrani, and why the hell hadn't Ibrani realized that? He needed to know what was going on, but he had no way, no way to find out.

Unless he went outside. Just . . . took a look. After all, Ibrani hadn't left instructions. Maybe he was supposed to look around. Maybe Ibrani had even left him another note.

One thing he knew for sure: He was done for if he stayed here alone. Sooner or later, the thing would attack his mind again, and he could defend himself only by scribbling equations and praying. But the fight would exhaust him, and he would need somebody to tie him down. Otherwise he would do . . . something else.

So, okay. One quick trip around the place, then back inside to reconsider.

He picked up his coat and eased out the back door just as a car pulled into the service drive. The driver could not have helped seeing him. He moved to duck back inside as the service door slammed shut with a final-sounding thunk.

And he'd left his keys on the big stainless steel table in the kitchen.

The car drew nearer, then stopped. The driver rolled down the window. "Get in here," Miss Pialosta said.

The gun in her hand made his decision pretty simple.

She drove away from the shelter.

"I suppose you're taking me to Goodmaster." With his own gun hidden in its shoulder holster, Tommy let bitterness sound in his voice. Since she hadn't shot him, and didn't seem about to, he could think about something other than going for his weapon and blowing her away.

This might not be the disaster it had first seemed. If Goodmaster's men had nabbed Ibrani, they would probably have taken him to the mansion. Miss Pialosta was, therefore, chauffeuring him to where he would have gone anyway. So he was glad he hadn't shot her back in the parking lot. "In for a penny, in for a pound," his mother used to say. Better to get Jason Goodmaster at the same time if he could.

She swung the car out through the turnaround circle, then confounded him, shoving the small nickel-plated pistol across the seat. "Take it," she said.

He just stared.

"I wasn't sure," she said apologetically. "Who you were or, when I recognized you, what you might do."

He nodded, considering. No one caught up in this —whatever this was—could be sure of anything. For example: Was she lying? Probably she was. She'd fooled him before. He'd better play along. She didn't know about his revolver, and that might come in handy at the mansion. "Miss Pialosta—"

"Call me Nicki, okay? Partners in crime ought to be on a first name basis, I think."

Yeah, sure. He tried to resist a sudden, strong impulse to trust her. Knowing it was only because he needed someone to trust, now. . . . And because he loved her. Had loved her, a long time ago. He frowned, thinking about how long ago it seemed. A wave of drowning discouragement washed over him. What good was staying alive if you couldn't trust anybody?

"Look, Tommy," she said. "I know what you must be thinking, and I don't blame you. I've started remembering. Some things I did, and some I almost did. And I just want to tell you, I'm so sorry. I wasn't myself."

He laughed in spite of himself. That put it pretty accurately. All at once he thought again how much he liked her. Had liked her.

Abruptly she pulled the car over and leaned her head on the steering wheel.

Uh-oh. Trust; don't trust. The conflict threw his gut into turmoil. "Nicki, I gotta tell you, you do one damn thing that strikes me too weird and I'll—"

What? Blow her head off? Kill her and shove her out of the car? The options kept coming, each more horrible than the last. Even worse was the realization that he would do them. He would. Because he couldn't afford to be a sap about her any more. He just couldn't.

She looked up at him, sad comprehension in her eyes. "Tommy. That shoulder rig you're wearing . . ."

He started unhappily.

She made a wry face. "It wasn't that hard to spot, Tommy. And the thing is this: If I do one damn thing that strikes you weird, I want you to do what you just almost said you were going to. I don't understand what's going on, but I don't want you to let me hurt you. If I try. . . ." Her voice trailed off. After a moment, she bit her lip and pulled the car back onto the street.

"I'm afraid," she said. "It's Goodmaster, isn't it? Somehow. I can feel him in my head. I keep remembering more, and I'm afraid he can get back in."

Tommy nodded. "Have you tried blocking him?"

She glanced at him. "How?"

Caution nudged him. Still, if she was lying, she already knew, because Goodmaster must know by now. And if she didn't, she'd better find out fast.

"It's a little hard to explain. You've got to fill your head up with something else, something really forceful. Something that clicks for you, something that pulls you in like he wants to. You've got to block his punch, see, really . . . block it." At the bleakness of her expression, he stopped miserably. "I'm probably not saying it very well."

"No," she said. "No, I know what you mean. It makes perfect sense; in fact, I think I've already done it once."

"But that's great," he said, seeing in her face that she didn't think so. "What did you—?"

Her laugh cut him off, if you could call that sound a laugh. "Despair, Tommy. This morning, when I knew I was going to come out here and get you, help you if I could, I was thinking of quitting."

He frowned, not understanding. "Quitting the *Bulletin*?"

She shook her head, glanced down at the little gun on the seat. "No. Quitting life. I was starting to remember already, see, even though I didn't want to. I knew I'd been used. Taken, invaded. Whatever. And it made me feel like I didn't want to bother living any more. To tell you the truth, I feel that way now. Just that it's all pointless."

"But you're here."

She shrugged. "Habit. Automatic pilot. Like the song —running on empty. I woke up to find I'd lost my hope, and now I feel hollow. A fake person. Nothing inside, only I weigh about a million pounds. I'm just walking through it, I guess, until I find a good place to sit down and . . . rest." She glanced at the pistol again, almost welcomingly. It gave him a chill.

"I thought," he said slowly, "that part of growing up was losing hope."

She shook her head. "When you grow up, you stop hoping somebody'll knock on your door and tell you a band of gypsies stole you at birth, and you're really the long-lost heir to Shangri-la. You stop hoping you'll win the Pulitzer just for showing up at work every day, or that Mr. Perfect is going to swing by in his Porsche, drive off into the sunset with you. What you don't do is stop hoping that you'll wake up the next morning. Because it's only going to get worse so why even bother?" She let her breath out slowly, painfully. "That's despair, I think. In fact, I'm pretty sure of it."

He turned to look at her. If this was an act, it was a damned good one. He didn't think it was, though, and suddenly found himself wishing he did. Because he wouldn't be able to save himself, to make her do or stop doing anything, by holding a gun to her head. She'd only smile and tell him to pull the trigger. Goodmaster had her for sure, now, even when he didn't have her at all.

Which brought him back to Goodmaster: how sly the man was, how powerful and evil. But not that powerful, or he'd have won already. And that made Tommy think.

"Nicki. You've seen the news today, right? I mean, from other places?"

She nodded tiredly.

"Are things going screwy there? In other towns, other cities, are strange things happening?"

"No," she said reluctantly. "But—"

"Then all we do is get ourselves out of town. Ibrani too, if we can find him." Briefly, he explained his recent alliance with the older man. "I'll bet anything that if we get away from here. . . ."

She sighed. "Tommy, I'm so tired. Why don't you just let me get out of the car? Go on if you want to."

He stared at her. Here it was, then, the moment he'd thought about and dreamed of for so long: time for him to assert himself, strong and masculine and decisive. Time for him to square his shoulders, deepen his voice.

But what he really wanted to do was curl up on the floor of the car and wait for a grown-up. Unfortunately, right now he was the grown-up in this group. And it didn't feel the slightest bit romantic.

Nicki kept driving; slowly, though, and aimlessly. Pretty soon he thought that she would stop. If he drove, he wouldn't be able to duck out of sight if he had to. Or do any algebra. He'd be helpless. He wouldn't be able to get her and himself out of town. He would never save Ibrani. And he had to do those things. He just had to. Somehow.

"Hey, Nick?"

"What?" Her voice was exhausted, toneless.

What the hell; he might as well try it. "Do what I tell you, okay?"

She shrugged faintly.

"I mean it, Nicki," he said, hearing his own voice grow forceful and feeling profound surprise. "I mean it, now. You put one foot in front of the other and do what I goddamn tell you, you hear me? You don't need hope, you don't need energy. You don't need one thing but to do what I goddamn say, when I say it. All right? Because if you do—"

His voice nearly broke; furious, he cleared his throat. "If you do, I'll get you out of this. If I can. Trust me, dammit. Just trust me, and have your breakdown later. Okay? Later." *If there is a later.*

She blinked. She bit her lip. She didn't look convinced. When she spoke, it was in a whisper.

"Okay."

Tommy sighed. "Good." He glanced out the windshield. "Turn here. We're going to pick up my mother, and then we're getting out of this town."

Five minutes later they stood on his front porch. The front door was locked. No one answered the bell. "I guess she's not home," Tommy said. "Come on, there's a key around back."

"Wait," Nicki said.

Tommy followed her glance up. At his bedroom window, the sheer curtain twitched. Then it twitched again. He recognized the familiar outlines of his mother's face. He turned to Nicki, grinning with relief.

And found her aiming the shiny little revolver at his midsection. "Get your hands up in the air," she said to him. "Mrs. Riley! Your son wants to say good-bye before I turn him in!" Then she grinned back at Tommy as his mother's step approached the front door. "One stupid move and I'll kill her, too. Oh, and by the way—"

She gestured unpleasantly with the pistol. "Thanks for the pep talk."

Meadbury

Jack O'Connor and Bernie Friedlander had been next-door neighbors for a dozen years. Best friends, honorary godfathers to each other's kids, chaste and honorable confidantes to each other's wives. Loving each other as well as men could, trusting each other.

Now each was losing it fast: sanity, equilibrium, whatever. Neither could stand the voices any more. Or the suggestions. Or the urges to do unspeakable, unthinkable things.

And each feared telling the other, or anyone, until Thursday night when they got deliberately, thoroughly drunk together down in Friedlander's paneled basement room, each thinking that maybe soused he could spill what he'd been going through. Just tell, and to hell with it. They poured booze into themselves in order, they hoped, that words might eventually float out on it.

"Jack," Friedlander said at last, staring owlishly over his

glass. "Lish—listen. If they come for me, take care of my kids. Take care of Mitzi."

O'Connor heard through a fog of Jack Daniel's. Mitzi. What a stupid name. Mitzi. Funny how you could kill for a woman with a name like that. A little chubby, too, and also a little bit dim, but he didn't care.

"Shit, yes," O'Connor said, and poured himself another belt. Next to Trish, he loved his friend's wife more than any woman.

"Jack, I'm not kidding." Friedlander stuck his glass out, waited for his refill, and gulped from it. "I'm scared." The confession seemed to unblock something; he rested his head on his bent knees and sobbed.

Tears clogged O'Connor's own throat. He couldn't believe his buddy had just said those words, the words he'd been about to say himself. Only it was just like Friedlander, doing that. The guy was fucking psychic, or something. Always had been.

"Funny you should mention—" O'Connor began, and produced a tiddly giggle.

Friedlander misinterpreted. "Please. I'm not joking, ol' buddy. Take care of Mitzi for me till I get out of wherever they finally put me. Will you do that for me, please? Huh? And the kids, I don't know. Jackie, you're my friend, don't look at me like I got bugs on my face, they're only in my head. God, I'm going nuts, me, who'd have thought. . . ."

"Hey!" O'Connor cupped his hands and intoned through them. "Earth to Bernie: Now hear this. Me, too. Me, too."

Friedlander stared. "No. You're shittin' me. Voices? Little bastard voices, like your conscience?"

Jack nodded solemnly. He had never felt so relieved in his life. Of course, he had not thought his way into this very far. Right now, all he cared about was that he wasn't going nuts, because Bernie wasn't going nuts, and if Bernie wasn't going nuts then he wasn't going—

" 'Smile,' they say," Bernie said. " 'Recycle your junk,' they say, 'get a haircut—' "

" 'Meadbury first!' " Jack raised his glass high. " 'Get your suit pressed'!"

" 'Vote for Gorman'!"

" 'Kill Ibrani'!" Jack cried, and snapped his mouth shut.

"Oh my God," said Bernie in a shaky whisper. "Did they say that to you, too?"

Jack blinked twice. "Yeah, they did." He stared at his friend. "Didn't say who he is, though."

"Jack," Bernie whispered, "we have got some kind of problem, here." All at once, he sounded sober. "Statistically, my friend, it's very unlikely we'd both go off the deep end at the same time, right?"

"Yup." Jack's voice trembled.

"And," Bernie went on, "if we did, the chances of our both going off into the very same nuthole are even smaller, right?"

"Yup." He closed his eyes so the fear wouldn't shine out of them.

They sat in silence. After a moment, Bernie got up and went to the refrigerator behind the wet bar, in the paneled basement room that Jack had helped him finish. He took two cans of Diet Pepsi out of the refrigerator and handed one to Jack. Both of them drank deeply.

"Uh, Jack. Check me on one more thing?"

Jack nodded, and Bernie began holding up fingers. "If we are neither one of us flip city, but we accept that the very same weird things are happening to both of us, and we accept that those weird things actually are real, not fig newtons or something of our imagination—"

"Then—" Jack finished Bernie's sentence, "we're maybe both in some deep shit. Although I've got to tell you, it beats me what kind."

Bernie gulped more Diet Pepsi. "Who cares? What we know is, it's got something to do with Meadbury—can't you feel that, too?"

Jack could.

"So let's get outta here," Bernie finished, "'cause I've got one more funny feeling that right now is our chance. We'll figure it out when we get to Boston."

Which was why, Friday morning, their identical Ford station wagons stood in their identical driveways, being loaded with belongings, wives, and children as fast as Jack and Bernie could load them. The wives were not identical. They were more like a negative and its print: Mitzi dark and Trish light. Also, the wives were not getting into the cars.

They stood on the snow-covered strip dividing their two yards, conversing earnestly and looking sidelong daggers at their husbands.

As Jack lugged the coffee thermos and the cooler full of ice and soft drinks to the car, Trish strode over to him. "I don't suppose you'd like to enlighten us about what you're doing? Me and Mitzi, I mean? We'd like to know, really we would."

Jack shoved the cooler in next to the suitcases. "I told you what we're doing, Trish. Bernie told Mitzi, too. We're getting ready to leave."

Trish smiled tightly.

Jack knew that smile, knew it only too well. Right now, though, he didn't have time to worry about it. Her foot was tapping, too. *Oh, Christ, please, not the foot-tapping.*

"But you haven't told us why, Jack. Have you? Have you told us why?"

"No." He looked down at her face, reddened now by the chill wind, and shook his head slowly. "No, Trish, I haven't. One, I haven't had a chance, and two, you wouldn't believe me anyway. But it's the right thing to do. It's the only thing to do. And you're doing it with me if I have to load you with the luggage. Got it?" He smiled tightly right back at her, turned around, and nearly walked into Mitzi Friedlander, who wore a tight woolen pullover sweater and whose unbelievable breasts, despite her plumpness or perhaps because of it, had the apparent lift and resilience of deep-water flotation devices. *Gotta save those. God, you could batter a man to death with those and he'd die happy.*

"Why?" Mitzi demanded. "You and Bernie in a hit-and-run or something?"

Jack reached out and took her by the shoulders. "Mitz, you know me, don't you?"

Mitzi nodded doubtfully, black curls bobbing.

"And you know Bernie and me, we'd never steer you wrong, or you either, Trish. Don't you know that?"

"Uh-huh," Mitzi said unhappily. "But—"

"Bernie's kids are crying their eyes out in their rooms," Trish said, "and you guys are acting nuts, and we want to know more. Is that so much, to tell us why you're getting out of town so fast, like the devil was coming after you?"

Bernie stopped tying cardboard boxes to the top of his

car, and stared at Jack.

Good old Trish always got right to the heart of the matter. "You want to know more?" he said. "All right, I'll tell you what more I've got time to tell you, which is this: I am leaving in ten minutes, and if you won't come, you may stay, but I am taking the children with me, and if you try to stop me from saving our children I will hit you until you fall down on the ground unconscious. That's the more, Trish. Do you understand me?"

Trish O'Connor stared through wide, shocked eyes. She moistened her lips with her tongue. She swallowed hard. "It's really that bad?" she whispered. "Whatever it is, it's that bad?"

Jack nodded slowly. "It really is. I'll tell you later, when we're not so rushed. When we can talk about it."

"So." She drew a deep breath and shook herself, as if coming out of a trance. "All right, then. I'll get the children ready." She turned and headed for the house.

Mitzi Friedlander didn't budge, though. "Yeah, well, that stuff might be all right for you two, but it isn't going to work with me. Who do you guys think you are, anyway? Boy, you know, you really make me mad."

"Hey, Mitz?" Bernie called over for all the world like he was going to ask her to bring him a beer.

She turned questioningly, out of habit, because Bernie sounded like he wanted something. And that was the thing about Mitzi: Maybe she was just a little bit slow on the uptake, and really stubborn, and maybe she did walk around behind those big bazooms like they were her tickets to the world. But if Mitzi liked you, she'd crawl through boiling brimstone for you. All you had to do was ask her nicely.

And Mitzi liked Bernie. She liked him a lot, because —aside from being a good father and a good provider and also, although Jack was not sure of this, probably fairly creative in the sack from what Trish said Mitzi said—aside from all that, Bernie Friedlander was also a complete mensch. The guy just loved women, and after thirteen years he was still absolutely nuts about Mitzi, who was also completely nuts about him. This state of affairs had simplified Bernie's life considerably over the long haul, and it did not fail to help him out of a crunch now.

"Uh, Mitz," Bernie said, "maybe you're right. Maybe this whole thing is a little crazy. In fact, it probably is. But, uh, I was wondering—could you just come with me? I mean just, uh, ride along with me? Please?" He spread his hands in simple appeal, smiling at her.

Then Mitzi sighed in that way she had, and shook her head and went over to let Bernie put his arm around her, just the way she almost always did. "You better have a good story for this," she said unconvincingly. Then, freeing herself from Bernie's arm, she spun on her heel and marched toward the house, calling, "Jeffrey! Marcia! Get your coats on, you two, we're going with Daddy!"

". . . don't wanna!" came a tearful voice from inside. Mitzi's voice rang out in the tone she used when she didn't want nonsense, and protest subsided.

Bernie looked over the car at Jack and wiped his brow in a gesture of mock relief. Jack gave him the A-OK sign in return, wishing he meant it. This whole thing just gave him the screaming willies, and now that they were almost ready to go, the feeling was much worse; he didn't know why.

About fifteen minutes later, he found out why. Bernie's car had been in his rearview all the way to the interstate. Now, though, with a hundred miles of plowed road in front of them, Bernie dropped back. "Come on, Bernie," Jack muttered, "put your foot down." Just a few more minutes until they left Meadbury behind, probably forever. Jack glanced at the shoulder again, watching for the road sign that would tell him they had entered the next town. Somehow he had his heart set on that.

When he looked in the rearview again, Bernie's car had fallen back half a mile. Automatically, Jack eased up on the gas.

Bernie began to gain again. Then, abruptly, Bernie's car lurched to the right, nearly spun, and careened left, kicking up sprays of snow from the edge of the median strip.

"Shit," Jack said. "Come on, Bernie, come on."

"What?" Trish turned, shoving the shoulder harness to one side. "What are they— Oh, my God."

Jack couldn't speak. He could only stare wordlessly into the rearview, and try to keep on the road himself.

Back in Bernie's car, two small sets of hands scratched and pulled frantically: the kids. Jeff and Marcia. Scrambling up over the back seat, kicking and flailing. Jack winced as a little fist, he couldn't tell whose, caught Bernie in the eye. Mitzi was slumped over sideways, unmoving.

The Friedlanders' car lurched left again, bounced off the guardrail, and fishtailed wildly. The rear tires caught and the car shot forward, gaining fast. Jack caught a glimpse of Bernie's face, contorted in struggle and pain, one eye staring in terror and the other—

No, Jack thought as his lunch flipped over. No.

Bernie's other eye was gone.

The two cars ran almost bumper-to-bumper now, and Jack couldn't tell for sure who was screaming: himself, or Trish and the kids. All he knew was that he had his foot to the floor.

When he looked back again, the Friedlanders' car was still right on his tail, but Bernie's face was not in sight. Where was he? There, there were his shoulders, arms . . .

Not wanting to, Jack suddenly remembered the surgical kit Bernie kept in the car, for emergencies. Because aside from his other talents, Bernie was a crackerjack general surgeon, and he always wanted to be ready for—

Emergencies. Jack whimpered, knowing now what he must be seeing and what that was, spattered and splashed.

Abruptly, the Friedlanders' car roared alongside. In the driver's window appeared Jeffrey's little face, red-daubed and grinning, Jeffrey's little hands clamped over his father's on the steering wheel.

Then the Friedlanders' car cut right, burst through a guardrail over the shoulder, and somersaulted down the ravine onto the Metro North railroad right-of-way.

Trish clutched Jack's arm. He shook her off roughly, snarling; she sank away from him in fright. In the back seat, the kids were howling their lungs out in uncontrolled terror.

"Jack? Jack, stop, we've got to—"

"No." He stomped the accelerator. A smoking pillar of flame rose in his rearview as the roadsign whipped by: Leaving Meadbury. Come Again!

Not on your life. Jack O'Connor hauled ass down the road with his weeping wife and his weeping children. Maybe sometime he would let up on the gas, but that was as far as it went. Maybe sometime. Maybe a hundred miles from here, or two hundred.

Not now, though.

Definitely not now.

Jason Goodmaster

No, he thought, staring at the four motelike crystals that were even now whirling away, escaping—away out of Meadbury's pattern and out of his influence. No. Then his eyes widened. "No," he repeated, but whispering now, as something greater than he had ever imagined began to influence him. Within moments he realized how short-sighted his inner eye had been, how narrow the range of his vision. And he understood, now, with a shriek of rage and pain, that however possible or impossible any escape might be for others, it was an especially hopeless idea for one person: himself.

Tommy Riley

Nicki Pialosta poked the handgun into his right kidney as, just inside the front door, his mother nodded grimly. "Couldn't listen, could you?" Mrs. Riley said.

Tommy looked into her eyes.

She didn't look back at him, though. Someone else did.

Disgust shuddered through him, and then a wave of grief. *Oh, Mom. Oh, good-bye.*

"Okay, you've seen her," Nicki said behind him. "Anything more you want to say to her?"

Numbly, he shook his head. He'd had such a clever plan to disarm Nicki, too: pivot fast, crack his right elbow hard on her wrist, straight left to the solar plexus, snatch his mother from the enemy's clutches—

Forget it.

"I warned you," said whatever was occupying his mother. He wanted to shoot it. "I told you what would happen if you broke the law, but you didn't believe me, did you? Well, now you're going to pay the price. I hope you're happy, Tommy."

He staggered backward, away from the monster, and nearly fell off the porch.

Grabbing a handful of his shirt, Nicki caught him, spun him about, and marched him away. "Are you okay?" she said in low tones.

"Fuck you. Just get me in the car." He couldn't see through his tears. She got him to the passenger side, opened the door, and made as if she were forcing him in.

The thing on the porch watched with tight-lipped satisfaction. Then it pivoted stiffly and went back into his mother's house.

"She's watching from the window," Nicki said. "Slide across. Drive."

He slid behind the wheel. "Where?"

"Tommy, just get us the hell out of here. Now." She waved the pistol menacingly at him.

So he drove, remembering his words of a little while ago. *Yeah, just do what I say. I'll take care of you. . . . Oh, Jesus, what a hoot.*

As soon as they turned the corner, Nicki slipped the gun into her purse. "How did you know?" he said when he could keep his voice steady again.

"I didn't. Not right away, anyway."

He glanced at her. "Then how—"

"She took too long to come to the door. You hadn't been home for what, a couple of days? She didn't know where you were, what became of you. Now she sees her darling boy from the upstairs window, and what does she do? She takes her time. She should have fallen down those stairs to get at you, Tommy. Instead, she took just enough time to dial 911 first, which is just what I'll bet she did. And when I saw how she reacted to you, I knew for sure."

"So all that stuff before about you being so knocked out, that was just an act?"

Nicki shook her head. "No. It wasn't. But when I came face to face with her . . . well. Naked fear is a wonderful energizer." Half turning, she touched his knee lightly. "I'm sorry, though. I just couldn't think of anything else to do that didn't involve hurting her."

If my mother is even there any more to hurt. But that thought was too terrible; if he thought about that he wouldn't be able to move at all. "So where are we going?"

"My apartment. It's risky, but we've got to have money. My cash and checkbook, even my bank card is there."

Grimly, he drove past the interstate access ramp and swung through the midtown traffic circle toward her place. She was right; they wouldn't get very far without money. The gas gauge, he noted, was pretty low.

"Hey," she said, "look at that!"

"Oh, my God."

In front of his market, Harold Roundtree perched on a six-foot stepladder, holding a huge cardboard sign that read, in red capitals, "LOYALTY!" As cars passed, Roundtree shouted and shook the sign at them. Behind the sign, he was stark naked. A block farther down, smoke wisped off the roof of a fire-gutted building. The words "Gorman for Mayor" were still legible on the single unbroken window.

Nicki gasped. "Up ahead. Look."

A middle-aged man toting a jug stumbled down the sidewalk. His mouth worked frantically; his free hand tore at his ragged clothes.

"That's Will Rifkind," Nicki said. "The *Bulletin*'s city editor. Tommy, the whole town's gone nuts."

"Or going—" Something poked him hard in the brain, like a nasty old lady with an umbrella trying to force her way onto a crowded elevator. He set his jaw, glanced at the speedometer, and began calculating the number of feet the car traveled in seventeen seconds.

Something stabbed him again, harder. His knuckles whitened on the steering wheel.

Nicki looked sharply at him. "I feel it too," she said. "Hurry!"

Ben Ibrani

He had started the day wondering if he or Tommy would survive; if Nicki would. If anybody would. But as the morning went on, he stopped wondering. His whole past life had fallen away like a snake's shed skin. Everything he had known and done paled to unimportance as the single question of his existence emerged, bright and compelling: Would he survive long enough to kill Jason Goodmaster?

He held in his mind a precognitive vision of the murder, a psychic snapshot focused so sharply that he could read the monogram on Goodmaster's cuff links as the old man raised his wrists before his terrified face. The next instant, though, and all the instants beyond: blank.

After all the running and plotting and hiding, it now seemed so simple. The cops were hunting a certain sort of fugitive, and only that sort. Pulling a blue woolen watch cap from his car trunk and tugging it over his hair, discarding his contact lenses for spare horn-rims from the glove box, deciding his three-day's growth of salt-and-pepper beard resembled the stubble made fashionable by a popular TV cop show, Ibrani made himself someone entirely different from that fugitive.

The car, of course, might still betray him. Ibrani drove it from the shelter lot, headed west on Edgewood Avenue into the park, and pulled it off a service road into the marsh beyond the ball field. Tall cattails swayed crisply as the big silver sedan shouldered through them.

When they blocked his rear window completely, he stopped, got out, and scrambled back. There were springs everywhere in this pond, and the car was already breaking through the soft, blackish ice. The water beneath ran some four feet deep, and when he turned it swirled in the wheel wells.

From the road, he watched the silver roof sink out of sight beyond the cattail tops. Then he went back, gathered up a bunch of the broken stalks, and stuck them into the snow so that the car's passage was not immediately evident. A determined search would spot it quickly, but Ibrani hoped it would not come to that. If he moved fast enough, no one would ever search for the car. Or for him.

Satisfied, he began walking. He feared nothing. On a winter day as fine and bright as this, no one would blink twice at a tall, distinguished-looking fellow who'd come out for a stroll to limber up his stiff leg.

At the edge of the park, he came upon a pair of teenagers grappling with a pile-driver, breaking up chunks of frozen earth and hauling them from what appeared to be a grave in the making. The stenciled "City of Meadbury Public Works

Department" on the pile-driver matched the emblem on the jacket sleeve of the body lying nearby. Ibrani gave the scene a wide berth, but the two teenagers did not even glance his way.

On Whalley Avenue, he skirted a two-car crack-up that had apparently sent one driver through the windshield. No victims or police or emergency vehicles were in evidence, though; only a few pedestrians. One was reaching through the driver's-side window of the more damaged car, dipping his finger into something inside, finger-painting his face red, then reaching in again.

Ibrani turned left, heading for the hardware store a dozen blocks up Whalley. If it was open, he could buy a hacksaw there. Otherwise he would find a way to steal one. Smash the window, maybe; it didn't look as if anyone would notice. He really did need the hacksaw, though, because while walking with a full-length shotgun concealed inside his coat was difficult, marching into Goodmaster Mansion that way would be even harder. And he did intend to go in with it. Absolutely.

As it developed, he did break the hardware store window, in the middle of a business day, in broad daylight. No one noticed. After all, he wasn't acting any crazier than anyone else. *For once in my life, I'm fitting right in.*

And all the while, as he shortened the blued-steel barrels and slipped the abbreviated weapon into his inside coat pocket, the moment beyond the murder became more evident to him, fleshing out and blooming like a tree in a fast-forwarded nature film. Once he had emptied two shells into Goodmaster, he would go back to the shelter, get his rifle, and end the infection once and for all.

At the railyard . . . yes. He could do that. He really could just . . . do it.

Possessed on this bright morning of the pure and simple happiness born of true purpose, he smiled to himself. He was going to die. He knew that perfectly well. Soon, too; very soon. But then, so was everybody else. Or almost everybody. His brow furrowed as another portion of his plan manifested itself, locking into place like a puzzle piece, making a satisfying little mental click! and adjusting the schedule of his morning only slightly.

Tommy Riley

Nicki Pialosta's apartment building looked like a trap: low and bunkerlike, with only one visible exit. Once they had gone inside, a ten-year-old with a butter knife could pin them down.

He had not wanted to stop, but Nicki said the car's gas gauge lied. Although it read one-eighth full, the tank might hold anywhere from a cup to five gallons of gas. They had to have gas, and they had to have money, so they had to go to her apartment.

Tommy supposed there must be a back entrance, a door out of the cellar, a fire escape, or something. He should probably locate all routes to and from her apartment before entering the building. It occurred to him that he was beginning to think like Mr. Ibrani, and that made him wish again that he could figure why Mr. Ibrani had taken off without saying anything.

At the moment, in fact, he wished he could figure out almost anything. But Nicki was halfway to the entrance, and he supposed he didn't have much choice but to follow.

He crossed the parking lot reluctantly. A lot of people must have skipped work; the lot was half full. He stopped, wondering if Nicki had something he could use for a siphon, just in case. Who knew, after all, if they dared pull into a gas station? The way things were going, who knew if the stations would even be open, or if the pumps would work, or if the attendants would be dancing naked around a bonfire of Goodyear steel-belted radials and DieHard batteries? Who knew? Glumly, he followed Nicki down the hall to her apartment. *DieHard. That's a good one.*

Except for these musings, the inside of his head had fallen eerily silent, increasing his unease. Was he being set up for something here? Loosening his jacket so he could get at the gun, he bunched his left hand into a fist. *Just let 'em try.*

Nicki unlocked her door, opened it, went in—then made the noise of a mouse having its tail stepped on.

He hit the door with his shoulder and drew his gun before he had cleared it.

Ben Ibrani sat calmly facing the door, his shotgun leveled at Tommy's midsection. A television set glowed in the corner, its screen showing the words "Please Stand By."

Tommy suppressed the impulse to giggle. *Yeah. Sure.*

"I had a feeling one or both of you might show up here." Ibrani's voice wasn't right. His eyes weren't right. Still Ibrani, though; not taken over. The paranoia proved it better than anything else could.

"Don't suppose you'd care to do me some math?" Ibrani said. "Right here? Right now?" It wasn't a request. "Find the slope and *y* intercept of a line that passes through points *x* equals two, *y* equals four and *x* equals four, *y* equals eight."

"Oh, Christ." More annoyed than frightened, now, Tommy relaxed. "First of all, you got those equations from me—by now we both know them by heart, so my doing them wouldn't prove anything. On top of which, has it ever occurred to you that other people know how to do them, too? Like maybe somebody who could already be in my head? Got there, maybe, while you were off on your solo mission?" Tommy shook his head. Ibrani was good, all right, but he couldn't think of everything.

Consternation clouded the older man's eyes.

"I told you before," Tommy said, "when you decide to shoot me, just shoot me. Never mind the pop quizzes, okay? And by the way, where the hell have you been?"

He turned to Nicki, who still looked stunned. "Go on, get your stuff. Cash is best; I've got a feeling the bank cards aren't going to work, anyway."

She didn't move, but eyed Ibrani's weapon doubtfully.

"Isn't that right?" Tommy said to Ibrani. "Goodmaster's making things nuts, somehow. Everything's—" He gestured helplessly at the TV, still not broadcasting. "I bet it's just the Meadbury station screwed up. Nowhere else."

Ibrani started at the motion. Then he sighed, and leaned the shotgun down against the sofa, but not out of reach.

Tommy approved of the half measure. Ibrani was right to be suspicious. And anything was better than having that sawed-off cannon aimed at his belly button.

"Yeah," Ibrani said. "That's right. Just Meadbury. 'The City That Cares.' " His laugh was ugly. "What about you?" he said abruptly to Nicki. "Why should I think you've suddenly got your head on straight?"

"Nicki and I have got a little agreement," Tommy told him. "Either one of us weirds out, the other one terminates our working relationship. So far, so fine. Get your moncy," he said to her again, "he's not going to hurt you." *I hope.*

She moved toward the bedroom.

"Wait," Ibrani said. "Tommy's right. You should stay in sight of each other. Here, I've got money. Take it." He produced a fistful of bills. "There's fifteen hundred." He eyed Tommy. "And let that be a lesson to you: Always keep a stash."

Slowly, Tommy reached out, took the wad of cash, and stuffed it in his pocket.

Ibrani's expression did not change: measuring, assessing. Memorizing as if he did not expect to get another look. And—wrong. Insane, actually.

It occurred to Tommy that this was what guys who thought they were Napoleon must look like. "You should come with us. Once you're away from Meadbury—"

Ibrani shook his head.

"Ben," Nicki said, "you can't stop Goodmaster on your own. Tell us what to do; we don't have to run."

"No," Ibrani said. "You do have to run, believe me. That's why I came. To tell you. And to say good-bye. Look." He gestured at the television set.

The screen now showed a local news program, the broadcaster smoothly dressed, well-fed, well-groomed, and serious.

"Rich," Nicki said, and in her voice was a yearning Tommy did not understand, but which tore at his heart. "I knew he was working down at the station, but— On camera? That seems awfully—"

"Fast. Exactly," said Ibrani. "And your brother's drunk sidekick, Reg Forsten, remember him?"

Nicki laughed sadly, her eyes still fixed on the television screen as if she wanted to reach through it.

"I saw him this morning, too," Ibrani went on. "In a cop car. Behind the wheel, that is. Wearing the uniform. Luckily, he didn't see me. Goodmaster's recycling them, Nicki. Only it's not just Goodmaster. It's the town itself now, I think."

He waved at the TV again. "It was all confused. But now

it's straightening itself out. Regrouping. If you don't run now, it'll catch you. And—" He glanced at his watch. "I haven't got much time, either."

"Like . . . a hive." Longingly, Nicki gazed at the TV image of—her brother, Tommy realized. That guy, she'd known that guy all her life. The idea made him all at once very unhappy, because brother or no brother, Rich Pialosta gave Tommy the crawling creeps.

"Taking them," Nicki said, "and making them into. . . ."

Ibrani nodded. "Things it approves of. Parts of itself."

Tommy looked from one to the other. "But how?"

"I don't know," Ibrani said. "But whatever Uncle Jason's been doing, I don't think that any person can do this. Which means—"

"Something else," Nicki whispered. "Something bigger. He might think he's doing it alone, but—"

"Remember what you said to me a long time ago?" Ibrani asked her. "About every town and city having its own personality?"

Wordless, she bobbed her head.

"Before the station went off the air," Ibrani went on, "I caught some earlier news. Ned Gorman's dead. They had an eyewitness who swore Gorman got burned at an invisible stake, by ghosts."

"Come on," Tommy said. "So some flako tells a story, so what?"

"So," Nicki said slowly, watching Ibrani, "what if he's not flako?"

Ibrani said, "Exactly. And you can bet it wasn't Jason Goodmaster's doing, even assuming he could do it. Gorman was his right-hand guy; Goodmaster would want to save him, not kill him. So who?"

"Or what," Nicki said.

Nicki's voice was getting that dead sound again. It made Tommy feel uneasy.

"Forget it," he said. Whatever they were talking about, he didn't want to know. And he didn't need Nicki spinning off on some Ibranified loop of nuttiness; not now, anyway. "What did you mean," he said to Ibrani, "about not having enough time. Time for what?"

"I told you things were getting reorganized again," Ibrani said. "And whoever or whatever's doing it, I think Goodmaster's still the focus. It's using him a little, still, I think, to get control again. For what, I don't know." He picked up the shotgun. "But I'm going to stop him, stop it. And then I'm going to make sure this town doesn't get reorganized. Not for a long, long time."

"You won't get within a hundred yards of the mansion," Tommy said.

"Yes, I will." Ibrani smiled. A smooth, dreamy smile, a mad smile.

The guy was hurtin' for certain. Pistachios. Yet—or, no, because—Tommy believed him absolutely. The whole thing was nuts, after all, wasn't it? The whole damn town was turning into a rubber room. A song from his childhood wavered in his memory—

> *Boom-boom ain't it great to be crazy,*
> *Boom-boom ain't it great to be nuts!*
> *Be silly and foolish all day through—*
> *Boom-boom ain't it great to be crazy . . .*

He shook the tune away.

"Yes, I will." Ibrani stood up. "Uncle Jason is calling me; he'll make them let me in. He wants me to come to him, you see, and I'm going to give him what he wants." The smile twisted. "I'm going to give him exactly what he's been asking for."

Swiftly, Ibrani captured Tommy in a wordless hug.

"Ben, we'll wait—" Nicki began.

"No." Ibrani turned and went out the door, which closed behind him with a final-sounding click.

"—for you. . . ." Nicki's voice trailed off.

Tommy shook his head. "He won't be back."

Boom-boom.

Boom.

Ben Ibrani

Frosted, glittering white with snow beneath an opal-blue sky, Goodmaster Mansion radiated an evil brilliance. Its windows shone like sheets of slick, black ice. Shards of sharp sun pricked the fanlight's diamond facets. Knives glinted in the brass door-trimmings, in the black-lacquered widow's walk, and in the copper flashings of the tall, red chimneys. From dully shimmering gutters hung enormous daggers of ice, ready to drop. At the head of the wide drive, Ibrani paused.

The estate thrummed to silent tension, like a held breath. No bird sang in the ancient, shadowy spruces that loomed behind the house. No thin thread of music drifted from the carbarn, no crunch of snow betrayed a footstep.

It waited for him, showing no flicker of curtain, no careless flare of sunlight reflecting from a gun barrel. No sense of distant cross-hairs shifting into focus on his chest.

One wisp of smoke curled up from the east chimney, drawing a question mark on the frigid air. Beneath the fanlight, the big front door swung open in soundless invitation.

Abruptly, dust filmed his skin.

Just as suddenly, it disappeared. An ugly chuckle rattled in his mind's ear. Joke, boy. Only a joke. Come inside, won't you? Come in here . . . with me.

Ibrani smiled to himself, only faintly shaken. *Joke. Right. You're such a funny guy, Uncle Jason. Only this time, the joke's on you.* Slowly, he approached the door's dark yawn.

Pulling off the stereo headphones he'd worn so long they'd begun to feel like part of him—*so long, Mick*—he mounted the front steps.

He didn't need music anymore, he realized. He didn't need headphones, or equations, or anything else, because his own purpose filled him now the way none of those outside things ever could. It was no longer a question of whether he would kill Jason Goodmaster, but only of when.

Do your worst, old man, he thought as he crossed the threshold. I don't need Mick anymore. I'm ready for you, now—all by myself.

Behind him the door swung shut with a smug thud.

"Hello, boy."

Heavy damask curtains blocked the tall windows of the second-floor library. A small fire sulked on the hearth, its sullen flickers sending murky red light into the shadowed corners. Ibrani stood outside, waiting for his eyes to adjust to the gloom within.

"Come in," Jason Goodmaster said thickly. "I don't bite."

All at once Ibrani quailed, wanting to bolt, for neither his purpose nor the shotgun slung inside his coat could defend against memories awful and obscene:

Himself, small and cowering even in adolescence, longing for his own good home, his good parents, and facing instead this wicked old man.

Himself, clawing at his own flesh, scrubbing his skin to a bloody mush in a vain, crazed try to be clean, sweet-smelling, pristine enough for this filthy old man.

Himself, obedient, cravenly cowardly, enduring the long shamed and shameful years of his slavery, his knuckling under to this helpless old man.

And Jason Goodmaster was helpless, now; his posture alone made that clear. He bent, slumped and feeble, tiny under the wings of his great armchair. He clutched a black shawl tight against himself and shivered.

"Do I, boy? Do I bite?" His voice emerged a gargly croak, as if something meaty were stopping some vital portion of his throat.

"No," Ibrani said. "You don't. Not unless I let you."

"You all let me, once, though, all of you. You wanted it. You needed it." Goodmaster's chuckle ratcheted into a deep and cavernous cough, a rattle of rotted lung tissues, airways muck-clogged and sodden with old blood.

"The hell I did!"

"That's what you say now." The old man spoke with difficulty, as though his tongue had swollen. A foul stench rose from his withered body. "You bite, though, don't you? Come here to take a bite of me." He peered at his ward. "What's in your pocket, boy?" he barked with sudden sharpness.

Ibrani jumped, hating himself for it. *Kill him. Just kill him and be done with it.*

Goodmaster nodded as if agreeing with the thought. "Mm. I suppose you would want to do that." He cocked one puffy red eye in a hideous parody of slyness. "You think I'd mind, boy?"

Just lift the coat and kill him, finish it now, finish him.

"You think I called you here to do anything but kill me, boy?"

Ibrani blinked. He hadn't thought of that. "What?"

"It turned on me. All those years, and it turned on me."

"What are you talking about?"

Goodmaster lurched to his feet. "I needed you, but I couldn't find you. Or young Ned," he whispered, taking a doddering step forward. Spittle dripped in glistening strands from his slack lips. "With just one of you at my side, I could have put it in its place. Just one of you; I only needed one of you!"

Ibrani backed away in spite of himself.

"But I couldn't touch you, couldn't find you, and so it got me."

Because music filled my head, jammed all the channels. But now there's no music, and if it's not stopping me now. . . .

"It put me on trial, boy. The audacity! Trying a Goodmaster for service to Meadbury!" Another spasm of coughing struck, bringing foamy blood to his lips. "It convicted me, boy. Said I had interfered with its damned pattern. Me! I gave it its goddamned pattern!"

. . . then it must want me here? Ibrani tugged out the shotgun and slapped it into firing position.

"Yes!" said Goodmaster. "That's right! Shoot me, boy! Now!"

The old bastard wants it, too. "Why? Tell me why, first."

"Because it sentenced me, you fool, sentenced me to interference with my patterns." Goodmaster groaned as he drew himself erect and let the shawl slide to the carpet. He wore a red velvet dressing gown over black silk pajamas. Beneath the silk, his body bulged in a dozen wrong places.

"It tampered with me, boy, gave me cancer. Inside and out." He tore open his robe and pajama top. Tufts of wiry black hair protruded from the gruesome tumor on his right shoulder. Between the tufts jutted half a dozen teeth.

The teeth snapped and chattered, then gaped apart, revealing a glazed, lidded eyeball that swiveled, stared . . . winked.

"Kill me, Ben." The old man's voice begged.

Ibrani cocked the shotgun. "Tell me something else, first." He heard his own voice break, and longed to pull the trigger. But he had to know. Uncle Jason had called him here, somehow, through the music. And it had let Ben come. So. . . .

"I'll tell you anything, anything, just—"

Look. Not Goodmaster's voice. Something else.

Ben Ibrani did look. And saw, in his mind's eye . . .

Uncle Jason, on his knees before the fire. "You can't, I forbid it," he bellowed in apoplectic fury. "You're not real, I'm the power, I am!"

He stopped, staring into the flames in growing horror. "No," he whispered, shrinking back. "I never . . . I never meant—"

Beneath the black silk pajamas, the horrid tumors sprouted like toadstools. He fell flat, squirming in anguish as sudden lumps bulked and lurched beneath his skin. His eyes, though, stayed fixed on the fire, in wonder and repulsion.

And terror. "So big," he breathed, "so . . . vast."

Suddenly he jumped up, scrambling for the library table, yanking open a drawer and jerking from it an antique dueling pistol, aiming it at his head.

"Oh, no," he said, "you'll not have me, not Jason G—"

Then he whimpered as his fingers unclenched from the gun. It clattered to the floor. He howled in frustration, staring down at it, then collapsed, scrabbling crabwise on the carpet until he was once more prostrate before the fire, and the thing within it.

His face contorted in hideous fright. "No! I served you, I served them, saved them—please." He whined. "Please, I won't interfere any more, I'll go away, I'll leave it all alone, don't, oh please don't do that, oh don't!"

The old man's voice spiraled up into a thin breathy shriek of bone-deep agony. Hopping and dancing as darts of pain pierced him, he flung himself up off the floor, pirouetting in mad anguish like a man being attacked by a swarm of bees.

Then, slowly, the picture dissolved, and Ibrani became aware again of the real room around him. But the show, it seemed, had not yet ended.

Goodmaster struggled to his feet, straightened as if in sudden pain. Eyes widening, lips curled back, frowning thunderously, he seemed for a moment to be the fearsome

Uncle Jason of old. In a sudden, desperate rush he flung himself across the room, snatching at the draperies and pawing them aside in his determination to be at the tall window—and through it.

Glass shattered and flew. Goodmaster's frail, bent body punched through the panes, seeming to sail out into the frigid air.

Then it stopped. The old man hung there a moment, legs waving uselessly, his body wriggling against the razor-sharpness of the remaining glass. His feet strained for the floor and began backpedaling, dragging him slowly but surely into the room again while he grabbed at jagged window shards with both bloody hands.

He thumped to the floor in a howling heap, still trying to scramble back into the window, but something would not let him. Something, it seemed, wanted him to go the other way—toward the fire.

Gusts of fresh air whirled through the broken window, spinning papers on the tables, flipping pages of toppled books, and whipping the flames on the hearth to sizzling brilliance.

"Ben," Goodmaster whimpered, "please. . . ." His spindly arms hugged at the carpet to no avail as his legs, of their own accord, kept stubbornly creeping him backward toward the hearth.

Struck dumb, imprisoned in a paralysis of terror, Ibrani watched as if from afar and began to understand what he'd walked in on: the last act of a play that had little to do with himself. Not directly, anyway. His part, he saw, was to deny the old man any release from it.

Meanwhile, the fire's crack and sputter rose to a horrid roar; the damper clanked hollowly open and shut as wind wailed up the chimney. And from the heart of that small hot inferno, something terrible looked.

And looked.

". . . nooo-o-o-o*o-o-o*!"

Under that gaze, Jason Goodmaster shuddered, scrabbled, and dove all unwilling at the flames. The smell of burning hair filled the room as the old man screeched in pain. Then he staggered back, for an instant freed by agony from the thing's hold.

"Please," Goodmaster groaned.

"How long will you last if I don't kill you?"

"By the blood of Christ, Ben, what are you thinking?"

"That if you don't answer me, I'll leave."

Goodmaster stared at his feet in horror; already they were twitching slyly, easing him back toward the flames. "I . . . don't know. It said it wants me to understand my sin before it lets me go, before it. . . . Please. Shoot me. Do it now."

Ibrani set the safeties on the shotgun and slipped the weapon back into his coat.

"Ben, I'm in agony. I beg of you."

"No." It delighted him finally to be able to say that to the old man.

"Ben! You'd put a rat out of its misery. You wouldn't let a roach suffer like this."

"Rats and roaches can't help what they are. You could have." He turned away without regret. He'd wanted to kill Goodmaster so badly, for so long. But now something else wanted it worse, something that had prior claim, and could do it better. It thought Jason Goodmaster ought to suffer a little longer before it dispatched him.

And for once, under no duress at all, Ibrani agreed with it.

"Ben!"

At the door he turned a final time as Goodmaster tottered once more toward the blaze, his face a mask of horror, his legs moving stiffly, against his will and out of his control. His arms struck the mantel, flailing; Ibrani heard the bones break with sharp, wet crunches. The silk pajama-shirt blazed up; Goodmaster wailed and slapped at it, twirling, falling. One of his ribs popped as he struck the floor, making a sound like a dry stick breaking. His hands now resembled half-cooked pieces of meat; one leg sprawled askew from a dislocated hip. And his feet began yet again their sly progress toward the fire. . . .

How many times? Ibrani wondered. *How many times before it finally kills him?* "So long, Uncle Jason," Ibrani said.

Goodmaster's screams followed him down the stairs, out the door, and into the yard.

Where it was already getting dark.

Meadbury

Harold Roundtree buffed another shiny, red Delicious apple on his sleeve, and set the apple on a growing pile in the new fruit bin of what would soon be his improved, expanded produce department. The new section of produce would stand where the magazine racks had always been, the magazines that now were smoldering on a pile, out behind the store.

Harold could almost see, already, the sacks of stone-ground meal and unbleached flour that would be stacked on the shelves once given over to muffins, bread, rolls: all poisoned, pre-packaged stuff. As soon as his new order of fresh vegetables came in, he could start moving out the frozen foods.

In the trash bin outside, next to the smoldering magazines, lay the wreckage of the stereo tape deck that had played by the registers. Harold didn't want it anymore, either.

Because, as everyone knew, all those processed items were full of dangerous, mind-altering chemicals, and the magazines were full of dangerous, mind-altering ideas, and the music was full of dangerous, mind-altering. . . .

Well, Harold didn't know what, but it was dangerous and mind-altering, he knew that much. And Meadbury didn't need to be tampered with any more. All of Meadbury agreed with him. All of it.

And that was how it would be.

Tommy Riley

Boom-boom.

"I'm almost ready," Nicki said.

He nodded, his eyes on the TV, where Rich Pialosta was informing the citizens of Meadbury that all was well. Four emergency first-aid centers were open; casualties entering them had fallen to a trickle. The fire department, rescue squad, and police emergency services were back in operation; street lights and traffic signals were functioning again in all but a few areas. Temporary food and shelter services were available at the former Meadbury Shelter for the Homeless.

Tommy laughed hollowly.

In front of the door, two carryalls stood packed and ready. Tommy's pockets and Nicki's purse were stuffed with all the money they could find. Somewhere, Ben Ibrani was doing something neither of them had wanted to hear about; if they didn't know, they couldn't be made to tell.

Nothing had attempted to invade his head, or to make him do or even think anything extraordinary, since the drive over. Nicki said she, too, felt as normal as could be expected, given thc circumstanccs. That made him nervous. Neither of them had thought it would be this easy, and he still didn't.

Nicki didn't like it either. "Why isn't it trying?" she said fretfully, belting up her coat. "God, it's almost worse than—"

"No, it isn't. It isn't worse. Don't say that."

She nodded. Her gaze wandered to the image of her brother. "He looks good, though, doesn't he? Just the way I always wanted to scc him." Her voice was wistful.

Tommy didn't answer, because if there was one thing Rich Pialosta didn't look, it was good. He looked dead, was what he looked.

Dead, or worse. The guy was creepy. Through his suit and tie, through his good haircut and wide, white smile, Rich Pialosta radiated a soft pulpiness transmitted without flaw by the miracle of television. He looked like if you shook his hand it would mush and squish out between your fingers.

"Maybe," Nicki said, "he'll come out of this okay, after all."

Tommy couldn't believe his ears; jeez, couldn't she see?

Boom.

Her head jerked up. "What was that?"

Tommy ran a quick internal inventory: not in his mind. Something real.

Boom.

"I don't know. Where's it coming from?"

"Outside, somewhere." She ran to the window and twitched a shade aside. "No one's there."

Boom-bump.

"It's coming from the front!" She started toward the bedroom.

"Stay here. I'll look. Keep watching out that window."

She stiffened, as if she didn't like taking orders from him.

Well, too bad. I don't like giving them, either, but my gun is bigger than yours and I've trained more with it. He crept into Nicki's bedroom, dropping to a crouch as he approached the window. She had left the shade half-open. Through a square of window showed the upper portion of a ladder.

He peeked over the sill. A man was climbing toward him and was almost two-thirds of the way up. Tommy leapt to his feet, threw the window up, and gave the ladder a shove that nearly carried him out, too.

The ladder sailed back through the frigid air. The climber shouted in panic just before he thumped into a snowbank. For a moment he lay in a rumpled heap, then slowly, painfully stood up. His face, white and ghostly, fixed Tommy with a blank, malevolent stare. He limped away and left the ladder behind.

Tommy closed the window, locked it, and went back to the living room. "Nicki. Were you supposed to be somewhere today? When you didn't go back to work, would anybody have missed you?"

Her fingers went to her lips. "Oh, my God . . . yes, certainly. I had two stories due for Will Rifkind and a staff meeting, too."

"I think playing hooky just turned into a hanging offense." He crossed to the window and peered out past her. "That was Will Rifkind making like a burglar. If he thought you'd let him in, he'd have come to the door, wouldn't he?"

Her shoulders sagged. "He knows."

Tommy ran through a mental checklist of the entrances he'd inspected. *Cellar door bolted but surely breakable. Trap door from the roof to the attic to the stairwell; a crowbar would do it. Front door, glass. No problem getting in there, either.* There was a fire escape, too, but pulling it down would be very noisy, which was probably why Rifkind hadn't used it.

Now that he knew they knew he was there, though, he

wouldn't care about making noise, would he?

He turned to Nicki. "How many people live in this complex?

She thought a moment. "Eighty or so. Not counting kids."

Eighty. My God. And that wasn't counting kids. . . . "I think you'd better count the kids." He didn't want to count them, though, because that would make, oh, Jesus Christ, more than a hundred, and he and Nicki had only the two guns, never mind enough bullets or enough bodies to cover all the windows, and that damn flimsy door.

"We can't do it."

She blinked at him. "Do what?"

"I'm talking about your neighbors." The apartment door itself would last about two minutes, Tommy figured. *Cellar, roof, front door, fire escape. Will Rifkind, where are you now?*

"There's a pay telephone down on the corner, isn't there?"

Nicki nodded. "But what's that got to do with—"

"I bet he's in it, that's what. I bet he's there, calling up all your friendly neighbors. Letting them in on the hottest neighborhood gossip: us. That's why nothing's been at our heads, Nick. Things have changed, it doesn't need to do things that way any more. Not as long as other people are around."

Her face paled in understanding as the telephone rang. She jumped. Then she reached out and answered it cautiously. "Hello . . . yes, of course I remember . . . uh-huh . . . mm-hmm . . . will you hold on for just a moment, please? I want to, uh, turn the TV down." She covered the receiver with her hand. "It's Madge Ackerman, from down the hall. I've barely ever spoken with her. She wants to come over and talk, she says. About what's been going on in town. She says she's scared."

"Tell her to come." Tommy tried to make his voice sound firm as he forced the words from between his dry lips.

Nicki assented with visible reluctance. "Sure, Madge. Just give me a minute to straighten up? Right. Okay." She hung up. "What are you going to do?" She stared into his face. "You're not going to— No. Tommy, I think she's really frightened. She could be all right, couldn't she?

Maybe lots of people are scared."

"Ackerman," he said. "Any Abelsons in the complex? Abercrombies? Abates?"

She shook her head. "No," she whispered.

"He's going down the goddamned phone book, Nick. Starting with the *A*'s. Her name came up first."

Nicki closed her eyes. "Oh, my God."

"Check the corridor before you unlock the door. I'll be behind the couch. Let her get all the way inside, then point toward me. Say, 'oh, look,' or something. And I'll do it. Don't forget to lock the door again."

Wordlessly, she agreed.

Tommy hunkered behind the floral-upholstered couch, listening to the footsteps come down the hall and stop outside the apartment door. *Dear God, I'm only nineteen and I suppose I could have this figured all wrong, and if I do I sure hope you can forgive me.*

There was a knock at the door. "Coming," said Nicki.

And if I don't have it figured wrong—

Silence as Nicki looked through the peephole. Then the chain rattled and the bolt rasped back. "Hi, Madge, come on in."

If I don't have it wrong, God, please help me shoot straight.

"Oh, look over there!"

He rose, braced, aimed, and fired the way he'd learned to. The gunshot clapped his ears. A small, round red hole appeared in Madge Ackerman's forehead, and she fell.

The small, middle-aged woman had had dyed-red hair, a freckled face, thin penciled-on eyebrows, and a pinch-lipped, dissatisfied expression, which she retained even in death. She wore a long, flowing-sleeved, navy-blue caftan of some velvety kind of material, and shiny gold house-slippers with gauzy gold roses on the toes of them.

Tommy crossed the room and crouched beside her. Inside one of the flowing sleeves he found an ice pick. Inside the caftan itself, held up by the caftan's belt, was a boy scout ax, the blade recently sharpened and glittering wickedly. The ax handle bore a burnt-in legend: Troop 1199.

Nicki reached out and took the ax, hefted it. "'Be prepared,'" she said dully.

She had the right idea, but Tommy didn't like her tone of voice. He closed up Madge Ackerman's caftan. The television screen still featured Rich Pialosta and the news. "Nicki. I don't care if you're ready or not. We have to go, now, before it tries something else."

Her gaze moved from Tommy to Rich and back again. A small crease appeared between her eyebrows. Her even white teeth nibbled at her lower lip. "No," she said. "No, I'm not going."

Meadbury

Horace Underholme sat in the railyard watchtower while the brisk offshore wind snapped the flags. He liked the sound. It reminded him of the way the pennants used to snap above the destroyer he had spent his first career on: painting and scraping, scraping and painting. Horace guessed he had painted that damn tub of steel in every ocean, sea, and port known to the mind of man. Its paint bills must have been twice as high as the fuel bills.

No more, though. Horace Underholme had retired from the Navy with twenty-five years service under his belt, and the first thing he'd done when he got home was get the contractor over to put up aluminum siding on his house. From that day to this he hadn't painted so much as the trim on a goddamn screen door. No, sir. No more.

All that paint had gotten him a nice pension, though. Actually he preferred bragging about the pension to thinking about it, but thinking would do in a pinch. Started right up the day he left, at age forty-three, not like that damn Social Security. And it was all his, too, while Social Security shrank down to nothing on anybody who had the gumption to go out and find another job.

One thing Horace Underholme had never been short on was gumption. Twelve years retired and now he was fully vested in the railroad pension plan, too. He snorted at himself. Some retirement. Alone in a creaky tower, babysitting railroad cars.

But it beat watching *Family Feud* or some such bushwa on the damn tube with his daughter Martha and her wimp husband and their whining, snot-nosed brats. Horace didn't like TV, and he didn't like kids, either; that was the long and the short of it. In fact, although he had plenty of gumption, he supposed most folks might say he was short on almost everything else.

Imagination, for example. Horace never had much use for it. He just went along taking the world pretty much the way it came. Feelings, too, or what passed for feelings nowadays. Without trying to be, Horace was damned near free of the ordinary run of guilts and neuroses, as well —mental haunts, he called them, when he thought of them at all.

Horace's mental and emotional landscape, in fact, was so smooth and nearly featureless, there were no knobs or dents or rough spots for mental haunts to get any handle on. He was, in fact, very nearly spiritually invisible—a thing he might have been proud of had he been introspective enough to consider it.

But Horace didn't like thinking about things like that. What he really did like, about the only thing he liked, was sitting up here, all alone and peaceful, high above Meadbury.

Yeah. That's me: above it all. He snorted at himself again. Still, he liked it.

This evening, though, he didn't like it quite so much as usual. For one thing, it was freezing. For another, it was raining. And for a third, lamebrain Martha had packed liver sausage sandwiches for his dinner. Horace Underholme would rather dance buck naked on the church steps than eat liver sausage sandwiches, and Martha knew it, only she'd forgotten it. Again.

Worse than the liver sausage sandwiches, though, worse than the weather, even, was the twilight itself. It felt . . . funny. Before he'd started painting the destroyer, he'd served on a minesweeper for a while; painted there, too, of course. Just painted; low rank. Saw nothing, heard nothing, said nothing.

Still, everybody aboard was equal in one way: If a mine got you before you got it, you were history, rank or no rank. Horace remembered very well the seemingly endless nights of silent cruising, just creeping along, almost wallowing really, everybody quiet and nervous and not wanting to admit it because that was bad luck.

This evening felt like that to him, somehow: bad luck. And those dozen goddamn chlorine tankers down on that rail siding didn't improve it any. He wished to hell those union guys up in Boston would stop striking long enough to get the poison gas out of Meadbury. After that, they could strike the rest of their lives, for all it'd mean to him.

It occurred to Horace that any man who passed a freezing night atop a railyard full of poison gas with a bagful of liver sandwiches in his lap—well, that man didn't need to worry about bad luck, did he? He already had it.

But never mind, never mind, it beat *Family Feud* and he was plenty hungry enough to eat the damn sandwiches, too. Leaning back in his wooden swivel chair, he swung his feet up onto the scarred wooden desk, turned on the radio, and unwrapped one of the sandwiches, hefting it thoughtfully. For all Martha's faults, she made a thick sandwich. And the bits of lettuce sticking out around the edges looked crisp and fresh.

What the hell. Horace bit into it.

From somewhere down below came a *crack!*

"What the—?" Frowning, he dropped the sandwich and heaved himself out of the chair. Peering down into the yellow-orange pools of light spilled by the rail yard's new high-pressure sodium-vapor lamps, he saw nothing. Just rusty tracks and tank cars gleaming in the rain.

But damn, it had been a familiar sound. Where had he heard it before?

Crack!

Then he had it: sea gulls! That second looey, what the hell was his name, on the fantail of that damned destroyer, shooting sea gulls! Forty years ago, shooting sea gulls with a rifle. Horace peered out the window again. Some damn fool was firing a rifle down there, now.

But there was no second looey in that railyard, and no sea gulls either, which brought Horace to the next question: why?

Crack! Crack! Crack!

He grabbed the phone. Let the cops deal with it. He had a pistol in a holster on his belt, but he wasn't about to hop on down there and try to use it. Only a turkey-necked jackass would wave a handgun at a sharpshooter, and never mind what the supervisor said.

Shit, he didn't hate liver sausage that much.

"You have reached the Meadbury Police Department," said the tape recording that answered the phone. "All our operators are busy right now. Your call will be taken by the first available operator in the order it was received."

"Well, dammit to hell and gone," he shouted at the phone. "I got me a nut case shooting up a yard fulla poison gas out here goddammit—"

Sugar-sweet music came over the line.

Cursing, hopping with impatience and still holding the receiver to his ear, he squinted into the darkness. And there the guy stood, on the trestle outside the yard, aiming again.

Crack!

Instinctively, Horace traced the line drawn by the rifle barrel. What he saw made him glad he hadn't bitten into the damn sandwich, because the sight made him want to puke. The line of fire ended just short of one of those tankers, in a yellowish cloud of chlorine gas which was already seeping downhill toward the roundhouse.

Downhill. Toward town.

Crack!

Another tanker sprang another pee-yellow stream.

Meanwhile, flags still snapped overhead, just as if everything were still okay. Good stiff breeze, Horace thought. On the telephone, the theme from *Summer of '42* ended and "Beer-Barrel Polka" began. Horace tried to remind himself that he was a grown man, a veteran, and the honorable earner of not one but two vested pensions.

It didn't help him much, though. Right now the grown-man part wasn't worth diddly-squat, and he would have cheerfully flushed the pensions, too, if he could have turned the wind around, which of course he couldn't.

And all the veteran part did was remind him of stories. On a destroyer, even painters heard stories, and some of the real old-timers on that tub had been in World War I. They'd told stories about chlorine gas, all right; terrific stories, practically in living color.

Horace tried now to forget what those colors had been, exactly, but he couldn't. Because chlorine gas was just exactly what that good stiff breeze was pushing; a cloud of death right toward the town, toward the stores and the restaurants, the card parties and political fund-raisers and school dances. Toward a lot of people sleeping, or eating, or watching TV.

Toward Martha, her wimp husband, her snot-nosed kids.

And toward the goddamn cops, who were still not answering the phone.

Pretty soon all those folks were going to be those colors.

Still holding the phone, Horace Underholme, grown man, veteran, and earner of not one but two fully vested pensions, began to cry, thinking that because of the direction of the wind he would be the only one left.

He didn't know that, for all practical purposes, he already was.

Ben Ibrani

He had left himself only two choices: run, uselessly. Or stand.

Tommy, Nicki. Run.

Steeling himself, he faced the yellow cloud as it rolled up to him and enveloped him. The blistering mist boiled his pores open, sizzled his skin off. Bundles of nerve endings flared, igniting like matchbooks. The taste of laundry bleach bubbled up, stopping his screams and his breath.

Clean. Clean clear through.

Tommy Riley

"Listen," he said with mounting hysteria, and for probably the hundredth time, "we have to leave. Rifkind's out there, a dead body's in here, and—"

"No." She pointed to the TV. "I won't leave my brother behind."

Abruptly, a test pattern appeared. A moment later it gave way to Rich Pialosta again, only now he did not look so smooth or self-assured. He looked furious. "—in your homes," he was saying sternly. He touched his earphone, and began, obviously, to repeat what was being fed to him through it. "To repeat: We have just received word that twelve tankers of chlorine gas have ruptured at the Meadbury railyard, south of downtown. There is no need for panic—"

The picture dissolved into flecks of snow again, and this time it stayed that way. Tommy grabbed Nicki's arm. "Nick, we've got to get out of here. Now."

She jerked loose and stared over his shoulder at the blank screen as if she expected the newscast to resume. Of course, he thought, he should have seen this coming. She was so hooked on the idea of her brother surviving somehow, she wasn't going to be able to just shake it off.

"Nicki," he said. "Nick, he's gone. You know the station's right down there on the south side, he's got to be—" Dead, he was going to say, but Nicki's eyes already rejected it. She just wasn't having any.

"No." Folding her arms, she backed away. "No, he's my brother and he's not dead. Don't you see, I've just found him again, he's alive, we can save him—"

He seized her shoulders. "You can't save him, Nicki. Even if you could, there isn't time. We've got to run. Ibrani broke those tankers open; he must have, and if I know him he did a good thorough job of it. In a couple of minutes, if we stay here, we're going to be gassed to death. Is that what you want? Is it? Is it?"

"I'm not going anywhere without my brother." Shoulders squared, chin jutting stubbornly, she stood with her feet planted and glared at the television screen, silently demanding that it restore her brother's face.

She had, Tommy realized, just lost her marbles on this topic, lost them completely. The thought crossed his mind that he could leave without her, but he knew he couldn't, not after all that had happened.

"Please?"

"No."

All right. He would lie to her, and worse. "All right. You win. We'll give it a try. It's a couple of miles from here to the rail yard. We've got ten, maybe fifteen minutes. Get your pistol and cover me from the window."

She looked relieved and eager as she scurried for her purse.

Which proved she really was bonkers. What he'd just said made no sense at all. If Rich wasn't dead now, he sure as hell would be in fifteen minutes. Slipping Madge Ackerman's ice pick into his pocket, he picked up the two waiting carryalls, and turned toward the door.

"What are you going to do?"

"I'm going to toss these in your car. Then I'm going to puncture all the tires on the other cars down there, even if it is broad daylight. That's why you have to cover me. Somebody might get real pissed. But we don't need anybody following us. Have you got some kind of plastic tubing? Anything at all? I'm going to siphon some gas if I can; we don't have time to stop, not if, um, we're going to pick up Rich."

She smiled thankfully. "All right. That's a good idea. I've got a plastic belt that's tube-shaped. Will that work?"

"You bet." *And then, I'm going to knock you unconscious and dump you in the trunk, and we're not going near that goddamn TV station on our way out.*

Later, he supposed, she would hate him. So he would worry about it when the time came, if it did.

The green Dodge Dart settled onto its wheels with a mournful hiss. That was the last. No one would drive out of that lot any time soon. Or ever.

Except me. Time to go. He glanced up at Nicki's apartment window. She was still standing there, protecting the guy who would save her brother for her. He rose from his crouch and waved to her to get on down right away.

A shadow appeared behind her. She vanished from the window. A hand tugged the shade shut.

Rifkind! Tommy smacked his forehead in disgust. When Madge Ackerman never reported back, Rifkind must have understood that his game wouldn't work. So he had gotten in somehow, to finish it himself.

Nicki Pialosta

"The boy is dangerous," Rifkind said. "He'll have to be rehabilitated. So much usefulness left in him; it would be a shame to waste it, don't you think?"

Nicki nodded speechlessly as the city editor followed her into the kitchen.

Without shifting his eyes an inch, Rifkind reached into his jacket and produced a straight razor. "You, on the other hand, you had your chance, didn't you? I'm afraid there really are very few options left, where you're concerned. You understand, don't you?"

She glanced from Rifkind to the door and back, measuring the distance, wondering if a quick break would do it. But no, he was already too close, following her glance and understanding it.

"Don't move." He raised the straight razor. "I'll kill you if you do."

And you'll kill me if I don't. He'd broken the bedroom window and swung inside before she could think. From the roof, she realized, on the fire escape, which made no noise if you didn't pull it down.

The shambling walk and vacant expression of this morning's street-wandering derelict had vanished. He moved with a sly grace the old Will Rifkind never possessed, easing his way toward her, not once taking his determined gaze from hers. Sly, determined, and something else. Something rotten, wrong. He reminded her of—who?

"I'm sorry," he said. "But you, Nicki, are a loose cannon. A wild card. And we can't have that. Not in a peaceful, well-run city like Meadbury. The town that cares just doesn't care for that. Won't have it, in fact."

"I thought Jason Goodmaster was—"

"Oh, he was. But we're under new management, now."

He was very near. The blade's edge twinkled. "Your brother," he said tenderly, "asked me to say good-bye to you for him."

Rich. That was who he reminded her of: Rich, on the television. Despite Rifkind's purposefulness, he had that same soft, unsupported quality, as if the real Will Rifkind had been cored out and discarded, replaced with something like a caterpillar or a slug.

It walks, it talks, it crawls on its belly like a reptile. . . . And Rich does, too, now. Or did. She hadn't wanted to admit it, hadn't even wanted to see it. But Tommy had been right.

Oh, Rich. All at once she was glad for what Ibrani had done. "My brother is dead."

Rifkind frowned. "No. Certainly not. He's providing a very valuable service."

"No. Dead. You don't know yet, do you? This whole town's going to die, and you can't stop it. But you killed Rich, really. You and your filthy, disgusting, unnatural—"

Still frowning, Rifkind took a step back. Clearly, he had not expected this reaction. He'd wanted cowering terror, not righteous fury. And the new Will Rifkind couldn't adjust quite as swiftly as the old one. Like the new Meadbury, the new Will Rifkind liked things neat and orderly. Predictable. According to plan. In fact, in his essence the new Will Rifkind was exactly what the old Will never would have tolerated.

"Boring," she said. "You, your life, your mind, your fucking perfect little boring town." Then, raising the .22 pistol he'd given her from the fold of her skirt where she had been concealing it, she did something she never had dreamed she'd be able to do: She shot the new Will Rifkind point-blank in his pulpy face.

He staggered backward, nearly tripping Tommy Riley as the boy came bursting through the door.

"Jeez," said Tommy as Rifkind fell.

"Now," she said evenly, "if it's all right with you I'd like to get out of here before a cloud of pollution brightens my colors and whitens my whites, okay?"

"Gotcha." He held the door for her.

"And we can forget the TV station, too," she said more gently as they clattered down the stairwell.

He said something she didn't catch.

In the parking lot, she realized he wasn't talking to her after all; he was just muttering the same thing over and over.

"Thank you, God," he was saying. "Oh, thank you, thank you, thank you."

She thought of asking him why, got a glimpse of the tire iron wrapped in a towel on the car's back seat, and decided she'd rather not know. "Can you drive fast?" she asked him as he slid behind the wheel.

His answering look of amusement surprised her. He'd gotten older, somehow, in the past few hours or days. Older and wiser.

"Vroom," he said, dropping the car into reverse. The tires shrieked.

Well, maybe not a lot older and wiser, she decided. He

drove, as a matter of fact, like an insane person. Considering the situation, though, that was perfectly appropriate.

Because it wasn't a matter of not being noticed, anymore. It was just a matter of not being caught. And it wasn't over yet.

Not by a long shot.

Tommy Riley

Cop cars, he figured, could probably go about 125, maybe 130.

The Toyota couldn't, which meant he needed a good head start if they were going to make it. No, they would make it. They would put Jason Goodmaster and the shelter and tests and murders and voices and dead bodies all behind them. Put Meadbury behind them—or die trying.

A vision of Rich Pialosta's face swam up before him: wide, dead smile proclaiming that everything was just ducky in zombie-land. But Tommy Riley was not going to go there, and he wasn't going to let Nicki go there, either. No matter what.

"Look out."

He swerved too late around a patch of ice; the rear tires spun wildly and swung out.

Ease back a little, let the tires catch, steer in, then out of it.

The Toyota howled, shot forward, righting itself.

Tommy gripped the wheel, stunned.

"Did you hear . . . something?" Nicki said.

"Um. Yeah." Ibrani's voice, Tommy realized, telling him what to do, helping him, from inside his head. As if in death they mingled together, perhaps for just a moment: Ben Ibrani and Rich Pialosta and maybe even Tommy's mother by now, Madge Ackerman and Will Rifkind and Jimmy Conklin, too, all existing somehow where the monster existed, where the path to Tommy's brain was accessible and the things people prayed to were real.

Thank you. But now there was nothing, only silence. As if Ibrani's voice had been the final spark of a dying fire. *Gone. He won't be back.*

Freezing rain began, building a film of ice on the windshield. "Crank the defroster, can you?"

"My pleasure." Nicki turned the knob.

The windshield cleared; nevertheless, he slowed because traffic was thickening: cars, trucks, even a few municipal buses. All moving normally; no speeding, no panic, because they didn't know. He wove from lane to lane, making his way slowly but surely past them toward the boulevard leading to the interstate on-ramp. They didn't know they were going to die.

The rain turned to snow, but no plows were out yet. No plows would ever clank out again. Behind them, invisible but real, a cloud of imminent death moved down on them, riding the northeast wind: toward the plow barn, toward City Hall, toward the stores and houses and officc buildings, the restaurants, garages, apartment buildings. Toward all of them. Within half an hour the drivers of all the cars would be dead.

Thinking about that, Tommy directed the Toyota into the lane marked "New York—95 South—¾ Mile. Keep Right."

At the next intersection, four cars had piled up; edging around the mess, he caught a glimpse of a tall, skinny man with no hat and a long grey beard. He lay on his side in the slush, curled into a fetal position, blood gushing from his mouth, nose, and ears as the drivers of the other three cars continued kicking him.

Biting his lip, Tommy pressed the gas pedal a little harder. "Nick. How fast does chlorine travel?"

"Depends on the wind, I think."

"Hmph." It was somewhere behind them, though. It would probably show when it got near. How close would it have to be for them to see it? A mile? A hundred yards? Ten feet? "What color is it?"

"Sort of a greenish-yellow, I think."

In the glow of the street lights, would it look different from mist and rain, sleet and snow? Could it be near them, almost upon them, this minute? Suddenly he was afraid again, and despite the iced street he pressed down on the gas again. The speedometer inched past thirty, past forty and fifty.

"Tommy!"

A road sign: sharp turn just ahead. "I see it!" He hit the brakes and the car went immediately into a skid, its rear end slipping to the right. But this time he needed no inner voice. He let the brake up, yanked the wheel right, and straightened out, still doing forty-five. Two hundred yards away and coming up very fast, the curve shone brightly under the sodium lamps: sheeted with ice.

Nicki moaned.

Pump the goddamn brakes, just jab 'em down. Up. Down. Up. Thirty-five going in, maybe still too fast, but he'd find out soon. "Hang on!" He dropped into first gear, spun the wheel hard right, and slammed on the gas.

Headlights glared at him, blaring past. Somewhere—too near—a horn blatted.

The car's rear fishtailed left, over the center line. The tires shrieked in protest but caught at last. He straightened it out, took his foot off the gas and smashed it back down hard again, missed an oncoming police cruiser by a skimpy two feet and came out of the turn at a fast sixty miles per hour.

"Tommy!" Her voice was ghastly.

"Yeah." His own voice trembled but he did not care. "I know. Sorry. I forgot that turn was waiting for us. But now I think we've got something worse to worry about."

She turned. Lights loomed up in the rearview. "My God! A gasoline truck. Is he crazy?"

"I don't know. Maybe he heard something. He's catching up, though. And I bet there's a cop behind him."

As if to confirm his unhappy suspicion, a siren wailed.

"Nicki," he said. "This is it. We're gonna run, now." He shoved the pedal down and swung around four cars. The tanker truck followed, evidently recognizing a smart move when he saw it. The Toyota's speedometer jumped to seventy-five, and then to eighty.

The siren behind grew louder, nearer. Now the whirling red light was visible, like a bloody smear in the wet night.

Meanwhile, the truck stayed right on his tail and then some.

Oncoming traffic clotted up, too: just what they needed. Beside him, Nicki clenched her fists. Ahead on the left, the twin towers of Meadbury General Hospital poked at the sky. Instinctively he eased up on the gas. Hospitals always had cars and ambulances zooming in and out, and Tommy had no desire to tangle with any of them. Not tonight, not with a cloud of poison gas closing in.

Daylight broke all at once inside the car: a crossfire of high beams from cars ahead and from the gasoline tanker fifty yards to his rear and closing fast. The dinosaur roar of its air horn would blast up his tailpipe any second now, and— "Shit! Oh, shit."

He'd had assholes driving at him before. He'd even had them driving at him doing sixty while he was doing sixty. But he'd never had one driving at him in the wrong lane, in his own lane.

"Oh, my God, I am heartily sorry," Nicki began, "for having offended thee."

"Shut up," he said very calmly, and sent the Toyota swerving hard up onto the sidewalk, slamming the heel of one hand onto the horn as they missed the oncoming moron by inches. "You are not going to die, because I am not going to die, and if I am not going to die then you—"

He glanced in the rearview and interrupted himself. "Oh jeez, look at that."

The car he'd just missed cut straight across the path of the gasoline truck. Mack kissed Chrysler. Chrysler couldn't take it. The big LeBaron spun around, rolled off the street, and took out a power pole. High voltage crackled and spat, arcing bluely on the black sky.

Then the truck lost it, too, skidding over the center line, brakes smoking as the driver tried to wrestle the big rig back under control and couldn't. Careening wildly, it crossed two lanes and jumped the curb, leaving a vacancy for the blue-and-white squad car screaming up behind it.

Siren hi-loing, roof rack flashing, the cruiser ignored the truck, the Chrysler, and the downed power pole to arrow after Tommy like some fast and intensely malignant parasite, seeking against all odds to catch him and fasten itself to him.

Meanwhile the big Mack rammed Meadbury Hospital's liquid oxygen storage tank, mingling liquid oxygen, gasoline, and enough sparks to set off a Fourth of July fireworks display. The result, however, did not resemble the Fourth of July.

It resembled the end of the world.

The fireball just kept growing. Orange and white, bigger and bigger, swallowing the truck, the storage tank, sixty feet of chain link fence, a concrete fountain, a pair of sliding glass doors, and the entire new entrance and waiting area of Meadbury General Hospital's outpatient clinic, along with half a dozen wooden benches that had recently been installed on the sidewalk by the bus stop.

The ground thundered. The force of the blast sent the little Toyota prancing like a headstrong pony, its nose veering this way and that. Bits of the truck, the tank, the fountain, the building, and the truck driver fountained and rained down. Things Tommy did not want to think about began pitter-pattering on the Toyota's roof.

And still the damned squad car kept coming, pulling up so fast it seemed the Toyota might as well have stopped. Just for an instant Tommy lost sight of it as flames from the explosion curtained the street, then fell back.

Tommy hit the gas as the flames surged again, throwing up steamy clouds of melted snow and ice. The squad car vanished once more into the billowing vapors, its flashers and headlamps haloed in steam. Tongues of flame licked down the pavement at it, searching and reaching—

Finding. The cruiser cut away, but an instant too late. A gout of orange and yellow engulfed it. Moments later its gas tank exploded, creating a small bright burst in the world of flames thundering at them now, huge walls of fire that bulked out and fell back. Tommy mashed the gas pedal flat on the floorboard, praying as yellow streamers raced up behind the Toyota, flared for an instant right on the rear windshield, then retreated for a few blessed instants. A half dozen secondary explosions *bumpbumpBUMP* went off in the hospital buildings on their left.

Tommy sucked back a sob and held the throbbing, bucking wheel of the Toyota as steady as he could.

And then, suddenly, they were clear. He glanced at Nicki, who looked as if she didn't quite believe it either. The fire was behind them, and so was Meadbury: just an orange glow dropping back in the rearview, burning hard. Burning hard, and fading fast.

Ahead was the on-ramp: I-95 South, New York, Keep Right.

Tommy Riley kept his eyes on it. Get there, he thought. Just get there. He had no idea what might be beyond that ramp, what else he might be required to do. But he hardly cared; that there should be a future at all seemed such an unimaginably generous and improbable gift. He put his foot on the gas, keeping his eyes on that ramp as if his life depended on it. Which, he supposed, it did.

Once I've made it that far, then I'll worry about the next thing, and the next. That's the way grown-ups do it, isn't it?

Yeah, he answered himself. Yeah, it was. He'd learned that much out of all this, anyway. All grown-ups really knew how to do, actually, was wing it. That was the secret.

And if it looks like a grown-up, and walks like a grown-up, and quacks like a grown-up. . . .

Quack, he thought, guiding the little Toyota up onto the interstate, out of Meadbury. Quack-quack.

Then he began, shakily at first, to smile.

FRIDAY, JANUARY 3

You are most cordially invited
to a celebration
honoring the reestablishment of
Meadbury

Saturday, January 18, 1:00 P.M.
Meadbury Shelter

children welcome

RSVP
